A MATTER OF TRUST

~

LUCY ANN HUXTER

First Published in Great Britain in 2023

A CIP catalogue record for this book is available from the British Library

Cover Design by Becky Warrak at Raven Crest Books

Typesetting by Book Polishers

For my husband Fred – without whom I couldn't write about fierce, burning, extraordinary love...

Chapter 1

ALL GONE. HOW COULD SOMETHING THAT HAD STOOD FOR SO long, and stood for so much, have simply ceased to exist in a matter of days?

Emma clenched her teeth to stop them chattering, as she watched another part of her life deconstructed. Yesterday the diggers had demolished the stable block, and today the tack room was becoming just one more unidentifiable heap of rubble. The bricks and stones that had formed its structure for a couple of centuries, were being loaded into the dumper, one enormous bucketful at a time. The mounting block still stood, strangely marooned in the middle of what had been the yard, detached from its mooring of the tack room wall, the stone of its steps pitted and worn from decades of use.

Maggie's house had been knocked down days ago, its crumbling walls no match for the relentless machines. Whoever would have thought that it was worth so much? Enough to buy a villa in Spain apparently. One with stables, and twenty acres, and even a pool. All for a tumbledown cottage and dilapidated stable yard. But of course, it was the land that made it so desirable to the developers; five acres of undeveloped land on the edge of suburban Basingstoke.

Already stripped of their green, the fields were now relegated to the uniform browns and greys of their surroundings. Where once the horses had grazed; chestnut, bay and strawberry roan, only mounds of bare earth stood. The air, once gloriously thick with the warm, sweet smell of haylage, saddle soap and dung, was now thick with brick dust.

The habit of coming here almost every day for the past thirteen years was proving hard to break. She wouldn't come again, there was truly nothing left now. The memories caught in her throat like the brick dust. Shoving her hands deeper into her coat pockets, Emma turned away. 'Stop moping,' she told herself. 'It's happened and there's absolutely nothing you can do about it.'

As she plodded on towards work, her hand closed over her phone in her pocket, but she managed to resist the temptation to check it again. She had already checked it twice for missed calls that morning. Really, she was getting quite neurotic. If Lottie were here, she would tell Emma to stop being so silly. But then, if Lottie were here, she wouldn't be worrying about it at all. They'd be zooming through the streets in Lottie's little red Mazda – late as usual – making plans for the weekend and moaning about their dreadful landlord. It would never have occurred to her to worry. But if the last few weeks had taught her anything, it was that she couldn't take anything for granted.

No Maggie, no Lottie…and without Lottie, she never would have met Edward. He was the only one left. It was as if all the pieces of her life were dropping out one by one, and there was nothing she could do to stop them.

She walked faster, bracing herself against the cold wind. Tomorrow she would go for a run before work – try and shake this mood she was in.

Her phone rang, sending vibrations up through her arm. She drew it out of her pocket eagerly, but it was just Maggie's name that flashed up on the screen. Huh. What bad timing. Pressing the "decline" button with a defiant thumb, she stowed her phone deep into her bag so she wouldn't be tempted to keep checking it.

It wouldn't have been so bad if Maggie could have just waited a few more months. After all, the developers had been after her land for years. In nine months, Emma would be leaving anyway. It would have been the natural end of an era; time to grow up, live in the real world, have a career and a mortgage, and all those other serious things… but she had thought she still had time. She would have spent every spare minute at Maggie's – every weekend that Edward couldn't make it, she would have stayed there. Then she wouldn't have minded so much. She wouldn't have had to go home to her parents when Lottie left to live with her boyfriend. It just went to show that you couldn't rely on anything – it could all change, just like that.

Reaching work, she was relieved to see the desk opposite hers was still vacant. Candice wasn't in yet; a moment of respite. Going into the kitchenette she made the usual pot of tea for herself and Candice, and coffee for the partners, which she took upstairs, before taking a seat at her desk. No sooner had she sat down than her phone began ringing again. This time she was more guarded, and sure enough, it was only Maggie again.

With a sigh of resignation, she answered. 'Hello Maggie…'

'Oh good, there you are at last! Have you read my email?'

Despite everything, it was comforting to hear Maggie's brisk no-nonsense tone.

'How are things? Are the horses settling in okay?'

'Yes, yes, they're fine – but I've not rung for a chat! You haven't got time to dither, I've told them you'll ring them straight away to let them know you're coming. It will be absolutely perfect for you, the answer to all your problems…'

'Maggie, you've lost me – you've told who? What will be perfect for me?'

'The job! Don't you read your emails, I sent it yesterday.'

'Job?' Emma asked, even more confused, 'Maggie…I have a job.'

'Huh! Which you hate.'

'I don't hate it,' Emma lowered her voice. 'It's well paid and, and…'

'And bores you to death,' Maggie interrupted. 'Listen, Malcolm's an old friend of mine, he rang me and asked me if I knew anybody who might be interested. They've been having some staffing problems; people keep leaving. They need someone reliable and hard-working who knows what they're doing. He can't afford to pay much mind you, and you'd have to really earn your keep –'

Emma laughed. 'Sounds delightful, when do I start?'

'You're missing the point. It's working with horses. Eventers! They're only a small yard and Malcolm's an old man now, but they still do some competing. Oh, read the bloody email will you?'

Emma was intrigued despite herself. Logging into her personal email account, she found it. Reading as fast as only an avid reader can, she soon had the gist.

'Dorset? Maggie, I can't move to Dorset, I'm moving to London!'

'It's only for eight months – just one season – so you'll be finished in time to move to London with….'

'Edward.'

'Yes, Edward. And accommodation is included, so that solves your problem of living with your parents until then – right?'

Emma had to admit, this was a huge plus. She read further …

'Bloody hell…!'

'Okay, I'll admit the hours and the money aren't great, it's more for the experience… but Emma,' Maggie sighed, her voice lost its impatient tone and became more heartfelt, 'it will be good for you. It will stop you moping and over-thinking, and resenting me… and don't say you're not, because I know you are,' she said, when Emma began to protest. 'You've always wanted to work in eventing again – this is your chance! Possibly your last chance to work with horses ever again.'

This was true. For three years, before she'd met Edward, Emma had groomed for Monique; a French-Canadian eventer who had kept her horses with Maggie.

Travelling around to horse trials, all over the country, had been some of the most exciting experiences of her life. She loved everything about it; the early mornings, leaving the yard in Monique's lorry, horses groomed to perfection, plaited, booted and rugged, swaying to the motion of the box, the atmosphere of excitement at the competition.

Emma had helped Monique get her horses fit and ready, and in return, Monique had given Emma lessons in flatwork and jumping. When Monique left, Emma didn't know whether she would ever be able to be part of that world again. Even now, the smell of warm crushed grass evoked a yearning for those competition days.

'Look, I'm not going to deny that life is a bit tedious at the moment,' Emma sighed, 'but running away to Dorset isn't the answer. Edward finishes in Oxford in nine months, I just have to suck it up; get my head down and put up with it.'

Maggie snorted. 'Is that your mother talking?' she demanded. 'If you don't live a little now, before you know it you will be up to your ears in babies and mortgages. Come on, it'll be an adventure! What have you got to lose?'

Emma heard the office door open. 'Listen, I can't talk now, someone will hear me.'

'Promise me you'll think about it?'

'I'll think about it,' Emma said to end the conversation, because Candice had walked in, and was hanging up her bag and coat.

'Did I mention that they also breed their own? There should be some foals soon,' Maggie was saying.

Emma's attention was immediately recaptured. 'Foals? Ooh! I'd love to see a foal born,' she couldn't help blurting out, making Candice turn and stare at her. Emma gave her an apologetic smile, and gestured with her hand to convey she was winding up the conversation.

'You see? What are you waiting for?'

'I'll call you later,' she said, hanging up. She turned with a bright smile. 'Good morning Candice, is your cold better?' she said, trying to avoid the inevitable questions.

Candice took a seat at her desk by the window and fished a damp looking tissue out of her pocket, dabbing ineffectually at her nose. 'A bit,' she said hesitantly, 'but now Mother's caught it, and you know how these things go straight to her chest.'

Emma did know – she thought she probably knew as much about Candice's mother's various ailments as the doctors.

'Who was that?' Candice asked.

'Just Maggie,' Emma said dismissively.

'Oh. I thought it was Edward, until you said "foals". Is he coming to pick you up tomorrow?'

Emma flinched. 'Er…I'm not sure…' she said, cursing inwardly.

'Hasn't he rung you yet?' Candice said, her eyes widening. 'Oh dear, I wonder why, I hope there's nothing wrong. If it were me, I couldn't help worrying – I mean, he's probably surrounded by pretty nurses, day in day out – don't you worry about hanging on to him?'

Emma forced as hearty a laugh as she could muster. 'No, of course not! It's just so hectic at the hospital – sometimes he doesn't get a minute to himself.' She got up quickly and poured them each a cup of tea, busying herself with milk and sugar to hide her misgivings.

'But it's Friday tomorrow – he's usually called you by now. He didn't come down last weekend either did he?'

Trying again to deflect her, Emma asked; 'You've got your date tomorrow night haven't you?'

'Yes.' Candice belonged to several dating sites, but never seemed to have much luck with men. 'But if Mother's chest is any worse, I shan't be able to go…' And they were back to her mother's ailments again. Emma knew that once she got started on this track she would need to go through the whole narrative, as she did every time. She logged back into her computer and mechanically started on some undemanding task, listening with half an ear to poor Candice.

Throughout the day – between working on autopilot and listening to Candice's chatter – she thought about Maggie's email. At least it was a welcome distraction from checking the clock, and her phone for missed calls. She just couldn't face another weekend at home with her parents. She realised, with a jolt, just how dependent she had become on Edward for her happiness. Something that Maggie – fiercely independent – had always warned her against. Possibly the reason why Maggie had remained single and childless all her life, although mother to many, like Emma and Lottie.

As a teenager, it had been Emma's dream to be just like Maggie; to work with horses…until the adult world of rent and bills started to bite. And then, of course, she'd met Edward. However – as Maggie said – the job was just for one season…and she would *so* love to see a foal being born!

At lunch time, she looked up the address Maggie had given her and found it on google maps. It was a small place, surrounded by farmland, but there was a train station nearby, which was lucky as she didn't drive. Coach House Stables – she liked the sound of that. She imagined an English stately home, and paddocks full of grazing mares and foals.

But the money was terrible – she was supposed to be saving up for their move – and she'd see Edward even less than she did now. Oh bother! It was pointless even considering. Her thoughts swung wildly between temptation and dismissing the idea altogether.

By four o'clock, Edward still hadn't rung, but Emma had made up her mind; if she still hadn't heard anything by five o'clock, she would ring up about the job. She just couldn't bear to become one of those needy, whining girlfriends whose life revolved around their boyfriend.

Having made this decision, she attempted to focus on her work. At least Candice was quiet – in fact so quiet, Emma thought she must have nodded off behind her computer screen.

At five to five her phone rang, loud into the silence of their tiny office. Candice, startled out of her snooze, looked about her in agitation, and sat bolt upright in her chair. 'It's Edward!' she exclaimed.

Emma picked up her phone. 'No,' she said in exasperation, 'just Maggie again.'

But Candice had got to her feet and was pointing out of the office window. 'No, it's Edward – there!'

Abandoning her phone, Emma jumped up and ran to the window. Sure enough, there he was, climbing out of his lotus; big, blonde and beautiful, a large bunch of flowers tucked under his arm.

Candice had turned scarlet and was busy smoothing down her hair and straightening her skirt. Emma went to the door and opened it, and in a second he was there, filling the office with his larger than life presence.

'What are you doing here?' Emma laughed, unable to contain her delight.

'I wanted to surprise you,' Edward said, kissing her. 'The hospital gave me an extra day off because I had to cover for Dr Benson last weekend. I've come to take you out to dinner,' he said, giving her the flowers.

'Beautiful! Thank you.' She was overwhelmed with joy and relief.

'Can you leave now?'

'Give me a couple minutes.'

'Okay, I'll wait in the car.' He looked over Emma's shoulder and raised his eyebrows. 'Oh, hi....er...Candice.'

Emma was amused to see that whilst they had been saying their hellos, Candice had applied more lipstick and taken off her spectacles. She had lifted her hand and was smiling brightly. 'Hi Edward, how are you?' she asked.

But Edward had already turned to go. 'See you in a mo,' he said to Emma.

Candice looked crestfallen. 'You are so lucky Emma,' she said, sighing sadly and putting her glasses back on.

'I know,' Emma agreed wholeheartedly.

Two hours, two cocktails and a glass of wine later, Emma was seated in front of fillet steak and chips at their favourite restaurant. Sealed in a bubble of happiness, she gazed at Edward in the candle-light, marvelling at how good she felt now, compared to how she'd felt earlier.

'Perhaps we could visit Lottie and Josh next weekend?' she suggested.

'Ah.' Edward put down his knife and fork, and reached across the table to take her hand. 'Sorry, hadn't got round to telling you – I might have to work again next weekend.' He smiled ruefully. 'The sad lot of the junior doctor I'm afraid.'

Emma tried to disguise her disappointment, taking a large gulp of wine. 'It's okay, can't be helped. I'll just go out with my other boyfriend,' she said, trying to laugh it off. Edward chuckled and went back to his steak – but the bubble had burst.

'I spoke to Maggie earlier,' she said, getting out her phone.

'Oh? How is the old girl?' he asked without looking up.

'Fine…she sent me this…' she said, hesitating slightly before handing him her phone with the email open.

He read it; his brows knitting together in a frown. Eventually he grinned. 'Wow, maybe the move was too much for her, she's finally lost it! Why would she think you'd want to move to Dorset?' Still reading, he laughed. 'I can't believe people can get away with paying so little in this day and age! Although come to think of it, Maggie never paid you anything,' he added under his breath.

'That's how I reacted at first,' Emma admitted, 'but accommodation is included, and it would be more for the experience – it's an eventing yard.'

'What is "eventing" again?'

'You know – what Monique used to do? All three disciplines; dressage, show-jumping and cross-country. Like a triathlon – but for horses.'

'Hmm, sounds dangerous.'

Emma smiled fondly at his worried look. His one attempt at riding – encouraged by Emma – had ended in disaster; a torn ligament and a bruised ego. 'It's true what they say about horses,' he'd said, 'dangerous at both ends and damned uncomfortable in the middle!'

She hadn't suggested he do it again, but admired him for trying.

'I wouldn't be competing, I'd just be a working pupil,' she reassured him. 'I doubt whether I'd even get to jump.'

'I bet all you'd be doing is shovelling shit from dawn 'til dusk.'

'That's a distinct possibility!' She grinned. 'But… I do miss the horses, and it wouldn't interfere with our plans, I'd be finished before we move.'

He put down his knife and fork and sat up, looking at her with surprise. 'Wow, it sounds like you're seriously considering it?'

She thought for a moment, then said, 'I just feel like this might be my only chance to do it – you know? And as Maggie said, what have I got to lose?'

Edward frowned. 'I just worry we'd never see each other. I've enjoyed not losing you to Maggie every weekend.'

She didn't state the obvious; that she spent many weekends without him, because she knew how important his career was to him, and she was determined to be supportive, but her silence made him lean closer and take her hand again.

'Look, I just don't want you to do something you'll regret, that's all. If you hate it, and you've given up your job at Hearnshaws, you'll have nothing to come back to. Just think carefully about it, that's all I'm saying. The reality might not live up to the dream.'

He made perfect sense, as always. But after Edward had dropped her off at home, and she was alone in her room, she got her riding boots and hat down from the top of her wardrobe where they had gathered a bit of dust. Just the feel of them in her hands, and the smell – still pungent with the smell of horses – made her long to be back in the saddle. Whilst she sat on her bed reminiscing and feeling nostalgic, her phone pinged. It was a message from Maggie, and she realised she hadn't called her back. It said: *Have you rung about that job yet??*

When Edward picked her up from work the following evening, she was fizzing with nervous excitement. 'I've done something a little impulsive,' she said, sliding into the leather seat of his lotus.

'Oh?' Edward raised his eyebrows.

'I've given my notice. I'm supposed to give a month, but Mr Hearnshaw said that if they can find a temp. to cover, I can leave in two weeks.' Edward's blue eyes widened. 'So, I rang the eventing yard and spoke to a lady called Cathy, she sounds nice. They want me to start as soon as I can.' She bit her lip whilst she waited for him to react.

Edward ran a hand through his hair, which was almost the exact same shade of blonde as her own and sighed. 'Well actually…maybe it's a good thing for you to get it out of your system before we move to London. And I guess I can come and rescue you if you need me to. I won't let you starve.'

'Thanks!' She laughed with relief, and thought again how lucky she was. At least she still had Edward.

Chapter 2

So it was, that at half past four, on an unexpectedly pleasant, spring-like afternoon in March, Emma stepped off the train onto the platform of a tiny station in West Dorset.

Lugging her bags out onto the road outside the deserted station building, she already wished she hadn't brought so many, but had found it impossible to pack lightly for a life she did not yet know.

The straps of her rucksack dug into her shoulders, and she regretted the number of books she had brought, along with the quantity of warm clothing, including a fluffy rabbit onesie that Lottie had given her. It was so bulky it took up nearly a whole bag on its own.

She put them in a heap on the ground with yet another bag which contained enough food to keep her going for a while; she wasn't sure what the arrangements for meals were – in fact, she wasn't sure of anything much. She waited, trying to ignore the prickles of anxiety.

After she'd looked up the train times, she had booked a taxi to take her from the station to Coach House Stables. But now, standing on the empty road, she wondered if she might have got the date or the time wrong. She glanced at her phone. No signal. She tried the door to the station office. Locked of course, it was Sunday.

'No point standing here,' she muttered under her breath, and shrugging her rucksack back onto her shoulders, she made her way up to where the tiny station road joined the main drag. She breathed a sigh of relief. Houses and – oh joy! – a pub. She could ask for directions in there, or use their phone.

It was a pretty pub, built from honey coloured stone – she thought it was called 'Ham Stone', although she had no idea why.

Big baskets full of bright flowers hung from the walls, and a wooden sign said, "The Chalk and Cheese."

It was shut. Glancing again at her watch, it was only ten to five. Country opening hours, it probably wouldn't open until six.

'Doesn't anyone live in this godforsaken place?' she grumbled.

She knew, from google maps, that Coach House Stables lay about a mile outside of the village. There was nothing for it but to hoof it.

Setting off with determination (in what she hoped was the right direction) she soon left the houses behind. The road became narrow and twisty, with ditches and tall hedges flanking either side. She was just beginning to wonder how far she should go before turning back, when she heard a vehicle.

It was a green Land Rover Defender, driven by a man on his own. To her unease it pulled up, and the window was wound down.

'You okay?' the driver asked, eyeing her bags. 'Do you need a lift anywhere?'

She looked at him. He didn't look like a murderer. He was young and fairly good-looking, not threatening at all, but then you could never tell, could you? It would be just her luck if she got murdered on her first day here.

'No, I'm fine thank you, I'm looking for Coach House Stables?' she said hopefully.

He nodded. 'Just up here on your right,' he said smiling. 'I go past it, are you sure you don't want to jump in?'

He looked even nicer when he smiled. He had that kind of open, honest countenance that made her want to trust him. But Emma knew only too well how looks could be deceiving.

'No, that's fine!' she said firmly, giving him what she hoped was a confident smile. She got out her phone as a precaution – just in case he was an axe murderer – still no signal, but he didn't have to know that. The man gave her the thumbs up and drove off. In the back windscreen he had a 'Vet On Call' sticker.

'Bugger!' Emma cursed. He was a vet. Bound not to have been a murderer. She'd always thought there was something inherently trustworthy about vets. Plodding on, she went up a hill and round another bend.

All at once, the thick hedges on her right gave way to post

and rail fences, revealing an open landscape of lush green fields, grazing horses, and further on, a house and out-buildings. Thank God, this must be it!

Sure enough, she came to a track on her right, and set into the grassy bank was a stone with, 'Coach House Stables' engraved upon it. She glanced at her phone. Now she had a signal. Typical.

As she walked down the track, she looked ahead at the place where she was to spend the next eight months with a mixture of excitement and apprehension. The fields were gently sloping, all fenced with pristine post and rail fences. The horses that grazed in them looked well cared for and well bred, mostly thoroughbreds she thought. Mature trees were dotted here and there, huge oaks and ashes all bursting into life with bright green leaves.

In a field to the right of the buildings, she could see some cross-country fences, and in front of the yard was a huge sand and rubber arena with some show-jumps at one end. At the back of it all was a large stone country house with white sash windows, and to the left of that was another low single storey building, which looked like a barn conversion. Might that be the staff quarters?

Approaching the house, she saw a side door with a sign on it saying 'Office', and through the window she could see a middle-aged woman with spectacles on a chain around her neck, sitting at a desk. When she spotted Emma looking through the window, she jumped up and came to the door.

'You must be Emma?' she said opening it.

'Yes,' Emma replied, feeling reassured. 'Cathy?'

'That's right, come in. We're so glad you've come. I'll go and find Malcolm.'

She bustled away through another door, reminding Emma of a squirrel, with her bright eyes and quick darting movements. Left alone, Emma looked around. The oak panelled walls were covered with pictures of horses, some framed photographs, some paintings. The furniture was a bit shabby, but probably antique.

Cathy came back with an elderly gentleman. He took Emma's hand in both of his, smiling into her eyes. He was slightly built but had a firm handshake.

'Welcome!' he said. 'So lovely to speak to Maggie after all these years – she's an old friend of mine,' he said with a twinkle in his eye, 'speaks very highly of you.'

She grinned, feeling instantly at ease with him, he reminded her of her granddad. 'And you!' she said.

'I do hope Kitty will still be here to show you the ropes,' Cathy said.

'I'll walk you down and find Kitty,' Malcolm said, picking up her rucksack.

For an elderly gentleman he certainly was sprightly, she had to hurry to keep up with him.

The stables were as impressive close up as they had been from a distance. They must have been built at the same time as the house, and from the same stone. They were set in a U shape with loose boxes down both arms of the U, and a tack room and feed room at the top end.

A few horses looked out over the half doors. Outside the tack room was a big, old, stone mounting block set against the wall. There was a concrete apron in front of the loose boxes and a grassy area in the middle, with gravel around the outside. An old-fashioned water pump stood in the centre and there were pots of flowers here and there. The daylight was fading and there was a light on in a few of the loose boxes and in the tack room, the door of which stood open. All together, the effect was cheerful and inviting.

Emma followed Malcolm through the tack room, adjoining which was a small kitchen and what Emma assumed was a staffroom with a battered old sofa, and a table with a few rickety chairs. Sitting on one the table with her feet on a chair was a girl, about Emma's age.

She was extremely pretty with long, straight dark hair, which came almost to her waist. She wore skin-tight black breeches, showing off a curvy figure, and a cropped tee-shirt with the slogan 'Moody Mare' written across her impressive bust. In one hand she held a bridle and in the other, a sponge. She was reading a magazine folded open on the table and a cigarette was burning in an ashtray next to it. She looked up with a sulky expression when they walked in. Was this Kitty?

'Simone,' said Malcolm, answering her question. 'This is Emma.'

Emma went forward with a smile, putting her bags on the floor.

The girl regarded her without enthusiasm, giving her an unsmiling up and down appraisal.

'I wish you wouldn't smoke in here Simone, I've asked you not to,' Malcolm said. 'Where's Kitty?'

'Dunno, probably sweeping up somewhere,' the girl replied, shrugging her shoulders and stubbing out her cigarette with deliberate slowness.

Malcolm went out onto the yard. 'Kitty!' he called.

Out of one of the loose boxes, came a girl of about seventeen or eighteen years old. She scuttled over to where they stood, eyes darting furtively. She was a small girl – smaller than Emma – with light brown frizzy hair, escaping from a messy ponytail, and she had round, wire-rimmed spectacles which she kept pushing up on her nose.

'Ah, good,' said Malcolm, 'you're still here. Kitty this is Emma.'

The girl gave Emma an uncertain smile, and Emma grinned back at her.

'Could you show Emma the ropes please, she's starting work tomorrow,' Malcolm asked her.

Kitty nodded quickly, making her glasses fall down again. She pushed them back up.

'Right I'll leave you to it,' he said. 'Make yourself at home Emma.' And he left.

Kitty seemed unsure where to begin, shifting from foot to foot.

'I've only worked here three weeks,' she said, 'but I'll tell you everything I know.'

She introduced Emma to some of the horses; there were some beauties. She showed her the feed room, where feeds were made up and ready to be taken round on a trolley.

In the floodlit arena, a man, also around Emma's age, was schooling a horse, about 16.2hh tall, thoroughbred type, dark bay with a pulled mane and glistening coat. The man was cantering him around slowly on a 20-metre circle and didn't look up when they went past. He was wearing faded jeans, a T-shirt, and no crash hat.

'That's Dan,' whispered Kitty under her breath, 'he's the yard manager.'

'Oh!' said Emma surprised. 'Should I say hello?'

'No,' said Kitty, flashing her a forbidding look. 'He won't speak when he's riding.'

'Right.' Emma supposed that was understandable if he was concentrating. Kitty hurried past, going across the yard and into the tack room, Emma followed. The room had a patterned, red brick floor and dark wooden beams.

She loved the smell of leather and the glycerine saddle soap that had sunk into the very pores of the bricks throughout the years, it reminded her poignantly of Maggie's. The walls above the saddle racks were covered in a multitude of colourful rosettes and silver plaques, along with pictures of horses, past and present.

It was rather a mess, with a huge box of bits – probably fifty or more – all thrown in on top of one another. A washing machine stood in the corner, and in front of it was a big pile of dirty saddle pads, boots and bandages. The bridles hanging on the hooks were obviously waiting to be cleaned, and there were dirty saddles on the saddle horse which stood in the middle of the room.

'We've been short staffed,' Kitty apologised, gesturing at the mess.

'So – is it just the four of us?' Emma asked.

Kitty shifted from foot to foot again. 'Should be five, but the last girl left two weeks ago.'

'Oh?' said Emma. 'Why'd she leave?'

There was a small silence. Kitty chewed her lip. 'I'll show you your room,' was all she said.

She led the way through the kitchen. Simone was still in there with the same bridle as before – not looking much cleaner – still reading her magazine, and she had another cigarette on the go. She and Kitty didn't speak as they went through.

Emma grabbed her bags, following Kitty through a narrow door and up a steep flight of wooden stairs. It was like going up to a secret attic. Upstairs was a corridor with three doors leading off it. One was a small shower room and toilet, the other two were bedrooms.

'This one's yours,' said Kitty, going to the first door on the left.

'Is the other one yours?' Emma asked.

'No, I live in the village.'

Inside, the room was tiny, sparsely furnished with a single

bed, a chest of drawers and a wardrobe. It had a sloping ceiling, bare wooden floorboards, and no curtains. It reminded her of Sarah's attic in the book 'The Little Princess' which had been one of Emma's favourite books as a child. It could have done with a lick of paint.

Putting her bags down on the bed, which was under the window, she looked out, straight down into the yard. Her heart lifted, at least she would be able to see the horses when she woke up in the mornings. It was getting dark outside, and the arena lights had been turned off. Kitty peered over Emma's shoulder and they watched the man, Dan, bring the horse he had been schooling back into the yard. Kitty drew back with a start.

'I'd better get down there,' she said, and disappeared, like a rabbit down a hole.

Out of the window, she saw Kitty appear below and scamper across the yard into the feed room. Emma went to the bathroom to use the toilet, noticing that there was men's shower gel and a razor in there. Her heart sank a little – had she got to share with a strange man? Oh well, she could keep herself to herself.

Going downstairs, she took the bag of food that she'd brought with her into the kitchen.

'Okay if I make a cup of tea?' she asked Simone.

Simone looked up with heavy lidded eyes and took a drag of her cigarette before replying. 'Knock yourself out.'

Emma was about to ask Simone if she wanted some, but just then the yard manager, Dan, walked in.

Emma went forward, holding out her hand. 'Hi, I'm Emma,' she said.

He had the kind of looks that ought to have weakened her knees and sent her heart into a flutter, but for Emma, one look was enough to put her instantly on her guard. He was olive skinned, with collar length, loosely curling brown hair, the ends bleached blonde by the sun; he looked more like a surfer than a rider. Deep set, rather wary brown eyes and a well-defined nose and jaw line, high cheekbones and a slightly downturned mouth gave him a look of perhaps having some exotic blood in him somewhere.

He gave her the same unsmiling, up and down appraisal that the girl, Simone had. Looking down at her proffered hand, he took it, shaking it once firmly before dropping it like it was red-hot, and stalking past her over to the fridge.

Disconcerted, Emma tried again. 'I'm making tea, would anyone like one?'

They both gave her matching disdainful stares, and Dan stood up from the fridge with a beer in his hand, cracking it open as he did.

'No thanks,' he said.

So six o'clock must be beer o'clock, thought Emma, feeling stupid and extremely self-conscious as she went about making her tea, although neither of the other two were taking a blind bit of notice of her. Her courage faltered at the thought of spending the next eight months in the company of their collective beauty and obvious contempt.

Kitty poked her head round the door. 'Okay if I go now?' she asked, her eyes flicking nervously towards Dan.

'Have you finished sweeping up?' he asked her.

'Yes,' she replied.

Dan nodded.

She gave Emma a fleeting smile and lifted her hand before ducking out, into the darkness.

'Night Kitty…thanks!' Emma called after her.

'You coming to the pub?' asked Simone, speaking to Dan obviously.

'Suppose so,' replied Dan without enthusiasm. Then he frowned and glanced at Emma. There was an awkward pause in which Emma pretended not to notice Simone rolling her eyes and pulling faces, before saying, 'You can come too if you want.'

'Me?' Emma looked at her in surprise and embarrassment. 'Oh no… thanks. I need to… er… get my stuff sorted,' she replied, thinking, '*Not bloody likely!*'

Left alone, Emma made a cheese sandwich and took it and her tea upstairs. She began to put her stuff away, setting her books out on top of the drawers and hanging her few nice clothes up in the wardrobe; then put her wash things in the bathroom.

She wondered whether to have a shower, then decided she

couldn't be bothered. Sitting on the bed, she tried to read a book but couldn't settle to it. Pulling out her phone she searched for a Wi-Fi signal. There wasn't one.

Feeling restless she went downstairs. After washing up her mug and plate, she wandered outside. It was too dark now to explore.

It was a fine night, chilly, but clear and still. Looking up, she gasped. There was a spectacular display of stars. You couldn't see stars like that in suburban areas because of the light pollution. Here, the sky was so black, each star had a halo of its own light.

She took a seat on the big, stone, mounting-block and tried to take in the unimaginable vastness of the universe.

She sat there for quite some time, and after a while, her eyes adjusted to the darkness. She could make out the shapes of the horses in their stables, most still munching at their hay-nets. Without wanting to disturb them she went from door to door, looking at each one in turn; she loved that they were right on her doorstep.

Some came over to the door with curiosity, some didn't. Some were already lying down in the straw, snoozing. A few stayed with her for a moment in a silent exchange of breath before going back to their hay.

Her solitude was disturbed by the sound of voices. Glancing at her watch, she realised it was late, and the other two, Simone and Dan, were back from the pub.

They came through the gate, him looking rather worse for wear, hands in pockets and struggling to walk in a straight line. She was hanging off his arm, holding on to him tightly and giggling. Emma shrank back into the shadows so they wouldn't see her. They went inside and up the stairs together.

So, they were a couple. Well, they definitely suited each other, that was for sure. At least Malcolm, Kitty and Cathy were nice. The other two… well, she could put up with them.

HALF AN HOUR later she wasn't so sure. Getting ready for bed she could hear their voices through the wall. Then, it became obvious from the sounds that they were doing more than just talking.

Argh! The walls were so thin she could hear everything. The girl seemed to be unnecessarily noisy; moaning and crying out, and something was banging against the wall – a headboard? – louder and louder. They must have forgotten she was here, at least she hoped they had. What if it was like this every night?

Hastily, she found her phone and earphones and put some music on – any music just to drown out the sound. Yuck. How was she going to look them in the eyes tomorrow over breakfast?

She listened to her music on full volume for a while before tentatively taking her earphones out. All was quiet, thank God! She got under the covers and lay, rigid, listening to the silence. What on earth would tomorrow bring? And still wondering, she fell asleep.

Chapter 3

THANKFULLY, IT SEEMED AS THOUGH SIMONE DIDN'T STAY OVER very often; she lived in the village and drove into work. Unfortunately, that was the only blessing. By the end of that first week, Emma was already wondering how she was going to stick it out.

She was not afraid of hard work, in fact she enjoyed it. But it was one thing to work as part of a team, knowing that your work was appreciated, and quite another to feel, every day, as if no matter what you did, no matter how hard you tried, it was never going to be good enough.

She soon discovered that Simone was bone-idle. She flounced around the yard, pretending to be doing something, avoiding any of the hard or menial jobs and sulking if she was made to do any real work. She wore the skimpiest clothes possible and then constantly complained that she was cold. Emma had to stop herself from snapping, 'Go and put some clothes on then!' Like a schoolmistress.

Dan worked very hard, but he had an absolutely foul temper. He wore a permanent scowl and it seemed to Emma that he went out of his way to find fault with everything they did.

Every morning they would start the day by mucking out the boxes after Dan had fed round. Emma was given six to do, Simone had six and so did Kitty. Dan had eight. Emma or Dan always finished first and then helped either Kitty or Simone, whoever was most behind.

Kitty tried her hardest, but she was hopelessly inefficient, and was constantly getting shouted at by Dan, which made her a complete nervous wreck. Once they'd tidied up and swept the yard, if they finished on time they would have a tea break. But more often than not they were behind, and Dan wouldn't let them have one.

Then it was grooming and tacking up horses for Simone and Dan to ride out, or for Dan to school and jump. While that was happening, Emma and Kitty had jobs to do such as scrubbing out water troughs, raking in the tracks in the arena and if there was time, cleaning tack.

If Dan was jumping, then Simone was helping him in the arena, setting up the jumps and putting back up any poles that were knocked down, but mostly just standing and watching him, whilst playing with her hair.

If they were hacking out, Kitty and Emma had to have the next two horses tacked up and ready by the time they came back, as well as doing their other jobs.

The two of them would ride into the yard, dismount, and hand their horses to Kitty and Emma. Then they would get on the next two and off they would go again, riding side by side, looking like an advert for 'Horse and Country TV', leaving Kitty and Emma to un-tack and wash off the two that had been ridden.

There was never a word of thanks, and always, Dan would manage to find something to criticise them for, whether it was a saddle pad not perfectly straight, a scrap of straw left in a mane or tail, or simply deciding that they weren't fast enough.

Simone got her fair share of these verbal attacks, but either she was used to it or just very thick skinned, because she didn't seem to care.

Then following a quick lunch break, the afternoons were filled with more of the same. Neither Emma nor Kitty got to even sit on a horse that first week. As part of their deal, being working pupils, they were supposed to have one staff-riding lesson a week. That didn't seem to be forthcoming, so Emma asked Kitty about it.

'While we're short staffed, we probably won't get one,' Kitty told her.

To be honest, Emma was so knackered she almost didn't care, but she felt that all she'd gained that week were new callouses on her hands, and a red raw hide where Dan had torn strips off her. She hadn't learnt anything.

At the end of each day she would force herself to eat something and have a shower, then fall exhausted into bed, too tired to even read. It was cold at night, and now she was glad of her rabbit onesie, which she frequently slept in to keep warm. When Dan was around in the evenings she stayed out of his way – bringing a book with her into the kitchen so she wouldn't have to talk to him – he ignored her anyway.

Whenever she saw Malcolm, which wasn't often, he would ask her how she was getting on, with his jolly smile and warm friendly manner, she didn't have the heart to tell him she was hating it. What made it worse was that when Edward called her, he told her he was going to see Lottie and Josh that weekend. She longed to tell him how awful it was; that she wanted to leave. But having taken this job against his advice, she couldn't bring herself to admit it.

Kitty got far more of the brunt of Dan's temper than Emma, because the poor girl was always making mistakes. It was constantly; *Kitty, why has Lynx got Merlin's bridle on? Kitty, Chance is still filthy, brush him again. Kitty, why are Harvey's boots on back to front?* And on top of that, being of a nervous disposition, she was terrified of some of the horses. Emma tried to help her out as much as possible, but there was only so much she could do.

On one occasion, there was a sudden clatter of hooves on the concrete. Emma looked out of the loose box she was in and saw the chestnut horse, Chance, trotting off loose across the yard. Now, Kitty had warned her about this particular horse, because you had to be careful to make sure his kick bolt, on the bottom of his door was kicked home, or he would undo his top bolt and let himself out – and he was a bugger to catch.

Dan came roaring out of the feed room.

'Who the fuck didn't bolt Chance's door?' he shouted, incandescent with rage.

Kitty's face crumpled and Emma knew instantly that she was the culprit.

Emma stepped out of the stable. 'Sorry, that must have been me,' she said.

Dan regarded her with narrowed eyes under dark brows. The truth was written all over Kitty's red, uncertain face.

'Is that right?' he said finally, chucking a head collar at Emma. 'Well, you'd better go and catch him then.'

It took her half an hour and half a bucket of nuts to catch him. Kitty was pathetically grateful.

'Thank you so much,' she said. 'I thought he was going to kill me this time.'

But her relief was short-lived, because later that same day, Dan sent Kitty to tack up Merlin; a huge black horse, which had recently arrived on the yard. Emma had learned quickly that you had to be really confident around him, or he could be a sod. He had already bitten Kitty twice, and Dan knew it.

'I want him ready in ten minutes,' Dan barked at her. Kitty paled.

'I'll do it,' Emma volunteered.

'No you won't,' said Dan, 'she needs to learn.'

She won't learn that way, Emma thought darkly. As soon as Dan's back was turned, she went to Merlin's stable.

Kitty cowered by the door, bridle in hand whilst Merlin regarded her warily from the corner. As she took a tentative step towards him, he swung his head at her, ears pinned close to his head, lips peeled back from his teeth and snaking his neck. He caught Kitty across the side of her head, her glasses flew off into the straw and she jumped back with a cry, ready to run out the door.

'Here,' Emma said, retrieving Kitty's glasses and handing them to her before taking Merlin's bridle out of her hands.

Walking straight up to Merlin's shoulder she lifted the reins to put them over his head. He tried to do the same thing to her; snaking his neck, he struck at her, teeth bared. With lightening reactions Emma lifted her arm defensively in a blocking motion, so all he managed to do was bang his nose against her elbow, hurting himself more than her.

'Get back, you bugger you,' she growled in her most threatening voice. 'Back!'

Merlin went back. Emma stayed level with his shoulder, then with a deft flick, swung the reins up over his head, and reaching underneath, got her hand up around his nose on the other side. Merlin knew he was defeated and allowed Emma to put his bridle on, his ears relaxed and he looked at them as if butter wouldn't melt.

'Oh, you're amazing!' enthused Kitty. 'I don't know how you do that, he's like a lamb with you.'

'It's just confidence,' Emma told her, giving Merlin a pat. 'If he knows you're scared of him he'll take the mick. Now quick, grab his saddle.' They finished getting him ready between them.

'Take him out,' Emma instructed her. 'I'll wait here in-case Dan's watching.' Kitty led Merlin out into the yard. Emma peeked out to see Dan walking towards them, if she went out now he would see her.

'Where's Emma, Kitty?' he asked. Poor Kitty resembled a mouse caught by a cat.

'I d-don't know,' she stammered.

'Emma!' he shouted. Emma had no choice but to show herself. His expression blackened as she emerged from Merlin's stable, and she braced herself for the inevitable, but he just turned away without a word.

So when he cornered her in the feed room that evening, as she was chopping up carrots, she immediately knew she was in for a pasting. She was right.

'Why did you tack up Merlin for Kitty when I specifically told you not to?' he started.

Emma put down the knife she was using and looked him in the eye. She wasn't scared of him the way Kitty was. He was just a bully like Merlin, and she knew how to handle bullies.

'She won't learn anything by having chunks taken out of her,' she said. 'She needs to be shown what to do, and taught how, or she'll never improve.'

He regarded her with a hard, cynical stare.

'It wasn't you who left Chance's bolt off either was it?' he asked in a chillingly quiet voice. Emma found she had to drop her gaze.

He shook his head slowly. 'Enjoy being shouted at do you?'

'More than I enjoy watching an unfair fight,' she said in earnest. 'You and Merlin take so many pieces out of her, there'll be nothing left in a minute.'

'You think you're doing her a favour by lying for her?' he asked, 'because haven't you thought how much happier she'll be if she realises this game isn't for her and quits?'

'Oh perfect! Then it'll just be the three of us left on the yard – oh sorry, two of us actually doing any work, while your girlfriend stands around watching her nails grow.'

His eyes darkened, his jaw clenched. She swallowed. For a moment she wondered if she'd gone too far. Maybe he would give her the sack, she thought, half hoping.

'She's not…!' he growled through gritted teeth – but then stopped and took a deep breath. He closed his eyes for a second and shook his head. When he spoke again, his voice was more controlled. 'Do you know how many people think they want to work with horses? There will always be another one, and another one after that. Girls like Kitty are easily replaced.'

As he said it, he looked her up and down.

'But everyone deserves a fair chance,' she said more quietly, 'and she's not getting one.'

His dark eyes bore into her for what seemed like an eternity. Her mouth went dry and all the hairs on her skin stood on end. Her eyes began to water with the effort of not blinking. But this time, she refused to look away.

Very slowly, the carrot that she had been chopping began to roll off the board. It rolled all the way to the edge of the feed-bin and fell on the floor between them. Still, Emma didn't move. Dan blinked and the corners of his mouth twitched. He looked down, and bent to pick it up.

'The vet's coming tomorrow to do some vaccinations,' he said, straightening up. 'I won't be here. You can take him round and help him with the horses.' He held the carrot out to her.

Emma let out a shaky breath. 'Okay,' she agreed, taking it from him.

He nodded and walked out abruptly, leaving Emma with the feeling that either she'd made things better, or a whole lot worse.

She sat on her narrow little attic bed with her phone in her hands; still a little shaky from her run-in with Dan.

She should just call Edward, tell him she'd made a mistake – that she wanted to come home. But did she? Really? One week – that was all she'd managed. How pathetic.

Her thumb hovered over the dial symbol on her screen under Edward's picture. One word from her and he would jump in his car and come and get her. She would feel foolish, but so what? She'd be going with him to see Lottie and Josh. They would go out to a restaurant – maybe some cocktails first. They would be celebrating because Josh had been promoted. It would be just like old times, right now, what wouldn't she give to go back? It was such a sad failing of human nature that it was only after things were over, that you realised just how good they had been.

Bzzzzz, bzzzzzz. Her phone vibrated, making her jump and very nearly drop it.

It was a text from Lottie:

Ed told Josh ur not coming to see us this weekend ☹☹☹ *Did he tell you about Josh's promotion? How amazing is that?!?! AND I've got a second interview for that job I applied for EEK!! Why can't you come??*

Emma groaned, replying:

Because I only get every third weekend off, and I've only done a week ☹

She hastily added: *But that's fantastic about Josh's promo/ur job!! I'm so happy for you.*

The little dots appeared on the screen to show that Lottie was replying…

That's crap!! Why don't you chuck it in the fuck-it-bucket and come anyway??? Can't they get someone else to shovel the shit for one weekend?

She'd obviously been talking to Edward. Emma hesitated. They would all be celebrating their various successes – and she would feel like a failure.

She stared at the words on her screen. Quickly, not giving herself too much time to think she typed:

Sorry, can't ☹ *Have a drink for me! xxxx*

She pressed send and flung herself back on the bed with another heartfelt, camel-like groan.

Chapter 4

AT TWO-THIRTY THE NEXT DAY, EMMA SPOTTED A GREEN LAND Rover pulling into the yard. She guessed it was the vet. Going to meet him, she had a moment of recognition when she saw the youngish guy getting out of the vehicle. It was the man who had stopped and offered her a lift on her first day here. That seemed like a lifetime ago. Emma saw that he had a similar moment of recognition.

'You got here all right then?' he said grinning. 'Joe Riley.' He held out his hand. 'Vet.'

'Emma Mathews,' she shook his hand, smiling in return. 'New girl.'

They walked down to the tack room together, where Emma picked up a pile of passports and the list of horses to be vaccinated. She held each horse in turn for Joe to vaccinate, before he recorded the date and signed its passport.

'So,' he asked her, 'how are you liking it here?'

Emma pulled a slight face. 'It's okay.'

'Oh dear – not enjoying it too much?'

'I love the horses and the work's fine…'

'But?'

She didn't know how much she ought to say, but decided he had the sort of face she could trust. 'Well, let's just say that working relations could be better.'

He chuckled. 'Hmm, I've heard that Dan can be a bit of a hard task master.'

'Yes, like Hitler was a bit of a fascist,' she said dryly.

Joe laughed. 'Dan's alright,' he said. 'He's good at his job, and the horses all do really well in his care.' Emma felt she couldn't say much in the face of these obvious truths, so she kept quiet. 'My advice would be, try and stick it out if you can – you could learn a lot.'

Emma walked him back to his Land Rover. 'Hope to see you again… if you're still here,' he said with a grin and a wave as he drove away.

All in all, there were 26 horses in, the rest were brood mares and a stallion, but they all lived out. Emma learnt that only two of them were competing already. Some were youngsters that either had yet to be broken or needed bringing on, and some were being prepared for competition.

On the wall in the tack room was a chart on which Dan worked out a training plan for each horse. Malcolm would come down now and then to discuss each horse's progress and decide, with Dan's advice, which ones were ready to compete or be sold.

Dan did all the schooling and, grudgingly, Emma had to admit he was a beautiful rider. He had that perfect natural balance and grace that made it all look so effortless, and was a joy to watch. He seemed to be able to communicate with each horse through some invisible channel, so you couldn't see the smallest aid that he was giving. Despite his obvious strength, he didn't use it against the horses. If a horse spooked or bucked, he barely seemed to notice, just sat quietly and sent it forward with a gentle squeeze of his legs, never grabbing up the reins or shifting in the saddle.

The two horses that were already competing were Lynx – a stunning, dapple grey thoroughbred mare – and Chance; the escapologist. On the Saturday, they were due to go to Larkhill; a fairly low-key event in Wiltshire. Simone always went with Dan to groom for him – needless to say – so that meant Emma and Kitty would be left on their own. It was supposed to be Kitty's weekend off, but she was coming in to help Emma muck out, like the good-hearted little thing that she was.

Dan and Simone were leaving early and wouldn't be back until much later in the afternoon. As Emma helped them get the horses ready and load up the lorry, part of her wished that she were going as well, although Dan was even snappier than usual. He bit Simone's head off after checking what she had packed and finding some things missing, and again when she let Lynx barge into Chance when they were loading.

Emma got her head down and tried to see where she could be helpful without being asked. At last they left, and Emma watched them go, with an odd mixture of envy and relief.

Kitty arrived on her pushbike and they got their work done quickly and cheerfully. At lunchtime, Kitty seemed in no hurry to leave.

'So, what are you going to do for the rest of the day?' Emma asked her.

Kitty hesitated. 'I don't know really.' She blushed. 'It's my birthday today.'

'Oh Kitty!' Emma exclaimed, 'why didn't you say? How old are you?'

'Eighteen.'

Emma couldn't help thinking it was a shame she had no plans on her eighteenth birthday.

'I know,' she said with excitement, 'go home and get your glad rags, and when I'm finished here, I'll take you to the pub for your first legal drink!'

'Ooh, could we?' Kitty squeaked. 'I'd love that!'

Once she'd left, Emma hurried through her afternoon jobs and made the yard clean and tidy; she didn't want to give Dan any excuse to yell at her.

It was four o'clock when the horsebox came swaying into view down the track. It drew up in the yard and Dan jumped out, slamming the door of the lorry with a force that made Emma wince.

'How did it go?' she asked cautiously, helping Simone to get the ramp down.

Dan ignored her.

'Oh, usual thing,' Simone said with her trademark shrug. 'Waste of time. Dressage judge was a bitch, marked them down for everything so we came nowhere, even though Lynx went double clear and Chance only had one pole in the show-jumping.'

After the lorry had been cleaned and the horses put to bed, Kitty came back and they went upstairs to get ready.

Emma decided to make a bit of an effort as it was Kitty's birthday, so she straightened her hair and put on some make-up, choosing a silver blue sleeveless top, which brought out the dark blue of her eyes, to go with her skinny jeans. Then she helped Kitty with her make-up, straightened her hair for her, and lent Kitty a scarf with little white horses on it that went well with Kitty's outfit.

'There,' said Emma with satisfaction, standing back to look at her. 'You look fab!'

'And you look stunning,' Kitty breathed in admiration. 'I'm so glad you came here Emma.'

Downstairs, there was no sign of Dan or Simone. They set off walking, Kitty pushing her bike, which she agreed to lend Emma to get back home later, saying she could walk to work on Monday morning.

The pub was warm and welcoming. On the inside it was a typical country pub with old oak beams and a dimly lit bar with horse brasses hanging on the wall. It had a pool table at one end and a juke box in the corner.

A group of men were drinking at the bar. They all stared at Emma and Kitty when they walked in, but then went back to their pints. They were a mixture of old and young and most of them looked like farmer types. It was obviously a drinking man's pub.

Emma couldn't care less; she was just glad to be out. Kitty had some kind of fizzy, sweet, alcoholic fruit drink, and Emma had wine. It seemed ages since she'd had a drink. The pub started to fill up and Emma was beginning to feel quite cheerful when, glancing up, she saw Dan and Simone walk in. Dan had changed out of his competition clothes and was in his usual attire of jeans and a T-shirt.

'Oh no,' Kitty said, 'I hope they don't come over.'

Emma thought they probably wouldn't. Dan was at the bar ordering drinks and Simone went to sit at a table on the other side of the pub by the pool table, so Emma couldn't be sure if they had seen her and Kitty or not.

A few more people came in; a woman and a couple of men. Emma recognised one of them as the vet, Joe Riley. He spotted her and lifted his hand with a smile, she grinned and waved back.

People shouted greetings across the pub and as the beer flowed and the banter escalated, it got noisier and noisier – everyone seemed to know each other.

Kitty got the second round, proudly producing her ID when requested, and the barman, a middle-aged chap with a big beer belly, noticing the date, had given her a free drink, much to her delight. But now they were running empty again, so it was Emma's turn to go to the bar. Someone had put some music on the jukebox and, after her second glass of wine, she was feeling quite merry. She thought she ought to slow down or she would fall off Kitty's bike on the way back.

There was a space beside Joe at the bar. He was talking to the pretty blonde woman who had walked in with him. Emma wondered if she was his girlfriend or possibly his wife. When Emma appeared beside him, he stopped talking and turned to her.

'Hi!' he said. He was wearing jeans and a checked shirt with the sleeves rolled up to the elbow, revealing muscular forearms.

'Hi,' said Emma grinning at him. He introduced the woman as Amy; the receptionist at the practice. She was attractive, a little older – thirty maybe – and seemed friendly enough.

'Special occasion?' Joe asked Emma, eyeing her appearance with obvious approval.

'It's Kitty's birthday!' Emma replied, having to raise her voice over the hubbub. She pointed over to where Kitty sat waiting.

'Wow, she doesn't look old enough to drink!' he exclaimed laughing.

'Eighteen today.'

'It makes me feel old,' he complained.

'Well yes, you must be all of what – twenty-eight?'

'Twenty-nine,' he said woefully.

'Oh, yes, ancient!' They laughed together.

Just then, Joe looked over Emma's shoulder. 'Alright Dan?' he said.

Emma turned. Dan was standing beside her, empty pint glass in hand. Her smile faded.

He gave a slight nod. 'Hi.'

'Hello,' she responded and turned away. Joe and Dan started talking, and Emma tried to attract the barman's attention.

It was busy, and the locals, who had the advantage of knowing the barman, were having a lot more luck getting served than she was. Joe and Dan were still chatting like old mates, Dan looking a lot more relaxed than he usually did, even laughing and cracking a joke. She didn't think she had ever seen him genuinely smile before, let alone laugh.

Amy, the receptionist, had visibly perked up with Dan's arrival. She turned now to join in the conversation between him and Joe. Emma tried, and failed again to get the barman's attention as he went past.

'What are you drinking?' Dan asked her suddenly.

'Er… red wine,' she said, caught on the back-foot. Dan made a gesture with his hand and the barman immediately came over.

'A red wine please Barry, and a pint of Carlsberg,' he turned to Joe and Amy. 'What are you two having?'

Well, this was awkward. 'It's Kitty's birthday,' Emma interjected, feeling a bit rude. 'She's drinking Hooch.'

Something flickered across Dan's face, it could have been amusement or annoyance, she couldn't tell.

'And a Hooch,' he told Barry the barman.

'Thank you,' Emma said, slightly embarrassed. She felt she ought to say something but couldn't think of a single thing. 'Well – I'd better not leave Kitty on her own any longer,' she said, picking up the drinks.

As she approached the table, she made a mock open-mouthed, astonished face at Kitty.

'Dan bought them!' she exclaimed, sitting down.

'Really?' Kitty looked amazed, and a bit unfocused.

Back at the bar, Amy was talking to Dan, who had sat up on a stool next to her. Emma glanced over at Simone who was sitting alone at the table, looking even more sulky than usual. Her eyes were on Dan.

Then as Emma watched, Amy put her hand on Dan's arm and leant closer, to say something in his ear. He smiled, revealing deep dimples and very even, white teeth. Was he flirting? Emma felt uneasy. Now, the look on Simone's face was so wretched, Emma could almost feel sorry for her.

Amy had got off her stool and was standing closer to Dan and, to Emma's horror, she put her hand on his leg. None of the others, Joe included, seemed to be taking a blind bit of notice.

'Oh my God, look!' Emma said to Kitty. Kitty looked.

Amy had positioned herself between Dan's knees now and was smiling up at him, coyly, her head on one side, her hand slowly moving up his thigh. Dan did nothing to stop her. Christ! Was he going to cheat on Simone, right in front of her?

At that moment Simone got up and walked out. Emma didn't like Simone but that was a horrible thing to have witnessed.

'I feel sick,' said Kitty.

'Yes, I know what you mean,' agreed Emma.

'No, I mean, I really feel sick,' Kitty said again. She looked a bit green, the colour of her Hooch.

'Oh! Quick, come on then.' Emma took her hand and dragged her to the toilets, only just making it before Kitty threw up into the bog.

When Kitty finally stopped puking, and they emerged twenty minutes later, Dan and Amy had disappeared. Joe had gone as well.

'Time to go home,' Emma said, with a sigh, realising she would have to walk Kitty home before making her cycle journey back to the yard.

Luckily for Kitty, she didn't have to come in on Sunday morning because she must have had a sore head. By the time Emma came downstairs, Dan was back, and feeding round. Emma was dreading the atmosphere on the yard that day. How would Simone be? Would she even come in? But sure enough, she turned up at the normal time and went about her work regardless, and weirdly, the atmosphere was not much different than usual.

Dan and Simone still rode out together. They didn't talk much, but then they never did. Emma rang Kitty at lunchtime on her mobile.

'Just wanted to check you're okay,' she said.

'I had a stinking headache this morning,' said Kitty, 'but I'm okay now. Thank you so much for last night, I had a great time,' she said.

'I'm sorry I let you drink so much, I should have known better since you weren't used to it.'

'Oh no!' Kitty protested, 'it was great! Can we do it again next weekend?'

Chapter 5

EMMA HAD THE NEXT DAY OFF. SHE WASN'T ENTIRELY SURE WHAT she was going to do with herself, it certainly wasn't worth going home for the day, and since Edward had gone back up to Oxford, there wasn't any point.

She had a short lie in but found that the noises from the yard below made her want to get up. From her room that morning she had already heard Dan shouting at Kitty, so she knew she was here anyway.

She made tea, and took a cup out to everyone, with the vague notion of starting the day on a good note. She got a grunt of thanks from Dan, and a wary 'Ta' from Simone.

It was a bright sunny day and Emma thought cheerfully that she might go exploring. Asking Kitty if she could borrow her bike again, she set off round the lanes. The scenery was breath-taking. From the top of the hills she could see the shimmering silvery ribbon of the sea on the horizon, but her legs had to work harder than they were used to.

She decided to go back via the village shop to stock up on groceries. Her sense of direction served her well, and more quickly than she had imagined she found herself outside the shop.

As she pushed through the door, rummaging in her purse to see how much of her measly weeks wages she had left, she nearly bumped into the man coming out.

'Oh, excuse me,' said Emma, looking up.

'Emma!' It was Joe Riley.

Emma brightened. 'Hi!' If they kept running into each other he was going to think she was stalking him.

'Day off?' he asked.

'Yes, just thought I'd have a look round,'

'How was it the other night?' he asked. 'I thought your friend looked a bit worse for wear, then you disappeared.'

'She had too much to drink. My fault really, she's not used to it. But it was a good night.'

'It's usually pretty lively in there on a Saturday night,' he said, 'most of the locals like a drink – how did you get home?'

Emma gestured to Kitty's bike. 'My trusty steed.'

'You should have called Ernie, much safer than riding that at night.'

'Ernie?' Emma said, puzzled.

'Our local cabby, lives in the village, he'll take you anywhere for a fiver. I'll give you his number,' he said, taking out his phone.

'Thanks!' Emma wished she had known this when she arrived. She supposed it was part of living in a small community, not what you know but who you know.

'Everyone seems to know each other,' she murmured, adding the number to her contacts.

'Small village,' Joe replied shrugging.

Emma couldn't resist saying what was on her mind. 'I think my boss went home with your receptionist,' she said, flushing slightly.

'Hmm, yes, it wouldn't be the first time,' he said, to Emma's surprise. 'Amy's always had a thing for Dan.'

'Really?' Emma said, her eyes widening in disbelief. 'But I thought that he and Simone were...you know, a couple.'

'No, not for years,' Joe said. 'Dan's what you might call... a free spirit, for want of a better word.'

'Right,' said Emma.

Actually, she would have used a different word, but didn't say so. The look on her face must have said it all though, because Joe chuckled.

'Dan's a mate of mine,' he said, 'a good mate, but I know he can be a bit marmite. You either love him or you hate him, and he's always been a bit on the wild side. You seem like you have your head screwed on though so you should be all right. Take care Emma.' And with a parting smile, he went on his way.

Back at the yard Emma unpacked her shopping. She couldn't afford to buy much, but it didn't matter. She could never be bothered to cook in the evening anyway and had been living on a diet of eggs on toast, cheese toasties and tinned soup. She would probably get scurvy.

At a loose end, she wandered into the tack room. It was still a bit of a state despite their best efforts that week. Well, she had nothing better to do; she might as well get stuck in.

Two hours later she surveyed her efforts with satisfaction. All the bridles were clean and hung in their proper places. The saddles all gleamed, their leather supple and shining with the glycerine saddle soap. All the bandages were rolled, all the boots in pairs and the washing machine was running with a second load of dirty saddle pads.

She had sorted through the box of muddled bits and one by one, cleaned and hung them on the nail board. Emma breathed in the smell of the clean tack. It was one of her favourite smells in the world.

'Wow!' Kitty was standing in the doorway. 'This place looks great!' She beamed at Emma, looking around in admiration.

Then Dan walked in with an armful of dirty tack from the last horse he had ridden. He glanced around and raised his eyebrows. Emma certainly wasn't expecting any praise from him – she hadn't done it for that – and she didn't get any. He put the saddle he was carrying on the saddle horse and hung the bridle on the now empty, dirty bridle hook.

'I'll do those later,' he said. 'Hurry up Kitty, you haven't got time to stand here chatting,' and strode out, Kitty scuttling in his wake.

The next day they got their first staff riding lesson.

Chapter 6

EMMA WAS TO RIDE A HORSE CALLED HENRY. HE WAS A SWEET bay gelding about 16.2hh tall. Uncomplicated to ride, but Emma had observed from watching him ridden by Simone that he had a tendency to be a bit lazy. Simone was on Chance and Kitty was on a quiet gelding called Paddy who belonged to a friend of Malcolm's.

Dan sat on an upturned bucket by the gate looking through his phone whilst they all warmed up. After five minutes he started watching them.

Unexpectedly, he was a good teacher; strict but fair. Kitty got shouted at a lot, and was very red in the face, but Emma had been able to see a visible improvement in her riding. Simone didn't take criticism too well and often had to be told something more than once.

After half an hour Emma's legs were beginning to feel like over-cooked spaghetti; it had been a while since she had used them so much, but she was happy. Henry had gone well, and she hadn't been shouted at too much.

'Tomorrow morning, I want to hack out first thing,' Dan was saying.

Emma grinned at Kitty; a lesson *and* a hack in the space of two days, things were looking up!

THE NEXT MORNING dawned fine and bright. They got started early and rushed through their mucking out to have their horses tacked up and ready to go by nine o'clock.

They set off down the lane two abreast, Dan and Simone in front with Kitty and Emma behind.

Merlin, Dan's horse, wasn't an easy ride. At first he crabbed sideways refusing to walk straight, breaking into a trot, spooking at imaginary objects, trying to catch Dan off balance, but Dan never moved.

Up the steep hills they made their horses work, pushing them forward, making them use their back ends. These Dorset hills must do wonders for getting the horses fit, Emma thought.

She and Kitty chatted with each other happily, it was great to be out and Chance, Emma's horse, was a nice ride. The sun was shining, and the spring air was sweet and fresh. They followed behind the two horses in front, trotting when they trotted, walking when they walked, the sound of their horses' hooves ringing sharply on the tarmac. Emma felt a deep sense of contentment. This was what it was all about. This made everything worth it.

Soon enough she had managed to see her second week through. Although nothing much had changed, at least now she was getting used to it.

But she still couldn't work out the nature of Simone and Dan's relationship. Since that first night Simone hadn't stayed with Dan in his room, thank God, but they had been out together and on one of these occasions Dan hadn't come back that night. Simone had been noticeably chirpier the next morning – but Dan had looked badly hung-over.

Emma and Kitty were talking about them on the yard one day when the two of them had gone out for a hack.

'My sister, Elspeth, is friends with Simone,' here Kitty giggled, 'well I say friends, Beth never has a good word to say about her, but she was in the same year as them at school. She says they used to go out with each other, then Dan started seeing another girl and they split up. But Simone always comes back for more, and Dan probably likes that because he's a sadi…sadi,' Kitty struggled to find the word.

'Sadistic?' Emma suggested.

'Yes! A sadistic bastard,' Kitty finished triumphantly. 'Beth says

Simone knocked a girl's tooth out once, at school, because she was flirting with him.'

'Really?'

'Yeah, Simone got suspended, but the girl never went near him again.'

'I'll bet she didn't.' Emma laughed, but actually, it was a bit sad. Why did Simone keep coming back for more? Didn't the girl have any self-respect? To love someone who was never going to love you back was so pitiful. Emma shook her head. 'Well, she needn't worry about me or you wanting to get near him anyway.'

'Not with a barge pole!' Kitty said vehemently.

At the end of that second week, Becky came to the yard. She was from Ireland, twenty years old, and Emma liked her immediately. She had long, wavy black hair and green eyes, a lovely bubbly personality and made a welcome difference to their rather miserable little team.

Becky cheerfully went about her work, joking with everyone alike and, even though Simone was foul to her – clearly threatened by her looks – it was like water off a duck's back. She didn't scare easily, not even seeming to mind Dan's sharp tongue. In fact, rather than avoiding him like Emma and Kitty did, she was obviously smitten by his looks.

'He can do what he wants to me with that tongue of his, if you know what I mean,' she told Emma loudly, not long after she started. 'I think he's absolutely feckin' gorgeous.'

Emma shushed her with a fearful look over her shoulder.

'Becky, seriously, you do not want to go there,' she warned. 'If Simone knows you're after him, she'll make your life a misery.'

'I don't care,' said Becky, in the same loud voice. 'I definitely wouldn't kick him out of bed for fartin'! May the best woman win I say.'

Chapter 7

EVERYTHING ACHED. MUSCLES, TENDONS, BONES; ALL THE structures which held her body together had been jarred and strained to within an inch of breaking.

'Get your bloody shoulders back Emma. *Sit!* Get your leg on him, don't wait for him to take charge. *Ride him!*'

Merlin bucked again, slamming her into the ground from a height of seven feet.

Barely giving her time to get her breath back, Dan made her get back on.

'He's trying to kill me,' she thought, as once again the ground rushed up to meet her, knocking the breath out of her body.

Dan crouched down beside her. 'Had enough?' he asked, a hint of challenge in his voice. It was nearly dark; the others had taken their horses in long ago. In answer, she slowly got to her feet and dragged her protesting body over to the huge black horse, hauling herself back up into the saddle.

'Get on with you, you old mule!' she growled through gritted teeth. With every ounce of strength she had left, she fought to stop him getting his head down. Denied the right to buck, he tried to rear, but this time she was ready for him.

Clamping her legs around him and pushing her bum deep into the saddle, she sent him forward into canter, not giving him time to react. For a long moment victory hung in the balance, just a matter of who could hold out the longest. Then, quite suddenly, as if he'd decided it wasn't worth the fight, he gave in, softening his jaw against the bit and cantering sweetly around on the circle.

She'd been on such a high afterwards, so full of her achievement at winning the fight, that she hadn't realised quite how sore she was. This morning, she was so stiff she could barely walk. Thank God it was her weekend off.

She sank down in the seat of Edward's lotus, easing her bruised bones into the soft, butter coloured leather with a deep sigh, relieved to be off the train.

'You look shattered,' Edward said with concern, starting the engine.

'I'm okay,' Emma said, suppressing a yawn. The prospect of the weekend ahead was blissful; real food, a proper bath, and sleep.

Edward hesitated at the station exit. 'Do you want to go and see your mother first?'

Emma sat up with a grimace. 'Oh God no, straight to yours,' she replied, 'I haven't even told her I'm home this weekend.'

Edward frowned, still not moving the car. 'You really ought to go and see her.'

Emma squirmed in her seat. She was just too exhausted to muster the energy required for dealing with her Mother. She looked at her watch in desperation and a welcome thought occurred. 'It's Friday, she'll be going to her music group soon.'

'All the better to go and see her now, the perfect excuse if you want to cut the visit short.'

As usual, his logic was infallible.

'But…she won't be pleased if we just "drop in". She'd expect me to ring first.'

'Of course she won't, you're her daughter.'

Emma groaned. 'I can't face another lecture about how irresponsible I was to give up my job at Hearnshaws, and how I'm wasting my life with the horses.'

Edward laughed. 'She's not that bad.'

Emma sighed with frustration and resignation.

In ten minutes she was at her parents' front door. Her father's BMW wasn't on the driveway, which probably meant he was away on business, as usual.

Steeling herself, she rapped on the door with a jaunty knock. Her mother answered, looking down on Emma from the top of the steps. Sylvia was a tall woman. Age hadn't softened her features and they were still as rigidly handsome as they had been when she was young.

'Goodness, what are you doing back so soon? Have you given up already?' she said when she saw Emma.

Edward stepped up before Emma could reply. 'Hi Sylvia,' he said, touching his cheek against hers in greeting, 'you look amazing, are you going out?'

Sylvia immediately smiled and brushed an imaginary speck of dirt from her skirt.

'Yes, it's my music group tonight…in just an hour actually. I wish you'd called and told me you were coming,' this last comment directed at Emma in an accusatory tone. Emma shot Edward an 'I told you so!' look, but he seemed oblivious.

In some ways she was glad that he was. It made it easier when he could be so charming that even her mother couldn't remain cold and disapproving. She responded to him in a way that Emma found quite amusing, becoming girlishly skittish and almost flirtatious in his company. Edward was a master of polite small talk, and because he hated any kind of conflict, Emma didn't allow herself to react, even though her mother's comments were predictably scathing.

'I suppose you're eating into your savings now you've given up your job at Hearnshaws, which you were so lucky to have, considering.'

'No Mum, I can live on what I'm being paid. It's not much but –'

'Still, I suppose you can't expect to be paid much for a job that basically anyone could do…'

Emma gritted her teeth and willed the hour to be over.

'She's only concerned for you Emma, you're her only child. Of course she wants the best for you,' Edward said when they were at last on their way to his parents' home.

'What she wants, is for me to conform to her idea of what is "successful",' Emma grumbled. 'She couldn't give a toss about whether I'm happy or not, she just wants me to "achieve" something, so she can boast about it at her music group.'

Edward fell silent and, seeing his injured expression, she relented, reaching for his hand. With a mother like his, it must be hard for him to understand, and the last thing she wanted was an argument. She and Edward never argued.

'I'm so glad you were there,' she said, genuinely grateful. 'It's always so much easier with you around.'

It was only a short drive to Edward's family home in the leafy, semi-rural suburbs of town. Sitting at the end of a quiet cul-de-sac, the house was large enough to accommodate their whole family, even now there were numerous grandchildren. Edward parked the lotus next to his father's Maserati convertible on the wide gravel drive.

'Emma love, come in!' Edward's Mum enveloped her in a warm, plump embrace, fragrant with soap powder and freshly baked biscuits. In the early days, Emma had found these frequent cuddles disconcerting, but now she quite looked forward to them.

Taking off her boots in the cream carpeted hallway, Emma began to pick up her bags to carry them up the stairs.

'Let Edward take those for you,' his Mum chided, 'they look heavy.'

Emma chuckled, thinking of the dozens of twenty kilo sacks of horse nuts she had unloaded from the feed delivery yesterday.

'Auntie Emma!' A small, warm body hurled itself against her legs, grasping her just above the knees; one of Edward's nieces – four-year-old Amelia.

'Whoa!' Emma grabbed hold of the door frame to keep her balance. 'And how's Amelia Bedelia?' she said, bending to scoop the little girl into her arms.

'I've got cheese and measles,' Amelia replied, scrunching up her nose.

'Pardon?' Emma giggled.

'You mean pins and needles,' Edward's Mum corrected. 'I did tell you not to sit on your feet.

'Is Arabella here?' Emma asked. Edward had two older sisters. Arabella, Amelia's mother, had three children. Sophie, the younger one, had two.

'She's got her Pilates class, so I've had the kids today – but she'll be back later. And Sophie's coming too with her brood. They're staying the night.'

Emma grinned with satisfaction; a full house, just how she liked it.

After a hot bath – in which she very nearly fell asleep – she went to see if there was anything she could do to help Edward's mum in the kitchen.

She found her pulling a tray of homemade Yorkshire puddings out of the Aga, while another of Arabella's children clung to her leg, and the youngest, a baby of only eight months, sat in a highchair next to the table, playing with a wooden spoon.

'Look at those Yorkshires,' Emma said, prising the limpet child from his grandmother's leg, and lifting him up to admire the puddings. 'How on earth do you get them so big and fluffy?' Her own mother had always bought frozen ones. In fact, most of their meals had come in frozen packages, courtesy of Marks and Sparks.

'I'll teach you how to make them. You'll need to know – they're Edward's favourite.'

The meal was delicious, roast chicken with everything; pigs in blankets, stuffing, leeks in a cheese sauce (homemade of course). Emma was glad she was sitting next to Sophie – who was a giggle – and at the opposite end of the table from Edward's father who was a little austere. Although always kind and solicitous towards her, Emma sometimes worried that he might not approve of her and felt like she ought to call him 'Sir'.

'Oh don't be silly!' Sophie protested when Emma confessed her worries over a glass of wine. 'You're so much nicer than Edward's ex, Adrianna. God, she was such a diva, Dad couldn't stand her. Always making out her career was so important. She once left in the middle of a family christening to "cover an emergency". She was only a journalist, not a heart surgeon – totally wrong for Ed.'

As she climbed into bed that night between the fragrant, freshly laundered sheets of Edward's king-size bed, Emma appreciated more than ever the comfort of being in the heart of his family. This was how a family should be. This was how she wanted her family to be.

Edward turned towards her for a kiss, just as a huge yawn took her by surprise. She quickly stifled it, with embarrassment.

'Are you too tired?' he asked her, stroking her arm with the back of his fingers.

'No, not if you're not,' she smiled, although if she were honest, she would have liked nothing better than to go to sleep.

As his hands began to move over her body, she tried to relax and respond in the way she knew she should, grateful that he didn't expect too much of her. He had never been very demanding of her physically, and soon she was able to close her eyes and give in to sleep.

The weekend passed in a pleasant blur of country walks, pub lunches and playing with Edward's nieces and nephews. But all too soon Emma was packing her bag to go back to Coach House Stables.

'I don't want to go back,' she admitted as Edward kissed her goodbye on the station platform.

'Well, you don't have to,' he said, kissing the top of her head, '– but I think it's nice that you have a hobby. Make the most of it before we move to London.'

*

It wasn't as hard to be back as she had feared. The yard was a much more fun place to be with Becky around, she was attractive and had an infectious laugh. Her riding was pretty good, and she was confident around the horses.

She had a beaten up old mini that she drove to work every day, much too fast, from the flat she shared with her older sister. It was covered in dents where she kept driving into things and made a habit of overheating.

One lunchtime, Emma was sitting with Kitty on the mounting block, her favourite spot, and Simone was sitting with Dan on the grass. It was late April and the weather had suddenly turned very warm. Becky had gone out, but on her return, steam was pouring out from under the bonnet of her car as she pulled up in the yard.

'Bloody thing's overheated again!' she swore.

Emma got up and went over to the car, which was hissing and spitting like an angry cat, while Becky scrambled inside to pull the bonnet's release handle.

After a minute Dan joined them. He surveyed the engine, waiting for the steam to subside before bending over to examine something down at the front. Becky nudged Emma and started to fan herself frantically with her hand. Emma stifled a giggle. Dan stood up, the perspiration running down his forehead.

'One of your radiator hoses is perished. It's leaking – that's why you keep overheating,' he said, taking off his T-shirt and wiping his forehead with it.

Emma averted her eyes, whilst Becky's were popping out of her head. Turning back to the car, he used his T-shirt wrapped around his hand to undo the radiator cap.

When his back was turned, Becky clutched at Emma's arm theatrically, pretending that her knees were giving way. Rolling her eyes up to heaven she mouthed, 'God give me strength!'

Emma had to turn and walk away, she couldn't supress the urge to laugh any longer. 'I'll go and get some water,' she managed to choke out.

In the kitchen she was able to chuckle quietly to herself; she just hoped for Becky's sake that she didn't really fall for him. Emma filled a jug with water and went back outside. Dan refilled the radiator and told Becky if she would get some radiator hose from the garage, he would fit it for her. Becky, of course, was extremely grateful.

Later on, Emma was alone in the tack room when Becky came in.

'*Sweet Jesus*, did you see that body!' she exclaimed. 'I swear I don't know how the *hell* you sleep with that in the next room!'

Emma was well aware of the perfection of Dan's physique. She had accidentally seen him half naked twice; once when she had come out of her room as he happened to be coming out of the shower with just a towel round his hips, and once when she had been on her way to the bathroom and he had been getting changed in his room with the door wide open. She had been quick to look away.

'How do you *not* fancy him?' Becky demanded. 'Emma girl – have you got no red blood in your veins?'

'Well,' said Emma, 'for one thing, I think he's a bastard,' counting on her fingers, 'two, I have a boyfriend, and three … did I mention that he's a bastard?'

'Yeah, but that body though!' said Becky dreamily, completely un-deterred.

Things had definitely improved; the extra pair of hands made light of the work, the weather was warm and sunny and now the horses' work regime had stepped up, they got a lot more riding. When she went home on her weekends off, she didn't dread going back to work the way she had before.

On one of these occasions, when she arrived back at the yard, it seemed awfully quiet. It was about 8 o'clock and there was no one around. She went to bed early.

The following morning, she got up and went downstairs to the kitchen to make tea. She could see Dan outside on the yard, feeding round. Neither Simone nor Kitty had arrived yet but Becky suddenly appeared through the side doorway, grinning from ear to ear like the Cheshire cat.

'Guess what?' she said.

'What?' said Emma, pleased to see her happy face.

'Dan stayed round mine last night!' she squeaked. Emma's heart sank, but she tried to look pleased for her.

'Have you seen him yet?' Becky asked, making herself a coffee.

'Not to speak to, he's feeding round, so – tell me what happened,' she said, as Becky was obviously eager to share.

'Well, Simone had to go early for some reason, so I stayed behind to help Dan finish off,' she began in a rush. 'Then I asked him if he wanted to go to the pub for a drink – so we did. Well, I like my whiskey – so does he – but we got into this argument over which was better, Jameson's or Grouse. I thought Jameson's of course but the pub didn't have any. So I said I had a bottle at home, why didn't he come back to mine for a couple and settle it once and for all,' she raised her eyebrows suggestively.

'Go on,' encouraged Emma, although she could see how this one ended.

'Anyway, we had a few and we might have accidentally got a bit tipsy, and somehow I ended up sitting on his lap!' she grinned. 'After that, things got a bit X-rated, but I have to tell you, he'd better take me off the market because I am *ruined,* for any other bloody man on this planet I can promise you, and I'm no blushing virgin!'

Emma cringed, she didn't want to hear any of the gory details.

'Did he drive in with you this morning?' she asked.

'No,' Becky replied, 'he left in the wee small hours.'

A warning bell went off in Emma's head.

'I haven't seen him yet,' Becky told her. 'I might pop out and say hello before the others get here.' She didn't need to because at that moment Dan walked in.

'Morning!' Becky said brightly, flashing him her ten mega-watt smile.

'Alright,' he said to no one in particular, looking straight through her. He filled up a bottle of water from the tap and left without a word.

Becky's radiant smile faded.

'Probably because I was here,' Emma said quickly. 'I expect he'll be different when you're alone.'

As the day wore on, it was obvious that wasn't going to be the case. In fact, it became apparent he was avoiding her. He sent them all out on hacks, and stayed in the school riding various horses all morning by himself. Then he disappeared somewhere in the afternoon, only re-appearing at the end of the day. He barely spoke to any of them.

Poor Becky was in agonies; she wasn't the type to bide her time. They were all in the kitchen, having finished their work when Dan came back. Heading straight for the stairs he ignored them all, but paused by the door, casting a wary eye round the room.

'Has anyone seen my phone?' he asked.

Whether she did it to get a reaction or whether it was an off-guard remark Becky replied without hesitation; 'Perhaps you left it at my place last night.'

Everyone stopped. Dan froze like a cornered wild animal. Simone went white, then red as she looked from Dan, to Becky, then back to Dan again. He turned quietly and went upstairs, shutting the door behind him.

The most awful slanging match that Emma had ever heard ensued in the kitchen.

Becky gave as good as she got, but Simone was brutal:

'You slag! You're not the first and you *definitely* won't be the last!' Simone.

'Well at least I'm not the last resort!' Becky.

'Funny how it happened while I wasn't here then!' Simone.

'Probably because when you are, you stick to him like a tick!' Becky.

Emma and Kitty made themselves scarce, but it was impossible not to hear them from everywhere on the yard. Eventually Simone came out and stormed off the yard. Emma went back into the kitchen.

'Well that was undignified,' said Becky, shamefaced.

Emma decided that perhaps silent empathy was the best course of action.

'Do you think I should go up and speak to him?' Becky asked.

Privately Emma thought Becky was on a hiding to nowhere.

'Couldn't hurt I suppose.' At least then she would know where she stood.

So off she went upstairs. She was back in less than ten minutes, white faced.

'He says he can't be doing with all the histrionics.'

'Wasn't worrying about that last night,' Emma thought darkly.

So that was it. All the fun went out of the yard with barely anyone speaking to anyone else.

At the end of another week, Becky was talking about leaving, for good. Emma couldn't blame her; the atmosphere on the yard was horrible, and if she left, Emma wouldn't be far behind her. It would serve Dan and Simone right if they all left, Kitty included. It was Becky's weekend off and she said she was going to look for another job. She never came back.

Chapter 8

A NOISE WOKE EMMA AT 2 O'CLOCK IN THE MORNING. AT ONCE she was wide-awake. Someone was moving around downstairs. Feeling uneasy, she got dressed and went downstairs to the kitchen. Dan was there, getting a drink.

'Oh, it's you,' she said, 'I thought I heard a noise down here.'

'One of the mares is foaling,' he told her.

'Oh!' said Emma, her eyes lighting up. 'Right now?'

'Probably in the next few hours.'

Emma's excitement temporarily overcame her antipathy towards him.

'Would it be okay if I come and watch, if I'm quiet? I mean – I won't if it will upset the mare or anything.'

'It should be okay, she's quite an experienced brood mare,' he replied.

He led the way next door where there were two boxes facing each other with a passageway in-between. They were larger than normal boxes; perfect for foaling. In the left hand one a deep straw bed had been laid, and in it was a bay mare that Emma had seen Dan bringing in earlier. She was standing quietly at the moment.

'Everything okay so far?' Emma whispered.

'I think so, it's hard to tell at this stage.'

He sat down on a sort of camp bed set up in the passageway. Emma looked around for somewhere else to sit, finding a bale of straw a little way away. They sat for a while in silence. Dan yawned, shifting his back against the wall.

Emma considered him in the dim light. She didn't like him, but she couldn't help respecting him. He was good at his job, hard-working and obviously experienced. She thought about what Joe Riley had said; that she could learn a lot.

'Do you always stay up with the mares when they foal?' she asked.

'Yup,' he shrugged. 'There isn't anyone else. Anyway – I enjoy it.'

'How long have you worked here?' she asked.

'Since I was fourteen.'

Emma was taken aback, that was a long time. Her natural curiosity started to get the better of her.

'And Simone?'

'She started here when we left school.'

'You've known each other a long time.' It was more a statement than a question.

He nodded. 'We were at school together.'

Emma could just picture them at school; they would be the 'popular' kids because of their superior beauty. That's the way it was in school. They were probably the kind of horrible bullies that had made her life a misery. She shuddered. The familiar flicker of defiance rose in her breast.

'I don't think Simone likes me very much,' she stated, without regret.

'She doesn't,' said Dan.

Oh! Emma thought to herself.

'She thinks you're stuck up,' he continued.

'Stuck up?' she protested, in a whisper.

'She thinks you look down your nose at her,' he explained, giving her a strange kind of sardonic look.

'Ridiculous!' Emma said. But secretly she wondered if Simone might have a point, after all, she did judge some of the things she said and did, didn't she?

'And you make her look lazy,' he added.

'A sloth would make Simone look lazy,' she replied without thinking.

He actually chuckled.

Encouraged, she asked, 'You've always lived locally then?'

'No, we moved here when I was eleven. My Dad used to teach, in Winchester.' She'd noticed before that he didn't have a West

Country accent, which she would have expected, and was actually quite well spoken.

'Does he still teach?' asked Emma.

'No. He gave it up.'

'Oh? Why?'

He paused, and Emma thought he stiffened slightly.

'He had a nervous breakdown after my Mum walked out. That's why we moved here.'

Oh. Emma felt suddenly like she had asked too much. She swallowed.

'I'm sorry,' she said, 'that must have been hard.'

He didn't reply.

Eventually they heard the mare moving around. Dan stood up and had a peek at her. Emma stood up slowly. The mare was getting down in the straw with a big groan. She shifted about uncomfortably, then she got up again. Suddenly there was a rush of fluid from her back end.

'Her waters have broken,' said Dan.

A few minutes passed. Something that looked like a transparent sack became visible, protruding from under her tail. She lay down, then got up again and moved around restlessly, only to lie down again a moment later.

'She's getting close now,' said Dan.

'Should we do anything?' Emma asked.

'Leave well alone,' said Dan.

Less than twenty minutes later, the foal was born. It had been a textbook foaling Dan said. Emma had watched, fascinated, as first one then the other of the foal's front feet had appeared, then its nose lying on its front legs. Emma had clenched her hands and given silent encouragement every time the mare had strained with a contraction.

Once the foal had flopped out onto the straw, Dan went quietly in and cleared the membrane away from its face, checking its airways were clear, while the mare lay still, her sides heaving. The baby took his first breaths, his tiny ribs visibly moving beneath his fine skin. It was a little colt foal. He started to move around, lifting his head, his long ears flopping. The mare sensed the movement and raised her head making a soft nickering noise, ears pricked, looking for her new baby. She got up and turned, her nose finding her baby's rump for the first time, begun to lick it. Minutes later, he was trying to stand in response to his mother's administrative tongue. Dan came out of the box, a look of quiet satisfaction on his face.

They watched the placenta delivered. Dan explained that if even a part of the placenta was retained it could lead to problems for the mare, so it needed to be checked.

The foal struggled to find his feet, at last managing to stand, all four wobbly legs splayed, and then after a few attempts, finding his mother's udder and taking his first noisy gulps of her life-giving colostrum. Emma was thrilled to the core of her being. She had never witnessed anything so raw and real.

'That was amazing,' she breathed.

All looked well, so they left the mare and her foal in peace.

As they climbed the stairs, Emma checked her watch. 4.30 am. Two hours and she would have to be up again, but it was so worth it.

'When the next mare foals will you tell me so I can come and watch?' she asked when they reached the top.

'If you like,' he replied.

Joe came the following afternoon. Watching him as he did all the necessary checks and declared mare and foal to be fit and healthy, it was easy to tell that he loved his job and was very good at it; he handled the mare and foal with a gentle confidence. Once he had finished, the little colt folded his legs and lay down in the straw, sighing with a grunt and closing his eyes.

'Tiring work being born, poor little fella,' Joe said, a soft look on his face.

'Are most foals born without complications?' Emma asked him.

'The vast majority,' he replied. 'And most minor problems an experienced stockman can sort out. Dan usually manages without me.'

Emma was besotted with the foal. He was so sweet with his big floppy ears and his bottlebrush tail, long gangly legs bent underneath him as he dozed in the straw. She spent every spare moment checking on him, and, for the time being anyway, she forgot about wanting to leave.

Chapter 9

On May 27th, Lynx and Chance were due to go to Millfield, One Day Event. There was the usual preparation the day before, horses bathed, rugged and hooded ready to plait in the morning. Tack cleaned and left ready in the tack room, all the gear packed in crates and also left ready for the morning.

Emma got up early to help when she heard Dan going downstairs. Simone arrived late, and went about her business in her usual unhurried way.

There was a sudden bellow from Dan, shattering the morning silence and very nearly making Emma drop the armful of the tack she was carrying.

'Why the fuck aren't Lynx and Chance plaited up?' he yelled at Simone.

'I've got plenty of time yet,' she looked at her watch in confusion. 'We don't have to leave for another hour and twenty minutes.'

Even that was cutting it fine with Simone's leisurely pace.

'We have to leave in fifteen!' Dan was livid. 'I said we had to *be* there at 9.30, not leave at 9.30.'

Simone went pale.

'*Shit!*' Dan swore. 'They'll just have to go un-plaited,' he gave Simone a look that would have made a less thick-skinned person quake in their boots. Simone pouted.

'I can plait,' Emma said. 'If that helps.' They both looked at her.

'How fast?' Dan asked.

'Twenty…twenty-five minutes,' she said, hoping to god that was still true, it had been a while since she'd done it.

He looked at his watch. '*Shit!*' he said again. Then seemed to consider something. 'Can you plait up in the lorry on the way there?'

Emma gulped, 'I can give it a go.' Talk about being dropped in at the deep end.

'I'll do it!' Simone piped up.

'No, you won't,' Dan said with a withering look, 'you can stay here and help Kitty. I'll do Lynx quickly now,' he said to Emma. 'Chance is easier to plait, he'll stand quietly in the lorry, you can finish packing the stuff.' Emma nodded.

Having anticipated a nice quiet day on the yard with just Kitty for company, she now had to move her brain up several gears in the space of a few seconds. Adrenalin kicked in.

Twenty minutes later, Dan had finished plaiting up Lynx (they weren't the most elegant plaits Emma had ever seen) and they were loading up the horses. They put Chance in first so he would be accessible from the jockey door in the cabin.

Emma stood on a round tub with the plaiting kit on a belt round her waist. She decided to sew the plaits in rather than use elastic bands, as bands could come undone if they weren't very secure.

Chance was a good boy; he stood quietly which made it easier. What didn't make it easier was the fact that Dan was obviously still angry and aware that they were running late, so his driving was a bit erratic. The horses were used to it and shifted their weight easily to keep their balance, but Emma had to grab hold of the rail to keep from falling off her tub, and twice she dropped her needle.

Luckily her fingers seemed to remember what to do of their own accord, and soon they were flying. She had them done in 45 minutes, despite the difficult circumstances.

She went back into the cab and sat down in the passenger seat. 'Thought you said you could do them in twenty?' Dan said.

Arriving at Millfield, Dan unloaded Lynx, and went to the secretary's tent to get his numbers. Back at the box, Emma started taking off Lynx's travel gear and getting the things out she would need.

She looked around at all the other horseboxes, the horses and people milling around, the sound of the voice coming over the PA system and the smell of warm, crushed grass; all so evocative of her former memories, she had a little shiver of satisfaction. At last she was getting to do the fun stuff.

'I have to go walk the course,' Dan said when he returned. 'The ground's bloody slippery – she's going to need studs in. I'll do them when I get back.'

'Just show me which ones you want and I'll put them in,' said Emma.

He hesitated. 'No, I'll do it. Simone never gets them straight and buggers up the screw threads.'

'You can't do everything yourself, let me do it – please?'

'Okay.' He sounded reluctant, but showed her which ones he wanted, nevertheless.

Left at the box, Emma cleaned out the stud holes in Lynx's shoes using a farrier's nail, then screwed in the studs (being extra careful not to cross the threads) and finished tacking her up.

Dan reappeared. He quickly came over and picked up Lynx's feet, checking the studs and nodded his approval.

'What's the course like?' Emma asked.

'Good,' said Dan, 'she'll make nothing of it. I'd better go and warm up.'

She held Lynx while he got on and helped him do his girth up.

'Good luck,' she said. He nodded and rode off.

Once he had gone, she set about getting Chance ready, finishing well before she saw Dan coming back. He didn't look happy.

'How did it go?' Emma asked apprehensively. Dan shrugged and slid to the ground.

'Won't know until I get my score. Bloody judges mark you up or down depending on whether they recognise your name on the score sheet,' he said, casting his critical eye over Chance. He didn't seem to be able to find anything amiss and springing lightly up into the saddle, he rode off to warm up.

If she hurried, she could get Lynx ready for the show-jumping and then go and watch Chance's test. She worked quickly and left Lynx tied to the lorry; the mare was quite settled now she'd been ridden in, and stood quietly resting a hind foot.

Emma set off at a jog towards the not-too-distant dressage arena. Chance was easy to spot amongst all the other horses with his bright chestnut coat and four, long white stockings. Dan was still warming up, but he wasn't riding in quite his usual relaxed way; he was scowling and looking very tense. Chance wasn't moving as well as Emma knew that he could either, clearly picking up the tension from his rider.

Dan's face throughout the test was set in a scowl, his mouth a grim line, and knowing how well he could ride, it was disappointing to watch.

In the show-jumping, Dan's riding was back to its best. He rode beautifully. Emma helped him in the warm up, doing the poles. When it was his time, Dan rode into the ring calmly and they jumped an effortless clear round. Emma ran to meet them coming out. She gave Lynx a big pat and a polo mint, feeling oddly proud.

'That was brilliant!' she grinned up at Dan. He looked pleased for a change.

Then came the fun bit, the X-country. Dan was right, Lynx made nothing of the course. Emma walked down to the start box with him, wished him luck and watched him jump the first few fences that she could see from the start. There was quite a nice inviting brush fence, then a short canter to a log pile. After that the ground sloped away down to a double of roll tops, followed by a big tree trunk.

Lynx was jumping with confidence and enthusiasm, giving the fences lots of air, which would have been a problem if she hadn't been going so fast as it wasted time. Emma lost sight of them as they disappeared out of sight into the country and waited anxiously for them to re-appear at the finish. They were round, clear, and well inside the time.

'Amazing!' Emma patted Lynx and beamed up at Dan. 'You were going bloody fast, I thought you were going to get penalties for going too much under the optimum time!'

Dan was fired up, the thrill of his ride giving his face an animation that Emma had never seen before. He grinned as he patted Lynx, his eyes bright with elation.

'She's bloody good,' he said getting his breath back quickly, 'I reckon she's ready to go intermediate.'

Dan got Chance ready for his X-country and went to warm up,

whilst Emma dealt with the hot and sweaty Lynx; washing her off, taking out her plaits and her studs, and finally poulticing her legs and bandaging them, ready for the journey home.

She just caught the end of Chance's round by the time she had finished and run down to the course. Chance was a less experienced horse; he'd had had one run out for twenty penalties at a skinny fence early on in the course.

'He's learning,' Dan told Emma, giving Chance a pat. 'It's only his second BE100. The run out was my fault, I didn't set him up properly and he didn't lock on.'

Back at the lorry, Dan stopped short when he saw Lynx.

'You've done her legs,' he said in surprise, checking her bandages.

'Yes, wasn't I supposed to?' Emma asked, worried.

'No, it's just… I usually have to do it,' he said.

Emma wondered what it was Simone actually did.

They both took care of Chance, and packed up all the gear. Dan was much more relaxed now the day's work was done. He was chatting to the guy in the neighbouring lorry who seemed to be a mate. They left both horses munching on hay nets contentedly, while she and Dan took a walk round the show ground. Emma loved every minute of it. Up until now she had been too focused on the task in hand to look around her and pay much attention to anything else, but now it was all over she could allow herself to fully appreciate her surroundings.

There were the usual shops in tents selling every kind of equestrian paraphernalia you could imagine, from saddles – which cost nearly a year's salary on Emma's current wage – to a humble bucket. She saw a couple of the more well-known riders walking about, and Rory Owens, one of her favourite riders even stopped and spoke to Dan. She was star struck. He seemed like such a nice bloke, Northern and down to earth.

'All right Danny boy?' he asked, stopping to slap Dan on the back. 'How'd you go?'

'Don't know yet,' grinned Dan, 'haven't seen the scores, but went clear on Lynx.'

'Is that the smart grey horse you were on?' asked Rory.

'Yup, that's the one – she's a cracker.'

They went on to talk about Lynx's breeding; Rory had a horse that had the same sire it seemed. Emma was dying to be introduced, but didn't want to seem pushy so stood back.

'This is Emma, my new groom,' Dan said. She was his "new groom" now was she?

'You want to watch yourself with this one,' Rory was saying, nodding at Dan. 'He has all the charm of the Irish. Managed to charm me out of thousands of my hard-earned cash over the years.' He laughed and gave Dan another friendly slap on the shoulder. 'If Malcolm wants to sell that grey, I'll have first refusal.'

'How do you know Rory?' Emma asked with excitement when they'd moved on.

'We've sold him a few horses in the past. You've heard of "Fool's Gold"?'

Emma nodded. 'Of course!' Fool's Gold was one of Rory's top horses.

'He came from our yard, Rory bought him a few years ago; the horse is syndicated now.'

'You're kidding?' Emma was impressed.

Dan nodded. 'He'll be after Lynx now.'

'Would Malcolm sell her, when she's doing so well?'

'That's *why* he'd sell her,' Dan explained. 'When a horse has proven itself and still has untapped potential, that's when it stands to make the most profit. It costs too much to compete at the higher levels and so much can go wrong, it's not worth the risk. If Malcolm gets a good offer for a horse, he takes it regardless.'

To Emma, the thought of losing a horse every time it started doing well sounded a bit soul destroying, but she didn't say so. Wandering around, they watched some of the last few rounds of show jumping that were still going on. Emma couldn't help noticing how much attention Dan got from all the girls they passed. Everywhere they went female eyes were on him. He seemed oblivious to it though.

'I'm starving,' Dan said, stopping at a burger van. He bought two bacon baguettes, giving one to Emma. She took it with thanks, realising she was famished. Still munching they went in to the scoreboard tent. Emma scanned the white boards for Dan and Lynx's score.

'There,' Dan said pointing. Emma looked.

Daniel Ryan - Balkan Lynx' Dr. 39 SJ. 0 Xc. 0.

It was only good enough for 16th. Chance's dressage was better, but the overall score was worse due to having a pole down and the run out. Dan turned away, shoulders slumped.

Soon afterwards, they set off. He drove much more steadily on the way home. Emma was studying his score sheets.

'So, it's a shame about Lynx's dressage test,' she began, giving him a sidelong glance. 'Disappointing when she jumped her heart out.'

'It's always the bloody same,' Dan growled, 'dressage judges shoot you in the kneecaps before you even get started.'

'Is it always the dressage which lets you down?'

'Yup. The trouble is its completely subjective, just a matter of one judge's opinion. Eventing isn't supposed to be a dressage competition, but so often that's what it comes down to.' He sighed. 'It's just one of those things, if your face fits, then you get a good score. That's why I love the jumping, it's completely objective. You just have to leave the fences up, and get over them without falling off.'

'So, why not do pure show-jumping?' Emma asked.

'I love the X-country,' he explained, 'and I like the fact that the horses have to be trained well for all three phases – it's the challenge I suppose.'

Emma thought for a minute, it was obvious that doing well meant a lot to him. 'Dan,' she said, 'if I say something to you, will you try not to bite my head off?' she said.

'Okay…' he said warily.

Emma took a deep breath. 'You rode like crap in the dressage,' she said.

Dan's eyebrows shot up, then his expression changed to something between amusement and annoyance. 'Fuck me Emma!' he exploded, shaking his head, 'don't spare my feelings, say it like it is why don't you…?'

'Wait, wait!' interjected Emma. 'I was going on to say…and perhaps I should have said this first,' she grinned apologetically, 'I think you're a brilliant rider, talented, gifted even.' Dan looked slightly mollified. 'But I didn't see any of that in your test, and looking at your score sheets, neither did the judges.'

'So, what are you trying to say?' asked Dan.

'Well, you only need to read the remarks to see what the problem is.' She ran her finger down the page. 'Resistance, going against the hand, rushed transition, early to canter,' she read in the remarks column. 'I mean, you got a five for your canter transition,' she exclaimed, 'you should be getting eights!'

'I suppose I get a bit uptight in the test,' he said. 'It's the judges; I hate the fact that they sit there, in their cars with their heated leather seats, drinking coffee and judging me, while I'm out there doing the hard stuff.'

'Well, that's kind of their job,' Emma said with a touch of irony.

Dan's forehead remained furrowed, his jaw tense.

'Believe me, I can sympathise,' she told him. 'I go to pieces in a test, any kind of test.'

'So, what's the answer?'

'Don't you have a trainer?' Emma asked him.

He shook his head. 'Nope, I can't afford one. We're primarily a breaking and selling yard. Competing serves mainly as a way to boost the value of the horses, it's not the main objective. I love it but…' he took both hands off the wheel momentarily in a gesture of frustration, 'there's nothing I can do about it. You need money in this game to do well, to be able to afford to keep the good horses, and for training and entry fees.'

'What about sponsorship?' Emma asked.

'You have to do well before anyone will sponsor you,' Dan said. 'It's catch twenty-two. It's difficult to get sponsorship competing at grassroots level, and every time a horse starts to do well, Malcolm sells it. I don't blame him; he can't afford to lose money.'

Emma did see the problem. She pondered for a while. 'So, do you have a plan?' she asked eventually.

He shrugged. 'Rob a bank?'

'Or, you could find a rich woman and marry her,' Emma joked, 'a rich widow who'll fall off the perch and leave you all her money.'

Dan grimaced. 'Maybe a young heiress.' He glanced at her sideways. 'You don't happen to be secretly rich do you?'

Emma snorted. 'Not a penny to my name, worse luck.'

'Oh well, you'd be too much of a handful anyway – too many opinions.'

'Ha! Too bloody right.'

Dan's mood shifted as soon as they were back home. He lost his easy-going demeanour and became his usual prickly self again.

Simone and Kitty had no-where near finished the afternoon chores. Kitty looked frazzled.

'What the bloody hell have you been doing all afternoon?' Dan shouted at them, and stormed around barking orders, making them scurry this way and that. At last the day was finished, all the horses put to bed, and Emma went inside to make a piece of toast. Dan came in and grabbed a beer.

'I was wondering, have you got any of your old score sheets?' she asked him.

He opened a drawer in the side-board which overflowed with crumpled, creased and torn score sheets; pink, yellow and green.

She pulled a whole bunch of them out, reading the remarks in the 'comments' column.

'So, am I right in thinking that if the total marks available are two hundred, then for each mark you lose, it will convert into half a penalty?'

'If you say so,' he said, running a hand through his tousled hair, and flopping into a chair. 'So what?'

'So – just looking at these – there's loads of ways you can claw back those marks…look at this one.' She pointed. 'You had an error of course, that's two marks for a start, one penalty.'

Dan looked. He frowned.

'Probably forgot which test I was doing,' he shrugged.

'Don't you practise your test at home?' She was perplexed.

'I do loads of flatwork.'

'Yes, but do you actually practise riding the test through, from start to finish, several times until you could ride it with your eyes closed?'

'No, I suppose not – it's boring. What usually happens is that I start to run through it, then get distracted by something like a bad canter transition, so I start working on my transitions and forget about the test.'

'Then here,' Emma pointed at the page. 'The judge has written; *Turned after 'A', Not straight down centre line,* which means you missed your marker, so she gave you a five whereas she probably would have given you a seven. Another easy two marks, one penalty.'

'Okay, I get the picture,' said Dan wearily, 'but what am I supposed to do? I'm obviously just crap at dressage.'

'But you're not!' protested Emma. 'If you rode the test like you do at home you ought to be getting eights and nines. I think you get stressed and irritable, the horses feel it, so they don't go so well, and you're rushing through it, trying to get it over with as quickly as possible.'

Dan said nothing, just looked down at his hands.

Emma sighed. 'The thing is, a trainer would be able to sort all these issues out.'

'It comes down to money again doesn't it?' he said bitterly, taking a slug of beer.

'But, if you wanted me to, I could maybe help by running through your tests with you at home. And, I could film them, at competitions, so you could watch them back yourself afterwards.' Dan looked up at her. 'If, I come with you to groom again, that is.'

He grinned. 'So this is just about you wanting to be allowed to come to more competitions?'

Emma smiled. 'If you like, then yes. It was fun, I enjoyed it.'

'Okay, I'll think about it,' he said. Then he got up yawning and stretching. 'I'm going to bed.'

Emma, catching it, started yawning her head off too.

He paused by the door. 'Night Emma,' he said glancing back over his shoulder.

'Night Dan.'

Chapter 10

THERE WERE SIX FOALS BORN IN ALL, INCLUDING THE FIRST ONE. Emma saw every one of them. The very last of these was a few days after she had groomed at Millfield.

It had been a cold wet day. After work, she had a hot shower and put on the rabbit onesie that Lottie had given her. Trying to get warm, she pulled the hood up and got into bed to read – but she must have dozed off because the next thing she knew, there was a knock at her door and she jolted awake with a start. Stumbling across the room, she opened it to see Dan standing there. Immediately his eyes widened, and he pressed his lips together, in an effort not to laugh.

'Why on earth are you dressed up like Bugs Bunny?' he asked her.

Emma blushed crimson, quickly pushing the hood off so the long ears flopped down her back.

'I'm not. My friend Lottie gave it to me, I was cold so….' She was hot now – with embarrassment.

'Okay, if you say so,' he said, still smirking. 'That mare's gone into labour.'

'I'll be down in a minute,' she said, closing the door gently in his face.

He had the kettle on when she arrived in the kitchen. Giving her a sidelong glance, the corners of his mouth twitched.

'I was rather hoping you weren't going to change,' he said. 'I used to like Bugs Bunny when I was a kid.'

'Ha, ha,' Emma said.

He made her a coffee.

'Thanks,' she said taking it from him. It was only early, 9.30. If all went well, she could be back in bed by Midnight.

It wasn't to be. This mare was a little overdue; Dan had been checking her for days now. She had a rather nervous temperament he explained, and sometimes they could put off foaling until they felt safe. Emma marvelled at Mother Nature and all her tricks.

'We just have to be careful not to disturb her too much,' he said.

She was restless, moving around, but her waters had not yet broken.

They sat and waited, drinking their coffee. The night wore on. Dan was yawning his head off.

'If you like, I could sit up and watch,' Emma offered, 'you could go get some sleep and I'll come and get you if things start happening.'

He shook his head. 'Tempting, but I want to keep an eye on this one.' He paused. 'Thanks though.'

Emma nodded and they continued their vigil.

The weather had settled after the wind and rain of the day. It was dry now and the wind had died down to barely a whisper. There was no noise except the rustling of the straw as the horses moved around, the quiet munching of hay and the occasional hoot of an owl. Emma was struggling to stay awake. After a while, she got up to make another cup of coffee. The mare watched her as she crept in and handed Dan his drink.

'You're not leaving then?' he asked suddenly, taking Emma by surprise. She hesitated, unsure whether he meant now, tonight, or her job at the yard.

'I thought you'd had enough a while back,' he went on. 'Didn't think you'd stick it out – after Becky left.'

She glanced at him sidelong. 'To be honest I did think about leaving,' she admitted, 'but the alternatives aren't that appealing either.'

He raised his eyebrows.

'My boyfriend and I are moving to London when he finishes his training,' she explained, 'but until then I was stuck living with my parents.'

He didn't say anything so she went on. 'My mother and I are like oil and water.'

'But why this job?' he asked. 'I would have thought someone like you could do something better paid.'

'The horses,' she said simply, and told him about Maggie, and how she'd persuaded Emma to take the job.

'I bet you cursed her when you found out what it was like,' he said with a small smile.

Emma shrugged. 'It's not so bad.... now. I wouldn't have wanted to miss this,' she said, gesturing towards the mare, who paused in her chewing to look at them, and then went back to her hay.

'Not many horses in London.'

'I know. I'm hoping I'll find somewhere I can ride, but I will miss being in the country.'

'I couldn't live in London,' he stated, 'no space.'

Emma had to agree with him, but she knew there was no choice; Edward had his heart set on London.

'What will you do for work when you move there?'

'Haven't got a clue,' she said. 'I used to work as a secretary back home.'

Dan shifted a little on his seat.

'If you don't mind me saying so, you seem smart enough, why not something better paid or more rewarding like a teacher, or a solicitor, or... something?'

Emma snorted softly. 'I don't even have A-levels, and I'm pretty sure you need a degree to do any of those kinds of jobs.'

Dan made a face. 'I haven't got qualifications either, but I thought...well, you always have your nose in a book.'

'I love reading, but I hated school. I hardly ever went, didn't even sit some of my exams.'

He raised his eyebrows. 'I didn't have you down as the rebellious type.'

'I wasn't. I was quite square really.'

A stray gust of wind blew a few blades of straw across the flag-stones. Dan seemed to be waiting for her to say something.

'I got sent to a private school. All my friends from Maggie's went to our local comprehensive, so I didn't know anyone, and I was a bit awkward and shy back then,' she explained.

Still he said nothing.

The quiet enveloped her like a cocoon. She thought back to those awful days long ago, the way she had felt such a misfit, so uncomfortable in her own skin. All the other kids had seemed so confident and self-assured.

'I was a bit of a late bloomer, never really fitted in,' she went on, feeling, as she talked, old emotion bubbling to the surface. 'Then, when I was fifteen, things got a whole lot worse.' She hesitated. Did she really want to be telling him these things? But, it was as if, now she'd started she needed to keep going.

A pressure had started to build in her chest and if she stopped now, it would sit there, forming a painful lump, like a tumour. Whether it was the silence or the near darkness, or something about the hour being neither one day, nor quite the next, it leant the atmosphere a strange sense of unreality. She took a deep breath.

'There was this boy,' she began. 'He was in the year above me at school, just sixteen,' although to her he had seemed so much older. 'He was one of those cool kids that always seemed to have dozens of people trailing round after him, typical good looking, sporty type, popular with boys and girls alike.'

As she described him, an image of him appeared in her mind. There he was, Todd McCarthy. His face perfect, handsome, arrogant.

'Anyway, for some reason I still don't understand, he started taking an interest in me. Sitting next to me, trying to talk to me, buying me lunch. And then he started to ask me out. I mean, I was fifteen but very young for my age, I was so shy, I didn't know how to speak to boys and I had no idea what he could see in me. Fresh meat I suppose.' She smiled ruefully. 'I was wary at first and avoided him but gradually he wore me down – wouldn't take no for an answer. Probably looking back, it was some stupid bet or something. So, I went out with him. He took me to the cinema and the school disco. I gradually warmed up to him, until, like the naïve little idiot I was, I thought I was in love with him.' Emma paused here, the familiar shame washing over her as she said the word 'love'.

'I thought he was amazing and I couldn't believe he seemed to like little odd me. It was great then, I thought. People who would never have given me the time of day started talking to me. I was 'in' with his group of friends, all super cool and confident. I was so stupid I honestly believed he liked me. He even bought me this gold necklace with a heart on it. Horrible cheap and tacky thing I know it was now, it turned my neck green. But at the time it was my most treasured possession; I never took it off. And for some reason, I thought it proved he really cared about me.' She paused again, but the words kept coming.

'Then, he started to want to get more serious, more than just a peck on the cheek and holding hands. I knew I wasn't ready for anything like that, so I avoided being alone with him. He kept inviting me round to his house after school and I kept making excuses… but he got pushier. And then, one of his friends, a girl called Nikki Abbott, invited me round to her house for a sleepover. I jumped at it thinking I was making real friends at last. When I got there, it turned out that she had told her parents that she was staying over at another friend's house, and they weren't there. Then Todd and another boy turned up. It was obvious what they were there for. I was terrified, but I didn't know what to do. I said I didn't want to do anything, but Todd's friend said if I didn't, everyone would say I was frigid. And Nikki told me not to be so square and went off with the other boy, so I was left alone with Todd. He said that he wanted me to show him what he meant to me. I was so scared of losing him, I couldn't think of a way out of it, I thought I had no choice. So I…slept with him.'

Her voice had become small and shaky. 'It was horrible. I cried the whole time, but in my mind I thought now at least I wouldn't lose him.' She had begun to shiver, convulsively. 'I couldn't have been more wrong. He dropped me faster than a used tissue. Literally, the next day at school he completely ignored me. So did his friends. Everyone was sniggering at me and talking behind my back. Apparently, he said some pretty nasty things about me, and you know what kids can be like.'

What Todd had actually said was, that she was a useless lay, and that she was too flat chested for him anyway, but she couldn't bring herself to say that out loud.

'I thought I must have done something really wrong for him to treat me like that. And I thought my heart was broken of course, so I bunked off most of the time and went to Maggie's. Got into a whole heap of trouble but I didn't care.'

She suddenly realized that she had been talking about herself for absolutely ages. She felt a rush of embarrassment. Dan hadn't spoken for the longest time. Perhaps he'd gone to sleep, she thought, half hoping that he had. She looked over at him. He had leaned his head back against the wall and his eyes were closed.

He must be asleep, thank God. She studied his perfect profile.

Suddenly he spoke, making her jump.

'It wasn't your fault, you know,' he said without moving, or opening his eyes.

'What?' she said, flustered.

'It wasn't your fault,' he repeated. Now he lifted his head and looked directly at her. 'You were only fifteen. That evil little shit should have been done for statutory rape.'

His words had a strange effect on Emma. She had never really looked at it like that before. The shame and self-loathing that she had carried round with her for years suddenly seemed unfair, unjust.

'If anyone had touched my sister at that age, I would have broken his legs.' His voice was low, his eyes dark pools under his brows.

An unexpected lump formed in Emma's throat, a sudden urge to cry taking her by surprise. She hastily swallowed it down.

Emma thought how differently she would have felt if she'd had a protective older brother to threaten to 'break Todd's legs'. Maybe the whole thing would never have happened in the first place. Even an older sister to talk to about it would have helped. Lottie was the only other person she had told about what had happened, years later. Lottie had listened and said, 'All men are bastards!' but somehow, that hadn't had the same effect as Dan's words.

She had never even told Edward. Part of her was scared that he would think less of her because of it.

At the time, she had felt that it was the end of her life. She'd taken refuge at Maggie's. Only around the horses could she feel normal again. Maggie turned a blind eye; knowing somehow Emma needed to be there. But then her mother had found out about her skipping school and had come down on her hard. She banned her from going to the yard, saying she needed to concentrate on her GCSEs. That had been a really dark time. All Emma had wanted to do was sleep. She would come home from the nightmare of school, fall on her bed, still fully dressed and go straight to sleep until dinnertime; mechanically eat her dinner, and then go back to bed. She never did her homework or studied; the school wrote concerned letters home. She lost all interest in taking care of herself. Her hair became lank and greasy, she got spots and didn't care how she looked. Her mother berated her for being lazy, told her she was ungrateful for all the money they had spent on her education. She was a lazy, stupid, ungrateful girl. Emma was beyond caring.

Then one day, for no particular reason, her misery turned to anger. Rage even. Anger with Todd, with the kids at school, with her mother, with the world in general, but mostly with herself. She was furious with herself. How could she have been so *stupid?* So pathetic, so weak. She wanted to punch someone, beat the living shit out of someone. That's when she'd started to run.

Perhaps in different circumstances, or if Emma had been a slightly different person, she might have turned to self-harm or drugs. But for whatever reason, she ran instead. She ran until her lungs screamed for oxygen and her muscles were on fire, and then she ran some more. Somehow the physical pain eased her mental pain.

She ran everyday, fast. Listening to her music. At least, even if she were mentally weak, she could be physically strong. And she was. She became fit and lean. She got up early in the morning to run through the empty streets, came home, showered and went to school.

The running enabled her to take control of her pain, and her body. She felt empowered. If she could find a tiny ember of anger, she could feed it until it became a raging inferno of pure energy, and running was a release. School didn't last forever. She started sneaking down to Maggie's again, she had friends there. Things got better.

But she swore to herself, that she would never, as long as she lived, let another person have a hold on her feelings like that again.

Emma cleared her throat. 'I'm an only child,' she said, 'I wish I'd had an older brother or sister, it would have made all the difference.'

'My sister might not agree with you there,' Dan replied dryly. 'She was worried she would never get a boyfriend. She said they were all too scared of me.'

Not hard to believe.

'My sister was only seven when my Mum left. Dad was…not really with it. I got very protective over her. And I was very angry, got into a lot of fights – a lot of trouble.'

Emma turned to look at him, feeling a curious kind of compassion.

'My Dad went all to pieces. I was scared that social services would take us away, put us into care. So I used to get my sister ready for school, walk to the bus, pretend everything was fine at home. I learned how to use the washing machine. We ate lots of beans,' he said, 'beans straight out of the tin. I can't stand them now.'

Emma couldn't speak. She had a vision of this little boy, getting his sister dressed for school, scared to death, but having to be so strong. A lump formed in her throat again. She sat still, not speaking for some time. Just feeling a strange, unexpected kind of empathy for him. She hoped he would sense it.

Soon afterwards, the mare started moving around; Dan got up and looked over the wall.

'Her waters have broken,' he said. Sitting back down they waited a little longer.

In response to sounds from the mare getting up and down, they both stood up to have a peek. She was on her side, the amniotic sack was protruding from under her tail and one tiny foot was showing.

'Hopefully won't be long now,' said Dan, settling back down again. After a few minutes he stood up and looked again, his brow furrowed.

Emma silently stood and had a look. Still only one foot showing.

The minutes ticked by. The mare was pushing hard now, they could hear her groaning with the effort. They both checked again; still only one foot showing. Emma looked at Dan's expression; there was a hint of unease. He looked at his watch, his face registering concern.

'I think the foal's not presenting properly,' he said, 'I'm going to have to help.'

Emma caught her breath. 'Is there anything I can do?' she asked.

'A bucket of warm water with some Hibbi-Scrub would be good,' he said. 'And Emma,' he stopped her as she was about to dash off. 'Get your phone, in-case we have to call the vet.'

Moving as fast as she could, she was back in less than five minutes with the bucket of water. In the stable, Dan had put a head collar on the mare and made her get up. He was moving her around the loose box. Seeing Emma come in with the water, he put the lead rope over the mare's neck and came out.

Quickly he stripped off to the waist, and scrubbed his hands and arms. Then going back into the stable, he went around to the mare's hind-quarters. He deftly pushed a hand inside her, feeling around the foal's visible foot. Then, biting his lip, with a look of deep concentration, he pushed further. His expression registered slight relief.

'It's just his leg, not his head,' he said. Then, his face contorting with the effort, he seemed to twist his arm and shoulder round, so he was turned away from the mare his arm extended out behind him, every muscle in his body contracted. The mare groaned. Emma held her breath, her fists clenching. After an anxious few seconds Dan drew his arm out, the mare strained. Two legs were now visible, one in front of the other. It wasn't finished yet.

Dan caught hold of the foals two legs and pulled down firmly, and again. The foal's nose made an appearance at last, and with another few pushes from the mare, the foal's shoulders were out. Emma let out her breath.

The mare strained again, a strong pull from Dan and the foal was out, lying stretched out on the clean straw. It was a big colt… but strangely still. Dan knelt down next to him, wiping his face and his nostrils clean, his movements quick and deft. Then moving both hands down to the foal's chest, he started massaging, his face anxious.

There was no obvious response from the limp body lying immobile and lifeless. Emma felt fear clutching at her bones. She covered her mouth with both her hands. Dan bent down low. Closing one of the foal's nostrils with his hand, he covered the other nostril with his mouth and blew into it. Suddenly there was a convulsive movement from the foal. Emma saw his rib cage lift and fall. He was breathing. Emma let out a small cry of relief,

'Oh, thank God, thank God!'

Dan sat back on his heels, breathing hard. 'He was just a bit shocked, I think,' he said. 'But he's so big, there might have been pressure on the cord.'

After that they did the usual checks, waiting for the afterbirth, and for the colt to get up and have his first feed. He did, after a while, and everything started to look more normal. At five o'clock in the morning, Emma finally fell into her bed.

When she woke, Emma was exhausted but strangely calm. The emotion of reliving those past difficult times, coupled with the drama of the mares foaling had left her with a sense of being purged, as if she had shed a layer of skin, and was very clean but slightly raw. She also felt a little awkward around Dan.

In the cold light of day, to have talked about something so personal with him seemed like a very odd thing to have done.

She was relieved, however, that he didn't seem to behave any differently towards her, and then, in the afternoon something happened which, bizarrely, put her at ease.

He had sent her into the feed room to slice up the carrots and start making up the feeds. She was staring at the chalk board and absentmindedly nibbling on a carrot, struggling to make sense of the scrawling, smudged lists that described what each horse had in its feed, when Dan walked in. He immediately cracked up laughing.

'What is it?' Emma demanded, startled.

'You, with your carrot,' he said. 'Are you sure you don't have a split personality? Turn into a bunny at night, a Ware rabbit maybe?'

'I think you might be slightly delirious from lack of sleep,' she said, shaking her head in bemusement.

Later, Emma had started to nod off at the kitchen table. Dan asked her if she wanted a coffee, and she didn't hear him at first.

'Oi! Bugs!' He prodded her with the spoon he was holding. She jerked awake.

'What?'

'Do you want a coffee?' he asked grinning at her.

'Yes – please… and don't call me that.'

But of course, the more she complained, the more it seemed to amuse him.

Chapter 11

As Dan had told her, the yard's business was predominantly breaking and selling. There were always lots of youngsters, most of them home bred. Dan did all the backing himself, on his own.

Emma found the whole process fascinating and whenever she could, she'd watch him with the young horses. It seemed to her that he never followed the same process twice.

'It all depends on the horse,' he said when she asked him about it, 'each one is different.'

'Wouldn't it be easier if you had another person to help?' Emma asked.

'Nope. On my own I can concentrate on the horse without worrying what the other person might do. The only accidents I've had backing horses were caused by someone else doing something I didn't expect. You can usually tell what the horse is going to do; it's people who are unpredictable.'

Once backed, they would be turned out again and brought back into work as four-year-olds to be sold. Malcolm would only buy older horses if he thought they had real potential and weren't too pricey; there wasn't a very big budget. Lynx had been bought as a four-year-old, and there was another horse called Arcturus; a six-year-old that he'd bought recently from Ireland.

Arcturus was the kind of horse that Emma would have loved to own. He was a big, strong, bold Irish bred gelding. He loved to jump and despite his strength, had a lovely trainable temperament. He hadn't been out competing yet, only to a few training shows with Dan, but showed lots of promise. He was due to compete in his first BE90 at Pontispool the following weekend. Dan had been schooling him over the cross-country fences at home but wanted to take him and Lynx out for a gallop before the weekend. Emma was to be allowed to take him.

'You'll need your body protector,' Dan told her when she was getting her crash hat from the tack room.

Emma felt a rush of adrenalin. 'Okay.'

They hacked out of the yard together, the two grey horses side by side. Lynx was taller than Arcturus and less stocky, she had the long legs and athletic frame of a true thoroughbred, whereas Arcturus probably had some Irish draught in him somewhere down the line.

The sun was shining, but the sky to the west looked black and threatening.

'Where are we going?' Emma asked.

'We'll go out to the Simonds estate,' Dan replied. 'It's good hunting country – there are some jumps – and Malcolm has an arrangement with the owners.'

It was about a thirty-minute hack to get there, enough time to get the two horses warmed up. They turned right, off the road through a wooden gate, then headed up a lane and through another gate.

They were at the foot of a hill, which was gently sloping at the bottom but got steeper towards the top. It was early in the day so the sun was behind them, but the green of the hill stood out starkly against the black sky ahead, and the earth here was very red.

They started off in trot along the bottom of the slope. Both horses knew what was coming and were on their toes. Emma could feel Arcturus's muscles bunching beneath her.

'He's going to get strong,' said Dan, 'but you just have to stay behind me, go where I go, jump where I jump.'

Emma nodded, the butterflies going mad in her stomach. Dan showed her how to bridge her reins across her horse's neck so he would be pulling against himself rather than against her.

'You ready?' he asked.

'When you are…'

He grinned at her over his shoulder as he let Lynx have her head and she leapt forward into gallop; Emma felt a ripple like a shockwave run through her.

Arcturus, giving a grunt like a warhorse beginning a charge, leapt to follow Lynx, nearly ripping the reins out of Emma's grip. She gasped – his power taking her by surprise, even though she knew it was coming. Just managing to stay with him, she stood up in her stirrups, taking the weight down into her heels and shortening up her reins; bridging them across his neck like Dan had showed her, and settling her knuckles firmly into a spot just above his withers.

All she could do was try to contain his power enough to stay behind Lynx. Dan started to turn up the hill, increasing the speed. He glanced over his shoulder at Emma, who was starting to feel more in harmony with her horse. They thundered up the hill and breached the crest, where they swung left, the wind rushing into Emma's face and whipping tears from her eyes.

There was a hunt rail in the fence up ahead, Dan barely slackened their pace, Arcturus took it in his stride so that Emma hardly felt it. Then there was a low wall with a ditch. Dan and Lynx flew over it, closely followed by Emma and Arcturus. They were going so fast now there was nothing but the blur of speed, the horses' legs going like pistons, as the ground and several more jumps fell away behind them.

They turned down-hill. Arcturus began to feel like a runaway train as Emma struggled to hold him. Relax. Breathe. She looked across at Dan.

He'd sat a little more upright, his lower leg more forward. Emma copied him, bringing her weight further back and she immediately felt more secure.

At the bottom of the slope there was a hedge. Surely they weren't going to jump it – it was enormous! Emma felt panic rising in her throat, but she had no choice. She was completely at Dan's mercy, wherever he went she had to follow.

He glanced back at her. 'Alright?' he shouted into the wind. 'You just have to trust him!'

'Okay!' she called back. Dan aimed Lynx at the lowest part of the hedge. For a second her grey ears were visible over the top, white against the black of the sky, then she rose like a bird taking off. Emma glimpsed her heels turned up to the sky, the sunlight behind them glancing off her metal shoes, then with a flick of her tail she was over and completely disappeared from view.

Arcturus was locked on to the hedge; one way or another Emma was going over. She sucked in a lungful of air, and then, if truth be told, she might have even closed her eyes. The next moment she felt Arcturus launch himself, their speed carrying them up, and up, and over, to land safely on the other side. Emma gave a whoop of triumph. Dan looked back, grinning at her delight.

Just then the heavens burst, and they were galloping through a torrential downpour. Dan took one hand off his reins and pointed up. Emma looked. Right in front of them a rainbow had appeared, arcing high over their heads. It seemed as though they could have galloped through the arch. Emma thought she had never seen anything so beautiful. She was euphoric.

Still they pounded on through the deluge, turning uphill again. The mud from Lynx's heels flicked back at her, hitting Emma in the face and streaking Arcturus's grey coat red. Over another hedge, not quite so big, and a fallen tree trunk.

At last Dan began to slow down, gradually sitting up and moving his fingers on the reins. As Lynx slowed, Arcturus began to pull up of his own accord, both horses breathing hard. Dan brought Lynx back to walk and began to circle her. Emma did the same.

She felt that she had never before known the true joy of being alive. Life seemed clear and simple to her then, it was all about this. The thrill of being.

'That was fantastic!' she said, giving Arcturus a big pat on his soaking wet neck.

'You look like you have war paint on,' Dan laughed at her. Putting her hand up to her face, Emma felt the mud that had flown into her face from Lynx's hooves, streaked by the rain. The rainstorm was sharp but short. As they hacked back to the yard, it had eased off a bit.

'Haven't you ever wanted to compete?' Dan asked her.

Emma shook her head.

'Why not?' he asked. 'It's a shame. You've got guts and the horses go well for you.'

Emma felt ludicrously pleased. 'Thanks,' she said giving him a self-conscious smile. 'But I don't do well under pressure; I go to pieces in any kind of test – it's why I don't have a driving licence.'

'Oh? Why's that?'

Emma sighed. 'My mother was very keen for me to 'do well' in something. Preferably something musical like the piano or the violin, because that was what she's interested in. So I learned both and she entered me for exams, but I was no good at either – I failed of course. She said it was because I was lazy and hadn't practised. When I got my results, she didn't speak to me for two whole days.'

'How old were you?' Dan asked.

'Eight,' Emma replied. 'After that, every time I had to take another wretched exam I got so nervous I would mess up even more, and it got worse and worse over the years. My Mother would make me practise a piece of music, and if I made one mistake, I had to start over again. Once I sat at that bloody piano for three hours with her sitting behind me, and I couldn't get it right.'

Emma remembered the rising feeling of panic, *I can't do it, I can't do it,* the sensation of being unable to breathe, that terrifying feeling of suffocation. Tears obscuring her vision so that she couldn't see the music or the keys of the piano. Her exams at school had been a nightmare. In a couple, she'd had to run out halfway through because she'd thought she was going to be sick.

'My Mother's never forgiven me for having nothing to show for all the money they spent on my education. She thinks I'm spoilt and ungrateful.'

It had been an often-repeated theme throughout Emma's childhood.

'It's probably all my own fault,' her Mother would always begin by saying, 'but because she was an only child, she was always spoilt rotten of course.'

Whoever she happened to be telling would usually nod in sympathetic understanding at this point. 'We always wanted to give her the best of everything which is probably why she has unrealistic expectations about life. If you have had everything handed to you on a platter, you don't appreciate it I suppose. When I think what I could have done if I'd had the education that she had. I was going to be a barrister you know, but I sacrificed my career to stay home and look after Emma. She doesn't seem to understand that in order to succeed in life, you have to be prepared to work for it.'

This narrative would vary a little in content and delivery depending on whom it was directed at. If she were talking to someone like Edward, or a relation, it would be toned down, softened and punctuated with a few 'dear Emma's', in consideration for the tender feelings of the listener.

When it was directed at Emma herself in the course of one of her Mother's fits of temper, it was stripped back to the bare bones and delivered without anaesthetic.

When she had been a young child, Emma had gone to great lengths to avoid one of her Mother's rages. She would watch her facial expressions anxiously for any signs of displeasure or censure. She would listen intently to her voice for any variation in tone, becoming hyper-sensitive to any slight tension or change in mood.

The assaults were only ever verbal – Emma was never physically hurt by them – but almost worse than these were the silences. Sometimes they would last for days. Often Emma would have no idea what had triggered them, or she would unintentionally say something, which would cause offence and her mother would simply not speak to her; would pretend Emma wasn't there, look right through her.

But she became very resourceful and self-sufficient, managing to do quite difficult tasks at a young age to avoid having to ask her mother for anything.

She never wanted for material things. Silvia took immense pride in having the best of everything, so Emma had a beautiful room, which had to be kept scrupulously tidy; not too many toys, only very tasteful ones, but lots of books to give the impression to anyone that visited, that they were all extremely well-read and clever.

Her Mother's friends were always so impressed by how well-behaved Emma was. What a 'good' child. What a well brought up, polite little girl. It was such a credit to Silvia what a well-mannered, pleasant child she was. Because Emma never pestered for attention, or made a fuss about anything and was desperate to please.

She wasn't allowed to watch television, but this had been a good thing for her, as it had meant that books had become her escape, and she loved to read. She devoured books one after another, feeling sometimes like the world she created in her head from the characters on the page was more real than the physical world around her.

Emma shook herself back to the present.

'Still, I guess it's a lucky person who gets through their childhood unscathed,' she said ruefully.

'What about your Dad?' Dan asked. 'Where was he?'

Emma shrugged. 'He wasn't around very much. He had to travel a lot for work and even when he was at home, I didn't really see much of him.'

She wanted to change the subject.

'Does your sister still live at home?'

'No, she moved back up to Winchester. She's got a baby now, eighteen months old.'

'Is she married?' Emma asked, thinking she must be quite young to have a baby.

'No, but her partner's a good bloke, he's older than her – looks after her. I expect she'll have dozens of kids.'

'How often do you see your niece….nephew?'

'Nephew. Not very often. Just after he was born and a few months ago when they came to visit.'

'I love my nieces and nephews,'

'I thought you were an only child,'

'I am – they're Edward's really but I've known them since they were born, so they feel like mine.'

He glanced at her. 'You've been with Edward a long time then?' he asked.

'Four and a half years,'

He raised his eyebrows.

Tentatively she asked, 'Has your Mother seen her grandson?'

His face became a rigid mask.

'Nope. She lives in Malta now. That's where she's from originally. Ran off back there with her latest bloke.' His voice was full of contempt. 'She'll say how much she wants to come back and see us and meet the baby, but she won't, it's all bullshit. It always has been. But for some reason, my sister always believes her. I can't understand why she opens herself up, just to be hurt over and over again. I think she must be stronger than me.'

'Or maybe she's not as hurt by it as you are,' Emma said softly, 'after all, she had you. You had no-one.'

He was silent and looked the other way for a few seconds.

When he spoke, his voice was hoarse. 'The last time, her boyfriend picked a fight with me. He was drunk and broke a bottle – slashed me across the ribs with it. I needed stitches.'

An icy shiver ran down Emma's spine.

'She promised she was going to leave him after that, but promises mean nothing to her. Maia and I were never her priority.'

Did a person ever fully recover from that kind of betrayal? Physical scars healed in time, but mental scars – they were harder to heal.

When they reached the yard, they put their horses away and went in for lunch. Dan pulled his soaking wet T-shirt off over his head, chucking it on the pile of dirty washing by the machine, then bent down to pull off his boots. Emma noticed a scar across his ribs on the right-hand side of his torso; it must have been a deep cut, close to the bone – it stood out white against his brown skin.

He straightened up, and with a start she realised she had been staring. Embarrassed, she began to peel off her body protector. She looked down at herself. Her T-shirt had become like a second skin, damp and clinging.

Dan grabbed a towel off the shelf and chucked it to her.

'Go and get changed before you get cold,' he said.

She ran upstairs to the bathroom and, catching sight of herself in the mirror, she got quite a shock. She looked like she had blood smeared across her face. Then she remembered the mud. She washed it off hastily and went back down.

Dan handed her a coffee, which she took gratefully.

'So, are you going to practise your tests this time? Or just hope for the best as usual?' Emma asked him.

'Bloody hell Bugs!' he replied. 'Have you always been this bossy?'

But later on, she saw him practicing.

On the Friday night, she and Simone were getting the kit ready for the next morning. Dan was snappy.

'Where's Lynx's French link snaffle?' he asked, looking blankly at the hooks where all the bits were now hung neatly.

Emma found it straight away and handed it to him. He took it without a word.

Simone, busy rolling bandages, asked, 'What time have we got to leave in the morning?'

'Six-thirty,' he said. Then, still with his back to her; 'Emma's going. You can have the weekend off.' Emma's heart gave a little thump. She risked a quick glance at Simone, to see her face darken with rage, before she chucked the last bandage in the crate and stalked out, her long dark hair swinging furiously in its ponytail.

Chapter 12

AT SIX-THIRTY THE NEXT MORNING THEY WERE PULLING OUT OF the yard in the horsebox. It came as no surprise that Simone hadn't volunteered to come in and help muck out, but Kitty, like the good-hearted little thing she was, had come in at six a.m. to make an early start.

'God knows what we'll come back to,' Dan grumbled as they set off. 'Malcolm needs to advertise for staff again.'

Emma didn't say what she was thinking; was there any point? Instead she asked; 'How did you come to be working for Malcolm?'

His scowl relaxed into a grin. 'When I was fourteen, me and a mate nicked a car.'

Okay, not what she had expected. 'You're kidding?' she laughed.

'Nope. We were always doing dumb stuff like that. Just joyriding, we didn't set fire to them or anything.'

Emma listened fascinated. In her world no one ever broke the law. 'Go on,' she encouraged.

'Well, this time, I didn't know it, but the car happened to belong to Malcolm. Anyway, I crashed it.'

'No! What happened?'

'I was trying to light a fag and drove into a tree.'

Emma chuckled. 'No, I mean – what happened? Were you hurt? Did Malcolm catch you?'

'Yup. My mate ran off. I had broken toes and couldn't run – Malcolm caught me. He made me sit on a chair in his kitchen and interrogated me. I lied about who I was, but he recognised me from the village and threatened to call the police. I had already been in trouble a few times and knew I was running out of chances.'

The lorries engine roared as they negotiated a steep hill. 'Malcolm said that if I came and worked for him, mucking out…. that sort of thing, I could work off the cost of the damage to the car.'

'That sounds like something Malcolm would do,' Emma said. 'He's so lovely.'

Dan gave her a sardonic smile, grinding the gears. 'He also threatened to break all the toes on my other foot, if I ever put one out of line again.'

Emma laughed.

'And he worked me bloody hard. I had to come every day after school and at the weekends. I had blisters on my blisters. But it kept me out of trouble. I left for a year when I was nineteen. Thought I wanted to be a jump jockey.'

'Didn't you like it?'

'I did, but I pretty nearly killed myself. Got had up in front of the stewards for reckless riding. Then I got into a fight with the head lad and knocked out his front teeth, so I got the sack.'

Emma felt like she had had such a boring life in comparison.

'Did Malcolm teach you to ride?' she asked.

'No, I could already ride a bit, I guess it's in the blood. Back when we were kids, our cousins in Ireland had ponies. We used to stay there every holiday. I didn't really learn anything except how to stay on, it was mostly jumping bareback, riding in head collars. Me and my cousins were pretty feral – I used to fall off a lot.'

'So, who taught you?'

'When I came to Malcolm's, the yard manager at the time – a bloke called Matt – taught me after I'd been here six months or so. I didn't want to learn at first, all my mates took the piss, said I was turning into a poof. But I found it came easy to me and I loved the horses.'

'What happened to Matt?' she asked.

'He ran off with the farrier four years ago, a guy called Jason. I think they're living in Brighton now. So Malcolm let me take over when I was just twenty. Honestly, if it hadn't been for him, I probably would have done some time by now.'

Emma nodded. It was funny how a person could come into your

life and completely turn it around. 'Like Maggie, for me.'

Dan chuckled, 'If it weren't for her you'd be in prison?'

Emma grinned. 'No. I just mean that meeting one particular person can change your life. I don't know how I would have survived my childhood without Maggie… and it's just chance isn't it, luck I suppose.'

Dan shook his head. 'I don't believe that,' he said. 'There's no such thing as luck. I think life gives you opportunities, and it's up to you to make the most of them. There's always a choice.'

When they arrived home that evening, Emma waited until Simone and Kitty had gone home, then got her phone out and showed Dan what she'd filmed that day. He watched the screen, a deep frown on his face.

'Christ, I reckon I should give up now,' he growled, chucking the phone on the table.

'It's not that bad,' Emma said, rescuing her phone. 'You just need to relax and slow it down, try to imagine you're riding at home, forget that it's a test.'

'Easier said than done,' he said raising an eyebrow at her. 'If it was that easy, you'd have a driving licence.'

Emma had to admit, he had a point.

'Let me film you riding at home tomorrow, then at least you'll be able to see the difference.'

He shrugged. 'Whatever.'

She took that to be a yes.

Merlin had a huge amount of potential, enormous scope and fabulous movement, but he wasn't an easy horse – in any way. Dan didn't think he was ready to go out competing yet, and, ordinarily, he would have the last say – but Malcolm didn't own him. He was owned by a local business man called Bret Andrews; a large man, red in the face and clearly prepared to throw his – quite substantial – weight around.

'And who are you?' he asked Emma, when he came to the yard, taking her hand and holding on to it too long. 'Danny's latest squeeze?' Another second and she would have snatched her hand away.

'You need to get that black bugger out earning his keep,' Andrews said to Dan. 'I don't pay Malcolm a bloody fortune to have a field ornament.'

'He's not ready,' Dan said in a matter-of-fact tone.

Andrews drew himself up taller and got a little redder in the face. 'I can always give someone else the ride on him if you're not up to it?'

Dan shrugged, his voice remained impassive. 'That's your choice,' he said.

'WE DON'T SEE him that often,' Dan told Emma after Andrews had gone, 'and it's mostly bluff – he knows no one else would want the ride on him.'

Emma could tell Dan disliked him, but apparently, Andrews paid a huge amount of money to Malcolm to keep Merlin on competition livery, so they couldn't afford to lose him. So Malcolm persuaded Dan to take Merlin to Bicton ODE with Lynx, despite his misgivings.

Lynx was in the Novice section and her dressage was first. Over the last few weeks they had been practicing, with Emma filming and then they would watch it back in the evening over a beer.

Dan had to admit it was working, his scores were consistently improving. Emma's heart swelled with pride as she watched them execute a bloody good test. It looked cool, calm and confident. Lynx was at her best, showing off her lovely athletic paces; supple and obedient. And Dan didn't scowl at the judges once. Emma kept her fingers crossed all through Lynx's show-jumping, praying for her to go clear. And she did.

Merlin's dressage was after Lynx's show-jumping. As Dan tried to ride him away from the box, the black horse was obviously unsettled by the unfamiliar sights and sounds. He didn't want to leave the safety of the lorry and napped, running backwards and trying to rear.

'Do you want a stick?' Emma asked anxiously.

'No…I can't hit him,' Dan replied through gritted teeth, 'it'll make him worse.'

Every time he tried to lift his front legs off the ground, Dan used either one rein or the other, catching him off balance so he couldn't get the stability he needed to stand straight up. Then he made him move sideways off his leg and turned him in a circle until Merlin wanted to go forward of his own accord. Now Merlin was going forward Dan kept him going, pushing him into a brisk trot. He looked like he had grown a whole hand taller and his body seemed to crackle with nervous energy. With his long sleek black body, built like a greyhound, he looked more like a racehorse than an eventer. He spooked, drifting dangerously close to other boxes and horses, then stopped and with a half rear, tried to spin back towards the lorry.

It took all of Dan's riding skills just to keep his four feet on the ground and keep him going in the right direction. Emma watched him go anxiously, but before following him, she couldn't resist nipping to the scoreboard tent. She looked for Lynx's dressage score. Holy crap! It was 24.5. They were lying in first place, just in front of Rory Owens.

Trying to contain her excitement, she ran off down to the dressage area.

Merlin was not looking much happier; Dan had taken him to a quiet corner away from the other horses, but it was obvious Merlin was having none of it. The circle they were on bulged out towards the other horses and he kept blasting out loud, frantic neighs, calling to Lynx back at the box. Emma glanced at her watch; he was running out of time. Bret Andrews had come to see his horse preform. He was watching from the opposite side of the arena in a group of his cronies.

Dan only just managed to get Merlin to turn into the arena at 'A' and then their progress down the centre line zig-zagged wildly one way and then the other. Their halt and salute never quite happened, but was more like piaffe – a trot on the spot – terminating in a half-rear. Dan took his hand off the rein for a split second to salute before hastily taking back the rein and sending Merlin forward before he reared again.

Emma didn't bother to film it. She was transfixed with dismay as Merlin did handstands all the way down one long side, and when Dan asked him for canter, he took off into a gallop. It took all of

Dan's strength to bring him back under control and turn him before he jumped the boards. Fuck.

Somehow, he got through the rest of the test, just about managing to stay in enough control to avoid elimination. Emma was full of trepidation as she went to meet them coming out of the arena.

Andrews was already there. 'Well, what a performance!' he boomed, making people nearby turn and stare. 'Perhaps you should go back to pony club and get some lessons.'

Emma didn't dare look at Dan as they walked back to the lorry. Given a long rein, Merlin finally walked sensibly. Resting a hand on his neck, she wondered whether it would be a good time to mention to Dan that Lynx was lying in first place. Tentatively, she looked up at him. His face was a picture of consternation, their eyes met and suddenly there was a light in his eyes, a twitching of the corners of his mouth.

Something snapped inside her and she dissolved into fits of helpless giggles. To her immense relief, Dan started laughing too. Merlin, startled, broke into a jog.

'That was truly impressive!' Emma choked, holding her side.

'Yep, knocked 'em bandy,' he replied.

They didn't stop laughing until they were back at the lorry, and the realisation dawned that he still had to show jump and go X-country.

Actually it wasn't that bad. Merlin seemed to have put his atrocious behaviour behind him and put in a creditable performance in the show-jumping with only two poles down. The round was very fast and looked a bit hairy-scary, but at least there was no uncontrollable bucking or bolting.

Due to the horses being in different sections, Merlin's cross-country was before Lynx's.

He was a bit nappy going into the start box, and Emma had to lead him in to avoid them missing their start time, but once they were galloping, Emma could see he was going to keep going. The fences weren't very big for a horse of Merlin's scope, it would come down to whether he liked the look of them or not.

Sure enough, they had two refusals. One at a slightly spooky fence (painted to look like a wagon, which Merlin obviously found suspicious) and one at the water, where, not wanting to get his feet wet, he'd ground to a halt, taken a couple of steps backwards before giving in and making a huge leap right into the middle, soaking both himself and Dan.

Once Emma had dealt with Merlin back at the box, she looked at her watch. Fifteen minutes until Lynx's cross-country round, Dan had taken her down to warm her up.

Emma had decided not to mention that he was lying in first place. If he went clear, no one could catch him. Off she ran on down to the course, her feet skimming the grass, light as air.

As she got there, Dan had just finished putting Lynx over the practice fences, he had just over five minutes before he would be called. Walking over to him, Emma saw him quickly dismount and start to undo his girth.

'What's wrong?' she asked him, jogging the last few steps.

'Saddle pads slipped back,' he said. He was a stickler for having everything just right. Lynx tried to put her head down and graze.

'Here, let me hold her,' Emma said, but it was just too late. Dan tried to pull her up, but in his hurry, hadn't noticed that she'd stepped forward and stood on her reins. She jerked her head up, snapping the leather just behind where it buckled on to the bit.

Dan and Emma looked at each other in horror. Their lorry was right the far side of the lorry park, there was no way Emma would make it back with a spare pair of reins before he had to start.

'Wait there!' she said, and sprinted off.

Going into the first tack shop she came to, she grabbed a pair of reins off a hook, and pulled out a couple of crumpled notes from her pocket. She slapped the money down on the table and ran out of the tent.

'Wait! Your change…' shouted the vendor after her.

'Keep it!' she called back, sprinting back to where Dan was holding Lynx.

'Where did you get those from?' He said, in amazement.

'Bought them,' she replied, getting to work to unbuckle the broken reins and attach the new ones.

'Quick thinking Bugs,' he said.

Luckily, Lynx stood good as gold whilst they fiddled with the stiff new buckles. They had it done just in time and, leaping on to her back, Dan cantered off.

Emma didn't think she had ever been more nervous watching him ride a course. Apparently, riders had been struggling to make the time, according to other grooms she chatted to. Lynx was fast, but now, Emma wished that she'd told Dan to put his foot down.

She needn't have worried. They flew round clear and inside the time – just.

As they rode through the finish, Emma ran up to them almost jumping up and down.

'You've done it!' she squeaked, 'you've won!'

While they were packing up, Rory came over.

'You beat me you bugger!' he bellowed in good humour, giving Dan a slap on the back. 'Must be a bloody good horse is all I can say.'

'She is,' agreed Dan.

'I'll have to up my game if you keep riding like that, I'm not ready to hang up my boots just yet,' he said, adding, 'remember to tell Malcolm if he wants to sell that mare, I want first refusal.'

Emma felt slightly uneasy.

Driving home, they had a good laugh about Merlin's test sheet.

'*Rushed transition*,' she read from the judge's comments column, next to the movement where Merlin had bolted.

'Obviously completely subjective,' she joked, 'judge clearly didn't know what she was talking about.'

Dan grinned. Considering Lynx's success, he could afford to be philosophical about Merlin's disaster.

'I think your judge had a sense of humour,' she laughed. 'Where he took off bucking she's put, *plenty of impulsion, incorrect bend (well sat!)*.'

They hadn't seen Andrews again after the dressage.

'I expect he was in the owners tent trying to flog Merlin to one of his cronies,' Dan said.

It was such a shame, all that raw talent, but impossible to train.

'I wonder what happened to make him the way he is?'

There was a pause, and Dan cleared his throat and shifted in his seat a little.

'I know part of it – his history. At least, I'm pretty sure I do.'

Emma sat up and turned to look at him, her curiosity instantly aroused, 'How do you mean?'

'Well…this is gong to sound weird, but…do you remember I told you that I got the sack from that racing yard, because I had a fight with the head lad?'

'Yes.'

'Merlin was the reason I hit him. It was six years ago, and he's changed a lot – including his name – but I'm sure he's the same horse.'

'That is weird.' Emma was intrigued. 'So, what happened?'

'He came to us for training. He was a bit tricky even back then, but no where near the cantankerous bugger he is now. I was his lad. In training he was outstanding – the kind of horse everyone was talking about, very exciting to ride, incredible jump. But every time he raced, he would nap so badly at the start that the jockey couldn't get him to the first fence. The head lad was a mean bastard, tried to beat it out of him. One day, he went into his stable and Merlin kicked him. So he tied him up, picked up a broom and started to beat the living shit out of him. I took the broom off him, pulled him out of the stable and showed him what it felt like to be beaten with a broom handle. That scar Merlin has, you know the one? On his right fetlock?'

'Yes I know the one!' It was a very old injury, long healed, but it would never disappear completely.

'That happened when he kicked through the wall in his stable, when the head lad was beating him up.'

'Jesus! Poor Merlin. No wonder he doesn't trust people!'

'Yes, so…' Dan sighed, 'he got sent away with that injury, and obviously I had to leave. But I found out he got sold on as a failed race-horse, and god knows how many times he's changed hands since then. Andrews bought him from an auction dirt cheap.' Dan hesitated, as if unsure whether to say what he was thinking. 'I swear he knew me though when he came to Malcolm's. Just the way he was with me…I don't know if that sounds stupid?'

'No. Not at all.' Emma sat and reflected for a minute. In a way it wasn't so strange that Merlin had ended up in Malcolm's yard; a good many race-horses are re-trained as eventers. Lucky though – very lucky for Merlin that he ended up back in Dan's hands. Luck, or something else; fate?

'Do you think he'll ever come right?'

'I don't know. But I'm not going to give up on him. This could be his last chance, the only place he is going if he leaves here is the glue factory.' His hands clenched and unclenched on the steering wheel. There was that grimly determined set of the mouth and jaw, the steely gaze out of the windscreen. Emma didn't doubt it for a moment.

Chapter 13

BACK AT HOME THAT EVENING, EMMA GOT SHOWERED AND settled down with her book. She heard Dan come upstairs and get in the shower. Twenty minutes later there was a knock at her door.

'Yup?' She answered. Dan put his head round the door.

'Want to come to the pub?' he asked.

'I thought you told Simone you didn't want to go?'

'Changed my mind. Besides, I feel like celebrating my win,' he said grinning.

'I suppose so,' she said, after a moment's hesitation.

Forty-five minutes later they were in the pub, Emma with a shandy, Dan with a pint of lager. It was a fine night, so they had walked.

The pub was quiet, they practically had the whole place to themselves. They took turns putting music on the jukebox, and played a few games of pool; Dan was horribly competitive and beat her every game. She noticed he was drinking really fast, and had a few whisky chasers when he went to the bar.

Huh, it was easy to tell who has the next day off. She stuck to her shandy.

Eventually they sat down, reliving the day and making plans for the next event. Dan looked relaxed and happy – in fact a little too relaxed. His eyes had that slightly unfocused look he got when he'd had too much to drink.

Emma was trying to think of ways they could stop Merlin's tearaway behaviour. After his horrendous performance in the dressage, he had settled down for the show-jumping, so she thought, perhaps, if they got him warmed up early, then let him chill out back at the lorry, then warmed him up again before his test, it might get him listening. As she explained her idea to Dan, and was earnestly describing some of the schooling exercises they could incorporate into his warm-up, she became aware that he was regarding her with a kind of lazy, unfocused, lop-sided smile.

'Are you taking any of this in?' she asked him.

He sighed. 'Aww Bugs, you're so cute,' he said, and put out his hand, trying to touch her face.

'Whoa!' she said, quickly ducking away from his hand. 'And you're so drunk! Time to go home,' she stated firmly, getting to her feet.

He got up, but instead of going to leave, he went back to the bar and ordered another double whisky.

'Dan!' she said in dismay. 'You're not going to be able to walk in a minute!'

'You'll have to carry me then,' he said happily, downing the whisky in one, and turning to leave. She wondered whether she should call for a cab, but he was already half-way out the door.

They wended an unsteady way home, Dan humming something unrecognisable. He kept insisting on putting his arm around her shoulders, but she stopped trying to get him to walk on his own when he nearly fell in the ditch – twice.

At last, they reached the yard. With relief Emma turned off the lights and pushed him up the stairs to his room, where he collapsed on to the bed. He was steaming drunk.

'Stay with me for a while Bugs,' he pleaded, trying to take her hand and pull her down onto the bed with him.

'Go to sleep,' she said, extricating herself firmly.

'Why don't you like me Bugs?' he said sadly, sticking his bottom lip out.

'I do like you Dan,' she said, shaking her head in bemusement.

His mouth stretched slowly into a grin. 'Help me get undressed then.' His hands went down to the buttons of his jeans.

She beat a hasty retreat out of the door and shut it resolutely behind her.

Once back in her room, she took a deep breath. Phew…God he was a handful! She would think twice before she went to the pub with him again – alone anyway.

She'd been in bed a few minutes when there was a knock on the wall. She ignored it, pulling the covers over her head. The knock came again louder.

'What is it?' she said crossly.

'Night Bugs,' she heard through the wall.

'Night Dan,' she sighed.

Next minute, loud snores could be heard. She put her pillow over her head and tried to go to sleep.

The following morning, he didn't appear until nine-thirty, clearly hung-over. Emma went into the kitchen at tea-break and he was there, drinking water out of a mug, looking like he'd slept in his clothes.

'I am *never*, taking you to the pub again,' she told him, putting the kettle on. 'I practically had to carry you home!'

He grinned a little sheepishly. 'Sorry Bugs,' he said.

She was instantly mollified; she didn't think she had ever heard him apologise for anything before.

'I don't remember getting home, was I being a twat?' he asked, not quite meeting her eyes.

She relented. 'Not really, you were just horribly drunk.'

He seemed cheered up by this. 'Good. Same again tonight then?'

'No chance mate,' she said laughing.

Chapter 14

EMMA'S PLAN SEEMED TO WORK. THE NEXT COMPETITION, THEY allowed extra time, to ride Merlin in.

Merlin was unsettled; his head held high on a tense neck, his muscles bunched and his back tight, drifting sideways and refusing to walk, his eyes goggling at all the other horses and strange sights around him. Dan warmed him up for twenty minutes and then brought him back, where Emma put him back on the lorry, leaving him to chill out by himself.

The second time Dan rode him away, Emma could already see he was much less uptight, and Dan worked him to bring his back down and release the tension. It did the trick. He actually did a pretty decent test with none of the histrionics of the previous weekend.

Emma was stoked. As they came out of the arena, she fell in beside them giving Merlin a pat and a polo.

'You're not such a bad old mule are you?' she said affectionately, pulling his long ears through her hands. He crunched his polo, looking pleased with himself.

'I reckon we've cracked it,' Dan said. 'He'll be top class if we can get him to concentrate.'

All in all, it was another fairly successful day. Merlin came 10th in his section, which had over thirty horses in it. Chance came 6th, again having a pole down in the show-jumping, and Arcturus, who was getting better and better, came 2nd in his section. They drove home in high spirits.

'Come for a drink tonight?' Dan asked her.

Emma hesitated, remembering the last time.

'I won't drink too much,' he said, apparently reading her thoughts. 'I promise.'

As they walked into the pub, they saw Joe, Amy and another vet from the practice called Mike, who Emma had met on one occasion when they'd needed a vet and Joe was away. Joining them, Emma slid into a bench seat in the corner and Dan slid in next to her. Amy sat between Mike and Joe on the other side.

Emma wasn't sure how she felt about Amy – she was always friendly enough, but Emma couldn't seem to get beyond polite small talk with her. The three men did most of the talking.

Mike got up to go. 'I've got a wife and kids to get back to, unlike you lot,' he moaned.

Joe and Dan went to the bar leaving Emma with Amy.

'So,' began Amy, 'Joe tells me you're Dan's new right-hand woman.' Her smile didn't quite reach her eyes.

'Did he?' Emma was surprised, but gratified all the same.

'Yes, apparently he thinks you're the best groom he's ever had.'

Emma blushed and glanced over to where Joe and Dan were stood at the bar, deep in conversation.

'Well, that's nice to know,' she said.

There was an uncomfortable pause, then Amy said, 'Emma, I hope you won't think I'm speaking out of turn, but you seem like a very sweet girl.'

Emma wondered what on earth she was going to say.

'You can tell me to mind my own business,' she went on, 'but I hope you aren't getting too…involved.'

Emma looked at her blankly.

'With Dan,' Amy said.

Emma felt a flush of embarrassment. 'Oh God no! I have a boyfriend.'

'Well that's okay then,' Amy said, but didn't sound convinced. 'It's just that, I know how easy it can be to…well, I think you know that I have had a bit of an on, off thing with him in the past. And I know it's never going to be anything more than that – and that's fine – I mean, he's not exactly the kind of man you want to take home to meet your father is he?' She laughed, but stopped when

Emma didn't join in. 'But seriously, he's not the type you want to let yourself get um… emotionally involved with.'

'Trust me, I know that,' Emma said, completely sideswiped by the whole conversation. Did she really look that naïve?

'Good. Well, I'm sorry if I'm out of line, but I'd hate to see you get hurt. Us girls have to look out for one another!'

There was a kind of forced bonhomie in her manner, which was a little patronising; she must think Emma was very young and stupid. It was a relief when the boys came back and sat down. This time Dan sat next to Amy, Joe next to Emma.

She and Joe chatted, and Emma thought again how nice he was to talk to. She kept her eyes firmly fixed on his, because in her peripheral vision she could see Amy pressing herself up against Dan, leaning closer to him to say something and brushing her lips against his neck. Her hands under the table did not seem to be kept entirely to herself.

Joe was telling Emma stories about the locals. Apparently, Ernie, the village cabby's real name was Steve, but everyone called him Ernie because he was a milkman, and drove a milk float in the morning, and a cab by night.

'But why Ernie?' Emma asked.

'Haven't you heard of Ernie? Drives the fastest milk float in the West? It's an old Bennie Hill sketch I think. Trouble is, he might drive his float fast but he drives his cab at exactly the same speed.' Emma laughed; she had noticed Ernie's driving was particularly slow.

'Talking of which, how are you getting home?' Joe asked her.

'Walking,' Emma said, suddenly wondering what she'd do if Dan went home with Amy. Would he leave her to walk home on her own? She glanced over at him to find him staring at her and Joe. He stood up suddenly.

'Drink up, we've got an early start in the morning,' he said. Amy's face fell.

'Oh, right,' Emma said surprised, downing the rest of her wine rather fast.

They all walked out together and said goodnight. Joe gave her a kiss goodbye.

They strolled home at a leisurely pace, not talking a great deal at first.

'So what are we doing in the morning?' she asked him eventually.

'Nothing much, I just want to get all the horses out for a hack,' he replied vaguely. 'What were you talking about with Joe for so long anyway?' he asked.

'Just this and that. He was telling me all about the locals; whose wife is having an affair with who, that sort of thing.' She giggled, which turned into a loud hiccup. 'Apparently, swinging is rife in the village. He's a bit of a gossip, our Joe, isn't he?'

'You seem to get on well with him,' said Dan, giving her a sideways glance.

'Yeah, he's a nice guy,' she replied.

After a pause. 'He likes you, you know.'

'Well, I like him,' Emma said plainly.

'No, I mean, he *likes* you,' he said again.

She stopped walking and stood still in the middle of the narrow road. Surely he was winding her up? 'Don't be silly! What makes you think that?'

Dan turned to face her, hands in his jean pockets. 'He told me. Tonight.'

Emma was completely nonplussed for the second time that evening. 'But, doesn't he know I have a boyfriend? You did tell him didn't you?'

'No.'

'But why not?'

'I thought that it was up to you to tell him,' he paused, '…if you wanted to.'

'Of course I'd want him to know, why wouldn't I?' she said impatiently.

'All's fair in love and war Bugs,' he said with a shrug as he walked on.

Emma hurried to catch up. 'What does that even mean?' she said, beginning to laugh. The whole thing was beginning to strike her as ridiculous, especially in light of the conversation she'd had with Amy earlier.

'Just that there are no rules, everyone's entitled to do whatever they have to do…or can do.'

'But that's nonsense, of course there are rules. You have to be fair in love or someone gets hurt. It's not war. I would never cheat on Edward, never!'

They fell silent again.

'So, do you fancy Joe?' Dan said after a while.

'No!' Emma said, shocked. 'I don't think you quite get this whole relationship thing; *I have a boyfriend!*'

'So what? That doesn't stop you fancying someone else, you either do or you don't.'

Emma didn't reply, hoping he'd drop it.

'You could do a lot worse than Joe,' he said after a minute.

'Dan,' she began, in frustration, 'I really like Joe. I do. He's a nice guy, good-looking, good company, what's not to like? But I've been with Edward for four and a half years, I'm not going to risk that for someone I hardly know, am I?'

'All right Bugs, I get the message,' he said laughing at her. 'You do take things seriously, don't you?'

They had reached the yard now. There was a pause, as they went through the gate.

'So, you think he's good-looking then?' he said moments later, a wicked glint in his eye.

'Oh for God's sake!' she huffed, rolling her eyes.

'Better looking than me?' he said.

'I'm not even going to answer that,' she replied, stomping up the stairs.

'So I suppose a goodnight kiss is out of the question?' he said when they reached her door, still smirking.

'No! I mean, *Yes! Of course* it's out of the question,' Emma spluttered in exasperation, stepping into her room, ready to slam the door in his face.

'Why? You gave Joe one,' he laughed, clearly enjoying her discomfort.

'Because it would be inappropriate! Something which you don't seem to grasp the meaning of,' she said, her voice rising, 'and if you keep getting drunk and being inappropriate, I won't be able to go to the pub with you anymore.'

His dark eyes became serious. 'I'm not drunk,' he said.

She faltered slightly, and then closed the door, slowly, shutting him out.

She heard him go into his room.

Alone, she put her cool hands up to her burning face. Her cheeks were on fire! She wanted to go to the bathroom and splash cold water on her face but didn't want to run the risk of bumping into him in the hallway.

She waited until she thought he'd gone to bed. He seemed to be taking an awfully long time. She heard him go into the bathroom and the 'ping' as the light went off, and eventually, silence. Quickly scooting through the passage into the bathroom, she washed her face and brushed her teeth.

Back in her room, she got into bed, but then lay there fidgeting, staring into the darkness. What a bizarre night. She couldn't imagine the conversation the boys must have been having at the bar, while she was having an equally strange one with Amy at the table. Again, it struck her as being ridiculous and she wanted to laugh out loud. She stuffed the corner of her quilt in her mouth to muffle the noise, realizing that maybe it was she who'd had too much to drink.

She turned one way and then the other, her thoughts and feelings in confusion. Snatches of half remembered conversations and images flashed through her mind as she tried to get to sleep; Joe's arm across the back of her seat, his goodnight kiss. Perhaps she *was* naïve.

A knock on the wall broke the silence, making her jump. She hesitated, then knocked back. She waited, holding her breath, but there was no sound.

Chapter 15

THE FOLLOWING THURSDAY, EMMA'S PHONE RANG AT TEN AT night, it woke her from a deep sleep.

She scrambled to answer it.

'Hello?'

'Emma, it's me,' came the answer in a voice, close to tears.

'Lottie! What's the matter, what's happened?' Emma said alarmed.

'It's Josh, we've split up,' Lottie wailed. 'I'm at my parents' house.'

'Oh my God! I'm so sorry, tell me what happened.'

Lottie began tearfully to explain how she had thought Josh had been cheating on her with a girl at work.

'He swears nothing happened – and he says he loves me, but if I can't trust him then we might as well call it a day, so I left.'

Emma didn't want to believe Josh was capable of cheating. He was a flirt, but then so was Lottie; with her vivacious personality and bright red lipstick she got a lot of male attention, and there had been a few times in the past where Lottie's flirting had bordered on infidelity.

'I really wish you were here,' Lottie said pitifully.

Emma had an idea. 'Why don't you come down here?' she said. 'You could stay the night and then we can have a proper chat and help you get some perspective on the whole situation.'

There was a pause.

'I suppose I could,' said Lottie. 'It would be good to see you.'

SO IT WAS arranged. When Lottie arrived the next afternoon, Emma ran out to meet her.

'Yay, you made it!' Emma ran and hugged her friend as she got out of her car.

'Phew!' said Lottie. 'You're way out in the back of beyond here, aren't you?'

Emma put her hands on Lottie's shoulders and looked into her face.

'Are you okay?' she asked.

'Oh, you know, soldiering on,' Lottie replied with a weak smile.

'Right, come on. Are we hitting the wine straight away or would you like a cup of tea first?' she asked her.

'Wine sounds tempting, but probably tea, please.'

'It's a bit smarter than Maggie's,' Lottie remarked as Emma led her across the gravel to the tack room. The yard was picturesque at this time of day, with the light fading and all the stable lights on.

Dan walked across the yard towards the feed room. Lottie watched him until he disappeared through the door, her eyes widening.

'Who's that?' she asked in a stage whisper.

'That's my boss,' said Emma.

'I thought you said he was old?' she squeaked.

'No, that would be Malcolm, he owns the place. Dan is the yard manager.'

'Wow – easy on the eye, isn't he?' Lottie said in admiration.

Emma raised her eyes to heaven. Here we go again. 'He's also bad-tempered, has questionable morals and absolutely no respect for women,' she said sternly.

'Oh.' Lottie looked chastened.

They reached the staff room kitchen and Emma put the kettle on.

'It's so good to see you!' Lottie said, giving Emma another hug. 'Are you sure it's okay for me to stay over?'

'Of course. I checked with Malcolm, he's the nicest man in the world.'

Lottie looked as good as ever; her mass of chestnut curls glossy and bouncy, her complexion glowing – maybe a little less animated than usual.

'You look great,' Emma said.

'So do you,' said Lottie, 'you're so slim and brown!'

It was funny how Lottie had always been envious of how slender Emma was, whereas Emma was envious of Lottie's curves.

Emma finished making the tea just as Dan came through the door, hanging up the keys to the feed room.

'Dan this is Lottie,' Emma said.

Lottie was sitting on one of the chairs at the table, her long brown legs in their white shorts crossed in front of her. When he came in, she un-crossed and re-crossed them and shook back her chestnut curls.

'Hi,' said Lottie.

'Hi,' said Dan.

'Do you want tea?' Emma asked him. He pulled a face. 'Beer o'clock Bugs,' he said and went out again. She went to the fridge and got a bottle of Peroni, taking the top off.

'Why'd he call you Bugs?' asked Lottie bemused.

'Um…ever since he saw me in that rabbit onesie you gave me,' Emma replied.

Lottie's jaw dropped open. 'How'd he see you in your onesie?'

'He lives here, upstairs as well.'

Lottie shut her mouth with a snap, her eyes wide.

Dan reappeared, and came into the kitchen, stepping over Lottie's outstretched legs. He grabbed his beer off the side.

'Are you going to the pub?' he asked Emma.

'Don't know yet,' Emma said quickly, shooting Lottie a silencing glance.

Lottie was staring at him. Emma watched as her eyes ran over him from top to toe; broad shoulders tapering down to slim waist, jeans barely sitting on narrow hips, long muscular thighs clad in worn denim.

His jeans often had holes in them, he definitely wasn't the smartest of dressers but it suited him somehow with his tousled, sun bleached hair and a tan that would be the envy of any surfer. He leant against the counter with an easy relaxed manner. Despite his uptight nature, his physical movements were never awkward or tense. He always moved with an effortless natural grace; quick without ever seeming to hurry, quiet without ever seeming unsure.

Emma had often thought that it was part of what made him such a good rider, that kind of supple agility which lent his every movement a pleasing elegance. Also, why women seemed to find him irresistible.

That and his face, which, in spite of herself, Emma sometimes caught herself studying, as someone might study a stunning work of art, trying to decipher just what it was that made it so appealing.

He wasn't handsome in that common kind of chocolate boxy, aftershave advert way, it was almost as if he was an artist's impression of the essence of masculine beauty, captured in just a few perfectly executed lines and shades of light and dark. The line of the jaw, the curve of the lip, the way the light caught the cheekbone, the definition of the nose, the lustrous downturned eyes beneath dark brows. That caramel skin.

His face was usually quite still, often with a slightly watchful expression, except when he smiled and then the kaleidoscope would shift and change almost every aspect and contour. If she had been an artist, Emma would have liked to draw him.

She wanted to throw something at Lottie to stop her staring. Although he seemed quite unself-conscious, he must be aware of the scrutiny he was under. Emma hoped he would leave soon.

'Right, see you later then,' he said abruptly, standing up and going upstairs.

'Can't he come with us to the pub?' asked Lottie, like a child asking for sweets.

Emma sat down opposite her at the table. 'Right, let's get one thing straight,' she said. 'That would be a very, *very* bad idea for so many reasons. For one: he is a man slut who sleeps around and treats the women he sleeps with like yesterday's dirty socks. Two: you are extremely vulnerable right now and liable to do something you'll regret. And three: you have only just split up with your boyfriend who, actually, you have no proof was unfaithful to you and with whom you really want to get back together. True?'

Lottie scrunched up her face with a pained expression. 'What was the middle one again?'

Emma laughed.

'But he would be such a nice distraction for me,' wailed Lottie.

'You invited me down here to cheer me up, and, success! I feel cheered up already.'

'No,' said Emma firmly, 'and let that be an end of it.'

'Oh, you spoil all my fun,' said Lottie, pouting.

'I GUESS THIS is the only thing for miles around,' said Lottie as they arrived at the pub an hour later. Luckily there was no sign of Dan.

'Actually, town's only a ten-minute cab journey,' said Emma, 'but this is fine if you just want a pint and basic pub grub.'

A few of the locals were standing at the bar. A couple of them acknowledged Emma and she smiled and put her hand up.

'Quite the local now aren't we?' Lottie teased.

Emma grinned. 'I've spent a lot of time in here recently.'

They ordered ham, egg, and chips; a meal, Emma was pretty sure, even the pub's chef could manage.

They talked, mainly about Josh and Lottie's current predicament, then about Edward for a bit.

'You must miss him so much.'

'I do,' Emma said, 'but I'm working so hard, I don't have time to miss him as much as I used to.'

'I miss Josh already,' Lottie said sighing.

'Let's have a game of pool,' Emma said trying to divert her.

'I'm useless at pool,' Lottie said.

'Oh well, no one in here knows you so it doesn't matter, come on.' She pulled Lottie to her feet.

They put some music on the jukebox and played. Lottie was right; she wasn't very good. Emma didn't play to the best of her ability, but she was still beating her.

'Told you I was rubbish,' Lottie said downcast, and then suddenly her face lit up. Emma followed her gaze. Dan and Joe had walked in together.

Dan had already clocked them. He lifted his hand and Lottie waved back enthusiastically. Joe was ordering them a couple of beers.

'Do you want to play again?' Emma asked Lottie.

But she wasn't listening, her eyes were on Dan as he and Joe came over.

Emma introduced Lottie to Joe; they smiled at each other with an obvious instant accord.

'Are you playing?' Joe asked Emma, gesturing at the pool table.

'Well…'

'Game of doubles?' Dan challenged. He always beat her.

'Okay.' Emma sighed at Lottie's eager nod.

'Boys against girls or...?' Joe asked looking at Emma, but Lottie spoke first.

'No, I'm rubbish and Emma's not much better, we need to even things out. How about me and Dan against you two?' She smiled, pleased with herself.

They began to play. Lottie was trying harder but playing even worse than before, bemoaning every missed shot and apologising to Dan. Then going into ecstasies of admiration when he potted something. She was flirting rather obviously.

Joe and Emma played well together; Joe kept setting her up for easy pots and they were beating Dan and Lottie.

'What am I doing wrong?' lamented Lottie, turning her big green eyes beseechingly up to Dan.

'Well, you need to space your hands out more on the cue for one thing,' Dan said.

'Like this?' she asked, still doing it wrong.

'Yeah, that's fine…if you're going fishing,' he said wryly.

'Show me then,' Lottie said smiling up at him, the invitation was implicit. Emma frowned at her.

Dan came around behind her and put an arm either side, taking hold of the cue, with his hands guiding hers. She blushed, the wicked smile never leaving her lips. Then bending her low over the table, he showed her how to line up the cue. He glided the cue back and forth over his guiding hand, which was over hers. Then with a final push, the ball shot into the pocket.

Lottie was gleeful, her cheeks flaming as they straightened up. Emma was not impressed. Somehow, she had to stop what now seemed inevitable. They all sat down at the table, Lottie right next to Dan of course – any closer, she'd be on his lap. Emma was beside Joe on the narrow bench, conscious of his thigh touching hers. They talked until Barry called last orders.

'Same again?' Dan asked.

'No mate, I've got to shoot off, I'm on call in the morning,' Joe said with regret, putting on his jacket. He said his goodbyes, kissing Emma and Lottie on the cheek, and left. Emma was sorry to see him go.

Lottie excused herself and, grabbing her handbag, headed for the ladies' loos. As soon as she'd gone, Emma turned to Dan.

'Dan, I need you to do me a favour,' she began, hesitating over her choice of words. 'Lottie's my best friend. I know she's behaving a little oddly tonight, but that's because she's just split up with her boyfriend. So I would appreciate it if you wouldn't…' Here she broke off, floundering.

He regarded her with a level gaze for a minute, letting her squirm.

'What you're trying to say is, back off. You don't want your best friend getting mixed up with the likes of me, right?' he said drily, with that look of his which was halfway between amusement and annoyance. 'Don't stress Bugs, you've got nothing to worry about,' he said, taking a pull of his beer.

'Thanks,' she said, genuinely grateful.

Lottie returned, fresh lipstick and perfume applied, and sat back down next to Dan. He immediately got up and went to the bar. Amy was there getting a drink and she went straight to him, her smile welcoming. He sat up on a stool next to her.

'Who's that girl?' Lottie asked, looking awfully put out.

'That's Amy, she's the receptionist at the vets.'

'Is she his girlfriend?' Lottie asked, clearly reading Amy's unmistakeable body language.

'Er – no. Dan doesn't have a "girlfriend", I did warn you. Joe says he's a "free-spirit", I say he's a tart.'

Lottie frowned. 'Has he ever tried it on with you?'

'No. Well, yes… kind of, but it doesn't really count because he was very drunk.'

'God, what a tosser,' Lottie said dismissively, taking a slug of her wine.

'Ha! You've changed you're tune!' Emma said, laughing.

Soon afterwards, Dan and Amy left. Together. Lottie's spirits had plummeted.

'Right, drink up,' said Emma, 'we're going into town.'

They took the short cab journey into town, where Emma had seen a kind of club when she had been out and about on her day off.

It was a while since they'd been out together on their own like this. They drank and danced. It was like old times, before Edward and Josh, when they used to share a flat and crawl home in the early hours of the morning. Then spend the whole of the following day in their pyjamas watching old movies on telly and eating junk food.

Finally, at one o'clock in the morning they'd had enough. Emma called a cab. Lottie had brought a roll up bed and a sleeping bag, which they put on Emma's floor. Just as they were dropping off to sleep, Lottie spoke in the darkness.

'I've decided I'm going to try to sort things out with Josh,' she said.

Emma reached down for Lottie's hand and squeezed it. 'Good for you!'

'I had a great time tonight, in spite of everything,' Lottie went on, 'but it made me realise, I don't want to go back to that world where everything is so uncertain and insecure. What Josh and I have is precious, I want to hang on to it if I can.'

'I completely agree, I think you're doing the right thing.' Emma was relieved.

'Thank you, for everything,' Lottie said.

Lottie didn't hang around in the morning. She left without bothering to say goodbye to Dan, who was on the yard, feeding round. Emma thought she was probably a bit embarrassed.

Chapter 16

IT WAS ONE OF THOSE SUBLIME AFTERNOONS WHEN EVERYTHING seemed to be right with the world.

They were on their way back from an afternoon hack, all four of them. Emma had Arcturus. Dan was on Lynx, Simone on Henry, and Kitty on Paddy.

Everyone was in a good mood, even Simone, who was probably pleased because Emma had the weekend off, meaning that she was going with Dan to groom at the competition on Sunday.

In a funny sort of a way, Emma experienced a twinge of regret when she had to miss a competition. But she was looking forward to this weekend, because it was her twenty-fifth birthday. She and Edward were going to stay with Lottie and Josh, and they were all going out on the town to celebrate – made even more special, because her two best friends had renewed their commitment to each other, and Lottie said they were closer than ever.

It was a gorgeous sunny afternoon, everything seemed to sparkle with new life after recent rain. The horses were still feeling fresh as they rode back through the home field where the cross-country jumps were.

'Anyone fancy a quick jump?' Dan asked.

Simone shrugged and Kitty looked doubtful, but Emma nodded with enthusiasm. She loved jumping Arcy; he was the rising star of the yard.

'Right, give them a canter round and let them pop over a few little ones,' Dan instructed.

Arcy was keen and took off miles before the fences, landing way out beyond the other side. Twice he put in a little buck after the jump. Emma didn't mind; it was just high spirits.

'Hold him into the fence Emma,' Dan was yelling, 'if he stands off like that when the fences are bigger you'll be in trouble.'

Emma tried to do as she was told but Arcy was strong.

The terror was plain on Kitty's face. She was keeping Paddy too slow so that he cat-jumped the fences. Simone was riding in her usual cool manner, but catching Henry in the mouth over every fence.

'Allow with your hands, Simone,' Dan yelled, 'keep catching him like that and he won't jump for you. Okay, Emma, Simone, the Trakehner,' he called, leading the way. 'Kitty…just stick to the tyre jumps.'

Lynx was fighting for her head, but Dan sat still, hands quiet, his focus on the fence. They cleared it by miles, making a beautiful shape over the hanging log.

Emma was next. She picked up the canter. Arcy was full of confidence, grey ears pricked. His canter was powerful, he met the fence on the perfect stride, Emma anticipated where he was going to take off and her face stretched into a grin of sheer delight as he soared through the air.

'Good Emma,' shouted Dan, 'but don't get ahead of him, if he stops you'll end up taking the fence without him.'

Emma wasn't entirely sure what he meant by "don't get ahead of him" but she was enjoying herself and couldn't imagine Arcy was going to stop. They jumped a couple of the other fences, another ditch, and a big log with a drop on the far side.

'Right, now for the log pile,' grinned Dan, 'you up for it?'

Emma felt a surge of adrenalin, the log pile was huge; she'd never been allowed to jump it before.

'I'll jump it first,' Dan said, 'get a good canter but don't let them go too fast, they will need to jump off their hocks for this one.'

Lynx thundered down to the log pile. Four strides out, Dan saw the stride he wanted, checked her ever so slightly letting her know where she had to jump, she responded, trusting her rider completely, three, two, one…and they were over. Emma was next.

She cantered Arcy in a wide circle, balancing in her stirrups, shortening her reins up slightly. Then she turned him towards the log pile and sat up.

Arcy locked onto the jump and got hold of the bit, picking up speed.

'Not too fast!' she heard Dan yell, but she was flying now and too close to the fence to do much about it. She couldn't see her stride. Helplessly she kept her leg on him and hoped Arcy would take care of it. She saw a long stride and felt the moment when he should have taken off. She folded forward in anticipation, but Arcy realised just too late that he was too far away to clear the big fence and tried to brake and put in another stride. The ground was slippery after the recent rain, he lost his front legs and skidded into the bottom of the fence, but Emma was already committed and flew straight over his head.

WHAM! She landed on her back on the unforgiving hard wood of the log pile, and then slithered to the ground and lay there quite still. Dan was off Lynx and beside her in a second.

'You still with us?' he said kneeling down next to her. She blinked at him but couldn't speak; the breath completely knocked out of her.

'You're winded,' Dan said, 'just lie still a minute.'

After what seemed to Emma like a horribly long time, but was probably just a few seconds, the air rushed back into her lungs. She gasped for oxygen, trying to sit up, but Dan held her down gently, his hand on her shoulder.

'Okay just breathe.'

She did as she was told.

'There, now you're a better colour.' He held up four fingers. 'How many fingers am I holding up?'

'Four,' Emma croaked.

'What day is it?'

'Thursday.'

'What's my name?'

'Dan… I don't think I banged my head. Where's Arcy? Is he okay?'

'He's fine. Simone has him. What hurts?' he asked, sitting back on his heels.

'Um… everywhere?' Emma managed a shaky smile. 'Can I sit up now?'

'Okay but slowly.'

Emma gingerly pushed herself upright. 'I think it's just my side, here,' she said putting her hand to her ribs round the back. 'And my ankle hurts.'

'Can you stand?' he asked, offering her his hand. She took it and he lifted her slowly to her feet. Kitty was holding Paddy and Lynx chewing her lip. Simone was standing by holding Henry and Arcturus, studying her nails.

'Ouch,' Emma said, sucking air in between her teeth as pain seared through her ankle, 'I think it's twisted.'

'Right – lean on me.' He put her arm around his shoulders and his arm around her waist. She tried not to lean on him too heavily. Dan shouted to Simone and Kitty to take the horses back to the yard. She and Dan followed behind more slowly.

Emma felt like an idiot. 'I'm sorry,' she said. 'It was my fault. Now I know what you meant by not getting ahead of him.'

Dan chuckled. 'We've all done it. Even the best riders get caught out sometimes. Confidence is good, sometimes you can just kick on and hope for the best and you'll get away with it. Today you didn't.' He paused. 'But you were riding well – you just need to sit up and wait for your fence. Your reflexes are good, you won't get left behind.'

Emma felt pathetically grateful for his kindness.

Somewhere on the slow, arduous, way back across the field, through the haze of pain and embarrassment, she became very aware of the warmth of his hand on her waist.

At last, they made it back into the yard. Dan stopped in the kitchen to grab an icepack and then helped her up the stairs, which was difficult because they were so narrow. Emma was shaking a little.

'I've some brandy in my room,' Dan said, 'it's good for the shock,' he insisted when Emma pulled a face. He pushed open the door and helped her to the bed. The room, although slightly larger than her own, was a typical boy's room with clothes strewn on the bare floorboards, more clothes and towels slung over the chair, and the duvet on the bed was thrown over in a haphazard way rather than made.

She sat on the edge awkwardly, while Dan knelt in front of her and carefully pulled off her boots. The ankle on her left foot was swelling fast. He lifted it up onto the bed and put the icepack on it. Then he went to the cupboard, found a half empty bottle of brandy and a glass and brought it back to the bed. Emma took a sip of the strong-smelling liquid and grimaced, but the effect was immediately warm and soothing.

Dan was back at the cupboard again. This time he came back with a white tube of something.

'What's that?' Emma asked.

'Arnica cream,' he answered, 'for the bruising. I use it on the horses all the time.'

'Great,' Emma laughed weakly.

He knelt down beside her. 'Let's have a look then.'

Emma hesitated.

He smiled wryly. 'Don't worry Bugs, I won't take advantage of you in your battered state. Do you want me to get Kitty?'

Emma shook her head and reaching round, lifted up her T-shirt, just enough to expose her bruised ribs at the back.

'Well I don't think anything's broken but they are going to be a pretty colour tomorrow,' he said bending down to examine her.

Squeezing some cream into his hand, he started to smooth some onto her skin, his touch surprisingly gentle – all the same, she jumped when he touched her.

'Sorry, does that hurt?' he asked, pausing.

She shook her head and took a large gulp of the fiery liquid in her glass, trying to concentrate on the burning sensation, because the feelings that were coursing through her body were disturbing, but not exactly unpleasant. In fact, quite the opposite.

He carried on; his hand warm, his touch sure. Emma felt herself blushing to the roots of her hair, her scalp tingled and her heart started to jump.

She looked around the room in an effort to distract herself and her eyes alighted on a picture on the nightstand. It was of a girl and a baby. The girl was the image of Dan, a prettier, much more feminine version of him, but there could be no mistake, she must be his sister. The little boy on her lap, probably around eighteen months old, looked up at the camera with solemn brown eyes under a mop of curly brown hair. Again, the family resemblance was striking.

'Is that your nephew?' she asked him, glad to have something to say.

'Yeah,' Dan glanced at the picture, his hand never pausing in its motion.

'He's gorgeous! He looks just like you.'

He raised his eyes to hers, a flash of amusement illuminating his features. 'Bugs! I think that's the nicest thing you've ever said to me.'

'Oh…I meant…' Now she was in danger of making a fool of herself, but he laughed.

'Don't spoil it,' he said, and straightened up. 'There, that'll do,'

But it wasn't over yet. He then sat on the end of the bed and lifted her foot carefully onto his lap, removing the icepack.

She couldn't cope; it was so strangely intimate. She wanted to snatch her foot away, but felt helpless. He examined her.

'Hmm, just a sprain I think, although if it's this swollen tomorrow, we should probably get it checked out.' He seemed oblivious to her turmoil, his head bent over her foot.

Again, he squeezed some Arnica cream into his hand and began to smooth it onto her injured ankle. She had started to shake again and was sure he must notice her breathing was not as slow and quiet as it should be for someone sitting down, she tried to hold her breath. What would Edward think if he could see her now? Sitting on a strange man's bed with her foot in his lap. Dan looked up suddenly, catching her staring at him.

'Did I tell you Edward's a doctor?' she blurted out in confusion.

'Is he now? Good for him,' Dan replied, raising an eyebrow, but his hands still rubbing her ankle.

'He probably sees injuries like this all the time, he would know if it's just a sprain.' Now she was just sounding ungrateful, she cursed herself inwardly.

'Right, you're done,' Dan said, putting her foot down on the bed and standing up. 'Keep that ice on it a while longer. You can stay here and rest if you like?' he offered.

'No,' she said a little too quickly. There was no way she could stay here, in his room. 'I'll go back to my room if that's okay?'

He shrugged. 'Whatever you like.'

He helped her back to her room.

'I'll check in on you in a bit. Are you sure you didn't bang your head? You shouldn't go to sleep if you did.'

She shook her head, wishing he would leave. 'I'm sure,' she said. 'I'll be fine.' He turned to leave – but now she stopped him.

'Dan…' Halfway out the door he looked back over his shoulder.

'Thank you,' she said.

ALONE, SHE TRIED to make sense of her feelings. Why had she reacted like that? And he, *he* had been so cool and professional. She cringed with shame, guilty and cross with herself. What was she going to do now? The thought of trying to manage the train tomorrow with her ankle like this was unappealing. Perhaps she wouldn't be able to go.

She must ring Edward and tell him what had happened – well, perhaps not everything that had happened. Her mobile was, thankfully, still in the little case she kept attached to her belt. Taking a few slow breaths, she touched Edward's number.

'Emma?' his voice came down the line.

'Hi Ed, yes it's me,'

'Everything okay?' he asked. Perhaps her voice had come out a bit squeaky.

'Yes, I'm fine. I just had a minor fall that's all. I'm absolutely fine, really, just sprained my ankle.'

'Fall? What kind of a fall?'

'Off a horse.'

'Oh! Have you seen a doctor?'

'No, there's no need, really. We think it's just bruising.'

'We? Who's we?'

'Oh…me…and D-Dan – my yard manager.' There was a pause. Emma chewed on one of her nails.

'Has he had any first aid training?'

'Yes, I'm sure he has, (she wasn't sure) – he gave me some ice to put on it and some cream for the bruising.'

'What kind of cream?'

'Arnica.'

Edward made a tutting sound. 'Do you need me to come and pick you up?' he asked.

She hated putting him out, 'Well, no…it's such a long way for you to drive down, and all the way back again. It doesn't matter, we can do it some other time.'

'No, everything's booked now, and I can't cancel the rooms…'

'Rooms? Aren't we staying at Lottie's?'

She heard him sigh. 'No, it was supposed to be a surprise – their flat's so small – I've booked us all into The Hilton,'

Emma gasped. 'Oh wow, thank you! In that case, if you don't mind, I'm so sorry.'

Now she felt even more guilty, he'd gone to so much trouble.

Chapter 17

THE ANKLE DEFINITELY WASN'T BROKEN. THE NEXT MORNING, the swelling was down, and she was able to hobble around. And although she couldn't help out on the yard, she spent the morning making everyone tea, and cleaning tack; singing along to her music whilst scrubbing bits and polishing leather.

'Is it okay if I finish early seeing as I'm not much use anyway,' she asked Dan at afternoon tea-break. 'Edward's coming down to pick me up.'

'The doctor?' Dan asked.

'Yes.' She handed him his tea.

'Whatever you like. Cheers Bugs.'

Emma frowned as a thought occurred to her.

'Dan?' she said. He raised his eyebrows over the top of his mug. 'Can you not call me "Bugs" in front of Ed?'

He laughed, nearly choking on his tea. Emma flushed.

'Why not Bugs?' he asked, highly amused.

Damn. She had probably just made things worse, he would do it on purpose now.

'Never mind, it doesn't matter,' she sighed.

TAKING HER TIME to get ready, she cleaned and tidied her little room, making it presentable in-case Edward came upstairs. She made the bed with her new, brightly coloured quilt over the top, and even put some fresh flowers that she'd picked from the garden in a glass by the bed. It looked nice; clean and cosy. After showering, she carefully did her hair and make-up, then wearing her best jeans and her favourite top, she hobbled downstairs to wait for him.

Dan was in the kitchen leaning against the counter eating a bowl of cereal. He gave a low whistle when she came in.

'You look nice Bugs,' he said.

She shot him a warning look. 'Edward will be here in a minute,'

'Going somewhere special?'

'Up to London, to meet with friends.' She hadn't mentioned to her workmates that it was her birthday.

There was a sound of car tyres crunching on gravel. Emma got up and went to the tack room window, which looked out on the driveway beyond.

'He's here,' she said, feeling strangely jittery. She limped outside and around the corner just as Edward got out of his Lotus.

'You found us then?' she said, going to greet him. 'How was the drive?'

'Long,' he said running a hand through his blonde hair. 'Traffic was awful.'

His shirt was a little crumpled from the journey, his smart trousers a little creased. Other than that, his appearance was effortlessly stylish as usual. He put his arms around her. 'You've lost weight,' he said.

'But I've put on muscle!' she said cheerily.

'Well don't lose any more, there'll be nothing left of you,' he said, releasing her.

'Come and see the yard.' She led the way.

The sun was slanting across the cobbles and the flowers in their pots looked bright and cheerful. Emma always thought the yard looked nicest in the evenings. She took Ed's hand.

'This is the tack room,' she said, leading him inside. She looked with pride at the rows of gleaming saddles and bridles, bits glinting in the sunlight, freshly washed towels and numnahs, all folded neatly on the shelf. Everything beautifully clean and ordered; the results of her efforts today.

Dan was still finishing his bowl of cereal, leaning against the worktop, ankles crossed in his favourite attitude.

'This is Dan,' Emma introduced. 'Dan, this is Edward.'

Edward stepped forward holding his hand out, perfect manners as always. 'Nice to put a face to a name,' he said smiling.

Dan stood up and shook Ed's hand. Edward was a little bit taller than Dan, and quite a bit heavier, although no broader across the shoulders. It was peculiar seeing them together, like two worlds colliding.

'Emma tells me it's you I've to thank for looking after her yesterday,' Edward put his arm around Emma's shoulder, all smiles. 'Glad to know she's in such capable hands. Perhaps I can leave it to you to stop her doing anything else silly?'

Dan glanced at Emma. 'It could have happened to anyone. Emma rides really well, she was just unlucky.'

'Oh. Well – maybe no more jumping? I'd like to get her back in one piece!' Edward laughed.

There was a small silence. Then Dan said, 'That's really up to Emma.'

Edward's smile began to fade. He glanced at his watch. 'We'd better get going darling,' he said, 'we've got a table booked at the Hilton for 8 o'clock.'

Dan turned away, putting his bowl in the sink.

'Come and see my room first,' Emma said. She led the way up the stairs; Ed took her arm to help her.

'You sleep up here?' he asked surprised.

'Yes.'

He frowned. 'I assumed you slept up in the house.'

They reached her room and went in. Edward had to duck under the low doorway.

'It's tiny!' he exclaimed, looking around in amazement.

'It's not huge I know, but it's cosy. Look,' she said going to the window. 'I can look down into the yard from my bed and see the horses first thing in the morning, and when it's clear you can see right across the fields, all the way to the sea.' Edward went to the window and looked out.

'Hmm,' he said. 'It smells of horse.'

They left shortly afterwards. Emma introduced Edward to Kitty on the way out. Kitty was so shy she barely managed to make eye contact, and when Edward held out his hand to her, she looked down at her own grubby little paw in mortification, wiping it on her T-shirt before taking his.

Simone walked past them as they crossed the yard. She stared hard at Edward but didn't stop to say hello.

'Friendly girl,' Edward muttered under his breath.

They reached London at about 7 o'clock and stopped first to pick up Lottie and Josh, before driving to the hotel.

'I can't believe we're staying at the Hilton,' Lottie said when she and Emma were squashed into the back seat of the lotus. 'Thank you so much Ed, it's really kind of you to treat us!'

'Yeah, very generous of you – you flash git!' Josh said with a laugh.

'Well, it's a special occasion,' Edward replied.

'He's definitely a keeper this one, isn't he?' Lottie said to Emma. She liked to take most of the credit for Emma's success in 'landing' Edward, seeing as he was Josh's friend. It was she who had introduced them.

Dinner began with champagne, and an 'amuse bouche', and finished five courses later with green tea ice-cream, sesame praline and chocolate mousse, punctuated by palette cleansing sorbets and a different wine with each course.

Absolutely stuffed, Emma was struggling to stay awake by 11 o'clock. They skipped coffee, and went up to their room, which was beautiful; large and sumptuously furnished. It must have been costing a fortune. She took her shoes off and scrunched her toes into the thick carpet. The bed was enormous with a soft, fluffy, goose down duvet. It looked extremely inviting.

Edward went for a shower and Emma lay back on the bed, wishing she could allow herself to sink into it, and into oblivion. But she supposed she had the sex to get through yet. She almost wished she'd forgotten to get her contraceptive implant changed, then she'd have an excuse. But Edward – ever the responsible doctor – had reminded her.

Oh well, it was never unpleasant with Edward; he was always very gentle and considerate, apologetic even. She owed it to him to be more enthusiastic. Despite her best efforts, by the time Edward came out of the shower, she was asleep.

She woke with a start, when the bathroom door closed. For a

minute she couldn't work out where she was. She had been having a dream – a nice dream. The sensation of it was still with her, although she couldn't remember the details, only that she'd been back in her room at the yard, on her bed and…no. In the way that half remembered dreams suddenly vanish, like water vapour, it had gone.

Edward smiled at her. 'Let's have a look at your ankle.'

She sat up, trying to refocus on her surroundings. He sat on the bed next to her and lifted her foot onto his lap.

Emma had a sudden vision of Dan, the day before, doing exactly the same thing, and with it came the memory of the sensations, which she had felt. An echo of her dream whispered through her mind and body. She swallowed guiltily.

Edward examined her ankle clinically, with expert hands. He declared it a sprain, and let it go. But he was more impressed with the colour of her ribs when she got undressed.

'Emma!' he gasped, 'how on earth did you get those bruises?'

'In the fall,' Emma replied in a small voice.

'You could have broken your ribs!'

Emma supposed so.

'It's crazy, you risking breaking bones for a few measly few quid a week! Thank goodness you've only got a few weeks left there.'

He was especially gentle with her in bed that night, on account of her bruises, and then he held her afterwards until he fell asleep. But for some reason, despite being so tired, Emma lay awake, long after Edward had gone to sleep. Edward was right, she only had a few weeks left. In spite of everything, she was starting to feel the way she had when she was a child, staying with her grandfather at his cottage in the country, and the summer holidays were coming to an end; a sense of time running out. And it was with a heavy heart that she finally drifted off.

*

'Happy Birthday.' Edward gave Emma a kiss on her cheek and produced a red velvet box from his inside jacket pocket. Lottie gasped, clapping her hands together.

Emma put down her glass of champagne. 'Not more presents Edward, you've done more than enough!'

She'd been thoroughly spoiled. First, they'd had a swim in the hotel pool, followed by a massage and a manicure for Lottie and Emma. Then Emma had got her hair cut at a celebrity salon and now, they were at some trendy wine bar; Emma wearing a new cocktail dress that Edward had bought, saying it suited her, although Emma secretly thought she would probably never wear it again. She felt slightly unreal, as if she were someone else entirely. Looking at the velvet box her mouth went suddenly dry.

'Open it! Open it!' Lottie squealed.

Her heart hammering, Emma opened the box. Inside were two huge diamond stud earrings. She let out a breath. 'I don't know what to say, they're absolutely gorgeous!'

'They?' Lottie leaned across to peer inside, 'Oh…oh, they're beautiful,' she said, in admiration, although for some reason, Emma thought she sounded disappointed, but she helped Emma put them on.

Later, the two girls snatched a minute alone in the toilets. They examined the earrings; Emma hadn't a clue, but Lottie thought they were at least a whole carat each.

'They're absolutely stunning – but for a minute I thought he was proposing,' she said. 'Weren't you disappointed?'

'No, not at all,' Emma said truthfully. 'It never occurred to me', she said – a little less truthfully.

Lottie was incredulous. 'But surely it must be something you've considered? Don't you want to get married?'

Emma considered, her feelings complicated. 'Yes, of course, but there's plenty of time for all of that – no rush is there?'

'God, if I were you, I'd snap him up as quickly as you can,' Lottie warned. 'If you don't, someone else will.'

AFTER LUNCH THE following day, Edward drove Emma back to Coach House Stables.

He parked the Lotus in full view of the yard.

Dan was riding Merlin in the school, cantering a figure of eight with a perfect flying change in the centre.

As he rode past them, Edward lifted his hand in greeting. Dan rode on without responding.

'Not the friendliest of chaps is he?' he said.

'He just doesn't want to break his concentration,' Emma assured him. 'He's not being rude.'

'I wouldn't have thought it would take much concentration just riding round and round in this arena,' he said dismissively.

'There's more to it than you think,' Emma replied, remembering Edward's own failed attempt at riding.

'What I mean is, it's not life or death, is it?' Edward said. The reference to his own job wasn't lost on Emma.

They went inside and Emma made them a cup of tea in the kitchen, carefully choosing him a mug that wasn't cracked. Edward looked oddly out of place in these shabby surroundings, sitting at the rickety old wooden table. She could see Dan bringing Merlin out of the school.

'So, perhaps we could find somewhere to go for dinner, and then I'll bring you back and go straight on,' Edward was saying.

'That will make it very late for you driving back,' she said, wondering how she was going to fit in another meal.

Dan came in.

'Do you want tea?' she asked him.

'No thanks,' he said, getting a glass of water from the tap, his movements hurried, as though he felt he was intruding.

'Merlin was going well,' she said, wanting to put him at ease.

Dan nodded. 'He's getting the hang of those changes – get his brain engaged before his next dressage.'

'Dressage?' said Edward. 'I thought Eventing was jumping? Isn't dressage just ballet on horseback?' he joked.

'Eventing is three phases,' Emma told him hastily, 'dressage, show-jumping and cross-country. Do you remember, I told you?'

'Yes well, I didn't think you got those bruises doing dressage!' Edward said, and then turning to Dan, 'You should see the bruises on her ribs she's got from falling off!'

Before she could stop herself, Emma lifted her eyes and met Dan's, pleading with him not to say anything. Dan stared straight back at her, until her face got so red, she thought any moment

Edward would feel the heat.

Thankfully Edward's mobile rang; he glanced at it. 'I have to take this, it's the hospital,' he said, going outside.

Emma cleared her throat and began to busy herself with rinsing out their tea mugs.

'Are you going to the pub?' she asked, for something to say.

'Maybe – are you?' he replied.

'No, I expect we'll go somewhere nice,' she replied, then cringed as she realised how that sounded.

Dan gave a sardonic laugh. 'There's always *The Pheasant.* I've never been there, but I've heard it's good. You need a credit reference to eat in there...but I don't expect that's a problem for the doctor.' He looked her up and down. 'And looking like that, you won't fit in down at The Chalk and Cheese.'

Emma turned to face him. 'Dan, I didn't mean...'

Just then Edward came back in. 'I'm going to have to go I'm afraid darling,' Edward said to Emma. 'They're having a crisis at work.'

'That's fine,' Emma said. 'I didn't want you driving back late anyway.'

'When you come home, we really need to start flat hunting,' he said. 'I don't want us to end up living in any old dump.'

Emma hoped Dan didn't notice the way he glanced around the room as he said it.

*

THERE WERE ONLY two more competitions before the end of the season; the first one was Bovington, the other was Aldon International's second and last fixture of the year.

They left for Bovington with Merlin and Arcturus at six thirty in the morning, before Kitty or Simone arrived. It was a cold, grey morning, and there was a light drizzle falling. Dan seemed subdued, a little distant, and after a few failed attempts at conversation, Emma was losing the battle to be cheerful. She felt chilled to the core.

Eventually Dan spoke. 'So, are you done with horses when you leave here? Giving it all up?'

'I guess so,' sighed Emma. 'I might be able to find somewhere to ride occasionally, but who knows.'

'And you're okay with that? You don't think you'll ever come back to it?'

'I don't see how I can,' she replied.

'There's always a choice.'

The drizzle had turned into rain; it splatted against the windscreen in big fat drops obscuring her view, before being swept away by the wipers.

She looked at him. He kept his eyes on the road.

'Is there?' she said with a frown. 'I don't see that. There are some things you can't change.'

'Of course you can,' he almost snapped at her. 'It's about getting your priorities right, what's important to you?'

Emma's defences rose. 'It's not all about what I want. When you're in a relationship you have to compromise, not just be selfish.'

Dan fell silent again. They arrived at Bovington, Dan parked up the lorry and opened his door. But then paused.

'Malcolm once said to me, if you want something enough you'll find a way, if you don't, you'll find an excuse.' Then he jumped out into the rain.

Chapter 18

Two days later, Malcolm called them all into the staff room.

'We have a horse arriving tomorrow,' he began, 'rather a special horse, it belongs to the grand-daughter of a very old friend of mine. She's American and wants to come over here to do the English Eventing circuit, she has huge ambitions apparently and this horse has already done the Kentucky four-star in America, although not with her. She'll be staying in the Coach House while she's here – I don't know how long for, could be indefinitely – but I want you to treat her as a guest.'

The Coach House was the barn conversion Emma had thought was the staff quarters when she'd first arrived; it was actually a guesthouse.

'Her horse will be on full livery, although we are under strict instructions that no one is to ride it except for her. She's arriving on Thursday.'

That was the day after tomorrow. Malcolm gave Dan a couple of sheets of A4 paper.

'This is the care sheet for the horse. I'll leave it to you to make sure it receives the right care when it arrives.'

When Malcolm had left, Dan sat at the table, legs up on another chair, reading the sheets and drinking a beer. Emma read over his shoulder.

They were headed *Angels Midnight Messenger*, owner *Caroline Hamilton-Barnes*. It had every conceivable piece of information about this horse, from how it was bred, down to when it was last wormed.

Dan seemed impressed by its breeding. It was by *Heraldik XX*, apparently one of the highest ranked Eventing Sires, out of *Dark Angel II*; an advanced event mare. It gave a list of its achievements to date – quite impressive – including coming fourth in the Kentucky five star, which is the American equivalent of Badminton.

'Wow,' said Emma, 'do you think this…' Emma read from the sheet, '…Caroline Hamilton-Barnes is a famous American eventer?' she asked.

'I've not heard of her,' Dan replied, 'but I can tell you one thing, if she owns this horse outright she must be minted, and you can guarantee she's paying Malcolm a small fortune to be here, which will be why he's warned us to be "nice" to her.'

'Do you think you can be?' Emma asked, seizing the opportunity to wind him up, wanting to shake him out of his recent mood.

'Be what?'

'Nice?'

'I'm always nice,' he said indignantly.

Emma snorted.

'What's so funny?' he asked her.

'I was thinking how much I hated you when I first met you,' she said.

'Bugs!' he protested.

'Even Joe says you're a bit marmite, and he's one of your best mates.'

'Marmite?' he asked.

'You know, people either love you or they hate you,' she explained, laughing at his bewildered expression.

'Well maybe first impressions aren't exactly my strong point.'

'No, but you're a grower,' she said, not wanting to push him too far.

'So, you don't hate me anymore then?' he said, a grin slowly illuminating his features.

'No, I don't hate you anymore.'

'And if you don't hate me, that must mean…?'

She quickly changed the subject. 'Hey! I've had a thought, this could be your big chance to land an heiress! This "Caroline" might be looking for a bit of English crumpet to waste her millions on,' she teased.

He snorted. 'I'm "crumpet" now, am I? Just a minute ago I was marmite,' he said. 'I don't know if I'm comfortable being objectified like that.'

Emma laughed. 'You might have to get over that if you want to be a rich woman's toy boy.'

'Well, she'd better be extremely rich if she's some old trout who wants to treat me like a lap dog,' he said.

'You never know,' said Emma archly, 'she might be gorgeous. You might fall madly in love with her.'

He gave her an odd look, his expression unreadable. 'You know me well enough by now Bugs,' he said, 'is that likely?'

She had to admit it wasn't.

The following afternoon, a huge horsebox drew in to the yard. Inside was the most beautiful black horse that Emma had ever seen. It came down the ramp like some mythical creature, wearing a dark grey rug with purple binding, its silken tail held high, delicate nostrils flaring, lustrous eyes wide and curious.

'What a beauty,' breathed Emma in admiration.

'Looks extremely high maintenance,' said Dan, disparagingly.

Once the horse had been unloaded, the biggest equine wardrobe imaginable was next to come off the lorry. There were rugs galore, a rug for every season and occasion, all brand new and still wrapped in their packaging. Boots of every description, brushing boots, tendon boots, fetlock boots, cross-country boots. Three saddles: one dressage, one GP, one jumping. And all kinds of other tack: bridles, breast-plates, saddle pads and sheepskin half-pads. Emma and Kitty's eyes got wider and wider, even Simone who practiced nonchalance until it was second nature, was a little awestruck.

Once everything had been unloaded, – including enough feed and supplements for three horses – a haynet had been filled with the special haylage that had come with it, and the new horse was safely ensconced in its loose box, they all gathered round the door to admire it. It was obviously fit and in peek condition; every movement screamed of quality and breeding.

'I wonder what its owner is like,' said Emma.

*

No amount of speculation could have prepared them for the reality of Caroline Hamilton-Barnes. Emma was completely blown away by how beautiful she was. It was no ordinary beauty; she looked like no-one Emma had ever seen before in real life. When she walked into the staff room and introduced herself, everybody stopped what they were doing and simply stared at her. Simone looked like someone had slapped her in the face.

Caroline was tall, only a couple inches shorter than Dan, and slim as a whip. Her legs, in the tightest of rust-coloured suede jeans, went on forever down to high heeled black leather boots, and up to slender hips. She looked like she had just stepped out of a catalogue for expensive country clothing, in a pale grey, cashmere, roll neck sweater and fitted dark jacket.

But it was her colouring that was so striking. Her long thick, glossy, layered hair was the colour of the autumn leaves, whilst her skin was white and flawless like porcelain. Huge amber eyes framed by thick, long dark lashes were further enhanced by smoky dark eye make-up, and her full lips were expertly painted scarlet. Next to her, Simone's beauty faded to mere common good looks.

Emma was the first to recover her manners; she stepped forward with outstretched hand.

'I'm Emma,' she said smiling up at her, thinking they must all look like a bunch of scruffy urchins; the grime of the day's work on their sunburned skin, hair in knots, filthy yard clothes smeared with dirt and stinking of horses and sweat. As Caroline took Emma's hand with her slim, white, fragrant, French manicured one, Emma cringed with shame at her own calloused, brown grubby paw. As no-one else said anything, Emma did the introductions.

Simone managed to shake hands, although her face resembled a smacked arse, Kitty gawped, open-mouthed and Dan's expression was inscrutable. Caroline turned back to Emma, obviously assuming that she was the one in charge.

'I'm so glad to meet you all,' she said in her breathy, rather refined American accent. 'Malcolm has told me how well you've all been looking after my boy for me, I can't wait to see him. Where is he?'

Emma led the way to where *Angel's Midnight Messenger* – already shortened to *Angel* – was stabled. The others all stayed where they were in the staff room.

Caroline was in raptures over him. She described how she had fallen head over heels in love with him the first time she had set eyes on him.

'My trainer told me he was perfect for me, I wanted a horse that will take me round Badminton and he told me this is the horse to do it.'

'Did you compete him in America?' Emma asked her.

'Oh no! I've only seen him once before he was shipped over here,' she replied. 'Golly, aren't your stalls small in England,' she exclaimed, referring to the standard sized loose box. 'Back home in our barn, the horses all have much bigger stalls.'

They continued round the yard, Emma introducing her to some of the equine characters. Caroline looked in the door where the foaling boxes were.

'Now these are a better size,' she enthused, 'perhaps Angel could have one of these instead?'

'They're actually foaling boxes,' Emma apologised, 'we don't use them as regular boxes.'

'They're not in use now though are they?' Caroline said. 'It would be much better if Angel could have one of these. Maybe we could move him tomorrow.'

Dan had come outside and was leaning against the doorframe of the tack room.

'No,' he said. 'They're just for the mares foaling, and occasionally if we have a horse in rehab.'

Caroline started when he spoke as if she hadn't noticed him standing there. She hesitated a moment and seemed to consider something.

'Well,' she said sweetly, putting her head slightly on one side and smiling at him. 'I'm sure it would be okay, I'll check with Malcolm, there's no need for you to bother about it.'

'You can,' Dan said evenly, 'but he'll tell you the same thing.'

Emma watched this exchange with interest. Caroline Hamilton-Barnes obviously wasn't used to being told 'No'.

'We'll see,' she said. Then, walking past Dan without another glance, she went into the tack room. Emma followed, giving Dan a helpless look. From inside the tack room Caroline was already exclaiming over her new tack.

'Phew!' said Emma, going into the kitchen once she'd gone. Only Dan was left in there leaning against the counter drinking a beer. Simone and Kitty had gone home.

'So, do you feel you made a good first impression?' she asked, tongue-in-cheek.

He shrugged. 'She's going to be a complete pain in the arse.'

'Yeah, I think you're going to have to up your game with this one,' Emma replied.

'Forget it,' he said. 'She's like her horse, way too high maintenance.'

'Very beautiful though,' Emma said regarding him closely. His expression was impassive.

She couldn't resist trying to get a reaction from him.

'Too much for you?' she persisted. 'Punching above your weight?'

Finally, some emotion flickered across his face.

'So, you're saying you think she's too good for someone like me?'

'No, I didn't say that,' Emma denied. 'I just mean, it might take more than flashing your dimples to impress her.'

For a second, she thought she might have touched a nerve, then he grinned insolently.

'There's more than one way to cook an egg.'

Unexpectedly, Malcolm put his head round the door.

'Dan, can I have a quick word?' he asked. Dan immediately got up and went outside with him.

They stood side by side in the dusk, the old man and the young man, leaning on the fence of the arena. Heads bowed in deep conversation. As Emma watched, Malcolm said something and Dan laughed. Malcolm put a hand on his shoulder, also laughing. It was somehow touching, witnessing these two very different men sharing a private joke. They parted, and Dan came back in.

'Did Caroline ask him about the foaling box?' she asked.

'Yup,' Dan replied, getting another beer from the fridge, 'she asked him about it alright.'

'What did he say?'

Dan grinned, 'He told her it was up to me.'

Chapter 19

CAROLINE'S EXTREMELY BEAUTIFUL NOSE HAD OBVIOUSLY BEEN put out of joint by that slight altercation on the first day. She completely ignored Dan unless she was forced to speak to him, and then would address him with a kind of haughty civility. She spoke mainly to Emma and Simone. To Kitty, she spoke in a rather condescending manner, as if she were talking to a child.

Caroline wasn't very hands on. She left Angel's care completely up to them, even asking Emma to tack him up for her before she rode him. She came down to the yard looking like a model from an Ariat Catalogue.

Emma brought Angel up to the mounting block for her and held him while she mounted.

The horse was obviously well schooled and extremely fit; he gave the impression of a coiled spring. There was power and energy contained in every step, but Caroline kept him very short and rather than allowing him to go forward, she kept shortening up her reins and he got tighter and tighter.

Although Caroline's position was very correct, there was something slightly peculiar about the way she rode which Emma couldn't put her finger on. There was nothing out of place, but it was as if she was riding by numbers instead of by the seat of her breeches.

For four days, she only rode him in the school and only in walk and trot. Dan was itching to say something. However, as Caroline never asked for any advice, he never gave her any, and she was still giving him the cold shoulder.

'I think that horse is far too good for her and she's scared of him,' he told Emma.

'But why?' Emma asked. 'He's so beautifully schooled, he never puts a foot wrong.'

Dan shrugged. 'He won't stay that way forever if she doesn't start riding him properly. He must be jumping out of his skin with frustration by now.'

His words were proved right the next day.

Emma and Dan had been out on a hack on Lynx and Arcturus, leaving Simone to get Angel ready for Caroline. When they got back it was early evening. They rode into the yard to find that the school was empty and so was Angel's box.

'Where's Angel?' Dan asked Simone.

'Caroline was riding him in the school and he was being naughty,' Simone said with barely suppressed glee. 'He bucked and you should have seen her face, she looked proper scared.'

'So where are they now?' Dan asked.

'Well, I thought he might be bored, just being ridden in the school, so I suggested she took him for a walk up the road.'

'By herself?' he asked.

Simone looked sheepish.

'I didn't want to get behind with our jobs,' she defended herself.

'Well, let's hope she comes back in one piece,' he said grimly.

Half an hour later, there was still no sign of them. It was starting to get dark.

Emma was rugging up Lynx for the night. The tall grey mare was tense; her head held high, her ears standing to attention. She stared out into the gathering gloom, then suddenly let blast a loud neigh.

'I'm going to have to look for them,' Dan said crossly, but just at that moment, the sound of a horse on the road could be heard. It was coming fast. The other horses around the yard all came to their doors excitedly, several of them whinnied. The next minute Angel came thundering into the yard, wild eyed and rider-less, sides heaving.

'Shit!' Dan swore, Emma quickly caught Angel and checked him over; thankfully he seemed okay.

'Walk him round, chuck a cooler on him but don't un-tack him,' Dan instructed.

Emma nodded.

Dan got the quad bike out of the shed and roared off up the track towards the road. Twenty minutes passed. Emma's ears strained for the sound of the returning quad bike. At last she heard the distant hum of the engine, and then saw the lights of the bike coming down the track.

Dan drove into the yard. Caroline was sitting behind him, her arms wrapped tightly around his waist. Her huge eyes were wide, black make up smudged around them and mud smeared up the side of her deathly white face.

'Thank God you found her,' Emma said to Dan, bringing Angel to a halt. 'Are you okay Caroline?'

'I don't know…I didn't know where I was… I didn't think anyone would find me.' Her voice was trembling.

Dan helped her off the bike.

'What happened?' Emma asked.

'I was walking him up the road to try to calm him down, but he got worse and worse. I started to get worried I wouldn't hold him so I turned him back to come home and…' her voice broke into a sob, 'he just bolted! Then he got spooked by something and took off into the woods alongside the road. He wouldn't stop, so I threw myself off.'

'I saw the marks on the road and the tracks into the wood where he must have spooked,' Dan said.

'It was so dark in the woods and I couldn't find my phone, I must have dropped it,' Caroline sniffed. It was so odd seeing her like this, usually so confident and composed, she now looked so young and vulnerable.

'Are you hurt?' Emma asked her.

'I don't think so,' she replied uncertainly.

'Would you like some tea?' Emma asked.

'Brandy would be better,' Dan said, 'and then, you're getting back on your horse.'

Caroline's eyes widened in terror. 'No!' she said, 'I can't.'

'Just in the school,' Dan insisted, 'but if you put him back in his box now after this, he'll do that with you every time you ride him.'

'He bucked in the school earlier, he's not the horse I thought he was,' Caroline wailed. 'I bought him as a schoolmaster!'

'He is a schoolmaster,' Dan said, 'but he's not a hobby horse, he's an event horse. You've got him on a huge amount of concentrated feed and he's fit. He needs to be worked.'

'I've ridden him every day!' Caroline protested.

'You have to do more than just sit on him in the school,' Dan said, not unkindly. 'A horse like this needs to be worked until he knows he's done something. He needs to hack out, gallop and jump.'

Caroline shook her head. 'I can't, I just can't,' she said, her big amber eyes pleading with him.

'I'll ride him then,' he said.

Caroline didn't argue.

'Emma can you get the brandy from my room?' he asked, going to switch on the school lights.

Emma ran off to get it. When she came back, Dan had already mounted Angel and was riding him around the floodlit arena. The horse was still unhinged from his mad gallop; he looked like a different animal from the one who had walked and trotted obediently round the arena for the past few days. Emma had brought a warm coat, which she put around Caroline's shoulders and gave her the glass of brandy.

Angel's back was up, his neck and his tail carried high, all his muscles bunched and solid. The two girls watched as Dan sent him forward into a trot. Angel bucked. Caroline gasped.

Dan never shifted an inch, just sent him forward again with his long legs. Angel shot forward into canter. Dan kept him in canter and started to turn him in a wide circle.

Caroline sipped her drink.

'He's a very good rider isn't he?' she said.

Emma nodded. 'If anyone can get to the bottom of a horse then he can.'

Gradually the horse's head started to come down, his muscles to relax.

Dan kept working him until he was cantering sweetly on both reins in a long low outline. Then he let him walk to cool down, finally coming to a halt and slipping down to the ground in front of the two girls.

'Will you ride him for me again tomorrow?' Caroline asked him anxiously. Dan considered for a moment.

'Okay, but what he really needs is a good long hack tomorrow. You can come on another horse.'

Caroline seemed relieved by this suggestion. 'Okay,' she agreed.

Over the next few days Dan rode Angel. There was no doubt the horse went exceptionally well for him. With Dan in the saddle Emma could see how good he really was. When he jumped him, his scope was obvious, lifting over fences well over four foot with ease. All the time Caroline watched with a rapt expression on her face. A few days after her accident, they'd been out for a long hack, Caroline on the quiet Paddy, Dan on Angel. When they got back, Dan took Angel into the school.

'Come in here a minute,' he said to Caroline.

'Put your hands here,' he said, gesturing to the saddle, she did as she was told, and when she was standing next to Angel facing him, Dan put a hand under the knee of her left leg, and with an expert jockey's lift, hoisted her up into the saddle.

She tried to protest, but in order to keep her dignity, had little choice but to swing her right leg over the saddle.

'Okay, now just walk him round,' Dan instructed.

Caroline started walking her horse around the outside track. Angel, sensing that this rider was nervous and, associating her with the fear and excitement of his uncontrollable gallop, started to tense up. Caroline immediately shortened up her reins, and tipped forward in the saddle, anxiety written all over her face.

'Leave your reins long, relax your weight down in the saddle. Give him a pat, reassure him,' Dan corrected her.

Caroline did as she was told.

'He's a very sensitive horse,' Dan told her, 'extremely reactive. If your body language tells him there's something to worry about, he's going to feel worried. He needs to get his confidence from you.'

Coming up beside her, he put his hands on the reins, and looked up at her.

'When you hold the reins, imagine you're holding the hand of a child, firmly but gently. Put your hands over mine, now ask him to walk on.'

Dan walked beside Angel, Caroline with her hands over his.

'If you want him to be soft and accepting with his mouth, you have to be soft and allowing with your hand. Now focus on your breathing.'

After twenty minutes both horse and rider were much more relaxed. Caroline dismounted. 'I don't know how to thank you,' she said, with a smile full of relief and gratitude.

*

It was astonishing to Emma just how much Caroline changed in her attitude. Before, Dan was definitely persona non grata, now, he was flavour of the month. It was Dan this and Dan that; Dan's such an amazing rider, Dan's such a good teacher. Caroline asked his advice about everything from what she should be feeding Angel to what bit she should use, and hung on his every word. It was almost irritating.

One afternoon towards the end of the week, Emma went into the tack room. Caroline and Dan were in the kitchen, alone.

'I just want to thank you for all your help with Angel,' Caroline was saying, '….so, tomorrow night? I'll book a table for eight o'clock?'

Wow. More than one way to cook an egg indeed.

'I don't know how you do it,' she said, going into the kitchen after Caroline had left.

Dan smirked.

'You're going to go out with her then?' she said.

'Why not?' he shrugged.

'I thought she was too high maintenance,' Emma said narrowly.

'Well, beggars can't be choosers,' he replied, grinning at her.

'Huh!' she said. 'Rory was right. You have got the charm of the Irish, or the luck of the Irish, or something. Where's she taking you?'

'*The Pheasant*,' said Dan, with feigned nonchalance.

Emma shook her head. 'I hope you know what you're doing. If you upset her, she'll go running off back to America and then where will Malcolm's bank balance be?'

Dan's smug look disappeared. 'You don't have a lot of faith in me, do you Bugs?'

'I have a lot of faith in you in many ways, just none when it comes to women,' Emma said bluntly.

'Why not? Why do you automatically assume that I'm going to upset her?'

'Er… because of all the others! Simone, Amy, Becky…'

'Becky?' He looked blank.

'Yes, Becky. Irish, pretty, black hair. Nice girl, you broke her heart, remember?'

She saw the penny drop. 'Becky!' he sounded indignant. 'She got me plastered and threw herself at me!'

Emma was incredulous. 'Oh right. So you're saying that she took advantage of you when you were drunk?'

'Yes! And as for Amy, she knows exactly what she's doing, believe me!'

She was slightly disconcerted at the intensity with which he said this.

'And this is different is it, with Caroline. You really like her?' she challenged him.

He dropped eye contact and turned his back on her, going to the fridge for a beer.

'It's just dinner Bugs, stop making such a big deal out of it,' he said moodily. 'And anyway, you're the one who said I should try to "land" her.'

'I was just messing about, I didn't think you'd take me seriously!' Emma objected.

'No, you just didn't think I could do it,' he said.

'Is that what this is about? Just about you trying to prove some kind of point? Because if it is, then that's even worse. We're not teenagers, and this is not some stupid game.'

'I don't understand why it bothers you so much! I didn't know you were a particular friend of Caroline's.'

'I'm not, but she's still a person with feelings, who doesn't deserve to get hurt. What if she really likes you? What if she cares about you?'

'Cares about me?' he said, suddenly losing his temper. 'She doesn't even know me!'

And he walked out, slamming the door.

Chapter 20

He barely spoke to her for the rest of that evening, or for much of the next day. Then, after lunch, Emma saw Simone getting Lynx ready in her travel gear.

'Where's she going?' Emma asked her, confused.

'She's been sold,' Simone said matter-of-factly. 'Dan's delivering her to Rory's this afternoon.'

Emma's blood ran cold. No. Not Lynx. Not after all Dan's hard work. Her heart in her throat, she went to find him. He was in the staff room.

'Simone said that Lynx has been sold to Rory,' Emma said, not wanting to believe it.

'Yup. I'm taking her over to him this afternoon.'

He was looking through the file now, for Lynx's passport.

'But she can't be, she's your best horse,' she said distraught. 'It's so unfair after you've worked so hard to make her the horse she is.' Tears threatened, and she fought to hold them back.

Dan turned to her, his face stony. 'Arcturus too,' he said. Emma shook her head, not wanting to comprehend what he was telling her. 'Malcolm has someone interested in him. They're coming to watch him at Aldon next weekend, and if they like him, they're going to buy him.'

This was too much for Emma; Arcturus was her favourite, and their second-best horse. She lost the fight not to cry. She didn't want to cry in front of Dan, so turned and fled upstairs. Flinging herself on her bed she gave way to the tears. She would never forget that wild ride in the pouring rain that they'd had on Lynx and Arcturus, when the red earth had made her look like she was wearing war paint.

There was a knock on her door. She sat up hastily, scrubbing at her face with her sleeve. 'Who is it?'

'It's me.' It was Dan.

'Come in,' she said sniffing, and wiping away the last tears.

He opened the door and leant against the doorframe.

'It's just business Bugs,' he said softly. 'You can't take everything so much to heart.'

'It just seems so pointless. Why care at all if you're going to lose them anyway?' An errant tear escaped from her eyes and rolled down her nose.

Dan came over and sat on the bed next to her. He sat forward resting his elbows on his knees.

'The point is,' he said patiently, 'we bought Lynx for three and a half thousand pounds, and Malcolm's just sold her for twelve and a half. We need the money.'

Emma wasn't consoled. 'Why does everything have to be about money?' she said in disgust.

'I guess because we couldn't do it otherwise,' he said reasonably. 'It's why I don't let myself get too attached. I've seen hundreds of horses come through this yard. They all get sold in the end.'

'How do you stand it?' Emma asked him. 'Losing them over and over again.'

Dan shrugged. 'I've been told I'm a heartless bastard,' he said with his wry smile, 'perhaps that's why. I've got no heart left to lose.'

She blinked away fresh tears and looked up at him. For a long moment he stared back at her. His words denied the hurt, but that's not what she saw in his eyes. He was the first to look away, getting swiftly to his feet.

As he reached the door she said, 'Maybe subconsciously you didn't want the horses to do well, because you knew that it meant you would lose them. That's why you used to screw up in the dressage.'

Dan turned and smiled. 'Nah, I was just rubbish.'

Emma managed a small smile.

'Chin up Bugs,' he said and left, closing the door behind him.

*

Later, when Lynx had been taken, everyone else had left, and Dan had gone out with Caroline, Emma had never felt more alone in her life.

She only had one week left. Next weekend was Aldon, and then she was leaving on the Monday morning. Her feelings were so confused she couldn't work out whether she wanted to leave, or if she couldn't bear the thought of it.

Everything seemed so hopeless. One moment, she longed to be back on familiar ground where things were solid and real, and she wasn't constantly bombarded by complicated and disturbing emotions that she struggled to make sense of. The next moment the thought of leaving this place, these people, these horses that had all become so dear to her made her want to cry.

Eventually, exhausted, she fell asleep.

Her last week was gone almost before she knew it, the time just ticked relentlessly on, however much Emma tried to be in the present moment, her thoughts fluctuated wildly between what was in the past, and what might be in the future.

Caroline was spending a lot more time at the yard; she and Dan always seemed to be together. Simone had a kind of defeated air about her, she knew she was beaten. Emma almost felt sorry for her again.

She went with Dan to groom at Aldon, Caroline came along as well. Arcturus came first in his section, that sealed the deal and he was to be collected on the Wednesday the following week. But by then, Emma would already be back in Basingstoke.

Kitty was quiet. 'It's going to be so horrible when you've gone,' she said miserably to Emma.

'What do you think you'll do? Will you stay?' Emma asked her.

'I guess so, I don't have anything else to do.'

Emma couldn't bear the look of dejection on Kitty's face.

'Look, when Edward and I have moved up to London, perhaps you could take a holiday and come and stay with us.'

That did the trick, Kitty perked up immediately. 'Do you mean it?'

'Of course.' Her own spirits were lifted by the thought of comforting her little friend.

Sunday morning, Emma spoke to Simone at tea break.

'Kitty and I are going for a drink tonight as it's my last night, will you come?'

Simone looked at her warily.

Emma went on. 'I know we haven't always seen eye to eye but I'm leaving tomorrow, and I'd like you to come.'

Simone hesitated.

Emma swallowed her pride. 'Please?'

'Okay,' Simone replied. 'I'll come.'

But when she asked Dan – his answer was cagey.

'I will if I'm back. Caroline has asked me to go and look at a horse with her this afternoon. I suggested she find herself a good grassroots schoolmaster to teach her the basics, in the meantime I'm going to keep riding Angel for her.'

Emma raised her eyebrows at him. 'So, that's worked out quite well then.'

He wouldn't quite meet her eyes. She didn't see him before he and Caroline disappeared off in her Porsche early afternoon.

Emma's leaving 'do' was a bit of a damp squib. Dan hadn't got back by the time they left for the pub, so it was just the three of them. Kitty really didn't like Simone, and Simone was never the liveliest person at the best of times, so it was down to Emma to make all the conversation and try to at least pretend she was having a good time. She was starting to wonder why she had bothered.

Every time the door opened Emma looked up. Simone caught her as, once again, the door swung open to admit another punter.

'He's not coming you know,' Simone said.

'Who?' Emma feigned ignorance.

'Dan. He's got other fish to fry now.'

Emma couldn't help thinking she sounded a bit smug.

'Oh well, who wants another drink?' Emma said quickly getting up, not wanting to let Simone see how pissed off she was feeling.

She went to the bar. Again, the door opened; it was Joe.

Oh thank God, Emma thought, the evening might be saved after all. He came over.

'Dan tells me you're leaving us tomorrow,' he said, 'I was hoping to find you in here.'

'I am,' she said ruefully.

'For good?' There was a slight implication in the question, which made her look up at him.

'I think so, yes,' she said, with a sad smile.

'Let me buy you a drink,' he said, as Barry came over. 'Where's Dan tonight?' He looked at the table where Simone and Kitty sat together, not speaking.

'Not here. He's out somewhere with Caroline – have you met her?' she asked, taking a large slug of her wine.

He nodded with a knowing grin. 'I met her the other day. It's not hard to see why Dan might be distracted,' he raised one eyebrow. Emma felt a twinge of something she knew she had no right at all to feel.

'Do you want to play pool?' she said, blocking the emotion. 'We'll have to play doubles with Cheerful and Happy over there, I'm afraid.'

She gestured towards Kitty and Simone, who were sitting, not talking, looking like Christmas had been cancelled.

Joe laughed. 'Why not.'

From then on, things improved. Simone liked Joe and cheered up considerably when he joined them. They had a few laughs and some of the other locals came over to say goodbye and to wish her good luck.

'I'm going to miss so many people,' she said as they were finishing the last of their drinks.

'Well, you know where we are,' Joe said. 'You can always come back and see us.'

Emma knew it was unlikely. How would she look back on this chapter of her life? Right now her feelings were so confused, it was impossible to tell whether she would remember it as the best or the worst of times.

Joe had to go; he was driving and had work in the morning. There seemed little point in prolonging the evening so the girls got up to leave as well.

'You want a lift home?' he asked Emma. She hesitated; thinking about what Dan had told her about Joe "liking" her. She looked up into his open, honest face. There was something in his eyes, a little like regret but also like hope.

'Thanks, that would be great,' she said.

'So, how are you feeling about leaving?' Joe asked, when they were in his Land Rover, heading back to the yard.

Emma sighed. 'I really don't know,' she admitted, 'it's been a bit of a rollercoaster. There's going to be a lot I miss.'

'Maybe hindsight will give you some perspective?' he suggested.

'I really hope so!' Emma laughed.

They reached the yard; it was in darkness.

Joe pulled up behind the stable buildings and turned to her.

'Thank you,' she said putting her hand on the door handle.

'Bye Emma,' he said, and leant towards her to give her a kiss. She leant forward to receive it. He left his lips on her cheek just a fraction longer than could strictly be called a friendly peck, and then drew back a little, but not quite all the way, his eyes looking for hers. Emma hastily pulled on the door handle and slid out of the seat out of the Land Rover.

'Bye Joe,' she said with regret, and shut the door. He lifted his hand and drove off, a slightly wistful smile on his face.

Emma's heart was pounding. She was sure that if she had hesitated, even for a second longer, he would have kissed her – properly.

*

She got ready for bed, but it wasn't really that late, and she didn't feel very tired. She finished her packing, ready for the next morning.

Despite what had happened with Joe, her thoughts kept wandering to Dan and Caroline.

She stood looking around her little room. Not hers anymore.

It felt strangely bare now with all her stuff gone. She wondered who would have it after her. Would they hate it, or come to love it like she had? Would they experience the same tumultuous journey of highs and lows? Sighing deeply, she got into bed and lay, staring into the darkness, thinking she would never sleep.

But she must have, because the next moment, she woke, and it was morning. There were sounds coming from the yard down below. Sitting up quickly, she looked out of her window. Simone was feeding round.

A feeling of unease settled around her heart. Although Dan officially had the day off, he would normally always feed round unless he had stayed out all night or was seriously hung over. Getting dressed quickly, she went downstairs. Simone was bringing the empty feed trolley back to the feed room.

Emma followed her in.

'No Dan?' she asked her.

'No, I haven't seen him,' she replied.

Perhaps she was imagining it, but Emma thought there was a hard glint of triumph in her eyes, a rather spiteful little smile hovering round her mouth.

Kitty arrived. 'When are you going?' she asked.

'Ernie's coming to pick me up at 10 o'clock,' Emma said. 'My trains at 10.22.'

Kitty's shoulders slumped. 'I'm going to miss you so much,' she said.

Emma gave her a hug. She made them all tea, but didn't feel like she could stomach any breakfast. Time started to fly past alarmingly quickly. She went up to the house with dragging footsteps to say goodbye to Malcolm and Cathy, who both gave her a big hug and told her she was welcome back any time. She left a tin of their favourite biscuits in the office, with a thank-you card.

Wandering around the yard, Emma said goodbye to the horses individually, giving each of them a polo mint. Tears were not too far away. She left Arcturus to last, giving him a kiss on his soft grey nose and then the whole of the rest of the packet of mints. The tears came now; there was nothing she could do to stop them.

'Be happy,' she told him. 'Be happy in your new home.'

Turning away, she walked quickly across the yard and up to her room to get her bags.

At 9.50, there was a knock on her door; for an instant her heart lifted.

'Come in,' she called. The door opened.

It was Kitty.

'Do you need a hand with your things?' Kitty asked.

Emma smiled shakily, swallowing her disappointment.

'Yes please, that would be great,' she said.

Giving her a couple of the lighter bags, she picked up the rest of her belongings, and, taking a deep breath, turned and walked out of her room for the last time, closing the door firmly behind her.

Having said a perfunctory goodbye to Simone, they carried the bags round to the front drive and put them in a heap.

'Don't worry about waiting with me,' Emma said, 'you'll get behind with your jobs.'

Kitty's chin began to quiver.

'Here,' Emma said, and quickly rummaging around in one of her bags, she found the scarf that Kitty loved; the one with little white horses on it.

'Keep this,' she said, putting it around Kitty's neck.

Kitty's eyes filled with tears.

'Stay in touch!' Emma said, giving her a hug, and with that Kitty ran off back to the yard.

Left on her own, Emma sat down on her small suitcase. She had less than ten minutes to wait.

Try as she might, she couldn't swallow the lump in her throat.

Was this it? Was this what it had come to? She was leaving, and he wasn't even going to bother to say goodbye?

She had thought… or at least… she had let herself believe, that they were friends – that her friendship might even mean something to him. That he might even care, just a little, for her.

She was helpless to stop the tears that were now coursing down her cheeks. She swiped them away in frustration. What an idiot she was.

And then it hit her, like a revelation. My God! She was such a fool! This is what he *did*, this was the way it always was with him.

She had known that all along, and *still* she had allowed him to get to her, allowed herself to care. She could almost laugh at herself.

And just like that, WHAM! Her barriers of self-preservation came slamming down around her heart. She stood up, looking at her watch.

'Hurry up Ernie,' she muttered, desperate to be out of there now.

The sound of a car approaching reached her ears. Phew, at least Ernie wasn't late.

But it wasn't Ernie's grey cab that swung around the corner, it was Caroline's red Porsche.

Emma blanched. Struggling to arrange her features into something resembling an acceptable formation, she ducked her head, pretending to hunt for something in one of her bags. Dan got out of the car.

'Bugs!' he called. 'Are you going already?' He came over, smiling.

She nodded, unable to muster up even the ghost of a smile.

'Are you okay, you look a bit pale?' he said frowning and trying to look into her face. Emma nodded again, finally forcing herself to give him a sickly smile.

'Just hung-over,' she lied. But he seemed to accept this explanation.

'You weren't going to leave without saying goodbye, were you?' he asked. Emma was gob-smacked by the ridiculous irony of this question.

She cleared her throat. 'My train leaves in twenty minutes,' she managed to say.

'Wait there, I've got something for you,' and he jogged off in the direction of the yard.

She stood watching him go, her feelings in complete turmoil. Caroline got out of the car looking absolutely stunning as usual.

'You're leaving are you Emma?' she said.

Emma nodded.

'We're just off to look at another horse,' Caroline said. 'Dan insisted on coming back to check the girls were getting everything done properly,' she said, rolling her eyes.

A rather unflattering word popped into Emma's head.

Just then Ernie pulled into the driveway.

'Well, good luck with everything in the future,' Caroline said breezily, getting back into her car.

Ernie got out and helped her put her bags in the boot of his cab. She looked around anxiously for Dan. At last he was coming back, and he was carrying something under his arm.

'Here,' he said grinning, handing her a bag. 'So you don't forget us.'

She looked in the bag. Inside was an over-sized, stuffed toy Bugs Bunny with long legs and arms and floppy ears.

'I saw it in town the other day and couldn't resist getting it for you.'

He grinned.

'Thanks,' she said, finding she was unable to look him properly in the face.

'God, you look green around the gills! What the hell were you drinking last night? At least if the worst comes to the worst, you can use the bag to throw up into on the train,' he laughed.

Caroline revved her engine. Dan glanced over his shoulder. He was standing between Emma and the cab, hands in his pockets, and still he didn't move.

'Well, I'd better go,' Emma said in consternation.

'See you later Bugs,' he said, 'take care of yourself.' Then, backing away from her towards Caroline's car, he pulled a face. 'Don't throw up in Ernie's cab,' he said and grinning, got into the car. They roared away down the drive.

With Ernie's driving she only just caught the train by the skin of her teeth.

Once she had installed herself and all her belongings in one of the almost empty carriages, she slumped in her seat, resting her forehead against the cool glass of the window and closed her eyes. She felt drained. She wished she were numb; she didn't want to feel anything anymore.

Emma was glad she was going home. What she needed now was to get her feet firmly back onto solid ground, leave all this behind her and get back some stability in her life. What she needed was Edward to hold on to, and even her Mother telling her to get a grip on reality would be welcome right now.

As the train left the Dorset landscape behind for the last time, Emma got the Bugs Bunny out of the bag and looked at it. It was so soft and very cute, but not tasteful at all. Not something Edward would ever have bought her in a million years. Turning to gaze listlessly out of the window, she watched as the last of the beautiful Dorset countryside slipped past the window and out of sight behind her.

Chapter 21

EDWARD WAS HOME FOR TWO WEEKS AND THEY STARTED FLAT hunting in earnest. They spent their days traipsing around London, looking at various places. Emma thought that any one of them would have done, but Edward was more discerning, asking sensible questions about ground rent and parking.

He had applied for a few positions in various hospitals around London; the hospital, which was his first choice, had some of the leading surgeons in the country and he badly wanted to train under them. But until he heard whether he had got the position, they couldn't make any final decisions about a flat.

Emma vaguely scanned situations vacant for a job for herself. Nothing grabbed her interest.

'There's bound to be something,' Edward said, 'anything's got to be better than being up to your knees in shit every day. It's so nice to kiss you without getting the faint whiff of horse.'

On the Friday night, they were going out on the town with Lottie and Josh.

The anonymity of London, the vast, impersonal crowds, unfamiliar faces and spaces were strangely, just where Emma felt like being in her current state of mind.

Here, she was just one of a million faceless people, seen in one moment, forgotten in the next. If she had been on her own with Lottie, she probably would have got completely shitfaced. That's actually what she felt like doing; drinking and drinking until she had blotted out all traces of any discomfiting thoughts or emotions that, if she allowed herself to think, even for a second, would come pushing their way into her consciousness.

She wanted to lose herself until she bore no resemblance to the girl who had cried on the train.

They stayed at Josh and Lottie's flat. Lottie and Emma stayed up talking until the early hours of the morning.

'You seem different somehow,' Lottie said, 'wiser, less innocent.'

'Really?' She definitely didn't feel wiser; she felt like she was no longer sure of anything anymore.

'I thought you were a bit quiet tonight,' Lottie went on, 'is everything okay?'

Emma hesitated.

'I'm fine really,' she said, 'I think it's just re-adjusting to reality. I've been living such a different life for the past few months.'

'I can understand how you feel. It was definitely "different" down in deepest darkest Dorset!' Lottie giggled, putting on a West Country accent.

'But I don't want to talk about Dorset,' Emma said hastily. 'Let's talk about the future.'

Lottie told Emma in a low voice that she secretly hoped that Josh might propose soon. She thought he was just waiting until they had saved a bit more money.

'At least you know Edward has the money, you can get married whenever you want, you won't have to wait.'

'True,' said Emma. 'I know I'm really lucky.'

When she crawled in next to Edward on the sofa bed, she snuggled up close to his back. He was so big and solid; in a way, it represented who he was. Reliable, dependable and stalwart.

The next day, they all went for lunch in a pub that Lottie chose, close to Lottie and Josh's flat. It was a fairly old pub, more traditional than some of the modern London bars. Inside, the girls found a table while the men ordered their drinks.

Lottie was slightly hung over; she'd drunk a lot more than Emma the previous night, enough to make her lively and amusing, but not like they used to drink in the old days when they were young and single.

As the men came to sit down, with their drinks and some menus, Emma spotted a Pool table on the other side of the pub.

'We should have a game. See if you've improved,' she teased Lottie, remembering the last time they played. An image of Dan and Joe suddenly popped into her head, and she was taken completely by surprise as, out of the blue, she was flattened by a wave of homesickness. She wasn't even sure you could you feel homesick for somewhere that wasn't your home. Mentally, she squashed the feeling into a little ball, and threw it away.

'Only because you know you'll beat me!' retorted Lottie.

'When were you two playing Pool?' Edward asked.

Memories flooded unbidden into Emma's head; memories of that night, of Lottie flirting with Dan, Emma, pleading with him not to take it any further. She glanced at Lottie wondering if she was remembering the same thing, but Lottie was completely composed.

'Oh, just when Lottie came down to visit me in Dorset,' said Emma quickly.

'Let's have a game of doubles,' said Lottie, apparently oblivious.

But Edward shook his head. 'I'm hungry, can't we eat?' So they abandoned the idea of playing.

It was warm in the pub and Emma took of her jumper.

'Look at your arms!' Lottie exclaimed, reaching across and feeling Emma's bicep. 'Look how toned they are, I know girls with personal trainers whose arms aren't as good as that. Look Josh,' she went on, 'feel Emma's bicep.'

Emma was acutely embarrassed as Josh reached across to feel her arm.

'Blimey,' said Josh. 'They're better than mine.'

'It's just working with the horses,' Emma said self-consciously glancing at Edward, but he was studying the menu intently.

'Give me an arm wrestle,' said Lottie, putting her arm up on the table. 'I go to the gym, let's see who's strongest.'

'No!' Emma protested, laughing, 'I'm not going to arm-wrestle you!'

'Go on!' said Lottie.

'No!' Emma insisted.

'Let's order some food,' Edward said, impatiently.

'Good idea,' Emma agreed.

Soon after lunch, they left, and Emma gave Lottie big hug goodbye.

'Won't be long and we'll be up here with you,' said Emma.

'It'll be fab, I can't wait!'

On the drive home Emma was introspective. It had been fun, she had enjoyed herself. Perhaps it would all be all right after all.

'It was a really good weekend wasn't it?' she said, smiling at Edward.

'Hmm,' he said in a slightly ambivalent tone.

Emma looked at him sharply. 'What? Didn't you have a good time?'

'Yes, it was fun…but sometimes I think Lottie is a little bit immature.'

Emma was instantly defensive. 'What do you mean?'

'Well, I know she'd had a lot to drink last night, but she was a bit loud didn't you think?'

Emma hadn't noticed.

'And then, today,' Edward continued, 'with the arm wrestling. It's all harmless I know, but I'm just saying… she's not the kind of girl you'd want to take home to meet your mother.'

Emma was incredulous. 'Well, Lottie thinks the absolute world of you.'

Edward sighed. 'I didn't say I didn't like her, of course I do! I've always liked Lottie. I just mean I'm glad you don't behave like her sometimes.'

Emma turned and looked out of the window. She didn't know why, but that made it worse somehow.

Chapter 22

EDWARD DROVE HER TO HER PARENTS' HOUSE. EMMA WISHED THAT she could have stayed at his parents', but as no-one had suggested it and he had to go back to work the following day, she had no choice. Her feet dragged up the path to the front door.

After she had eaten dinner and spent the required amount of time making polite conversation with her parents, she excused herself and went up to her room. Her bags that she had brought back from Dorset were still in a heap where she had dropped them, two weeks ago. She couldn't avoid dealing with them forever.

She unzipped her rucksack. The smell of horse assailed her nostrils immediately and with it came the inevitable feelings of homesickness and nostalgia.

While she had been with Edward, in London, it had been easy to stay numb for the most part; feeling so far removed from anything to do with her recent life had helped her to gain the sense of detachment that she had so wanted. But now, on her own, with each and every one the objects in front of her evoking memories, it was impossible to remain detached.

Sighing, she put some music on and began to unpack, and was instantly transported back to her funny little attic room. Her clothes, which needed washing, still had some horsehair on them: black, bay, chestnut and grey. Her boots, when she took them out of their plastic bag, had some mud on them – Dorset mud, slightly tinged with red.

Her bright bedspread that had been on her little bed smelt of the very essence of her room; old wood, the earthy pungent smell of the outdoors and fresh air, and a hint of saddle soap and leather which had seeped up through the floorboards from the tack room below.

She missed it. Badly.

In the last bag was the Bugs Bunny that Dan had given her. She ran its soft ears through her hands and sat it up on her bed – then something made her move it over to her chest of drawers.

Surrounded by her things, she took her phone out and started looking through the hundreds of photos and videos on it. There was Lynx, sleek and elegant, Chance, bright chestnut with his four white socks, Arcturus, solid and powerful with his handsome roman nose, and of course Merlin, with his long black limbs and belligerent expression.

She watched a video of Dan schooling Merlin in the arena, practising one of his tests. As he rode past, he turned to smile over his shoulder. Emma quickly shut down the video and turned it off.

That night, she had the strangest dream.

She was walking through the streets of London on her own, looking for something, but she didn't know what. She looked around trying to read the writing on the signs that were everywhere, but the words kept changing before she could work out what they said. The names of the places she could make out were all unfamiliar. She walked and walked, looking for something, some place that she recognised, but she was struggling to open her eyes properly, her eyelids were so heavy, she could hardly see at all. She felt completely lost. Then she heard a voice, a familiar voice saying; 'Emma, where are you going? Just stay with me.'

And she knew that as long as she could hear that voice, it was going to be okay, she would be fine.

*

With Edward back at work, and no job to occupy her, Emma was slowly going insane with boredom. If she'd had some more money she would have loved to go and visit Maggie for a couple of weeks, but she would need her savings to be able to contribute towards things for the new flat.

She spent her days trying to stay out of the house as much as possible; running, reading in café's, wandering aimlessly around town and dwelling in the past, far too much.

She felt horribly isolated, far more so than when she had been out in the middle of nowhere in Dorset. Several times she wished she had her driving licence.

Thinking about how Dan had conquered his issues in the dressage and improved so much. If he could do that, even though he hated it, she ought to be able to conquer her anxiety.

She, who could sit on half a ton of horse, and jump over a hedge so big that she couldn't even see over it. She had done that. She ought to be able to do this.

The thought was exhilarating. She would be able to go anywhere she wanted; could go and see her Granddad, Lottie, or even.... yes, she would do it! She would take her driving test! It seemed ridiculous to her now that she hadn't done it before.

She rang Edward in her excitement, not wanting to lose another minute; hopefully he would take her out for a practice next time he was down.

'There's hardly any point now,' he said. Her excitement took a nosedive. 'It's a pain having even one car in London, let alone two.'

'But I could drive yours,' she suggested.

He laughed. 'Have you any idea how much it would cost to insure you on the Lotus, having just passed your test? Even if it was safe for you to drive it?'

Emma didn't.

'Well, it's not worth it. You won't need to anyway once we're there. Everything's within walking distance, you just hop on and off the tube.'

Emma couldn't argue with his logic, but giving up the idea caused her more than a small pang of disappointment and, if she were honest, a tiny bit of resentment.

Edward still hadn't heard whether he had got the position he had applied for and until he knew, she was in limbo.

So when he called her a few days later sounding excited but anxious, it was unnerving, but also a relief from the interminable waiting and wondering. He said that he needed to talk to her about something serious, something that would affect them both.

He drove down to see her on the Wednesday night, even though he had to be back at work on the Thursday morning, and took her out to their favourite restaurant. He was on edge, which was uncharacteristic of him. She was both uneasy, and intrigued.

She could hardly wait to know, but he wouldn't tell her until they had ordered their food and had their drinks.

'Emma,' he began. She held her breath. 'I've been offered a job, something that would be an incredible experience as well as furthering my career.' He paused.

'Go on,' Emma encouraged, 'what is it you'd be doing?'

'Well, that's the thing…it would be abroad, Germany more specifically.'

Emma raised her eyebrows. 'Wow!'

'A senior doctor at my hospital heard about it through a contact he has in Berlin. It would be working with one of Germany's leading surgeons, very similar to the position I wanted here, and I would get the specialist training I need.'

'That sounds amazing!' Her mind was quickly computing the possible implications.

'But of course, it would mean that we would have to put our move to London on hold…and I would be away for months at a time.' He paused. 'It might be a while – and I would be busy – but once I was settled, you could join me.' It wasn't a question, more of a statement.

Emma's brain was working fast, going through such a range of conflicting thoughts, occurring one after another it made her head spin.

'When?' she asked.

'I would have to go fairly soon,' Edward continued, 'shortly after Christmas in fact. There is a house share already in place for the position, then once I was there, I could look for a place for us.'

Germany. Berlin. It would be something new, and anything would be better than staying here with her parents, and…there was something else; a glimpse of a possibility.

Edward took her silence for disappointment.

'I know you must be disappointed, and I'm sorry, but this is really important for my career, a massive opportunity.'

Emma at last found her voice. 'Of course you must take it, I would never forgive myself if you missed something like this for me!'

Lottie was upset when she heard the news of course.

'I was so looking forward to having you both up here with us!' she cried in dismay.

'So was I,' Emma consoled her, 'but it's still going to happen, just not right now.'

'Why don't you come up anyway?' suggested Lottie.

'I can't afford it, I haven't even got a job.'

'You could stay with us until you get yourself sorted!'

Emma was grateful for the offer, but for the moment, wanted to keep her options open.

THEY SPENT CHRISTMAS at Edward's parents' house as they had planned. It was lovely as always. Such a contrast to the Christmases she remembered growing up; just herself and her parents sitting around the long, formal dining table, with, 'Pass the sprouts,' the extent of the conversation. Edward's house was rammed, both his sisters and their husbands and children were all staying.

There was nothing like waking up on Christmas morning to the sound of excited children's voices, all squealing with delight over their stockings. Edward's mum said Emma had got too thin and set about feeding her up with a continuous stream of delicious food.

Climbing the stairs to bed one night, Emma paused to admire a painting, halfway up, one that she had always been drawn to. It was a country scene, in watercolour, of a farmhouse with an orchard in the foreground. Chickens scratched around the foot of the trees, pecking at the fallen apples; big fluffy fat hens, brown and white. And the artist had been particularly skilful in depicting the way the sunlight glanced through the branches of the trees, casting dappled patterns on the ground beneath. There were several similar paintings around the house which appeared to be by the same artist, but this was Emma's favourite.

Edward had followed her and stood on the step below.

'I love this painting,' Emma said, 'I've noticed your parents have several of these around the house. Do you know who the artist is?' she asked, peering at the initials painted in the corner; they were hard to make out, but they looked like S F.

Edward laughed. 'Yes, as a matter of fact I do, Sarah Farrington – my Mother.'

Emma gasped and turned quickly to look him. He was smiling, hands in pockets, leaning against the wall.

'You're serious? Your Mum?'

He shrugged. 'Yes.'

'But – I didn't know she painted, I mean, I've never even seen her pick up a brush! When…where does she paint?'

'Oh, she doesn't do it anymore – not for years, I can't even remember her painting.'

'But why? She's so good, these are beautiful, why on earth did she stop?'

'No particular reason, just family life and kids. I don't think she had the time when we three came along,' he laughed, 'and I think Dad used to get fed up when he'd come home after a long day at work, and the house would be a mess, and there would be no food because she'd been lost in her painting all day. She would get so absorbed in what she was doing, she would completely lose track of time. She never made any money at it – could never bare to part with any of her paintings – so there wasn't much point in doing it really.'

Emma was incredulous. It was such a tragic waste of talent. And for her to have given up something that she was so obviously passionate about – it made Emma feel almost angry.

Around the dinner table two days later, the talk was all about Edward's trip, when his father spoke to her directly, just as she'd put a large forkful of roast beef in her mouth.

'So, Emma, what are you planning to do before you can join Edward in Berlin?' Everyone looked at her.

For what felt like an excruciatingly long time, Emma couldn't answer, frantically chewing until she could swallow her mouthful.

So far, she had managed to avoid the question of what she was going to do, finding a vague, 'Oh, I'll probably do some temping,' served as answer enough for most people.

Now, looking round at their expectant faces, she knew she would have to give them something more specific.

With difficulty she managed to swallow her food. 'Well, I thought I might to go back to my old job,' she said.

To her surprise, Edward nodded his approval and went on cutting up his beef. 'Good thinking. Hearnshaw's might want a temp, have you already asked them?'

A murmur of approbation went around the table.

'Actually, I meant…' Emma began, but Edward's father was already replying.

'The important thing is that it's got to be something you can leave as soon as Edward is settled,' he said nodding. 'I always think having secretarial skills is so useful for a girl, you can put it down and pick it up whenever you need to.'

'Mmm, actually…' she tried again, but Sophie piped up.

'At least you don't have to go back to that place in Dorset!' she exclaimed. 'Didn't they pay you something pitiful like one hundred pounds a week?'

Arabella joined in. 'Oh God yes! And you always came home covered in bruises, what an awful place!'

Emma took a deep breath and said loudly. 'That is where I meant actually; not Hearnshaws. I'm going back to Coach House Stables.'

Everyone stopped eating and looked at her. Edward and his father wore identical frowns.

She turned to Edward. 'I've spoken to Malcolm, I rang him yesterday. He said they could do with someone to help out, someone who knows what they're doing – like me.'

It had been a brief telephone conversation, short and to the point. Malcolm had clearly been delighted that she wanted to come back; 'Fantastic Emma! Come whenever you want. We could do with someone who knows the ropes, we're a bit short handed at the moment.' Some things never changed.

'I don't think that's a good idea,' Edward said, 'it was a dreadful place – ghastly people.'

'I loved it there – I loved the people.'

Around the table there was an exchange of glances. Edward put down his knife and fork.

'I want to leave you where I know you'll be safe, under your parents' roof. I would feel much happier…'

'But I wouldn't,' Emma said softly, and Edward broke off, mid-sentence.

There was a silence. Edward and Emma stared at each other.

His mother got to her feet, serving dish in hand. 'More potatoes anyone?' she said briskly.

*

A week before Edward left, it was Lottie's birthday; Josh had organised a party for her in a club in London. All their friends were there, and Lottie had sparkled all night in a floor-length sequined dress, in her element as the centre of attention. Emma would have hated it.

Then, glasses of champagne were handed round and everyone knew something special was afoot.

Josh got down on one knee and proposed to Lottie in front of everyone. Emma knew this was just what she would have wanted and was absolutely over the moon for her friend.

'It'll be you next!' Lottie said, when Emma hugged her. Emma smiled, but privately thought she would die if Edward proposed to her in front of everyone like that.

The day of Edward's departure dawned, and his Dad drove him to the airport. Emma went with them to see him off. He was excited to be going, buzzing in anticipation of his journey.

'I'll call you when I get there,' Edward said, hugging her.

'Yes do.'

Kissing him goodbye, Emma felt desolate as he walked away from her through the departure gate, but she knew that his father would be embarrassed by a public display of emotion, so she managed not to cry.

The moment she got home, she pulled her rucksack out from under her bed and started to pack, wasting no time. She was going back to Dorset.

Chapter 23

There it was, nestled between the soft, Dorset hills, the low winter sun casting a rosy hue on the yellow stone of the buildings as it sank into the sea in the distance.

Emma released her seatbelt and sat forward on the edge of the passenger seat of Ernie's cab, as they made their way down the long drive towards the house, barely able to contain her excitement – or was it nerves – or both; it was hard to tell the difference.

'Emma! So good to see you.' Cathy came out to greet her, giving her a kiss on both cheeks.

'How is everyone?' Emma asked.

'Absolutely fine! There have been a few changes, but we're all fine.'

Emma didn't like the sound of that; she wanted everything to be just the same.

There was a brand-new VW golf parked on the drive, which she didn't recognise, apart from that, everything looked exactly the way she remembered it.

'I know someone who'll be pleased to have you back,' Cathy said.

'Oh?' Emma asked.

'Kitty!' Cathy said.

'Ah, Kitty. She's still here then?'

'Yes, Kitty's still here unbelievably, and Simone of course,' Cathy said with a little less endearment. 'I don't think she'll ever leave.'

'Hmmm,' said Emma knowingly.

'But you haven't met Rachel,' Cathy went on.

'Rachel?' Emma said.

'Yes, she's the acting yard manager now – she's very good.'

Emma's heart paused in its rhythm. 'Oh really?' she swallowed. 'Where's Dan?'

'He's not here,' said Cathy.

This matter-of-fact statement gave Emma a rather unpleasant reality check. 'Not here?' she echoed.

'No, he's away skiing with Caroline, we're not sure exactly when they'll be back. You remember Caroline?'

'O-of course I remember…who could forget her?'

This was a lot of information for Emma to take in. At least her heart had started beating again with an uncomfortable bump. But *skiing*? With *Caroline*?

Somehow, she had just assumed that Caroline would be long gone by now, it had never occurred to her that she might still be on the scene.

'Well, anyway, Rachel is very good, as I said, she keeps everything running smoothly.' Cathy was saying.

'So, what does Dan do now if Rachel is yard manager?'

'He still works for Malcolm…' Cathy hesitated, '…to be honest I'm not entirely sure what arrangement they have, but Caroline has got three horses here now, all on competition livery. Between you and me,' Cathy lowered her tone in a conspiratorial air, 'the money comes in very handy, more than covers the extra staff wages – and Dan is still basically running the yard, he's just…' she made a vague gesture with her hands. 'Anyway, whatever arrangement they have, it seems to suit everyone. And it's good that Dan is finally getting some time off – he never has before you know, he's always worked so hard,' Cathy said with real affection. Emma did know.

'Well,' Emma said, 'should I take my stuff down and see the others? Am I in my old room?'

'Yes dear,' Cathy replied.

A thought occurred to Emma. 'And does Rachel have the other one?' she asked.

'No, she lives locally,' here she lowered her voice again. 'The room is officially still Dan's, although everyone knows he spends most of the time staying in the Coach House!' she gave a little laugh.

'Ah, I see.'

'Anything you need, you know where I am,' said Cathy, going back to her desk.

Emma thanked her and went back outside.

Picking up her stuff, she made her way down into the yard.

It was just the same, if a little more wintery, there was still frost on the ground even though it was mid-afternoon.

As she crossed the yard, Kitty appeared out of a stable and gave a little cry of joy. She ran across the grass and flung her arms around her.

Emma laughed, dropping her stuff where she stood and returned the hug.

'Cathy said you were coming today!' Kitty exclaimed.

A girl came out of the feed room; she was probably a couple years older than Emma, tall and well-built, long brown hair in a ponytail and wearing a Toggi baseball cap.

'Rachel, this is Emma,' Kitty introduced her.

'I've heard all about you from this one,' she nodded at Kitty, holding her hand out for Emma to take. She had a northern accent, possibly Geordie, and a friendly manner. 'She's been that excited about you coming back.'

'I'm excited to be back,' Emma said.

Simone walked across the yard,

'Hi Simone!' Emma called.

'Alright?' Simone said, as she came past. It looked like she was attempting to smile but the expression she achieved was more like a grimace; it was obvious she was less than thrilled to see Emma again.

Kitty helped her with her bags whilst she chatted away, telling Emma everything that had been going on.

'Rachel seems nice,' Emma said.

'She is,' said Kitty cheerfully, 'she started a couple of weeks before Christmas, before Dan and Caroline went away.'

'They've been away that long?' Emma said in disbelief.

'No,' laughed Kitty, 'that was the time before – they went to the Caribbean or somewhere for Christmas.'

Emma was taken aback. 'They're quite serious then?' she said, as they reached her room.

'Seem to be,' Kitty said shrugging her shoulders. 'Caroline bought him a car for his birthday.'

Emma's jaw nearly hit the floor. 'What? Oh my God, not that brand new Golf!'

'Yep, that's the one,' Kitty giggled. 'Rachel calls them Posh and Becks behind their backs.'

Emma smiled, but she was finding all of this rather unsettling. She had wanted everything to be just the same as before and it was quickly becoming obvious that things were different – very different indeed.

LEFT ALONE IN her room Emma closed her eyes and breathed in deeply. Ooh that smell. At least her room looked and felt the same.

The rug that she'd left was still on the floor, and it didn't look like anyone had changed anything. She put her bright quilt on the bed and arranged her books on the chest of drawers remembering how heavy her heart had been when she had packed them up to go home last October.

When she had finished unpacking, she went down to the kitchen and put the kettle on. Wandering outside she began to get reacquainted with the horses. Not all the boxes were occupied – and she couldn't see Chance – but spotting Merlin, she immediately went to him, relieved to see a familiar face. She knew better than to try to give him a kiss – he might take her face off, so she settled for giving him a rub on his forehead. He put his ears back but didn't try to bite her. In the next box was Angel. He was so beautiful, he had a kind of ethereal quality about him, like a creature out of a fairy-tale.

The girls were just finishing off and sweeping up.

'I guess you know most of the horses?' Rachel said, coming over.

'Some of them. There's a few I don't recognise.' She stopped by a dark bay horse in the next box. It was also very beautiful. And huge; well over seventeen hands.

'This is Beau, he belongs to Caroline,' Rachel told her.

Emma raised her eyebrows. There was a smaller, lighter bay gelding in the box which used to be Chance's. 'And that one?'

'That's Charlie, he belongs to Caroline too.'

Emma rubbed Beau's nose, almost afraid to ask. 'Where's Chance?'

'Chance? Oh, you mean that chestnut gelding with the four

white socks? He was sold over the winter. To be honest I was glad to see the back of him, he was constantly escaping!'

Chance gone as well. Emma concentrated on the softness of Beau's nose to ward off the tears that were pricking her eyes and making her nose tingle. It was as though Caroline had taken over the whole yard.

'Does Caroline spend much time on the yard now?' Emma asked.

'Whenever Dan's here, she'll be here. To be honest, neither of them are here that much. They've been away a lot of the time.' The way she said this gave the impression that this was the way she liked it.

'When are they getting back?' Emma asked.

'We're not sure, we haven't been told,' Rachel said, with a slight edge to her voice.

That night, Emma shivered under her quilt. She'd never been here in freezing weather before. Her room was perishing. There was an old storage heater but it didn't seem to kick out much warmth. Even though she was wearing her rabbit onesie with the hood up and two pairs of socks, she was still freezing. It occurred to her there might still be a duvet on the bed next door.

Getting up, she padded into the corridor. The door of Dan's room was shut. She paused with her hand on the handle, stupidly feeling like she ought to knock, although she knew no-one was in there. Turning on the light she glanced around. Everything was very tidy; no clothes strewn on the floor, or towels slung over the back of the chair, it had an un-lived in feel, but still something lingered – a faint scent…

She tip-toed over to the neatly made bed. Cathy had said Dan rarely slept in here anymore, but she recognised the quilt. It was his. She could borrow it and put it back, no-one would even have to know that she'd taken it. But as she stood there, the feeling of wrongdoing became so strong that she couldn't bring herself to touch it. Quickly, she turned and left, shutting the door behind her.

When she woke up in the morning, it took her a minute to realise where she was. It was early but the noises let her know that there was already someone out on the yard, feeding round. Jumping out of bed she got dressed as quickly as she could; the cold was vicious.

She wanted to make a good impression so, forgoing breakfast, she pulled on her coat and boots and went outside. Grabbing a wheelbarrow and some tools she asked Rachel where she wanted her to start.

By the time Kitty and Simone arrived both Emma and Rachel were on their second stable; Rachel was extremely efficient, the morning's work was done in no time at all.

The sun came out, and after a tea break, they all went for a hack together. It was a lovely crisp, bright day and it was fantastic to be riding again.

Malcolm was waiting for them when they got back. He greeted Emma with his customary good-natured, kindly manner, his twinkly blue eyes reminding Emma of her Granddad again.

'Wonderful to see you!' he said.

Emma beamed back at him. 'It's wonderful to be here!' she told him truthfully.

'Back in the saddle, eh?' he said, 'knew you couldn't stay away for too long.'

'Ha! You may be right,' she said laughing, 'I'm a hopeless addict.'

They exchanged a few more pleasantries, and then he turned to Rachel, asking her if she'd done the feed order. She went into the feed room and came back with a list, then asked him about booking the farrier for the following week.

It was strange; they were all things that he would have talked to Dan about. It was as though he no longer existed. But there were ghosts of him everywhere, from his writing scrawled on the board in the feed room, to his boots sitting by the door in the tack room. Being there without him was like listening to a favourite song and finding that all the lyrics had changed.

Rachel ran the yard confidently and efficiently. She did things a little differently to the way Dan used to, and seemed to be fond of a shortcut. She was a fairly good rider, but admitted that she hated riding Merlin; he had put her on the floor a couple of times, so she usually opted to lunge him instead – if she worked him at all.

At least the weather was fine, and when she was working, Emma didn't feel the cold, just at night when she was trying to sleep. And it was good to be working again; doing something physical, using her hands. The workload was not too heavy, and she had to admit they worked well as a team. It was a far cry from the early days when she had first started nearly a year ago.

Kitty was a lot more competent than she used to be, she had a year's experience under her belt now and made fewer mistakes. Simone was still lazy and kept sneaking off for sly fags when she thought no one would notice, but Emma thought she was a little less arrogant and spiteful.

They all got to ride out a lot, and there was no shouting or slamming of doors. They didn't finish the day exhausted and miserable. But even though it was undoubtedly a more peaceful, harmonious yard now, Emma still had a kind of wistful yearning for the bad old days.

After everyone had gone home in the afternoons, the yard seemed very quiet. There was a Super Ser gas fire down in the staff room, so she stayed up after she'd made her dinner and sat on the sofa in front of it, reading her book, delaying going up to her freezing room as long as possible.

She thought about Joe and wondered if she would see him anytime soon. Right now, she would have given anything to go back to the days when they were all in the pub together; talking, laughing, playing pool, getting mildly tanked up. It seemed like another lifetime. Perhaps you couldn't go back, recapture the past, things would never be the same.

After another bitterly cold day, she made herself some tomato soup for warmth, and a cheese toasty for comfort, and tried to distract herself with her book. Then, dressed in a big baggy jumper that used to belong to Edward, jeans with tights underneath and thick woollen socks, she lay on the sofa with her feet stretched towards the fire, reading. At least it was warm and comfortable down here; she wouldn't go upstairs just yet.

Although it wasn't late, her eyelids began to get heavy. Her book drooped in her hand and the print blurred in front of her eyes. She shook herself. She mustn't fall asleep, she really ought to go to bed. But it was so comfortable and cosy – she would have just five more minutes, then she really would go to bed…

In her dream, she was walking through the streets of London again, looking for something. She thought that it was just around the next corner, but no, she realised she had made a wrong turn. She tried to find her way back to where she'd started, but couldn't read the writing on the signs. It was all blurred and the words didn't make any sense. Her eyes were heavy and wouldn't open properly, she couldn't see very well at all.

Then she heard the voice again. 'Emma, where are you going? Stay with me.' But it was very faint, fading into the distance.

'But where are you?' she called back.

'Don't you know it's dangerous to fall asleep with the fire on?' Much closer this time, right next to her in fact.

Emma's eyes snapped open with a start. The voice was here, was now, was Dan's.

Real, living, breathing, Dan. He was crouched down next to her, his elbows on his knees, grinning at her.

She sat up so fast she nearly fell off the sofa.

'Dan!' she exclaimed. 'You're back!'

'Emma!' he said, laughing at her, 'you're back!'

'I wasn't asleep,' she said frantically rubbing her eyes, and trying to pull herself together.

He stood up, picking up her book where it had fallen to the floor, and put it on the table.

'Good thing too,' he said dryly, 'I fell asleep in front of that fire once and set fire to my socks.'

Emma giggled. 'When did you get back?' she asked.

'About,' he glanced at his watch, 'fifteen minutes ago. I just came down to check on the horses and heard this terrible snoring coming from in here…'

Emma gasped. 'I was not snoring!'

'Okay, if you say so,' he said picking up the kettle. 'Want a coffee?'

'Yes, that would be good,' she said, pleased. It looked like he was going to stay and chat.

It was slightly surreal – as if she might still be dreaming.

She got up and sat at the table as he got two mugs out and put instant coffee in each of them.

He looked good, tanned, and wearing smart jeans and a black

jumper. While his back was turned, she ran her hands through her mussed-up hair and scrubbed at her front teeth with her finger in case any tomato soup had lingered.

'How was skiing?' she asked.

'Good,' he replied. 'Caroline's an expert skier,' *(of course she is)* 'so I had a lot of catching up to do. I'd never done it before, but I was hitting the black runs by the end of the first week.'

Emma could imagine him being very competitive in that, just like in everything else.

'What about you,' he asked, 'didn't fancy London after all?'

'Well not quite.' She explained about Edward getting the job in Berlin. Dan sat down at the table handing her a coffee.

'So, you thought you'd cool your heels here until he clicks his fingers for you?' he said, with his wry smile.

Ignoring the implication, she nodded. 'Pretty much, yeah. Malcolm said I was welcome to stay on as long as I can. It's good to be back. I missed it.'

They went on to talk about the horses. 'I can't wait to get going with Angel, see what he's capable of,' Dan said, 'he's going to be the serious contender this year.'

'So, has Caroline given up the idea of riding him herself, altogether?' Emma asked.

'Yup,' he replied, 'she's going to have a crack at some BE90's on the bay gelding, Charlie, but I think she's realised that Angel's too much horse for her, she's happy for me to ride him.'

Emma raised her eyebrows, taking a gulp of her coffee.

'What about the other one… Beau?' she asked.

'He was a bit of an impulse buy,' Dan explained. 'I saw he was up for sale and mentioned he was a good horse, I've seen him around on the circuit. So Caroline bought him.'

'For you to ride, or for her?' she asked.

'For me.' He grinned – did he look the tiniest bit sheepish?

She knew that he would know what she was thinking, but she kept her mouth shut. It might be too soon to start teasing him just yet.

'I've never started a season with two such good horses,' he said.

As he said it, she saw in his eyes that burning ambition, that hunger and fierce determination. 'If I can't start winning with these two, I might as well give up.'

He touched the wood of the table as he said it.

Sitting at the rickety table across from him, drinking coffee out of the cracked old mugs, the smells and noises of the horses all around them, Emma felt a deep sense of contentment.

Eventually, she glanced at her watch and yawned. He didn't seem in a particular hurry to go anywhere, and she would quite happily have stayed there chatting all night, but it was getting late.

'Well, I suppose I'd better go on up to my ice locker,' she said reluctantly, getting to her feet.

'Are you cold upstairs?' he asked, frowning.

'Let's just say, when I woke up this morning, my eyelids were frozen shut,' she replied.

'Why didn't you take the heater out of my room?'

She hadn't spotted a heater. 'I wouldn't just go into your room and take it.' She took the mugs to the sink.

'Why not?'

And getting up, he disappeared up the stairs. Emma hesitated to follow him, so she wandered around tidying up a few things. The door to the tack room opened and Caroline appeared.

'Oh, Emma,' she said surprised, 'I didn't know you were here, have you seen Dan?'

'Er – yes. He's just nipped upstairs,' Emma said.

She'd forgotten how strikingly beautiful Caroline was. She hadn't got a tan from skiing like Dan, but was glowing and ravishing in a green cashmere sweater and designer jeans.

'What's he doing upstairs?' Caroline asked.

'Just sorting the heating out I think,' said Emma awkwardly. 'How are you? How was skiing?'

'Oh yes, very good thank you,' Caroline said, recovering her manners. 'How are you? Back for long this time?'

'I'm not sure yet, I've got no definite plans,' Emma replied as Dan came back down.

'There, that should sort it. I've changed the settings on the storage heater so that it will give you some warmth in the evenings and you've got my heater on a timer as well.'

'Thank you,' said Emma, gratefully.

'You've been ages!' Caroline said with a little laugh.
Emma glanced at Dan, but he looked insouciant.
'Well, I'm going to bed now,' said Emma, 'see you tomorrow.'
And saying goodnight, she went on up the stairs.

Chapter 24

When she woke up in the morning, she lay still for a moment, savouring the sensation of being warm and cosy. The warmth she felt wasn't just on the outside; it went all the way through to the very core of her being.

The noise of a horse whinnying, and another banging its door, alerted her to the arrival of somebody down on the yard. It was incredible how horses always seemed to know what the time was, and would kick their doors impatiently if they weren't fed on time. Sitting up and looking out of the window, she saw Rachel going into the feed room.

'I gather Posh and Becks are back,' Rachel said, when Emma joined her. 'Caroline's Porsche is back on the drive.' She didn't sound exactly overjoyed.

'Yes, I saw them last night,' Emma told her.

'Oh well, hopefully they won't feel the need to make an appearance today.'

Emma didn't reply. She thought she maybe ought to say something to let Rachel know where her loyalties lay, but Rachel went on.

'I expect they won't be able to resist coming down to interfere and make a nuisance of themselves, let's hope it's later rather than sooner,' she said.

In fact, Dan arrived shortly afterwards. He was on his own though, and went into the tack room, appearing a minute later with an armful of tack and headed straight for Merlin's box. Emma was in one of the other box's mucking out. She watched as he brought Merlin out and took him into the school.

Merlin wasn't the easiest horse to ride at the best of times, but as Dan warmed him up, it was clear he was being a sod. He wouldn't walk on a long rein but kept shooting sideways, spooking at imaginary things on the fence line, and then finding excuses to buck and mess about. When Dan kept his leg on and asked him to stay straight Merlin stood up in a half rear. As soon as he touched down Dan sent him forward, but the black horse took off around the arena, head high in the air, eyes rolling and ears back. Emma gasped as a couple of times he slipped going around the corners and she felt sure he must fall, but he was an athletic horse and managed to keep his footing.

After his first wild burst of speed had been spent, he started to slow up, but Dan sat deeper in the saddle and rode him forward, keeping his lower leg firmly around him. His long sensitive fingers started playing on the reins, asking Merlin to soften his jaw and accept the bit in his mouth. Little by little, Merlin lowered his head and began to round his back, finally starting to listen to his rider and yield to his aids.

Emma realised she had been staring for the last fifteen minutes and hadn't done a stitch of work. She gave herself a shake and speedily went back to her mucking out.

After another half an hour's schooling, Dan let Merlin have a long rein and walked him round to cool him off. As he brought him out of the school, his expression was black. Putting Merlin back in his stable, he called to Rachel as she passed.

'Can I have a word please Rachel?' he asked, his tone ominous. Emma held her breath and stopped to listen.

'Did Merlin get ridden yesterday?' he asked.

She went pink. 'No, not yesterday,'

'The day before?'

'No… but the day before that I lunged him.'

'He needs to be worked every day, I thought I'd made that clear.' Dan's voice was harsh.

'He's such a sod to ride,' Rachel complained, 'even in draw reins I struggle…' she didn't get to finish her sentence.

'Draw reins!' Dan exploded, 'You've been riding him in draw reins?'

Rachel quailed, her face bright red now.

Emma knew that in Dan's book, draw reins were a big no-no. He believed that if you had to force a horse's head down into a fixed position with gadgets and gimmicks, you had no business riding it. If she'd seen Rachel using them, she would have warned her.

Dan didn't wait for an answer; he stalked off in the direction of the tack room. When he came out, he had the offending draw reins in his hand.

'I won't have fucking draw reins on my yard!' he shouted, and taking them over to the dustbin by the feed room, he opened the lid and dropped them in.

'Hey! Those are mine,' Rachel protested.

'Then take them home with you, I don't ever want to see them on my yard again.'

And, goodbye to peace and harmony, Emma thought.

Rachel fished the reins out of the bin with trembling hands, then walked stiffly to the tack room. Emma followed her in and shut the door.

'Are you okay?' she asked.

'I'm fine, he's just such a bastard.' Rachel's voice was shaky.

'Believe me, there was a time when I thought the same thing,' said Emma sympathetically, 'but he just likes things done a certain way, he's really not so bad when you get used to him.'

Rachel stared at her as though she'd lost the plot.

'He does know what he's talking about, you'll just have to trust me on this one. I've learnt a lot from him...'

Just then Dan came in with Merlin's tack. Rachel walked out without acknowledging him. Tight lipped, Emma took Merlin's saddle from him and he looked at her with narrowed eyes.

'Well?' he asked.

'Well, what?'

'I can see you're dying to say something so – spit it out.'

Emma sighed. 'It's just...Rachel's done a pretty good job of looking after the place while you've been away.'

He gave a derisive snort, but Emma went on undeterred.

'She has. And you could maybe cut her a bit of slack.'

'I'm not compromising when it comes to the horses.'

'You don't have to,' Emma said. 'Just try not to be so abrasive – try explaining why you don't use draw reins rather than biting her head off, then she might understand.'

'Okay, I'll try not to be so 'abrasive', whatever the fuck that means!' he said, and went out, slamming the door.

Just like old times, Emma thought ruefully.

Caroline came down shortly after that and she and Dan rode out together on Angel and Charlie. Then after lunch they rode out again on Beau and Henry.

They hardly spoke to anyone else all day.

Emma got up early the next morning in the hope of getting some breakfast before she started work. Although it was only just light, it was going to be an absolutely gorgeous morning; blue skies and sunshine, cold and crisp.

Thinking she was alone, she jumped when Dan walked in to grab the keys to the feed room.

'Tea?' She asked quickly before he could leave again.

'Okay,' he said unsmiling, and went off to feed round.

She made two teas and took his out to him.

'If it makes any difference, I did back you up yesterday,' she said.

He took his tea without saying anything, but looked at her warily.

'I told Rachel you knew what you were talking about, and that you just liked things done a certain way, which – in my opinion – is the better way. I think you're right about the draw reins.'

His frosty look began to thaw.

'And it's obvious that Merlin has gone downhill from not being ridden properly, so I don't blame you for being a bit cross,' she said. 'But now you're back you can sort everything out, and… and my room is a lot warmer, so, thank you,' she said, watching the last bit of resentment leave his face.

'Right, come on then,' he said, draining his tea. 'Let's get mucked out and then you can ride Beau out with me and Merlin.'

He helped her rush through her share of the mucking out and in less than an hour, they were riding down the road towards the village.

Beau felt enormous. Emma had been a little disconcerted at

first by his size – she didn't think she had ever ridden anything quite as big – but she soon realised that he was a gentle giant, and perfectly schooled.

'Nice, isn't he?' Dan said.

Emma nodded her enthusiasm. 'Where did you get him from?'

'Bill Hannon.'

She had heard of Bill Hannon, he was a fairly high-profile rider. 'Why was he being sold?'

'Money, I think,' Dan shrugged. 'Bill's getting married, moving to a bigger house, bigger yard, needs the cash.'

Emma leaned down and stroked Beau's silky neck, it shone dark bay like a conker. His perfectly pulled black mane was as shiny as a model's in a shampoo commercial, his neck supple and well-muscled. She knew he couldn't have been cheap. It made her feel slightly uneasy, the thought of how much he must have cost.

Merlin had settled after yesterday's wild behaviour, he still had his habitual belligerent expression, but he seemed to be – if not happier – at least resigned to the fact that the boss was back.

They passed the "Chalk and Cheese".

'How's Joe?' she asked casually, 'have you seen him recently?'

Dan gave her a sly look. 'You'll probably see him yourself tomorrow, vaccinations are due. But he's fine. More than fine actually, he's seeing someone.'

How fast things changed.

'Really?' said Emma. 'Who?'

'A girl who runs a stud farm a couple miles away,' he replied. 'She's nice, I've met her a few times.'

'That's good, I'm glad for him,' Emma said firmly.

Dan gave her a quizzical look. 'Yeah, I'm afraid you might have missed that boat Bugs, if that's why you came back,' he said. 'You should have grabbed him while you had the chance.'

Emma rolled her eyes at him. 'That is absolutely not why I came back,' she said.

'Really?' he wasn't to be deflected. 'Your boyfriend has left you high and dry and you thought, why not come back and see whether a vet might suit you just as well as a doctor?'

'Argh!' Emma protested in exasperation, 'I'd forgotten how

annoying you are!'

'So why did you come back?' he challenged her.

'I told you,' she said, 'I missed it here. I missed the horses, the place, the people…' She knew what was coming almost before she finished speaking.

'D'you miss me?' he asked, his smile wicked.

'I didn't miss you winding me up, that's for sure,' she said, 'shall we trot?'

And without waiting for an answer, she pushed Beau into a trot up the hill.

He caught up with her in seconds, laughing. 'But it's so easy! You always bite. And I enjoy watching you go red.'

She shook her head in disgust. Maybe it was time to get her own back.

'So,' she began, 'I feel sorry for all the single girls round these parts now, with the two most eligible bachelors off the market.'

He didn't say anything, so she carried on. 'Who would ever have thought it, Daniel Ryan in a 'serious' relationship.' She stole a glance at him, but his expression remained impassive.

'I have to say I'm impressed; I didn't think you could behave yourself for this long. Must be a challenge for you. What is it; four months?'

No reply.

'Still, I guess a car is a pretty good incentive…'

His face broke into a grin. 'Okay, you got me Bugs, you can stop trying so hard now,' he laughed. 'I knew you couldn't resist mentioning that sooner or later.'

At the top of the road, they turned through a gate into an open field. Dan kept Merlin in trot, but Emma wasn't ready to drop the subject yet.

'She must like you an awful lot,' she said.

He shrugged.

'I mean, to give a gift like that she must be pretty serious, she must feel like it's the real deal…don't you think?'

'I try not to,' he said. 'Let's canter.'

And with that he pushed Merlin into a gallop, leaving Emma behind.

She let Beau follow on. He was well mannered and not strong, his long stride covering the ground easily. She let him gallop on until he drew up alongside Merlin, then slowed him until his stride matched the black horse's. Emma's mouth stretched into a broad grin.

This is what she loved. It felt so good to be out again, the sun on her back and the wind in her face from their speed, the sound of hooves pounding on turf. She balanced in her stirrups, feeling in perfect synchrony with her horse. Beau had a beautifully soft mouth, the slightest feel on the reins was enough to have him flex from his poll and round his neck so she was careful to keep her hands light, her elbows elastic.

They slowed to a trot after a short while, and then a walk as the horses weren't fully fit yet.

'There's a hunt fence up here,' Dan said, 'do you want to pop it?'

'Okay,' said Emma, praying she wouldn't mess it up on this amazing horse.

'Tuck in behind me, but don't get too close in case Merlin kicks out,' Dan instructed. 'It's pretty upright, so keep him short and bouncy.'

She nodded, dropping back behind him. He moved Merlin up into canter from the walk, making him get his hocks underneath him, Emma copied.

The fence was fairly big for a hunt fence, nearly the height of the post and rails. She sat up and used her seat to keep Beau on a short, bouncy stride. Merlin popped neatly over it, making it look like nothing at all, and she focused her attention on the fence.

Beau was so responsive she barely needed any leg. He met it perfectly and was over almost before she felt it. He must make an Intermediate course feel like pony club stuff.

'Well done for not interfering with him, you ride him well,' Dan said.

'He's in a different class!' Emma said, her heart swelling with his praise.

She felt unbelievably privileged to be able to ride such an amazing animal. He was gorgeous. *Don't fall in love,* she told herself firmly. He belonged to Caroline. She mustn't get attached, like she had to Arcturus.

They rode on in companionable silence for a while, on their way back home now, Emma happy just to be there. Until she became aware that Dan kept glancing over at her with a questioning look in his eye.

'What?' she said eventually.

'Just...are you really fine with Edward buggering off to Germany? Waiting around for him to call when he decides he wants you?'

She shrugged. 'It's important for his career,' she replied. 'It's not about me,'

'But aren't you worried he might find a bit of German skirt to keep him warm?'

Emma tutted. 'No. Edward's not like that.'

'He's a man isn't he?

'Yes, but he's not like you – I can trust him.'

'Ouch! You know what to say to hurt a man don't you?'

'I didn't mean...Oh! You know what I meant.' She didn't believe he was actually hurt for a second.

'What about him though. Isn't he worried you might replace him whilst he's gone?'

'No. He's not in the slightest bit insecure. It's about trust – and commitment,' she looked at him sidelong. 'But that's something you wouldn't know anything about.'

He chuckled. 'Okay. So you are both completely committed to each other. I get that. But how do you know? How do you know what you want now is what you will want in a year, or even in six months. How do you know he's "the one"?'

She squinted at him, trying to gauge whether he was taking the piss or not.

'Because I do. Edward's kind, and honest, and a good person...'

Dan burst out laughing. 'I didn't ask for a character reference Bugs!'

'Okay then,' she said, annoyed. 'Because he is something solid and real to rely on, because I know he will always be there if I need him, and I don't have to worry about anything when he's around. And because he's the only thing in my life which makes any sense.'

There was a pause. Then Dan said; 'Hmmm.'

'What do you mean, "hmmm"?'

'Nothing. What do I know about it anyway?'

'Exactly. Just what I was going to say – at least we agree on something.'

Neither of them spoke as they walked on, the two horses on a long rein.

'Anyway,' she said after a while, 'in my opinion, the most important thing in a relationship is respect,' she said giving him a hard stare. 'And in-teg-ri-ty,' she stressed each syllable. 'But I guess different things are important to different people.'

He grinned. 'You're very sensible aren't you?' he said. 'Most girls want hearts and flowers – to be swept off their feet with big romantic gestures.'

'None of that's real,' she said. 'None of that lasts, it's what you've got left after all that's gone that matters.'

'Like a big bank balance?' he asked, teasing her.

'Hardy har ha,' she said. 'You're sooo funny.'

'So truthfully, that doesn't matter to you at all? You'd be just as committed to Edward if he was broke?'

'Yes, absolutely, I don't care about that. Money isn't important, you can't buy happiness.'

He grinned. 'No, but you can buy horses,'

She couldn't argue with that, so she said nothing.

As they rode into the yard and dismounted, the others had finished their mucking out and were sweeping up.

The two horses had mud splattered under their bellies from their canter across the hill. It was too cold for the hosepipe, so Dan asked Kitty if she would get some warm water from the kitchen, and a sponge. She scampered off to get them.

Emma noticed that he didn't seem to shout at Kitty anymore, which was good, and he even thanked her when she came back with the steaming bucket of water.

'Here Bugs, catch,' he said, throwing Emma the sponge that was absolutely full of water, completely soaking her as she caught it.

She shrieked, but at least it was warm. She washed Beau off carefully and dried him with a towel so he didn't get sore.

When Emma went to put her tack away, she had nearly reached the door of the tack room when she heard her name being used by someone inside. It was Simone. Emma hesitated by the door.

'I like the way Emma gets out of mucking out to go for a hack,' she was saying bitterly.

'Doesn't matter – she'd done her share,' came the reply; that was Rachel.

'Only because *he* helped her,' Simone complained.

Emma's blood rose. She walked into the tack room and Simone left abruptly, brushing past her, but Rachel greeted her with a smile.

'Good hack?' she asked.

'Lovely thanks.' Emma returned her smile.

Rachel lowered her voice. 'I'm sorry, I didn't realise you and Dan were such good mates, or I wouldn't have said the things I did to you yesterday.'

'Don't worry about it,' Emma reassured her, 'much worse things have been said on this yard, believe me.'

At tea break, they were all around the table except Dan, who was writing something on the board, when Caroline appeared. She was wearing cream breeches and long black leather boots. She put a finger to her lips as she tiptoed up behind Dan and put her arms around him, kissing the nape of his neck.

'Why didn't you wake me?' she said, 'I would have ridden out with you.'

Emma looked away hastily. For some reason such a public display of affection seemed completely inappropriate here. She glanced at Simone who had turned her back on them with a look of disgust.

Simone was never openly hostile towards Caroline from what Emma had seen, in fact quite the opposite; she had become almost ingratiatingly friendly towards her. As a consequence, Caroline seemed to like her the best out of all of them. If she wanted help with anything it was always Simone she asked, and Simone seemed only too happy to oblige.

Chapter 25

AFTER LUNCH, THEY BROUGHT ALL THE THREE AND FOUR-YEAR-olds in from the field, ready for their vaccinations the next day. Over the next few weeks Dan would begin the process of backing the youngsters and bringing the older ones back into work to be sold.

Everybody got to work putting fresh beds down in the empty loose-boxes, and filling extra hay-nets.

She was glad, but slightly apprehensive that she was going to see Joe. Would he have changed? Did he even know she was back? She really hoped things wouldn't be awkward between them and they could still be friends.

They all went down to the field with head-collars and a bucket of pony nuts.

It took a while to catch them all, because although they were fed every day, none of them had been handled much through the winter so they were a little wild. It took two trips to get them all in.

At two o'clock the following day, Emma was sorting through the stack of passports in the tack room, realising it must be almost exactly a year since she'd first met Joe. It was impossible not to think of the last time she saw him and wonder whether he might remember that too.

She heard a vehicle approaching and the crunch of gravel as it swung onto the drive. Eagerly, she looked out the window, but it wasn't Joe's green Land Rover defender, it was a blue Discovery. And it was Mike, the older vet from the practice who got out.

Emma almost laughed out loud at herself. All that nervous

speculation and it wasn't even Joe. Shaking her head at her own foolishness, she went out to meet Mike.

FOR THE NEXT week or so, they would be getting the youngsters used to being handled again, teaching them stable manners, grooming them and starting to build a relationship of trust before the backing process could begin for the three-year-olds.

It occurred to Emma that Dan had probably brought every one of them into the world, and now he would be the first one to ride them. She thought how much she would love to be the first person to have that special partnership with a young horse. And how much more that would mean if she had also seen that horse being born.

There was one of the three-year-olds that Emma took a shine to immediately. She was a chestnut filly; quite small, only about fifteen-two hands, finely built and had the sweetest nature. Dan said she was Chance's full sister, and there was a look about her which reminded Emma of Chance. She was very gentle and a little timid. Emma set about making friends with her, filling her pockets with grass nuts and spending time in her stable grooming her and getting her to pick up her feet when she asked, then Emma would reward her with a grass nut. She called her Penny.

The filly soon learned that Emma often had treats and would whinny whenever she saw her.

'Do you want to have a go at backing her?' Dan asked her one day as he saw her coming out of the filly's box.

'Really? Me, on my own?' Emma said nervously.

'I'd help you.'

'Do you think I could?' She was excited at the thought.

'Well, she's already beginning to trust you, that's where it all starts. And it makes sense, she's quite small for me really, she needs someone light like you.'

So, over the next week or so, Emma took her time; leaning across Penny in the stable while she was grooming her, scratching her itchy spots and letting her become accustomed to her weight, until she could sit on her without the mare reacting.

'Remember, training horses is all about association, that's how they learn,' Dan told her. 'If they associate a certain sound or action with something, they will always expect that. That's why it's so important that they enjoy the experience of being backed. Then they will turn into horses who enjoy their work and love being around humans – it will set them up for life.'

Emma was incredibly gratified that he thought she was up to the job. She started to teach Penny to lunge and long-rein, gradually introducing the tack, giving her voice commands and rewarding her when she responded correctly, teaching her what the aids from the bit meant, and how she should yield to pressure; first from the long reins, and then from the leg.

'Trust is a two-way thing,' Dan told her, 'if you want her to trust you, you have to show her that you trust her. If you take the time to get this bit right, the rest of it will be easy and there shouldn't ever be a reason for her to feel fear or worry.'

She knew she was learning from the best. He stayed close by, offering his advice and practical help if Emma asked for it, but didn't interfere too much.

'It's important to allow them to react in the way that comes naturally to them,' he told her, 'not try to control them with fear and punishment, or you will never know whether they have truly accepted it. You have to feel when she's ready for the next stage.'

Emma had never seen him punish a horse in all the time she had watched him back the youngsters, he seemed to have endless patience when it came to them – if nothing else.

Seeing Penny gain confidence and begin to enjoy her work was so satisfying and rewarding, and Dan let her help with some of the others, which she took to mean she was doing a good job.

One day she was riding Penny in the school and everything just clicked. The little horse was going so well, she only had to think something and the mare would respond; the lightest touch of her leg, the merest shift of her weight, and Penny would answer, tuned into the same frequency. She was so absorbed that she didn't realise Dan was watching until she'd finished, giving Penny a long rein and a pat.

'You've got her going really well,' he said.

Flushing with pride, Emma tried to make light of it. 'Well, she's an easy horse…'

'No easier than any other,' Dan contradicted her. 'Just accept it, you're good at this.'

'I have a good teacher.'

'Emma – some things you can't teach, you're a natural.'

Coming from him, this was the best compliment she'd ever had.

But the evenings were long and boring for Emma; she had only been to the pub with Rachel and Kitty once. She had hoped she might see Joe, but despite the pub being really busy, he hadn't been there. Maybe now he had a new girlfriend they went somewhere else. She couldn't help but feel envious when she saw Dan and Caroline going out.

One night, Emma saw them leaving – there was a new swanky wine bar opening in town, and it was the first night party, a black-tie affair. Caroline was wearing a floor length, off the shoulder black silk dress, which showed off her creamy skin and willowy figure. Dan was in a suit and black tie. They looked like a couple of A-list celebrities going to a premiere. They roared away in Caroline's Porsche, Dan driving.

On the evenings Edward rang, she tried to keep him on the phone as long as she could, but he was often tired after a long day.

'I'm sorry, I haven't had any time to flat hunt yet,' he apologised.

'It's fine – I'm fine. You need to concentrate on your work at the moment. Don't worry about me.'

They took Merlin, Charlie, Angel and Beau, to a few training competitions as well as jumping them at home. Both Angel and Beau were exciting to watch; Angel had masses of scope and was very careful, but Beau was bolder and made nothing of the bigger fences.

Caroline had found a trainer to come once a week for herself and Dan for flatwork, and another one for jumping. Dan was finally getting the training he needed.

The first event was of the season was Aldon International. Many of the top names were there, and because the one-day event ran alongside the three-day international event, it was much more glamorous than some of the smaller competitions.

In the dressage warm up, it was clear that Angel was in a class of his own. He attracted lots of admiring and envious glances from other riders. His paces were fluid and elastic, and the union of his poise and elegance with Dan's natural grace as a rider was awe-inspiring.

It was easy to tell that Caroline was enjoying being associated with this dreamy partnership and could be heard on the side-lines talking loudly about "Her horse" and "Her boyfriend". She had the most amazing talent for striking up conversations with people she didn't know. Perhaps because she was so beautiful, people were only too willing to talk to her, and she was so obviously classy and sophisticated, she seemed to attract a certain type of people; people like her, with money and status.

The regular training that Dan was having was definitely starting to pay off. He kept his cool and rode a spectacular test. Emma was thrilled.

Beau's test was nearly as good. The big horse wasn't quite as elegant as Angel, but extremely well-schooled, allowing Dan to be really accurate.

In the show jumping, neither horse put a foot wrong, both going clear. Then the moment of truth arrived. Would Angel be as good cross-country as he promised to be in his schooling sessions? The look on Dan's face was intense and focused, Emma knew adrenalin would be pumping hard through his veins as he circled Angel at the start.

Emma silently wished him luck as Angel left the start box, quickly finding his rhythm and, ears pricked, cantered towards the first fence. Meeting it on the perfect stride, he lifted over it in a fluid arc, and then picking up the pace, galloped on to the next fence. It was a faultless round, Angel made it look easy. The course was well within the scope of both horses. Beau came back triumphant as well, two perfect rounds.

Leaving Emma to take care of the horses, Dan and Caroline went to check the scoreboards, Caroline taking Dan by the hand. Emma noticed that whenever they walked anywhere together they turned heads, there was no doubt they made a beautiful couple.

'So, where did you come?' Emma asked when they came back. Dan had brought her a hot chocolate and a bacon roll.

'Second on Beau,' he said.

Emma squealed with delight. 'And Angel?'

A huge grin rose, like the sun, on his face. 'First.'

'Holy shit!' Emma yelled, nearly spilling her hot chocolate.

Caroline was obviously feeling the love for 'her boys' as she called them in their victory. When Dan went to collect his prizes she went with him, holding tightly to his hand, smiling round at everyone and hardly stopped talking the whole way home in the lorry, her hand on Dan's thigh while he drove. It was getting dark outside long before they reached home. It had been a long day; Emma was exhausted.

'I want to celebrate!' Caroline was saying. 'How about we go to that new restaurant down at the bay? Emma, will you take care of the horses when we get back, so I can take Dan out?'

'Yeah, sure,' Emma replied, turning away to stare out of the window into the gloom. It was too dark to see anything except her own reflection, but she kept her face turned away all the same.

Chapter 26

Over the next few weeks, they were at a competition almost every weekend. With the backing of Caroline's money, they could afford to compete as much as they wanted to. Some were a long way away and they had to stay overnight, and sometimes they stayed the whole weekend, with horses competing on different days. Emma would accompany them to groom, and would sleep in the lorry, while Caroline and Dan stayed in nearby hotels.

The regular training was making a huge difference. Both Angel and Beau were quickly moving up through the grades as they got placed at nearly every competition.

Malcolm's lorry, although not top of the range, was cosy. It had a toilet and a shower, a small kitchen and a comfortable bed over the top of the cabin. Emma enjoyed camping overnight, and she made friends with some of the other grooms. There were two that she became particularly friendly with: Sarah, who was younger than Emma, very petite, blonde and bubbly, and Toby, who was hilarious, and who fancied Dan like mad.

'Are you sure he's not even a little bit gay?' he would keep asking Emma.

'Not even a little bit I don't think,' Emma would reply.

'What a waste,' Toby would say, sighing.

In the evenings she sometimes went around to one or other of their lorries for a drink and a chat. They were like a little nomadic community.

Dan was starting to get a name for himself, as people noticed his increasing success. It was impressive to witness how focused he was – how single-minded.

There was a new confidence in his step, a squarer set to his shoulders. And it was obvious he was determined to make it work. Caroline was in her element, whisking Dan away to celebrate in the owners' tent, toasting his prowess with endless glasses of champagne.

But not everyone was happy. Merlin's owner, Bret Andrews, gave Malcolm an ultimatum; either he started to see some results on his horse, or he was going to sell him – send him to auction.

'He's heard that you've been out and about, winning everything on Angel and Beau,' Malcolm told Dan one evening when they returned late from another successful day. Rachel and the others had gone home and it was just Emma, Dan and Caroline left in the staffroom.

Caroline hung around, clearly curious as to what Malcolm had to say.

'He wants to know why he's not seeing the same results on his horse. I told him Merlin's a completely different animal, he needs time and work to get to the same level, but he wasn't having it.'

Dan frowned and rubbed his hand through his hair – but before he could answer, Caroline spoke.

'To be honest, I can't blame him. I wouldn't want to go on throwing my money at a horse that's never going to be any good. And he's dangerous,' she said to Dan, 'you should let him take him, then you can concentrate on Beau and Angel.'

Malcolm and Dan exchanged glances.

'His next competition is in a couple weeks time. I'll have to pull my finger out and make sure we get some results,' Dan said. Caroline pursed her lips.

'Good lad,' Malcolm seemed satisfied with that. 'I know he's not an easy horse, just do your best – or we're going to lose him.'

When they had all gone, Emma went out to see Merlin. It was dark in his stable. She could barely make out his outline, he was so black. She switched his light on.

Had he been neglected because Angel and Beau were such super-stars? Maybe a little. He went on eating his hay, but his ears flicked back and his eye was on her as she approached his shoulder. She reached up to his neck, just in front of his withers where he often had an itchy spot and started scratching. Merlin stopped eating and his ears relaxed. As she worked her fingers deep into his mane, he started making little grunting noises, his top lip twitched and his eyes glazed over. Sheer heaven. Emma chuckled.

'You're not the fearsome beast you make out to be are you? You're just a big softie underneath it all.'

She stopped scratching and Merlin turned his head towards her. For a few moments, he rested it against her shoulder. Emma's heart melted. She reached up and rubbed his forehead, and he sighed gustily and went back to eating his hay.

As she let herself out of his stable she heard an engine start on the drive and the noise of wheels spinning on the gravel. Someone was leaving in a hurry. Curious, she nipped out to the front to have a look. Dan's car was gone.

She was going up to bed an hour later when Caroline appeared at the door.

'Have you seen Dan?' she asked. Her eyes were red and her face pale.

'No, he hasn't been down here,' Emma replied.

'If you see him…t-tell him I'm looking for him will you?'

'I shouldn't worry, he'll be back.' Emma reassured her.

He did come back, but not until six-thirty the next morning. He came into the kitchen and collapsed at the table, plonking his head down on his arms, hiding his face.

'Good night?' Emma asked, getting up to make him a coffee. By the looks of him, he had been out all night. Emma set his drink down and waited.

Eventually he lifted his face and looked at her with bleary eyes.

'I had a row with Caroline and went into town,' he said.

Emma nodded. 'She came down here looking for you.'

He winced, closing his eyes; whether from his hangover, or from something else. 'It all started over Merlin. Caroline wants me to give him up.'

Emma waited for him to go on.

'I know he can be a git, but there's something there…I don't know what it is. I just know, he could be incredible. That fire, that energy. If I can get hold of it – not tame it, but channel it – he would be unstoppable.' He paused. 'I know if he gets sold, he will just get passed from hand to hand until he ends up as dog food. I can't let that happen. Caroline says he's dangerous…that it's not my problem…that it's a stupid risk.' He lowered his head back down onto his arms again.

Emma swallowed a mouthful of her coffee, choosing her words carefully.

'Maybe Caroline does have a point,' she said. 'Maybe Merlin will never change, maybe his start in life was so bad that you can never repair the damage, and it isn't worth the risk.' She paused and Dan sighed. 'But it's all about taking risks this business isn't it?' she said. He raised his head to look at her. 'And I feel it too, there's something special about him. He could be so much more than he is. If you want me to, I'll ride him whenever I can as well – give him some extra schooling in between competitions – if you think it would help?'

He looked directly into her eyes. 'I'd appreciate that,' he said. Then suddenly he lifted his open hands and smacked them down on the table, spilling his coffee. 'Aargh! I don't know if I can do this Emma.'

'Do what?' she asked, alarmed.

'It's not just about Merlin. Caroline wants to have a say in everything – wants to be with me all the time, it's exhausting. She wants to know where I am, what I'm doing, *all the time*. I just don't know whether I'm cut out for this whole committed relationship thing.'

Emma knew, that with someone like Dan, the tighter you tried to hold him, the harder he would struggle.

'When she learns that she can trust you…'

'She's right not to trust me,' he cut in, 'I don't even trust myself.'

In the silence that followed, a strange tingling ran up and down Emma's spine, making her feel a bit sick.

A car pulled up on the yard outside; Rachel, arriving for work.

Dan took a deep breath and got to his feet. 'Better go and face the music.'

No one saw either Dan or Caroline for the rest of that day, but Rachel was full of gossip.

'Guess what,' she said to Emma in hushed tones while they were finishing mucking out that morning, 'One of Simone's mates saw Dan out drinking last night, without Caroline – but he wasn't alone, if you know what I mean.'

That odd tingling sensation came back.

'This could be the end of Posh and Becks!' Rachel giggled.

The next day however, they were back on the yard together, Caroline as chirpy as ever. And in the afternoon, a saddle fitter came to fit Beau and Angel each with a custom-made Butet jumping saddle, which Emma knew cost an eye-watering amount of money.

Everything seemed back to normal, and Emma didn't dare question herself too closely, because there was absolutely no legitimate reason why she should feel disappointed. And yet she did.

Rachel had no such reservations though. 'God I wish they'd split up,' she said. 'I can't stand their smug togetherness anymore – Caroline's always so bloody pleased with herself.'

For some reason, Rachel's bluntness made it all better. Maybe it was okay to feel the way she did.

And then the following morning Dan was first down on the yard again early, before the others got there.

'Oh, you're up,' he said coming in to grab the keys to the feed room. He started to go out the door, but then stood, fumbling with the keys in his hand.

'Everything's all good with Caroline then?' she asked, when he didn't say anything. He let out a breath and came back into the room a little further.

'We've sorted it out. Basically, she's not going to interfere when it comes to the horses, but I've got to promise not to go out drinking again. She's older than me – pushing thirty, she says she doesn't want to waste her time with me if I'm just messing about. If I stay out all night again, it's over.'

In the past, she would have made a joke, teased him about it. But now her heart wasn't in it, so she just said, 'Good.'

'I thought about that lecture you gave me about integrity and commitment.'

Had she given him a lecture? She drew her eyebrows together, puzzled.

'You know – when we rode out, the first time after you came back? You said you were committed to Edward no matter what. That you could trust him?'

'Oh yes.' Now she remembered. It seemed like a long time ago.

'I know you probably think I didn't listen but.... well, I saw the look on your face yesterday.' He twisted the keys in his hands, looking at the floor. 'The thing is, you were right. I don't want to fuck things up, I can't afford to. This might be my only chance. And I want you to know that – whatever people might be saying – I didn't do anything wrong the other night. I mean, I stayed out drinking, but that was it, I didn't...I stayed the night at Joe's, on his sofa...alone.'

She didn't know why, but it was a relief to know that he hadn't cheated on Caroline. He looked up from the floor and seemed to be waiting for her to say something.

She tried to smile. 'You won't fuck it up if you don't want to,' she said, meaning it.

A wry smile lifted his mouth. 'I thought you didn't have any faith in me when it comes to women?' he said.

She swallowed. 'But I do have faith in the fact that you can do anything you put your mind to,' she said firmly.

It almost looked as though he were blushing. 'Have you noticed? It's easier to believe in yourself when someone else does?' he said.

Emma was disgusted with herself. Caroline had done this for him. Given him this self-belief. She not only believed in him, but was prepared to back him all the way – with all her millions. Words were cheap. Anyone could be generous with words. And she, Emma, had been wishing that they would split up. What a horrible person she was. She made up her mind that – no matter what her feelings towards Caroline were – she would be happy for Dan and do her best to support him, as his friend.

Trying to make her voice sound casual, she said, 'I never really doubted you.'

His smile appeared again and this time it was genuine. He chucked the keys up in the air and caught them again as he went out the door.

Chapter 27

So Emma did her best to ease the pressure on him, riding Merlin whenever she had the chance – often after work when everyone had gone home. Knowing what he could be like she was apprehensive at first, but the more she rode him, the more she began to enjoy it. She felt they had come to an understanding. He was beginning to trust her, and she him. There was something there – a connection – similar to the one she had with Penny.

It was the time of year again when the mares were foaling. Chance and Penny's Dam was due, and showing signs that foaling might be imminent. For two nights Dan had been keeping an eye on her and on the third night, Emma couldn't sleep as she lay in bed. She lay awake listening for noises that would tell her if the mare was foaling.

Eventually she got up and crept downstairs. As quietly as she could she tiptoed next door. There was a dim light on in the passage. That must mean Dan was in there. Hopefully that meant the mare was foaling and she could sit with him and watch – her heart gave a little skip. Putting her head around the door, she saw the chestnut mare standing calmly in her box.

On the camp bed, Caroline lay curled up next to Dan with her head on his chest, fast asleep. Her red hair fanned out beneath her white cheek. He was half sitting, half lying back against the wall; his eyes were closed and he had his arm around her. They looked so beautiful and peaceful, Emma couldn't help but stop and stare for a moment.

Then she became aware of an emotion that she wasn't familiar with pushing its way into her consciousness. Not a very nice feeling at all.

Going back upstairs, it was as though something was dragging at her – pulling her down, a weight in her chest, a tightness in her throat. I'm just lonely, she told herself. I'm missing Edward. And no wonder, she spent so much of her time alone. At least with the birth of the foal, she would get to see Joe again.

But she had a sudden wave of apprehension when she saw the dark green land Rover pull into the yard the following morning. Given her current state of mind and the strange way her emotions kept getting the better of her, how was she going to feel?

Telling herself to stop being so stupid she went out to meet him.

'I heard you were back,' he said with his warm, friendly smile as he came towards her. 'It's really good to see you.'

He looked just the same, his gaze direct and honest, and thankfully, her pulse remained normal. She had only the tiniest pang as he kissed her cheek in greeting, and she was able to look him directly in the eye without blushing. Soon they were chatting easily like old mates. Thank God for that. Whatever it was that had been eating her recently – she was over it.

On the Wednesday afternoon, Caroline announced that as Dan was only competing on the Friday morning, they were going up to London over the weekend to meet up with some friends of hers, who were over visiting from America.

Another boring, lonely weekend. She considered asking Kitty and Rachel if they wanted to go to the pub, but the one time they had gone, it had been a bit of a disaster. Rachel was a drinker and seemed to undergo a complete personality change when she drank. So professional and business-like at work, after a few vodkas she lost all her inhibitions.

Emma found it quite funny at first, until Rachel invited three blokes they didn't know to join them. Resulting in Rachel going off with one of them, and leaving Kitty and Emma unable to get rid of the other two, until they were forced to pretend they were going to the loo and slipped out through the back door.

Normally Edward rang her on a Thursday, but she needed to speak to him, so she called him that evening from the funny old-fashioned phone in the kitchen.

'Hi, Ed…it's me,'

'Emma – is everything okay?'

'Yes – it's just…have you managed to look for a place for us yet?'

There was a pause and he sighed. 'I've been absolutely flat out here – the hospital is hopelessly understaffed at the moment, I'm sorry.'

'It's fine, I'm sorry to nag you. I'm just a bit fed up with it here, that's all.'

'Look, why don't you come out for a visit. We couldn't stay here – the house is really cramped, there's five of us sharing – but I could book us into a hotel.'

'That would be good, I'd like that.'

'I'll see when I can get some time off. I'll call you tomorrow – hopefully I'll know by then.'

Emma sat at the table and read her book while she waited for Edward to call her back the following evening. Dan came in to grab his car keys, which he'd left on the side.

'We're going out,' he stated as he was going out through the door. 'Can you check round for me?'

Without warning, resentment against him rose in her breast. 'It'll have to wait,' she snapped. 'Edward's going to call.'

Dan stopped in his tracks, paused and then turned and came back.

'What's up Bugs?' he asked, coming to sit at the table.

Now she felt awkward. She wasn't sure she could explain to him how she was feeling without sounding whiney and sulky.

'I've been thinking I might take a week off and go to Germany.'

Dan frowned. 'If that's what you want to do,' he said hesitantly. 'Any particular reason?'

Emma sighed, her mutinous feelings subsiding in the face of his obvious solicitude.

'I don't know, perhaps I just need a change of scene. I feel like I'm … ' she couldn't find the right words. But he seemed to get it; he nodded in understanding.

'Go if you need to,' he said eventually. 'But you'll be missed.'

All of a sudden she felt ridiculous tears pushing their way up behind her eyes.

'I know I don't say it enough but…I do appreciate you Emma.'

Jesus, she was going to burst into tears! She was saved from answering by the phone ringing. It rang once, then twice. But Emma was unable to move, battling with her feelings.

'You'd better get that,' Dan said, getting up. 'I'll check round, okay?'

Emma nodded, having to swallow hard several times. He left, and she took a few deep breaths before answering the phone. Edward had managed to get some time off the following week; only a weekend, but at least she would have two days. It meant she would miss grooming for Dan at Merlin's crucial event – but for heaven's sake! She needed to start getting her priorities right.

'Great,' she told Edward, 'I can't wait.'

That Friday morning they had a local competition to go to, but they were back by the afternoon. They got the other horses done early and then Caroline and Dan left, presumably to pack for their weekend in London.

Emma heard the Porsche roar away down the drive at about six o'clock, as she and the other girls were finishing work. So she was startled when Dan appeared shortly afterwards in the staff room.

'I thought you'd gone,' she said. For a second she was caught out by his unexpected appearance and tried not to notice her heart, pounding in her chest.

He grinned. 'I'm not going. I told Caroline I thought the grey mare would foal tonight. So, do you want to come to the pub?'

Confused, Emma's forehead furrowed. 'We can't if the grey mare's going to foal, can we?'

Dan laughed. 'False alarm, she's not even due.'

If Caroline found out Dan had been to the pub, she would be livid. She groaned silently. 'I don't think we can.'

'Why not?' he asked.

Emma sighed. 'Because there are too many reasons why it wouldn't be a good idea. You've got too much to lose.'

He raised an eyebrow at her. 'What about if I ask Kitty and Rachel to come too?' he said dryly.

Emma hesitated, a worried frown on her face and Dan started to laugh at her. 'You worry about everything too much Bugs! Come on, you know you want to – I'll even ring Joe and see if he can come.'

It was too tempting. 'Okay,' she grinned.

'Go and get ready,' he said, 'I'll ask Rachel and Kitty.'

Emma privately thought that Rachel and Kitty would be amazed at his invitation, but to her surprise, they accepted and arranged to meet at the pub in an hour's time.

Emma hastily showered and got dressed, agonizing over what to wear. She didn't want to look like she had made too much of an effort, but at the same time, she wanted to look nice. She finally settled on her black skinny jeans and a light grey, fine knit sweater that draped softly over her shoulders.

They walked to the pub and met the other two girls. Rachel was a bit stiff with Dan at first but, as she was straight on the vodka, drinking shots – much to Dan's amusement – she soon began to loosen up. Kitty was drinking cider; she hadn't touched Hooch again after her first night out with Emma. Although she didn't dislike Dan anymore, she was still a little in awe of him.

'How did Dan get you to come out?' Emma asked Rachel while he was ordering their drinks.

'He told us you needed cheering up,' Rachel replied. Emma was touched.

Shortly afterwards Joe walked in with a girl, maybe a little older than Emma with longish curly brown hair. He spotted them and came over, giving Emma a kiss and Dan a bear hug.

'Nice to see you in here for a change,' he said to Dan with a grin. 'Thought the bar was going to fall over without you propping it up!'

Emma turned her eyes to his girlfriend. Joe introduced her as Hannah, putting his arm around her waist in a sort of protective gesture as he said her name.

She had a sweet, pretty face, and a wide-eyed, very direct gaze, which gave her an almost innocently childlike appearance. Her smile was broad and genuine. There was something instantly endearing about her and Emma decided she was going to like her.

She wanted Prosecco, and since that was what Emma was drinking, suggested they share a bottle between them. Now it felt like a celebration. Rachel and Hannah knew each other through the horsey world and soon, the three of them were deep in conversation. Kitty had a big smile on her face, obviously enjoying being part of this lively group.

After having a good catch up at the bar, the boys went over for a game of pool, and the girls grabbed a table nearby, except Rachel who went back to the bar. She was drinking beer now but still having the odd vodka chaser and was already a little drunk.

There was a loud 'Whoop!' from Joe as he potted the black and beat Dan.

'You're out of practice,' laughed Joe.

Dan grinned good-naturedly. 'You won't do it twice,' he said, flicking a beer mat at Joe.

While he was setting up again, Joe came over and asked them if they wanted another bottle of Prosecco. Emma was surprised to realise they had finished the first bottle.

'So, how does Dan come to be out tonight?' Hannah asked taking a sip of her drink. 'I've never seen him without Caroline.'

'She's in London,' Emma replied. 'Do you know her?'

She was curious to know whether the two couples socialised with each other.

'Not well,' Hannah replied. 'Dan used to bring her in here occasionally when Joe and I first started going out, and we all went out for a meal together once.'

Emma felt that new unfamiliar emotion again, it wasn't at all pleasant – a sinking, rather sickly feeling in the pit of her stomach.

Joe returned with another bottle, two more pints for himself and Dan, and a whiskey chaser for Dan.

'Come on Emma,' he said. 'Dan's seriously in need of your help, he's forgotten how to play. He needs someone on his side, come and have a game.'

The two girls got up and Emma was alarmed to find that the wine had gone straight to her legs, making her wobbly. She wasn't going to be able to play at all.

She looked around at the faces of her friends, all smiling and joking with each other, the music on the jukebox playing, and felt her happiness, like the Prosecco, fizzing inside her. If only it could always be like this.

Considering she was a bit drunk, she didn't play too badly and Dan cleaned up, pocketing the black with an exaggeratedly casual, behind the back shot.

'Show off,' said Joe, feigning disgust. But Dan was looking towards the bar, where Kitty was trying to get served. It was busy and she was so tiny, she was having trouble getting herself noticed.

A large man with a sweaty face pushed in front of her, leaning across the bar to get Barry's attention. Dan instantly got up and went to the bar. He tapped the guy on his shoulder and said something to him. Emma couldn't hear what he was saying but the man stood up to his full height, puffing his chest out, taking a step closer to Dan. But Dan held his ground. Kitty stood by, shifting from foot to foot and chewing her lip. Dan leaned in a little closer towards the sweaty man and said something else, quietly, in his ear. Immediately, sweaty man's face fell. He deflated like a puffer fish, backing off hastily and gesturing to Kitty to get in front of him. She took her place back at the bar, and Dan called Barry over. Kitty ordered her drink, flashing Dan a shy smile of gratitude.

As he came back to the table, Emma caught his eye. He held her gaze for a long moment, until something fluttered in her chest, and she found she had to look away.

They played another game of pool, the wine and beer flowed, as freely as the conversation and banter.

Emma noticed Simone come in with a bloke Emma didn't know. She walked past them, somehow contriving to nod in greeting to Rachel, Joe and Dan whilst regarding the rest of the group with a hostile stare. Emma couldn't care less, she was really feeling quite merry now, but at least she wasn't as drunk as Rachel who was laughing raucously at something Joe had said. Topping up Hannah's glass and her own, she couldn't remember if it was their second or third bottle of Prosecco.

Ed Sheeran '*Shape of You*' came on the Jukebox. Hannah squealed with delight and went to dance with Joe. They seemed to have abandoned the game of pool, so Dan and Emma kept playing against each other, both of them missing easy pots. It was Dan's turn and Emma stood to one side, dancing to the music.

He took his shot but his eyes were on her, and he missed, setting her up for an easy pot.

But as she danced past him to take her shot, Dan caught her around her waist. She pushed him away with a smile and a shake of her head and tried to take her shot, but he came up behind her and blew in her ear, making her miss completely.

'Whoops! Terribly sorry about that,' he said.

'It's alright, I won't hold it against you,' she said, taking the shot again and this time potting the ball.

'I think he wishes you would hold it against him!' cackled Rachel, who was watching.

Emma tried to look disapproving, but when a moment later, he caught her again, this time pulling her to him and moving with her to the music, she found she didn't mind. Not nearly as much as she should have. In fact, she didn't want him to stop.

The physical contact felt good. His touch felt good. She looked up into his face. The expression in his eyes wiped the smile off her face and her pulse quickened.

She couldn't catch her breath and the room was beginning to spin. Oh God, she was horribly drunk. She put her hands on his arms, as if to push him away, but instead, found herself pulled closer until their bodies were touching. She knew she should have tried harder to extricate herself – but her knees had given way, and he was holding her against him, swaying to the music.

Just then, out of the corner of her eye, Emma noticed Simone, staring at them with an expression that was a mixture of pure malice and, oddly, a kind of smug satisfaction.

It was like a cold hard slap in the face. Emma pushed Dan away – she found he released her quite easily – and staggered into the ladies' toilets. Splashing cold water on her face she stared at herself in the mirror. 'What the hell are you doing?' Her blurry reflection accused her.

She closed her eyes, blocking herself out. 'It's just the alcohol, it's just the alcohol,' she told herself. But with her eyes closed she could still feel his hands on her body, still feel his body, hard against hers. Whoa! She'd nearly toppled over, standing as she was, at the sink with her eyes closed. Feeling foolish, she dove into the nearest cubicle.

She fumbled with her clothes, which had become complicated

and difficult to manage, collapsed onto the toilet and had a pee, then got herself dressed again with difficulty.

When she came out, she found Simone reapplying lipstick in the mirror. She looked perfectly sober. Emma took a deep breath and tried to pull herself together. She stepped forward to wash her hands. Inevitably though, Simone had something to say.

'Well, well,' she began. 'It's funny how you can be so wrong about somebody.'

Emma turned and gave her the most direct look she could manage, but her gaze kept sliding around all over the place.

'What d'you mean?' she asked.

'Oh, I don't know,' Simone shrugged carelessly. 'I never thought that you would be happy with being just another notch on the bedpost. I always thought that you believed you were a little too good for that. A little bit better than the rest of us. But it turns out you're not. And you with a boyfriend as well.' She tut-tutted, shaking her head.

'I would never cheat on Edward,' Emma said, with a conviction that her guilty reflection belied, 'and Dan would never cheat on Caroline.'

Simone threw her head back and laughed. 'If you believe that then you're an even bigger idiot than I thought!'

Then, clicking her bag shut, she took a last look at her pretty, spiteful little face in the mirror, and walked out.

Emma immediately felt more sober. 'Get a grip!' she told herself, straightening her clothes. And giving herself another stern look in the mirror, she walked back out into the bar.

At some point, Joe and Hannah had left. Emma couldn't even remember seeing them go.

'I need to go home,' she announced as soon as she joined the others.

Dan was looking at her, a quizzical expression on his face.

'I'm not going home yet,' he said. His eyes were glittering with the alcohol. 'I'm going into town.'

Now she had a problem. If she got into the cab with him, would they end up going into town? Would she be able to stop him?

'I can't go into town,' she pleaded. 'I'm too drunk.'

'Clearly not drunk enough,' Dan said. His voice was low and the look in his eyes was dangerous.

Thankfully, Rachel came to her rescue.

'You can stay at mine tonight if you want, and drive into work with me in the morning.'

Emma let out her breath. 'Yes please, if that's okay?' she said gratefully.

Dan was on his mobile, presumably calling Ernie. Everybody finished their drinks – except Emma who didn't touch another drop of hers – and went outside. The fresh air was a relief. Her head started to clear.

Ernie was already waiting in the car park. The others were saying goodnight, but Dan stopped Emma, taking her hand. She pulled it away.

'Come with me,' he said.

'Only if you're going home.' She was worried about him now; he'd had far too much to drink.

'This is my only night of freedom,' he said. 'I'm not ready to give it up yet – maybe never – stay with me Emma.'

Emma shook her head, 'I can't.'

'Can't or won't?'

'Both,' she replied.

'What are you scared of?' he asked her softly.

How on earth to answer that question? A thousand answers flashed through her mind all at once, none of which she could say out loud.

'You coming Emma?' Rachel called.

She realised Dan had taken her hand again, and was gradually pulling her towards him.

'Dan, please. Go home,' she pleaded, 'you're going to regret this tomorrow morning.' Looking at his eyes, though, she could see he was way beyond the point of reason. Giving up, she pulled her hand out of his.

'I'm coming,' she called to Rachel and shaking her head, she backed away.

'What was all that about?' Rachel asked, swaying slightly.

Emma looked over her shoulder to see him get in the cab.

'He always gets like this when he drinks too much, then regrets it in the morning. It's all right, I can handle him,' she replied.

But as she said the words, she no longer knew whether they were true. It seemed that slowly but surely, she was losing her ability to handle him.

Chapter 28

After an uncomfortable night spent on Rachel's sofa, they drove into work the next morning, feeling more than a little worse for wear.

'It was a fun night though,' Rachel giggled.

Emma had to agree, but she was furious with herself for getting so drunk and letting things get so out of hand with Dan. Her memory was a little hazy surrounding some of the details.

There was no sign of him when they got to the yard.

'Typical,' said Rachel, 'he can just take the day off. He's probably in bed sleeping it off, unlike us who've had to drag our sorry arses into work!'

Emma ran upstairs to get changed and brush her teeth. She desperately wanted a shower but there wasn't time.

Simone arrived shortly after they had fed round, closely followed by Kitty, who hadn't got drunk last night and was especially bright and cheerful.

They went about their work doggedly until, at about eight thirty, Emma heard a shout and a laugh from Rachel.

'Look what the cat's dragged in!' she called to Emma.

She turned and saw Dan stagger through the yard gate. He looked a right state, and by the way he was walking, was still drunk. He didn't stop but went straight in the tack room door. Emma put down her tools and followed him in.

The door to the stairs was open and she could hear him going into his old room upstairs. Oh well, let him sleep it off. At least Caroline wasn't coming back until tomorrow.

They got through the morning somehow getting all the horses exercised and all their jobs done.

Just before lunch, Emma heard a car pull up on the gravel. Oh *shit!* It sounded like Caroline's Porsche. Sure enough, Caroline came tripping lightly through the gate, bright eyed and bushy tailed.

'Where's Dan?' she asked, looking round at them all.

Simone opened her mouth to answer, but Emma was too quick for her.

'He's out on a hack,' she stated hoping Caroline wouldn't notice that all the horses were in their boxes. 'He's only just left,' she added, wanting to buy some time.

'Oh,' said Caroline. 'Well, when he gets back, can you tell him I'm home? I came back early, it was no fun without him,' she said, and went on up to the Coach House.

Emma went straight upstairs to Dan's room. She didn't bother to knock because the door was wide open. He was lying face down on his bed, fully clothed except for his jacket and boots, one leg hanging off the bed as if he'd just fallen onto it. She went over to him and shook him gently by the shoulders; she could feel his skin was hot underneath his T-shirt.

'Dan, wake up!' she whispered loudly. 'Caroline's back and she's looking for you.'

He groaned. She opened the window wide letting the breeze in.

'Wake up!' she said, shaking him again, but he didn't move. She went back downstairs and shouted for Kitty before putting the kettle on. Kitty came in looking worried.

'We can't let Caroline find him in this state,' Emma told her. 'Can you make a strong black coffee and bring it upstairs?'

'Okay,' said Kitty, nodding her agreement, although her eyes were full of doubt.

Emma ran back upstairs.

'Come on Dan,' Emma pleaded, as she knelt down next to him and shook him again a little harder. 'You've got to wake up or you're going to be in so much trouble.'

She felt at fault in more ways than one. Maybe he wouldn't have gone out at all if it hadn't been for her.

At last he stirred a little and turned over on his side towards her. Slowly, he opened one eye and a grin spread across his face.

'Bugs!' he said happily.

'We need to get you in the shower,' she told him firmly.

She heard footsteps on the stairs and panicked in case it was Caroline, but it was only Kitty bringing coffee.

'Here, drink this,' Emma took his hands and tried to make him sit up, but he collapsed back on to the bed.

'No. Sleep,' he said, snuggling back down.

It was clear he wasn't going to cooperate.

'Oh why do you do this to yourself?' she said in exasperation.

'Perhaps we should just leave him,' Kitty said anxiously.

Emma ignored her. 'You're going to have to help me get him in the shower.'

Kitty's mouth dropped open, aghast, 'I'm not…' she began to protest.

'With his clothes on,' Emma reassured her hastily. 'If we can find some clean ones. She looked in the chest of drawers. There were a few clothes in there. She found a pair of jeans and a T-shirt; old, but they would do.

She managed to get one of Dan's arms round her shoulders and lifted him into a sitting position.

'You take his other side,' she ordered Kitty.

Then, puffing and panting they half carried, half dragged him into the bathroom.

'Come on Dan, work with me now,' she said as they tried to get him into the shower. It wasn't easy, but finally they managed to get him propped up against the wall and let him go, whereupon he slithered down into a sitting position, his chin falling forward onto his chest.

'I'm sorry to have to do this, but it's for your own good,' she apologized, and turned on the water, hard.

He swore, gasping under the cold water, standing up so fast that he nearly slipped over as he tried to get out, but Emma stood in his way pushing him back in.

'No, you stay in there until you are good and sober. Caroline's looking for you and if she finds you like this, you're a dead man. Now, have a shower and drink the coffee,' she ordered.

'Okay, okay,' he spluttered. 'I'm awake!'

Kitty fetched the coffee, which he drunk down in one, and then, as he did seem to be more awake, they left him to shower. One hour, and two more strong coffee's later, he was sitting downstairs at the kitchen table, looking more human, but very grumpy.

In a way Emma was glad he had been so out of it. Hopefully he wouldn't remember last night too well either.

'I'm never drinking again,' he groaned.

Emma chuckled. 'I'll remind you of that next time you want to go out.'

'There won't be a next time,' he swore, and then after a pause. 'I'm sorry if I was being a tool…again,' he said despondently.

Emma flushed. 'You just had too much to drink, but so did I – we all did.'

But his eyes were downcast.

'Look,' she said, 'I had a really good time last night. Maybe we were being idiots, but I can't remember the last time I had such a good laugh.'

He looked up at her, from heavy lidded eyes. 'You're a good friend Bugs.'

Emma wasn't so sure she was.

'Heads up.' It was Rachel. 'Caroline's on her way down.'

Simone wandered in, never one to want to miss anything.

Dan got up from the table, taking his mug over to the sink and seconds later Caroline bounced in.

'There you are!' she said to Dan, going over to him and putting her arms around him. 'Did'ya miss me?' she asked, kissing him.

He gave her a slightly sickly smile.

Caroline drew back and looked his face. 'Baby! You look terrible, are you okay?'

'I was up all night,' he replied.

'With the grey mare? Did she foal?'

Simone made a noise very much like a snort. Emma shot her a warning look.

'False alarm,' Dan said.

'You're kidding? So you could have come with me after all,' Caroline said in dismay. Dan shrugged.

'How boring for you!' cried Caroline.

'Oh, I don't think he was bored,' muttered Simone.

Emma pushed her chair under the table with a loud scraping noise. Everyone looked at her.

'Sorry,' she apologised. 'Right, we'd better get on with some work I suppose.'

When Caroline and Dan had disappeared up to The Coach House, Emma, Rachel, Kitty and Simone finished the afternoon chores.

Emma felt guilty. She'd lied, and behaved appallingly; it didn't sit well with her conscience.

What made it worse was Simone taking the moral high ground. The sneering looks that she directed at Emma made her squirm, and she was painfully aware that if Simone wanted to make trouble, she had as much ammunition as she needed. And she wasn't going to let this opportunity pass, without making the most of it. She came into the feed room when Emma was making up the feeds and chopping the carrots.

'If Caroline asks me about last night, *I'm* not going to lie. She deserves to know what's going on,' she said to Emma in a loud voice, so that if anyone happened to be passing, they would be sure to hear.

'Oh get off your high horse Simone,' Emma snapped; she'd had enough of her duplicity and was feeling ratty. 'Firstly, there's nothing going on, and secondly, you don't care about Caroline, you just want to make trouble.'

Simone's air of superiority dissolved into naked hatred.

'You think you're so special don't you?' she hissed. 'You think he really likes you? You must do or you wouldn't be sneaking around, lying for him – acting like you're Snow White, when all the time you're going behind Caroline's back!'

Emma put down the knife she was using and turned to face Simone, her skin was prickling all over and she felt quite sick. But Simone wasn't done yet.

'I know Dan better than anyone; better than you; better than Caroline. And I know he won't be able to keep this up forever. Sooner or later he is going to slip up, and when he does, Caroline is going to leave him, you will go back to your posh boyfriend – and I will still be here. Everyone finds their own level eventually.'

The exchange left Emma shaky and nauseous. It wasn't just that she seemed to have made a formidable enemy out of Simone, it was the terrible worry that what she was saying might be true.

No sooner had Simone left, then Rachel came in with a furtive look over her shoulder.

'Simone's properly got it in for you hasn't she,' she said, her eyes bright with intrigue, 'she thinks there's something going on between you and Dan.'

Emma's hung-over nerves were in shreds. 'Well, there isn't,' she said, picking up her knife again and chopping with unnecessary force.

Rachel gave her another sly smile. 'It's okay, you don't have to tell me.'

Emma had had enough. She stopped chopping and turned to face her.

'No really! There isn't! I would have to be a complete idiot,' she barked hoarsely, waving the knife around. 'Dan and I are friends, nothing more than that. I'm not as stupid as everyone seems to think I am.'

'Okay, okay! Don't chop my head off, I believe you,' Rachel laughed. 'I told her I thought you had more sense than that.'

It was a very good thing she was going to Berlin the following weekend. She needed to get away from here, because clearly she couldn't be trusted to behave in a sensible manner at the moment. She would never allow herself to be the reason Dan ruined his chance of success and destroyed the yard's best source of income. And although she might have convinced Rachel that she wasn't an idiot, she was having a harder time convincing herself.

Chapter 29

IT WAS THE NIGHT BEFORE SHE WAS GOING TO BERLIN. EDWARD WAS going to call to go over the final arrangements for taxi's to and from the airport.

Only Dan was still there, checking round and locking up. 'Waiting for the doctor to call?' he asked her as he came in to get the keys to the feed room.

'Uh, huh,' Emma replied.

While she waited she cleaned the kitchen and emptied the rubbish bin, keeping busy to stop herself over-thinking. She had found it necessary to keep herself busy a lot recently; it seemed the only way to prevent her thoughts from veering off onto crazy paths.

The phone rang, and she answered it with relief.

'Hello, may I speak to Emma Mathews?' a female voice said. Emma balked. It was her Mother.

'It's me Mum,' she said, with trepidation – her mother never called.

'Oh at last! I've been trying to ring you on your mobile but you never have it turned on. I had to look up the number on the Internet and then the woman who answered gave me this one.'

'I'm sorry,' said Emma, 'my mobile doesn't hold its charge very well, it keeps turning itself off.'

'Hmmm,' said her mother.

'Is everything alright?' Emma asked.

'Well, I didn't know whether to bother you with this really, but your grandfather's in hospital, he's had a heart attack.'

Emma sank down onto the nearest chair, weak with shock.

'A heart attack,' she echoed. 'Is he okay?'

'Well no, obviously not, or he wouldn't be in hospital, but he is stable and on a ward.'

Emma was silent for a moment. She couldn't imagine her Granddad in hospital. The only way she could picture him was sitting on the bench outside his cottage in the sunshine, or feeding his chickens, or in his vegetable patch digging potatoes. She hadn't seen him in so long. What if he died before she got to see him again?

'Are you still there?' her Mother's voice sounded querulous.

'Yes, yes. When are you going up to see him, I'll come home and then I can come with you.' She would have to cancel her trip…

'Oh, we've already been up to see him. It happened three days ago. We won't go again unless things take a turn for the worse.'

Emma was horrified. 'Three days! Why didn't you ring me before? I would have come home, I would have come to see him!'

'Don't shout at me Emma,' her Mother said coldly. 'As I said, I have been trying to get hold of you. Anyway, I didn't know whether you would be bothered to go all the way up to Suffolk to visit him. I know how absorbed you are with the horses.'

Emma was up on her feet again now, pacing back and forth. 'Of course I would have come! Of course I would want to see him!' The inevitable tears of injustice welled up in her eyes. She wiped them away in frustration. 'Never mind,' she went on, taking a deep breath. 'Tell me which hospital he is in and the name of the ward, and I will get up there, somehow.'

She hastily found a bit of paper and a pen and scribbled down the details. 'I have to go,' she said abruptly when she had written it all down. 'Edward's going to call.'

Her Mother sighed. 'There's no need to make such a fuss Emma, I did try to get hold of you.'

'Not hard enough,' Emma growled and slammed the phone down. It rang almost immediately.

'Emma?' came the voice down the line. It was Edward. 'I've been trying to ring for ages; the line's been engaged. I nearly gave up.'

An overwhelming sense of weariness threatened to engulf her and she leant against the table.

'My Mother rang. Granddad's in hospital, he's had a heart attack.'

Her voice was weak and unsteady. She needed Edward's reassurance that it would all be okay.

'Oh dear, poor old chap. Is he stable?'

'Yes, and not in any immediate danger apparently, but I need to get up to see him. I won't be able to come to Berlin. I'll have to get the train up to Suffolk – God knows how long that will take. My Mother has only just told me, and it happened three days ago. They've already been up to see him, she said she couldn't get hold of me!' She waited for Edward to be suitably outraged on her behalf.

'Well you can hardly blame her for that,' Edward said. 'I'm sure she tried to get hold of you, she wouldn't have done it on purpose.'

This wasn't exactly the response Emma had hoped for.

'Yes she would!' Emma exclaimed. 'That's exactly what she would have done. She would have done it to make me feel bad, to make it look like I didn't care, because she knows how close I am to Granddad, and she's jealous!'

'Oh Emma, not this again. You shouldn't say things like that about her. She's your mother and I'm sure they're not true. Be reasonable.'

Her self-control cracked. 'I don't want to be reasonable!' she shouted. 'I want you to understand how I feel! I want you to be on my side. And what's more, if I had taken my driving test when I wanted to last year, I could have driven myself up there!' She stopped, breathing hard, listening to the shocked silence at the other end of the phone.

When he spoke, his voice was controlled and subtly aggrieved. 'I'm very sorry to hear about your grandfather, and I sincerely hope that he's okay. But today, we had a patient die on the operating table, and another go into cardiac arrest, and there was nothing we could do to save them. So, I'm sorry, but I'm not really in a frame of mind to be shouted at. I'll call you later on when you've calmed down. Bye.'

Emma held the phone to her ear for a moment even though she'd heard the click as he'd rung off. She'd gone too far, he was upset. Her instinct was to call him back immediately and apologise. She was already dialling the number when the resentment kicked in. Resentment like nothing she'd ever felt before. She slammed the phone down again.

'Fuck it!' There didn't seem to be a better way of venting her frustration. 'Fuck it, fuck it, *fuck it!*' But even this didn't seem to be enough, so she kicked the empty rubbish can as hard as she could – it was an excellent kick. It flew through the air hitting the doorframe with a crash, narrowly missing Dan as he came through the door.

'Whoa!' he ducked with lightening reflexes.

Emma clapped her hands over her mouth in mortification. 'Oh! I'm sorry, I'm so sorry. I completely forgot you were here!'

'Something vexes thee?' he gave her a quizzical smile.

Emma sat down heavily on the chair again, rubbing her face with her hands. 'Oh God. I've had a row with my Mother…and with Edward.'

Dan checked his watch. 'All in the space of twenty minutes. Impressive!'

Emma's answering smile flickered and died.

His expression became serious. 'Tell me,' he said, pulling up a chair.

She explained about her granddad and her mother. Then she told him what Edward had said and the resulting row. 'I really should call him back and apologise.'

He listened quietly, without comment, then shook his head.

'Why? Because you were upset about your Granddad? Because you put your own feelings first for a change, instead of supporting him?'

'No, I really was out of order. I even blamed him for not having my driving licence…kind of.'

Dan didn't reply immediately. Instead, he went to the fridge, fetching a beer for each of them.

'Don't call him back,' he said, handing her the open bottle and then leaning against the countertop, ankles crossed in his favourite attitude. 'Trust me, he'll respect you more if you don't.'

Emma looked up at him doubtfully. 'You don't know Edward like I do. He absolutely hates that kind of out-of-control behaviour.'

'So, you're not allowed to have a bad day?' He narrowed his eyes and took a swig of his beer.

'I guess it's because he never loses his temper, he expects other people to have the same self-control.'

'Well, you don't have to worry about that around me,' Dan laughed. 'You can shout and curse and kick cans around as much as you like.'

Emma smiled. 'It's okay, I think I've got it out of my system.'

She took a deep breath and pushed the hair away from her face. 'So now… I'm not going to Berlin obviously. I'm going to have to catch a train up to Suffolk to see Granddad – God knows how long that's going to take – and find somewhere to stay up there.'

It was all going to cost a bloody fortune and she had no idea which train she would have to catch once she was in London. She would have to get the first train up to Waterloo in the morning and find out from there. And then just hope she would be able to find a taxi to take her to the hospital once she reached Bury St. Edmunds…and somewhere to stay…

'I'll drive you,' Dan said, his words cutting through her misery.

'What?' she was startled. 'But it's miles away, it's Bury St. Edmunds. I couldn't ask you to do that.'

'You're not asking, I'm offering.'

She didn't know what to say. The offer was so unexpected and so, *so* tempting. To just get in a car and be driven. She would get there in half the time. She could see her granddad and be back at the yard by the evening without the bother of trains and unfamiliar stations, and taxis to find the hospital at the other end. But could she possibly accept?

'Do you really mean it? It would take the whole day.'

'Yes,' he said simply.

'But what about the horses, you're competing Saturday and Sunday. And what about Caroline and…' she could think of a thousand reasons why it would be too difficult for him.

'Simone, Kitty and Rachel can hack the horses out tomorrow. Caroline will probably want to come – go shopping, or sight-seeing…' he pulled a face, 'or I could tell her I'm doing something else.'

Emma's hope faded. Maybe she couldn't accept his offer after all.

'No Dan, if you can't be honest with Caroline about this then I can't let you do it.'

He gave her a wry smile. 'Are you trying to save my soul Bugs?'

'Only you can do that,' she said.

'You have to do things the hard way, don't you?' he asked.

'Yup, sorry,' she said.

He sighed. 'Okay, have it your way.'

Chapter 30

Caroline couldn't come although she had wanted to; she had a spa treatment booked for that afternoon. It wasn't until they were speeding up the A303 that Emma realised that she had forgotten to ring Edward back the night before.

Dan drove the way he rode, fast but smoothly. Emma was usually a nervous passenger but for some reason she didn't feel worried, despite the speedometer creeping above 90mph a few times. At Stonehenge they hit a bottleneck of traffic, enabling Emma to have a good look out of the window at the huge standing stones. They stopped once on the way for Emma to buy some of Granddad's favourite shortbread, but they were still there in less than four hours.

With time to kill before visiting hours, they grabbed a coffee and a sandwich from a nearby café, and walked around the Cathedral gardens to stretch their legs. The gardens were full of people on their lunch breaks; pasty, white people in office suits, blinking in the bright sunlight after hours spent in artificially lit offices.

Amongst them, Dan stood out with his tanned skin, sun bleached hair and striking good looks. But also in these strange surroundings, comfortingly familiar to Emma.

He hesitated when it was time to go in to the hospital.

'You don't have to come in if you don't want to,' she said. 'But Granddad loves company – I'm sure he'd like to meet you.'

'Okay, I'll come in if you like.'

They found the ward and asked the older of the two nurses there, where they had to go. Emma tried not to look too hard at the figures beneath the white hospital blankets on either side of the room as they followed her down the ward. Most were old, and most looked so thin and frail. Emma couldn't imagine her own Grandfather in so fragile a state. She was glad she wasn't alone.

The nurse led them to a bed by the window at the end of the ward. In it was an old man, just like all the others, propped up on his pillows and apparently fast asleep. It was Granddad, undoubtedly, but a much smaller, older looking version of himself.

But then he turned his head and opened his eyes and seeing her, his whole face lit up, his dark blue eyes sparkling.

'Emma!' he said, pleasure instantly giving his face life and vitality.

'Granddad!' she gave him a hug. 'I'm so sorry, Mum only told me yesterday, I came as soon as I could.'

'She and your father were here a couple of days ago. She said you weren't coming – luckily I ignore most of the things she says nowadays,' he chuckled. 'I knew you would come if you could.'

Emma was relieved to hear his voice sounding strong and he still had his sense of humour.

'How are you feeling?' she asked him.

'Absolutely fine,' he waved his hand dismissively. 'Never felt better, it was only a bit of a stutter. Got to expect it at my age.' He grinned, then turned his eyes towards Dan with interest.

'This is Dan,' Emma introduced him, 'he's a good friend of mine.'

She watched as Dan stepped forward to shake her granddad's hand, a complicated emotion heating her face.

'I drove Emma up,' he said.

Granddad took Dan's hand in both of his own. 'Thank you for bringing my girl up to see me.' Then he gave Emma a stern look. 'Have you still not got your licence?'

She shook her head with a grimace.

'Get on with you girl!' he turned to Dan again. 'Will you get after her to take her bloody test, I don't see her often enough.'

'I'll try,' Dan answered with a grin, 'but she'll do it when she's made up her mind to do it.'

Granddad laughed. 'You're right. It's a clever man who can influence a woman's mind – I could never make any impression on Emma's grandmother at all!' He leaned closer to Dan, his eyes narrowing. 'So what do you do boy? Are you a rider too?'

'I am,' replied Dan.

'A jockey?'

'Used to be, once upon a time, but now I event.'

Emma could see her grandfather's interest was piqued. He'd been an amateur jump jockey in his younger days and still loved his racing. Emma had always assumed that was where she'd got her love of horses from. Out from underneath his bed, he fished a newspaper, looking around furtively as if it were contraband. It was open at the racing section of the sports pages.

'I've got my favourite nurse to put a fiver on for me in the four o'clock at Kempton,' he said, jabbing a gnarly finger at the page. 'What do you think?'

And they were off; chatting about racing, swapping stories about the various races they had ridden in as if they'd known each other for years. Both their faces animated by their common interest. Relaxing in her chair, any awkwardness forgotten, Emma was content to let them talk, leaving her free to look about her.

One of the nurses, the younger prettier one, walked down the ward with a vase of flowers. As she passed by, she was staring at Dan so hard, she nearly collided with the bed opposite. On her way back, she gawped again. A moment later she returned, to fluff up the pillows of the occupant in the bed next to them, fussing around, but all the time she was gazing at Dan. The two men were oblivious, but Emma began to find it a little irritating. She managed to catch the girl's eye and raised her eyebrows with a questioning look. The nurse blushed and bustled away with an officious air.

Eventually, Dan got up, saying he had to check the parking on the car.

'I like this one!' Granddad said, almost before he was out of earshot. 'Much better than the last one – what was his name – Edward?'

'No Granddad! I'm still with Edward,' she explained hastily. 'But he's in Germany at the moment doing some more training, and I'm joining him there soon. Dan's just a friend, we work together.'

'Oh?' he frowned. 'But this one's far more interesting, he's got a bit more about him. I always thought that Edward was a bit dull for you Emmy.'

'Granddad!' Emma protested.

'Well, if you don't say what you think at my age you might not get another chance,' the old man said impatiently.

'I'm very lucky to have Edward,' she scolded. 'He's kind, honest, hard-working and generous…'

'Yes, yes, that's all very well, but is he a good kisser?' he replied earnestly.

Emma fell about laughing. 'You're supposed to get wiser as you get older.'

'So, what's wrong with this boy then? I don't pretend to know what girls want these days but he's a good-looking fellow. And he's a rider Emmy.'

Emma looked nervously over her shoulder in case Dan was coming back.

'Nothing's wrong with him, but he's got a girlfriend for one thing.'

'And yet he's here with you, visiting an old, sick man in hospital.'

'Yes, but he's also unpredictable, and unreliable; always looking for trouble and generally finds it.'

Granddad chuckled. 'A bit on the wild side, eh?'

'Yes.'

The old man was thoughtful for a moment.

'It's your choice I suppose, and you must know what's best for you.' He took her hand in his and pulled her a little closer. 'But don't go getting married or anything silly like that until you're sure it's real love. Until you've experienced real love, you haven't lived. Don't make the same mistake your mother made, it's made her the woman she is today. Believe it or not, she was once a sweet girl, full of life, now she's so bitter and twisted, I hardly recognise her. She settled for your father because she got scared. She wanted to be a barrister, but she failed the Bar exam and was too afraid to keep going.'

Emma was taken aback. 'She's always told me she had to give up her career because she got pregnant with me.'

'No, that's not how it happened at all. She failed her exams and used you as an excuse to stop trying. Too scared to fail again. So she married your father because it was the easy option; he had money and could support her, but she's resented him for it ever since. And she's resented you Emma, truth be told.'

Emma was gobsmacked as she digested this information.

'I blame myself,' he went on. 'I never taught her what's important in life, because I didn't know myself back then. It's when death starts breathing down your neck that you realise what truly matters.' He squeezed her hand tightly. 'Be sure to know your own mind Emmy! Know what it is you want. Be honest with yourself, even when it's painful. Never settle for anything less than extraordinary.'

His dark blue eyes, although faded with age, were still piercing and his words were deeply affecting. Her own eyes filled with tears.

'With Edward, at least I know my heart is safe,' she said in a small voice.

Granddad patted her hand. 'Of course it's safe,' he said gently. 'He can't break your heart if he's never really had it.'

Emma blinked back the tears. 'But… he loves me.'

Granddad smiled at her fondly. 'Does he? A man gives his heart to a woman who makes him want to be a better man. I get the feeling that your Edward thinks he's good enough already.'

At that moment Dan came back. 'I've put another hour on the ticket,' he said.

Emma got to her feet, hiding her face from him. 'I'll go and get us some tea.'

Her grandfather's words threatened to crack the very foundations upon which she was building her life. This man who cared about her more than anyone else, and whom she trusted, beyond anything, had called into question everything she thought she knew to be true. She'd lost her point of reference, and her defences were beginning to crumble.

She came back with the teas to find the two men deep in conversation. For a second, she wondered if she had been wise to leave them alone together.

'Dan's been telling me about all these horses that you ride where you work.'

Granddad said, as she handed him his tea. She breathed a sigh of relief. 'He's told me about this superstar horse – Angel was it? – that wins everything.'

'And there's Merlin,' Dan grinned at Emma. 'Everybody's frightened of him except Emma. He's very talented – amazing scope – but he's temperamental and unpredictable; not the easiest ride.'

'Horses like that are the interesting ones,' Granddad said. Then he turned and said pointedly to Emma: 'I'd rather have a tricky one like that any day. You might suffer a few knocks and bruises on the way, but the difficult ones are more rewarding in the end, wouldn't you agree Emma?'

'Mmm,' she murmured, refusing to meet his eye.

Granddad creaked with laughter at his own private joke, his eyes twinkling. Emma looked around for some form of distraction, and thankfully, her eyes alighted on the tin of biscuits.

'Shortbread anyone?' She handed it around, taking some herself.

The taste took her straight back to her Granddad's cottage. Every summer as a little girl as young as five, she would stay with him for a few weeks. Feeding his chickens and collecting the eggs in the morning, the fondest memories of her childhood; the excitement of lifting the lids off the nesting boxes, spilling the morning sunlight onto the warm brown eggs nestled in the golden straw – like finding treasure.

Too soon Emma realised they would have to leave if they were to be back home at a reasonable hour. There was no stopping the tears as she hugged Granddad goodbye. It was so hard to leave him there.

'Promise me you'll take your test and come to see me again soon, when I'm back at home,' he insisted before he would let her go.

'I promise I will,' she said, knowing now she had promised, she would have to do it. She wished they could take him out of there now. Take him out in the fresh air and the sunshine, home to his own cottage. She had the unsettling feeling that time was running out, and that opportunities could slip away without you even noticing, until it was too late.

Chapter 31

Emma was quiet on the journey home. Her grandfather's words were playing around the edges of her consciousness. Questions that she hadn't dared ask herself were forcing themselves to the surface of her mind and demanding an answer. *Be honest with yourself – even when it's painful.* She could have been in Berlin right now, but if she were honest there was nowhere she'd rather be than in this car, with the long journey ahead of them. She didn't really want it to end.

'You okay?' Dan asked, glancing across at her.

She nodded. Today, despite the circumstances, had been a really good day, and there didn't seem to be a way to express to Dan how grateful she was to him. She'd said thank you – more than once – but the words felt inadequate, and he refused to take any money for fuel.

It had clouded over and started to rain. After the heat of the day, everything smelt damp and earthy and there was the odd rumble of thunder. It was very close.

'Music?' Dan suggested.

Emma pulled out her phone but it had died again. Luckily she had remembered to bring a charger, so she plugged it in and connected it to the stereo. As it came back to life, the screen lit up and it vibrated. Several missed calls from Edward and two new voicemails. Whoops. Automatically she touched the screen to listen to the voicemails, but then hit cancel just as quickly. She wasn't in the mood to listen to them now. She would wait until she was alone in her room.

Emma shook off her shoes and curled her legs up underneath her, turning a little sideways in her seat towards Dan. She yawned.

'Go to sleep if you're tired,' he said.

'No, that's hardly fair on you,' she said. 'I need to keep you company.'

The car was warm and the music mellow; "*Don't Stop Now*" by Crowded House. Despite her best efforts she felt herself drifting off, but she fought it, opening her eyes every so often to watch him as he drove, his eyes on the road.

She felt an overwhelming sense of gratitude towards the man sitting next to her. Gratitude and something else – affection. *Be honest with yourself Emmy.*

It was more than mere gratitude, or affection. It was…love.

The innocuous little word slipped into the inner world of her consciousness from the outer world of her sub-conscious, where it had been waiting for a very long time. Waiting for an opening, a slight weakness in the hard, outer shell of her defence. Love. She was in love with him.

It was both shocking and liberating to finally admit it to herself. To say the words in her mind; to give up the fight. And now she was drowning in her emotion. It was like she had opened an artery, and the blood was flowing faster and faster, and she couldn't stop it.

All at once she wasn't drowsy anymore, not at all. She sat up suddenly, her eyes wide open.

He glanced at her questioningly. 'What's wrong? You look like somebody who's just remembered they left the gas on.'

She cleared her throat. 'I…I just don't want to fall asleep, that's all,' she said in confusion, picking up her phone and scrolling through her music. 'This music's putting me to sleep.'

She put her iPhone on shuffle. Immediately Ed Sheeran, "*Shape of You*" came on. Oh Christ! That was worse. She had a sudden flashback of being in the pub. His hands round her waist, pulling her to him, his body against hers.

She risked a glance at him, regretting it immediately as her stomach somersaulted into zero gravity.

He was leaning back in his seat, his right hand on the steering wheel, elbow resting on the top of the door, his other hand resting on the gear stick, long legs relaxed, knees apart. He looked lost in thought, but there was a smile hovering around his mouth. That heartbreakingly beautiful mouth.

She felt a kind of pulling sensation in her stomach and closed her eyes again, trying to control her emotions and her breathing.

She was in love with him. What a fool she was. All this time she had been lying to herself, and everyone else; Rachel, Amy, Simone; they'd all been right. She was just as stupid as Simone thought she was. Oh God, she should never have come back! She knew that now. Now it was too late.

She imagined the look on his face if he knew how she was feeling. The thought was mortifying. He was going home to a woman who loved him, who was making all his dreams come true. He must never know. No one would. Not Kitty – not even Lottie. She would take it to her grave. The strength of her conviction was enough to allow her to gain some control over her feelings, enabling her to look and speak normally.

Soon, they were off the main road and the country they were passing through became more rugged and wild. Emma knew they were nearing home. The light was fading and the headlights showed hedgerows filled with wildflowers. It had stopped raining. Another half an hour and they were pulling into the driveway.

The lights of the Coach House were on. Instead of parking up in front of the house, Dan drove down into the yard. He switched the engine off, the stereo went silent and they were in complete darkness. They sat, as if mesmerized by the stillness.

Emma knew she had to speak, to try to express at least a small part of what she actually felt. Feeling a lump form in her throat and unwanted tears beginning to spring up underneath her eyelids, she was terrified she might say something stupid.

The darkness seemed to gather and become more dense. The silence became charged with a kind of static hum, like a high voltage electricity cable. Still, he made no move to get out.

Dan's phone vibrated, making them both go through the roof. The screen lit up with Caroline's name, filling the car with her presence. Dan silenced it, but it jolted Emma enough to enable her to speak.

'I don't think you'll ever know how much it meant to me… what you did for me today,' she said, and her voice was remarkably steady. 'Thank you for being so kind and talking to Granddad the way you did. I know how much he enjoyed it.'

Quickly, and before she could let herself think about it, she leant forward and kissed him on the cheek. Acutely aware in that split second of the feel of his cool, hard cheek against her mouth, the days growth of dark stubble that grazed her lips and the heady, spicy scent of his aftershave. Then with her heart in her mouth, and before he had a chance to say anything she slipped out of the car and was running through the yard.

Once in the kitchen, she leant against the table breathing hard, her heart pounding. Was this the way it was always going to be now? Was she ever going to feel normal around him again?

Going upstairs to her room she realised to her dismay that she had left her phone in his car. Now, she wouldn't be able to listen to the voicemail from Edward, or ring him back.

Part of her was glad she had a reason not to ring Edward back right away. She needed to get her head straight. She got into her nightclothes – pyjama shorts and a crop top. Despite the rain it was still too hot for anything else.

She left the door open to let in the breeze. Leaving on her bedside light, she lay on top of her bed staring at the ceiling. She had some hard thinking to do.

This love. Fierce, burning, sharp. So different from what she felt for Edward. Her heart was going to be broken, there was no doubt about that. But she couldn't regret it, because although it was painful, in a strange way it also felt deeply nourishing, like a very beautiful, but very sad song. The music they had been listening to in the car played over and over in her head as she fell asleep.

She was on her back, in a river. At first she was alarmed and tried to swim. But then she realised that if she just kept still, she could stay on top of the water, she was floating. In the dream she lay back and relaxed, allowing the flow of the water to take her downstream.

The water was warm and the current was strong; it was taking her faster and faster. But the sensation was so pleasant, she wasn't scared in the least. It took her over little waterfalls and round bends, flowing this way and that, she had no way of knowing where she was going to end up, but she didn't care.

There was a gentle breeze blowing softly on her face, it was warm and smelled sweet and reminded her of something achingly familiar. It made a soft whispering noise as it blew gently across her cheeks, and as it touched her forehead, it almost felt like a kiss.

She didn't want the dream to end, but her consciousness started to push its way up to the surface. Lying quite still, she clung to the sensation as long as she could, but it was no good, she was awake. She reached over to turn off her lamp. As she did so, something caught her eye.

Her phone was on her bedside table. Her breath caught in her throat. That could only mean one thing. Dan must have brought it down and put it there while she was sleeping. He had been in her room. Now, she could swear she could smell his aftershave, very faintly in the air around her. She closed her eyes and breathed it in deeply. It was unmistakable.

She put her phone on charge and the screen flashed on with the message from Edward, but she turned it face down on the bedside table. She didn't want to break the spell that her dream had woven around her.

Turning off her lamp and getting under the covers, she tried to hold the lingering scent as long as she could and remember the delicious sensation of her dream. Because the two seemed to be inextricably linked, and somehow they eased the ache in her heart.

Chapter 32

BECAUSE SHE'D HAD TO CANCEL HER TRIP TO BERLIN, SHE WOULD be able to groom for Dan at the competition the following day and be there for Merlin's crucial event on the Sunday. Funny how things worked out.

When she woke, the first thing she did was dutifully listen to Edward's message. He actually apologised. She couldn't believe it. He apologised for having not been more sympathetic and said he'd been trying to get hold of her for most of that day.

Dan had been right about not calling him back straight away. It had obviously given him something to think about. The message also asked her to call him back as soon as she got it.

It was still very early but they were out all day, and if she didn't call Edward now, she might not get another chance until this evening.

She dialled his mobile but it went straight to voicemail. She had another number; the landline of the house where Edward lived. She'd never rung it before, but decided to give it a go. Dialling carefully, she heard the unfamiliar ring tone of the foreign line. It rang and rang. She was about to give up, when it was picked up the other end.

'Frieda Baumann, hallo?' A female voice, in German answered.

'Oh. Hello.' Emma said disconcerted. 'Sorry, I'm trying to reach Edward Farrington?' She hoped the person speaking would understand English.

There was a pause.

'Edward is not available at the moment,' said the voice. 'Can I take a message?'

'Yes, please. Can you tell him that Emma called?'

Another pause.

'Okay, I will tell him.'

'Thank you…' Emma said, but the line had gone dead.

Perhaps – whoever she was – had been annoyed by the phone ringing at such an early hour. But then, wasn't Germany an hour ahead of English time? Oh well, at least she could say she'd tried.

She glanced out of her window. Most of the horses had their heads over their doors, looking eagerly towards the gate for someone to arrive with their breakfast. Any second, Dan might appear at that gate. In a very short time, she would be face to face with him.

'It's just a morning like any other,' she told herself, closing her eyes and taking slow, deep breaths to calm her nerves.

Immediately, there was a clamour of excited whinnying from all the horses and a clattering of hooves banging against doors, setting Emma's heart banging against her ribs. Her eyes snapped open in time to see Dan walk across the yard to the feed room; all equine eyes fixed on him.

'It's like that wherever he goes,' Emma thought to herself gloomily. 'Except usually it's all female eyes.'

He had finished feeding round by the time she went downstairs and was in the kitchen.

'Morning,' he said, smiling at her as she came through the door from the stairs, just like he'd done a hundred times. But this morning it had the effect of making Emma's face heat up, and immediately she felt jittery and self-conscious.

'Morning,' she replied, looking anywhere but at his face.

She went over to put the kettle on, just as she always did, except now she had lost all coordination and her hands were shaking. He was standing, leaning against the sink, eating a biscuit, and when she leant across to fill up the kettle, he didn't move, so she had to reach across behind him to turn on the tap.

Then, as the kettle was filling, he stretched an arm out round her, leaning across to grab another biscuit from the tin, brushing her arm as he did so.

She dropped the lid of the kettle into the sink with a noisy clatter.

'Sorry,' she said, her face getting hotter. Trying to turn the tap off, in her confusion, she turned it the wrong way, and the water suddenly gushed out soaking them both.

'Sorry!' she said again.

'I think you'd better sit down and let me make the tea this morning,' Dan said with a laugh, taking the kettle from her and handing her a towel. 'I don't feel safe standing here if you're going to be chucking boiling water about. Is something wrong?'

Emma shook her head, trying and failing to meet his eye, and instead watching his mouth as he smiled at her.

'Thanks for bringing my phone up last night,' she said, very carefully getting two mugs out of the cupboard.

'I took it up to the house with me, but then it rang, and I saw it was Edward trying to call you. I didn't answer it in case he wondered why a man was answering your phone at ten o'clock at night – although I was tempted.'

'I tried to call him back this morning, but he didn't answer,' she told him, trying to ignore the implication behind his words.

'Do you always sleep like that? With the light on, on top of your bed?' he asked. 'You looked like sleeping beauty, waiting for prince charming to kiss you and wake you up.'

'I was just hot,' she said hastily, her embarrassment deepening as she remembered what she had been wearing…or not wearing, more to the point.

He raised his eyebrows and nodded slowly in a way that made her have to concentrate very hard on pouring the boiling water into the mugs.

'Maybe you shouldn't leave your door open if you're going to wear so little at night.'

'Hmm, well I didn't know there would be wolves prowling around,' she replied.

He gave her a mischievous grin, but before he could say anything else Rachel walked in, which Emma thought was a very good thing. How had their conversation strayed onto such dangerous ground so quickly?

'You're early birds,' she said, in her usual cheerful manner.

Emma got another mug out and made her a coffee and the talk turned to the day ahead.

Just as they were leaving for the competition, Emma's phone rang. It was Edward. He sounded anxious, not at all like himself.

'Are you okay?' he asked her. 'I was trying all day yesterday to get hold of you.'

'Sorry,' said Emma, with a pang of guilt. 'I went up to see Granddad in hospital.'

'Oh good, how is he?'

'He seems fine, but he has to have more tests before they will let him go home.'

'Yes, he would have to. Where are you now?'

'I'm back at the yard…Dan drove me up there and back.' She faltered slightly over is name, aware that Dan and Caroline had already got into the lorry and were waiting for her.

'Dan?'

'Yes, you remember? My boss.'

'Oh yes…I remember. Look, I'm sorry about this morning.'

Emma was momentarily nonplussed. She glanced over to the lorry. Dan had started the engine and was looking at some paperwork, probably the timesheet, but Caroline was staring hard at Emma and drumming her fingers on the dashboard.

'This morning?' Emma questioned, walking towards the lorry.

'Yes. I was still asleep when you rang, I was working late last night,' he said in a rush. 'Frieda gave me the message, she's a friend of one of the guys I house share with.'

'Oh, right – listen, I need to go, the others are waiting for me, can we speak later?'

There was a pause.

'Okay, I'll call you later,' he replied, still sounding anxious, but Emma had no time to worry about that now. She said goodbye and rang off, jumping into the lorry.

'The doctor?' Dan asked.

'Yes,' Emma replied.

Caroline who had been looking decidedly po-faced at being kept waiting, looked a little more forgiving.

'Oh yes, how is your grandpa?' she asked.

'He's okay thank you,' Emma replied. 'That was Edward, my boyfriend,' she added, realising Caroline's misassumption.

Caroline looked confused.

'Emma's boyfriend's a doctor,' Dan explained.

'Oh,' said Caroline, sounding surprised and none the wiser.

'He's in Berlin,' Emma told her, hoping to enlighten her.

'In Germany? I thought he was in Suffolk?' Caroline asked even more befuddled.

'My granddad is in Suffolk – Edward's in Germany,' Emma explained.

'Then how is he taking care of your grandpa?' Caroline asked, her bewilderment was quite comical.

Dan started to laugh.

'He's not,' Emma replied, trying to suppress the urge to giggle.

'Then why would he be calling you to tell you how your Grandpa is?' Caroline said, starting to look cross.

'He wasn't, he was asking me how he was.'

'You English people are weird, surely he should be telling you, if he's the doctor!'

Dan laughed even harder and Emma had to turn and look out of the window, her shoulders shaking with the effort of trying not to.

'I don't see what's so funny,' Caroline said haughtily.

'Look, Emma's boyfriend's a doctor in Germany, and Emma's Grandad's in hospital in Suffolk, the two things are entirely unconnected,' Dan explained.

But poor Caroline was clearly feeling very put out.

The familiarity of the day's work helped Emma to feel more normal, and by the time they got home that evening, she had her nerves back under control. Everyone else had already gone. Caroline left them to unpack the lorry. Dan went to unlock the tack room door carrying an armful of dirty tack, whilst Emma was carrying another load behind him.

As he opened the door and went into the darkened room, he nearly fell over something just inside.

'What the fuck…?' he swore.

'What is it?' Emma asked.

'Some idiot's left a small florist in here,' he said turning on the lights.

Sure enough, just inside the door there was an enormous bouquet of flowers.

A mass of dark red roses, deep purple hyacinths, and green foliage.

'Who are they for?' Emma asked.

Dan picked out the heart-shaped card that was stuck in the top.

'You,' he said, handing it to her. 'From the Doctor.'

'Oh!' Emma said in surprise.

'Guilty conscience?' Dan suggested.

Emma put the tack down that she was carrying and picked up the flowers. She carried them into the kitchen. They were so huge she could hardly see around them. It was a little embarrassing. There wasn't a vase anywhere, so she put them, rather incongruously, in a bucket on the table.

'Beautiful,' Dan remarked, smirking.

'What the hell am I going to do with them? I can't take them upstairs; they'll take up half my room.'

'They won't fit through the door for a start,' said Dan.

'They'll have to stay there then. I'll give them to Cathy in the morning.'

The phone rang. Dan, who was closest, picked it up.

'Hello, Interflora,' he said into the phone.

Pretty sure it would be Edward, Emma tried to take the phone from him. He gave it to her after a small scuffle, still smirking.

'Hi,' she said quickly.

'Emma?' Edward's voice came down the line. 'Who was that?'

'Just Dan being an idiot,' she said, sticking her tongue out at him. He grinned and left the kitchen. 'Thank you so much for the flowers!' she said. 'They're beautiful.'

'Oh good, you got them.'

'They're lovely, I just wondered…what are they for?' Emma asked.

Edward sighed.

'This last year has been hard.... on both of us,' he said. 'Spending so much time away from each other. I want us to get back on track. Get back to where we are supposed to be, because I'm worried that if we keep going the way we are, things might fall apart.'

Emma was silent for a moment. What he was saying was true. Things had changed, her feelings had changed. And if they didn't do something about it, she wasn't sure they would ever be able to get back to the way things were. Tears sprang into Emma's eyes. It was uncanny, almost as if he knew…

'Emma? Are you still there?' He sounded a little desperate.

'I'm here,' she said.

'Do you understand what I'm saying? We need to remember what's real, what's important. Not let things come between us.'

'I understand Ed,' she said shakily. 'I'm not going to deny that things have been difficult, I have been feeling… confused. But I will try to think about what's important.'

She heard him breathe a sigh of relief.

'I need you to know, it's you I'm thinking of, okay? Promise me you'll hang in there and stay strong.'

'I will. I'll try.'

'I promise you that things will be fine, I'll make things better. Trust me?'

'Okay, I believe you. I trust you.' She wiped a tear from her eye.

'Good. Alright, speak to you on Thursday.'

They said goodbye and Emma hung up. She sat down at the table, leaning her elbows on the table, her head in her hands. She had never felt more confused in all her life. Oh God! What a mess.

There was a noise in the tack room next door, and she realised Dan was in there putting things away. He'd probably overheard some of their conversation.

What Edward said was true. She needed to make the utmost effort to pull herself back from the brink of something crazy. She had been allowing herself to stray down a very dangerous path and if she didn't stop, who knew where she was going to end up.

Chapter 33

The rain hammered on her window. She lay without moving in the early morning gloom, knowing in a minute she would have to get up and face the day. It was the last of everything: Merlin's last chance to come right, or he would be sold, Dan's last chance to save him – and her last event. The last event she would ever groom for him.

She had made the decision last night, as she had tossed and turned on her narrow bed. How many girls had fallen for him over the years? She was just one of a hundred other girls who had become infatuated and had their hearts broken. As Simone had said – she was nothing special; she was a cliché.

She would do this one last event today, be there to support Dan and Merlin, then she would tell Malcolm she was leaving.

Forcing herself to get up and get going, she made her way downstairs and donned her wet weather gear. This was just what they didn't need; Merlin hated getting wet.

What a day it was. The weather changed from bad to worse, the wind got up and the rain got heavier. Dan and Emma worked together in grim determination whilst Caroline sheltered in the lorry.

Everywhere Emma looked, horses zigzagged through the horizontal deluge, refusing to stay straight, spooking and shying at the gusts of wind.

'Go out there and show them all how it's done, eh?' Andrews boomed, turning up just before Dan went in to do his test. 'Just a bit blowy, nothing to be frightened of.'

'Oh, please leave him alone,' Emma pleaded under her breath, the last thing Dan needed was more pressure. Merlin swung his quarters into the wind, forcing Andrews to jump back out of the way. He slipped on the wet ground and swore.

'I'll do what I can,' Dan said, touching his leg onto Merlin to send him forward.

'You'll do more than that,' Andrews spluttered, his dignity injured, 'you'll get a bloody result!'

All things considered, Merlin's test wasn't too bad. He hated the rain and the wind, which made it very difficult to keep him straight and in a rhythm, but then, most riders were having the same problem, and he didn't buck, and he didn't take off, which was better than they could have hoped for. Andrews didn't stand with them to watch, but stood in the entrance to the owner's tent, drink in hand.

'So far so good,' Emma said as she walked back next to Merlin after his test.

'Must be down to all that extra schooling you've been giving him,' he said, smiling down at her. 'We're a good team Bugs.'

Her heart twisted. She wished he wouldn't say things like that. 'Don't go thinking you're special,' she told herself sternly. Simone's words rang like a warning bell in her head.

Caroline went off, ostensibly to look at the scores, but probably to get a hot drink in the dry. Emma put Merlin back on the lorry out of the rain. They had a little time before he had to jump, so Dan helped her untack him and dry him off as best they could before they rugged him up warmly.

She and Dan stepped around each other, the confined space making it inevitable that they should be close. Emma was acutely aware of the nearness of him, and also, that this was probably the last time they would be alone together. She knew she ought to tell him that she was leaving while she had the chance, but told herself it would be better to wait until he had finished riding. But really, it was because she couldn't bring herself to break this feeling of closeness – not just yet.

She was quiet, her mind on all the things she wanted to say but couldn't. He was quiet, his mind on…who knew what. Whenever they worked together, they fell into a natural rhythm and barely needed to speak; he wanted a dry towel, she was already passing it to him, she reached underneath Merlin's belly for the cross-surcingles, he met her halfway, handing them to her.

Now, he came around to her side to help her get down an extra rug from the overhead rack. As he reached up, he leaned into her, his chest touching her shoulders. Oh! It was too much. She couldn't deal with her body's reaction. With a sharp intake of breath, she leant as far away from him as possible, pressing herself into Merlin's bulk to escape from him and from her feelings.

He looked down at her with a frown. 'Sorry,' he said, moving away quickly.

She battled with her emotions until Caroline came back and the opportunity to talk to him had gone.

'The event organisers are on the brink of cancelling – there have been loads of withdrawals,' Caroline said, opening the door from the cabin. 'I can't believe you're still going to jump in this.'

All the while they had been taking care of Merlin the weather had been worsening with alarming speed. The wind battered against the sides of the lorry, making it rock like a boat on an angry ocean.

'I don't have a choice,' Dan said.

There was a sudden loud banging on the side of the lorry. 'Anyone in there?' It was Bret Andrews. Dan swore and jumped out to speak to him.

'Not going to chicken out are you?' she heard Andrews say in his foghorn voice. 'With all these withdrawals you might actually win for a change.'

She couldn't hear Dan's reply, it was too low, but Andrews' answer came back even louder and more forceful. 'Now look here, I can promise you – if you don't go out there and get a result, I will be at the yard to collect him tomorrow, and he will be at auction on Tuesday, understand?'

When Andrews had gone, they sat in the cab, three abreast (Caroline in the middle), staring out into the rain; the mood as sombre as the weather.

'This rain!' Caroline exclaimed in disgust, never one to appreciate silent contemplation. 'And this is your summer! Next week, we should take a few days off and go somewhere for some sun – don't you think Danny?'

'Next week we're at Barbury, for the two-star,' Dan murmured.

'The following week then, or next month?' Caroline was nothing if not persistent.

'I can't leave the horses in the middle of the season.'

'Just a few days, they'll be alright. Emma can keep them ticking over,' she turned to Emma, 'can't you Emma?'

Why was it that every decision she tried to make for the best, came back to bite her in the arse? What could she say? She had no choice but to tell them. 'I…I can't actually. I'm not going to be here.'

Dan snapped his neck around to look at her. 'What?'

She winced at his expression. 'I'm leaving – after today.'

'When did you decide this?'

'Last night.'

'After speaking to Edward?'

'Yes.'

'He's found a flat for you?'

'No…b-but…' Emma stammered.

'That's very inconsiderate of you Emma,' Caroline piped up, 'to leave us in the lurch like this! Especially as Danny's been so kind to you, driving you all the way up to visit with your grandpa…'

'Then why?' Dan cut across her.

'I'm sorry,' Emma couldn't bear that he might think her ungrateful. How could she possibly explain? She could hardly tell him the truth; that every second around him her heart was slowly bleeding to death, she needed to get away from him so she could heal. 'I…I just need to get my priorities right.'

This seemed to make things worse. 'Your priorities?' He recoiled as if she'd slapped him. 'And when were you planning on telling me this?'

'Today, after you'd ridden.'

Dan stared at her and the look on his face made her want to cry.

Caroline huffed and shook her head. 'Well, no matter. Simone will have to groom for us, and we'll just find someone else to help Rachel on the yard. It's not the end of the world.'

Emma couldn't sit there any longer, she was in danger of breaking down. 'I'll get Merlin ready,' she mumbled and escaped out of the cab. Now she was glad of the rain. She turned her face into the wind to wash away the tears that were stinging her cheeks.

Dan didn't come to help her with Merlin. She got the horse completely ready; stirrups down, girth tight, so all Dan had to do was jump on and get going. She threw a rug over the top of his tack and stayed with him, talking to him, soothing him, putting her cold hands under his rug for warmth.

She could hear Caroline talking to Dan in the cabin whilst he was changing and hoped she would be calming him in the same way. His state of mind was crucial to the way he rode.

Eventually, she heard the door closing and the ramp being lowered. Untying Merlin she led him down, risking a glance at Dan. His face was stony and he wouldn't look at her. He just folded back Merlin's rug and mounted without a word. She wanted to tell him to take it slowly and just get around in one piece.

But it was Caroline who voiced what she was thinking. 'Please be careful!' she said.

'I can't afford to be careful, I have to win,' he answered, touching his heels into Merlin's sides. The flat tone of his voice and the steely look in his eyes chilled Emma to the bone.

'Good luck,' Emma called after him – but the wind whipped the words away from her lips, so she couldn't be sure he'd heard her.

The arena was a quagmire, the take-offs and landings treacherous. One fence had been removed from the course because it had blown over twice.

In the warm-up, Merlin wasn't fighting Dan too much, and cleared all the practice fences, giving Emma a glimmer of hope. At home, when she had been schooling him, Emma had concentrated on slowing him down; riding circles between the fences and making him jump from a trot. Emma prayed that he would remember, and so far, he was jumping well.

But it was the look on Dan's face which was scaring her. He had a fixed, almost kamikaze look in his eyes, and was riding with a kind of reckless abandon, as if he had nothing to lose.

The bell rang for his round to begin. Standing at the entrance to the ring with Caroline, she cheered inwardly as he cleared the first four fences, but he was picking up speed. The fifth had been removed due to the wind blowing it over, then there was a big oxer followed by a double on a one-stride distance. He would really need to check his speed for that one.

As he approached the oxer, Merlin's ears were pricked, locked on to the fence. There was no doubt that he was trying for Dan, and Emma could have cried with pride and love for them both. But just as he was four strides out, an advertising banner broke free from its mooring on the arena fence and blew straight in front of him, making him skid very nearly to a halt.

Caroline shrieked and clutched Emma's arm. By some miraculous feat of superhuman strength, Dan held Merlin onto his line, jumping the fence almost from a standstill. Even so, he cleared it with inches to spare, but it was only with a massive gymnastic effort in the air that Dan stayed with him.

Unsettled, Merlin bucked after the fence, surging forward into a gallop. The reins were slippery, and Dan fought to hold him. They were going much too fast.

'Oh, circle him, circle him!' Emma cried; it would cost them faults, but who cared? He just needed to get around safely. It was clear however that Dan was in no mood to play it safe. He kept going. Straight for the double. She couldn't watch – neither could she bear to look away.

Merlin took off in front of the first fence, inevitably landing much too close to the second to get a stride in. He saw the second fence and his black ears met in surprise. Going at that speed, Dan did the only thing he could do; he kept his leg on and gave the horse his head.

Merlin, instead of jamming on his breaks and refusing, took off from the spot where he'd landed, attempting to jump the second fence as a bounce. It was the bravest, most magnificent jump.

'He's going to make it!' Caroline shouted – and he very nearly did.

But no horse could have made that jump. He came down on the back rail, bringing the fence crashing down. There was a terrifying crack, as one of the poles splintered. Merlin kicked out, trying to free his back legs from the mess of poles and wings, but his front legs couldn't find purchase on the slippery ground. He took a nosedive straight into the mud, his momentum carrying him forward in a complete somersault.

Merlin thrashed around, trying to right himself, Dan somewhere underneath him. 'No!' Emma shouted, and Caroline screamed.

Ducking under the arena fence, Emma started to run towards where Merlin had finally found his feet. He instinctively turned towards the exit, galloping straight towards them. Caroline, close behind her, screamed again.

'Shut up!' Emma yelled at her, fear making her forget all sense of decorum. 'We have to catch him.'

Stepping into the path of the galloping horse, she put out her arms to check his speed.

'Whoa Merlin, whoa the horse,' she called, trying to sound calmer than she felt. Merlin heard her and recognised her, he slowed a little, nearly skidding into her but she dodged, and managed to catch his dangling reins as they flew past her face.

'Steady the horse,' she soothed him, his nostrils were blood red pits in his black, rain slicked face as they drew in the air. His eyes were wild and showing a lot of white, his ears flicked crazily back and forth. Blood poured from a cut on his hind leg, just below his stifle.

Caroline ran past her to where a couple of stewards crouched on the ground at the spot where Merlin had fallen. Emma followed, getting as close as she could, dragging the reluctant Merlin, who pulled back to the length of his reins.

Over the steward's shoulder, she saw Dan lying motionless on the ground, his face white beneath his hat, caked with black mud. There was blood mixed with the mud. A lot of blood. Her own blood drained from her face and her legs threatened to buckle.

'Is he alright?' she said but no one was listening to her. She needed to know that Dan was okay – that he was breathing. *She couldn't see if he was breathing.* Panic seized her by the throat. She couldn't hear what the stewards were saying over the shrieking of the wind. She stood by helplessly, trying to steady Merlin who was fretting at the end of his reins.

The paramedics arrived, bringing with them a stretcher. Now there were too many people around Dan to even see him. When they parted, Emma could see he had been lifted onto the stretcher on a back brace, a thick pad of wadding partially covering his face. They carried him towards the waiting ambulance.

One of the medics turned towards them. 'Who's with him?' she asked.

'Me!' Caroline cried, going forward, wringing her hands.

'Good, you can come with us.' The medic put an arm around Caroline's shoulders, guiding her gently in the wake of the stretcher.

Emma was left standing on her own in the rain, watching them go.

'Are you the groom?' Someone was speaking to her; a hand touched her arm. It was one of the stewards. She nodded dumbly. 'You ought to get the vet to look at your horse, he's injured,' the steward was saying.

Emma shook herself and turned her attention to Merlin. She walked him a few steps. Although his leg was still bleeding, he didn't appear to be lame.

On the way back to the lorry, people kept stopping her to ask if Dan was all right, but what could she tell them; she didn't know. And who was going to tell her? She was only the groom. She wanted to be alone so she could cry in peace.

Finally reaching the box she examined the wound on Merlin's leg, terrifying thoughts crowding her mind. Riders died from falls like this; brain injury, broken necks, smashed spinal cords. It wasn't that uncommon.

'So, that wasn't exactly a resounding success,' a voice boomed. With a start she looked up. Andrews loomed above her. She stood up, but still her eyes were only level with his chest.

'It was an accident, it could have happened to anyone,' she said.

'I said it was his last chance – and I'm a man of my word,' Andrews replied with a pompous jut of his chin.

Emma was incredulous. 'Don't you even care if Dan's okay? Or your horse for that matter?'

'It's the nature of the game, everyone knows the risks.'

There was obviously no point in expecting any understanding from him. Emma turned her back on him in disgust.

'I'll be at Malcolm's tomorrow morning to collect the horse.'

She spun round to face him again.

'You can't,' she protested, 'not with Dan in hospital, it's not fair!'

'Don't tell me what I can and can't do girly,' Andrews drew himself up even taller. 'It's my horse, I'll do what I damn well like.'

In anguish Emma gestured at Merlin's torn leg. 'But he's injured, he'll never sell with an injury like that,' she said, trying to buy Merlin some time, but her words spectacularly backfired.

'How bad is it?' Andrews peered at the leg without stooping for a closer look, wary of Merlin's back end. 'I'm not being saddled with weeks and weeks of vet's bills on top of the bloody fortune that Malcolm charges me. I'll send him straight to the knacker's yard, worthless beast.'

The knackers yard. He was going to have Merlin killed. She couldn't let that happen. In a moment of sheer desperation, she heard herself say, 'I'll buy him from you.'

Andrews snorted. 'Will you now?' he said. He narrowed his eyes and the tip of his tongue flicked between is lips. She could see him calculating how much he could salvage from this situation. 'Okay, five grand, and you can have him,' he said, putting his hands in his pockets and rocking back on his heels.

She didn't have five grand, no-where near it. 'I'll give you three.'

'I'll take four, and that's my final offer.'

'You just said he was worthless!'

Andrews' lip curled in a leery smirk – he really was the most repulsive man. 'Obviously not to you,' he said.

She would need all her savings, and more besides. This was crazy, but she couldn't stop herself. 'Okay, I'll try and get it by the end of the week.'

Andrews shook his head. 'No. Tomorrow morning. I want it in cash – I don't have time to mess about.' He turned on his heel and walked away as he said, 'I'll be there tomorrow morning – have the money, or I'll take the horse.'

Chapter 34

THE NEXT FEW HOURS WERE GRUELLING; SO MUCH TO DO AND organise, trying to think straight when her brain was clouded by a fog of fear and misery. She called Malcolm first and told him what had happened. He told her he would find out which hospital Dan had been taken to and go straight there himself.

She had the course vet look at Merlin, and one blessed relief was that the cut on his leg wasn't too serious; not much more than a deep scratch. The rain must have made it look like there was more blood than there really was. She prayed the same was true for the blood on Dan's face.

Cathy dropped Rachel off to drive the lorry back to the yard, Emma feeling useless because she couldn't drive herself. Then the arduous journey home; trying to hold herself together while she told Rachel all that had happened, and not bawl her eyes out, when she was sick with worry about Dan.

What if he was so badly injured he was in hospital for weeks? What if he was so badly injured he couldn't ride ever again? Or worse. She couldn't bring herself to even think about that possibility.

They arrived home just after six, and she had to go through the whole story again for Kitty and Simone.

At last she was alone and spent the evening in Merlin's stable, re-dressing the wound on his leg and making sure he was comfortable, but really because she wanted to be close to him. He was the nearest thing she had to a connection with Dan.

By eight o'clock she still hadn't heard anything. She paced around the kitchen constantly checking her phone had a signal, her anxiety increasing with every minute that passed. She tried to ring Malcolm but got no answer. Eventually, worn out, she collapsed on the old sofa.

'Emma love, wake-up, you should go to bed.' It was Malcolm.

'Have you seen him? Is he okay?' Emma asked, rubbing her eyes, gritty with sleep.

'Yes, he's okay. Concussion, a dislocated shoulder, and he's not quite as pretty as he usually is,' Malcolm chuckled, 'but nothing broken. The doctor said he was very lucky – he must have strong bones.'

Emma burst into tears. It was all too much; the worry and the relief. Malcolm took her arm and sat her down at the kitchen table. He handed her a clean handkerchief from his pocket and sat with her, waiting until her first burst of emotion had exhausted itself.

'Is he coming home?' she asked when she could speak again.

'He's got to have some minor surgery on his shoulder, but he should be able to come home in the next couple of days I think.'

'Oh.' She was overcome by a fresh bout of sobbing. Malcolm watched her with concern.

'Emma, are you okay?' he asked after a minute.

'I'm fine,' Emma managed a smile and blew her nose. 'It's just been the worry and…' she took a few deep breaths and scrubbed at her face with the handkerchief. 'It was mostly my fault – the accident.'

Malcolm drew his brows together. 'Of course it wasn't.'

'It was…. you see, I told him that I was leaving just before he had to ride. He and Caroline were really angry that I'm leaving them in the lurch, and you know what he's like when he's angry.'

'Emma, no. You mustn't blame yourself for that – but, you say you're leaving?'

Emma nodded. 'I have to I'm afraid,' she blinked to ward off fresh tears. She told him about Edward, and that she had to join him in Berlin as soon as she could. 'I shouldn't have come back really, I was being foolish…' she only just stopped herself from admitting too much.

Malcolm's expression was troubled. 'I'm sorry you're so unhappy, of course you must go whenever you want, you mustn't feel guilty.'

She thanked him. 'But it's not just that…it's Merlin.' And she told him how Bret Andrews wanted to take him, and that she'd offered him money that she didn't have, to save him from being shot.

When she had finished Malcolm shook his head and smiled. 'You have got yourself in a pickle haven't you?' Emma nodded. 'Well, I can help you there at least – I'll make Andrews an offer for Merlin, then we'll see if he comes right. I can always sell him again…'

'No, you see, that's just it – I want to do this. I've got most of the money, just not quite enough. I want to give Dan the opportunity to buy him from me. Because then I know Merlin will be safe.'

Malcolm frowned. 'But what if Dan doesn't want to buy him?' he asked.

'I know he will,' Emma insisted. 'He thinks he has as much potential as I do, he could be something really special – he just needs someone to believe in him.'

He gave her a sad smile. 'You really care about him, don't you?'

For a second, Emma didn't know if he meant Merlin – or Dan. She nodded, her chin trembling.

Malcolm sighed. 'Well, if you've made up your mind to do it, then I'll help you sort out the money side of it.'

Emma was so grateful and relieved, she thanked him over and over again. He told her to go to bed, and that he would drive her to the bank in the morning.

*

She had more money in her account than she thought, and Malcolm only had to subsidise her a little. He offered to pay more but she wouldn't take it – she wanted to make sure that Dan would have the opportunity to own the largest share of the horse.

Malcolm kindly said he'd deal with Andrews, who came mid-morning, signed the change of ownership form and took the cash without even bothering to ask after Merlin, or Dan.

She and Malcolm had agreed that – for the time being at least – they would keep her ownership of Merlin a secret. There was an unspoken understanding between them that it might not be a good idea for "certain people" to know, for which Emma was extremely grateful.

Caroline hadn't forgiven Emma for shouting at her the day

before, and was absolutely furious that they were keeping Merlin. 'After he nearly killed Danny!' she cried when she found out. 'You'll have to ride Merlin seeing as he's such a pet of yours,' she said to Emma. 'The least you can do is to stay now until Danny is better.'

So Emma agreed to stay and help ride all the horses until Dan was fit again. Caroline went to the hospital and stayed there all day; the devoted girlfriend. Malcolm found out that Dan was out of surgery but would probably be kept in another night.

That evening, Emma took Merlin's passport and went to sit in his stable to look through it. She thought she would send it off to have her name put on it as his new owner, even if it was just for a short time. She never thought she would own a horse – and certainly not in these circumstances. What would Edward say if he knew that she'd blown all her savings on a horse? He would say she was wild and reckless – and perhaps she was.

Getting a spare rug off the wall, she wrapped it tightly around herself and watched Merlin eat his hay. Her horse. She liked the sound of that. Why was possession so important? To be able to say that something was yours? She didn't know why, but it just was. And hugging the passport to her chest, she snuggled down underneath the blanket.

She was having the most lovely dream. She could hear Dan's voice saying her name – *Emma.* She could almost feel the warmth of his hand on her arm; could smell his scent in the air. She smiled in her sleep.

Emma. 'Emma, you're going to have to wake up. You should go to bed, and I can't carry you with one arm.'

Prickly straw underneath her face; damp night air in her lungs; course blanket wrapped around her. Where was she? 'Dan….?'

'You probably shouldn't stay in here, you might get savaged in your sleep.'

It wasn't a dream, he was right there, close beside her. 'Where… what are you doing here?'

'I couldn't stay another night in that hospital, so I signed myself out. I came to check on Merlin.'

She scrambled to try to stand, but before she could, he'd slid down next to her, wincing with pain. His right arm was in a sling and the bruise on his left eye was vivid, the gash above his eyebrow stitched.

'Stay here a minute,' he said.

She wasn't ready for this, seeing him so unexpectedly. She needed time to prepare herself – shore up her defences. The way she felt now, she was entirely vulnerable, and she must look a state. Her hair was full of straw, she hadn't had a shower and the day's make-up was probably half-way down her face. She was glad the stable light was dim.

'H-how's your shoulder?' she stammered.

But he'd picked up something that had fallen into the straw. 'What's this?'

'Merlin's passport. Did Malcolm tell you – we're keeping him?'

'Yeah.' She smiled at how pleased he sounded. 'I was pretty out of it yesterday when I saw him, I wasn't sure I'd heard him right. I never thought Malcolm would buy Merlin – too much of a gamble. And he's okay?'

'He's stiff, but not too bad. What about you? Is your shoulder painful?' she asked.

He gave a tiny shrug and winced again. He was sitting so close to her that she could feel the heat from his body. Every part of her wanted to lean closer to him, wanted to so badly it was like a hunger, deep in her bones. She started to shake a little.

'Is it true you're staying until I'm fit to ride?' he asked.

'Yes, I promised Caroline I would. She said it was the least I could do considering…' she tailed off, but he sighed and shook his head.

'I'm glad I found you in here because I wanted to talk to you alone,' he said.

Her trembling became more violent. 'You're shivering,' he said and made a small movement of his left arm, as if he was going to put it around her…Oh God!

'Daniel! What are you two doing here?' Without warning, Malcolm appeared at the door, he sounded almost angry. Startled, Emma jumped to her feet. 'Dan, you shouldn't be down here, Caroline's looking for you. And Emma, you should be in bed.'

'I'm just going,' Emma said, going to the door.

Dan got to his feet more slowly, grimacing with pain.

'Come up to the house Dan,' Malcolm said. 'I want a word.'

Turning Merlin's light off, Emma went up the stairs alone. Going into the bathroom she caught sight of her face in the mirror. It was pale and grubby, and her hair looked like it hadn't seen a brush in weeks. She pulled a piece of straw out of it and washed her face, staring at her reflection.

It was no good. She was trying to do the right thing, but she was falling at every hurdle. If this was some kind of test, then she was bound to fail. Because, if Malcolm hadn't come along when he did, and if Dan had put his arm around her, there was no way she would have stopped him.

*

Desperate to find out what Dan had been going to say to her if Malcolm hadn't come along when he did, she waited impatiently for the next opportunity to speak to him alone. But, aside from a staff meeting with Malcolm and Rachel to discuss the plan going forwards, he wasn't on the yard at all the next day. Or the next. It always seemed like he had somewhere else to be, and when he was around, Caroline was always with him.

Days passed without them having a single conversation, it was as if when she walked into a room, he walked out. Almost as though he were avoiding her.

But then, when she and Kitty returned from a hack one afternoon, Rachel took Beau from her as she dismounted. 'I'll take care of him,' she said, 'the boss wants a word with you, he's waiting for you in the staff room.'

Her pulse and her thoughts immediately took off, galloping uncontrollably on a wild flight of imagination – what was he going to say?

She stopped short in the doorway to the staff room. It was Malcolm who was sitting at the table. Not Dan.

He got up when he saw her. 'Ah, Emma good. I want to talk to you. Come and sit down.' She went forward and sat down at the table obediently, folding her hands in her lap.

'So,' he began, 'I haven't forgotten about our conversation the other night. I know you agreed with Caroline to stay until Dan is fit again – and that was very good of you – but I've found someone to replace you! They can start whenever we need them to, so you're free to go off to Berlin to join your boyfriend with a clear conscience whenever you like. You don't have to give any notice.' He smiled benevolently at her.

'Oh! Malcolm…thank you…and I really appreciate that, but…' she began, but he held his hand up to stop her.

'It's okay,' he said. 'I had a word with Dan – I told him he had no right to pressure you – no right at all!'

She felt suddenly desperate. 'B-but there's Merlin…I'd like to stay until Dan can ride him again…'

Malcolm opened his hands. 'Whatever you like,' he said.

So that was it. She was to be replaced. Easily, apparently, because she was nothing special – she was just a cliché. One small comfort was that Dan had no idea what her feelings were, so at least he couldn't pity her. He would carry on with his life as if she didn't exist and she would stumble around looking for the pieces of her broken heart.

He seemed oblivious in fact. And why shouldn't he be? He was totally focused on getting fit again. There were some owners of a horse-wear company who were interested in sponsoring him due to his recent success at the higher levels. They had several meetings with a Mr Davies; an elderly gentleman with white hair, and his son. They were keen to watch Dan compete at a few events before offering him a deal, so he was determined to be fit again for Hartpury International; the next big three-day. Emma had no doubt he would do it and when that time came, she would no longer have any excuse to stay.

Simone had done an excellent job of ingratiating herself with Caroline, who confided in her – and she in turn told Rachel, who told Emma – that Caroline wanted to take Dan back home to meet her folks after the season.

'Simone says that Caroline wants to take him to meet "Ma and Pa" before they officially get engaged.' Rachel told her when they were hacking out together one day.

Emma didn't respond to this gossip. She just felt cold and numb. So often at the moment she had a pain, like a cold leaden weight in her chest, that she wondered if she had something physically wrong with her heart like Granddad, who was, thankfully, out of hospital, and back in his own home.

So she was glad to be busy, keeping all the horses fit, schooling and jumping Angel and Beau, riding a few of the up and coming youngsters. As soon as Merlin was sound, she took some pleasure in riding him because now he was "her horse". She was in no hurry to get her money back.

She rode all day, every day until she was so exhausted, she could only fall into bed and sleep. On her rare days off, she took long runs through the fields, going to visit Penny, who was now turned out with the other three-year-olds. The weather was beautiful, and she would lie in the grass in Penny's field and go to sleep.

Two weeks before Hartpury, Dan was back in the saddle, riding out on a few of the quieter horses. Every day he got stronger and fitter, and each one brought them closer to the day when Emma would no longer have any excuse to stay.

She was aware of the days rolling past, like stations on a railway line, heading towards a dreaded destination. As each one passed, she got closer and closer, helpless to stop the relentless forward motion – until she had run out of track.

Chapter 35

HARTPURY WAS A HUGE SUCCESS. DESPITE HAVING ONLY BEEN able to ride for a fortnight before the competition, Dan rode at the top of his game and both Angel and Beau were placed in the first ten.

There was a party after the event. Everyone was invited; riders, owners, sponsors, grooms and hangers on. Emma was in no mood to party and had no intention of going, especially as she knew Dan and Caroline would be there.

Sarah and Toby, her fellow grooms, had different ideas however.

'You've got to come!' cried Toby. 'It'll be a giggle and think of all the free booze!'

'I've brought nothing to wear,' protested Emma.

'I've got a dress you can borrow,' Sarah piped up. 'I brought two because I couldn't choose.'

They wouldn't take no for an answer and eventually Emma agreed to come.

She managed to wriggle into Sarah's dress, which was shorter, tighter and more revealing than she would have chosen, but very flattering and a beautiful deep blue colour, which matched her eyes. At least her legs were brown from sunbathing in Penny's field. She didn't have any heels, but she had brought her ballerina pumps luckily, so they would have to do.

It was a lovely warm evening. They walked arm in arm from the lorry park, and down the lane, the short distance to where the party was being held.

Sarah was very keen on one of the young male riders; a guy

named Tom, who she knew was going to be at the party, so she was excited.

When they got there, the place was packed, the music loud, and the atmosphere was already heating up.

As soon as they walked in, Emma clocked Dan and Caroline over by the bar, surrounded by other competitors and their partners. They were part of the elite group of demi-gods that everyone wished they could belong to, but that only the privileged few ever got to be part of.

'Ooh! There's your boss,' said Toby, gazing at them with longing. 'He's looking particularly delicious tonight.'

Emma had to agree. Everyone was dressed up, and there was no shortage of good-looking men in the room, but he had that quality, so hard to define, which turned heads wherever he went and made all the women – and some of the men – light up when he was around.

'God, he is lush!' said Sarah, who had a strong West Country accent.

'That Caroline is ravishing though,' Toby added, sighing. 'Lucky girl.'

'Let's get something to drink,' Emma said hastily, taking Toby's hand and dragging him away.

Sarah was already heading over to a table where there were buckets of ice filled with bottles of Prosecco. They helped themselves to a glass each.

Although it was still early-ish, some people were up and dancing, a sure sign that there was plenty of free alcohol. Sarah was rubbernecking, trying to spot the guy she fancied. Once she did, they all had to go and stand nearer to where he was, with his group of friends.

Toby grabbed a full bottle of Prosecco and brought it with them.

Emma kept finding her eyes drawn over to the bar area. Caroline, wearing a halter-neck, backless, emerald-green silk dress, was pressing herself up against Dan, the fingers of her right hand interlinked with his.

Emma took a large gulp of her wine. She decided jealousy was the most disgusting of emotions. It was quite sickening.

'Loads of talent in here tonight,' Toby said, looking around excitedly. 'It's a shame you've got that boyfriend Ems, I'm glad I'm single.'

'Ooh! I just got a terrific eye-meet from Tom,' Sarah suddenly squealed.

Now Caroline had her hands locked around Dan's waist; he was talking over her head to someone else, but his brown hand was on the very white, very perfect skin of her back.

Sarah followed Emma's gaze.

'I can't stand that can you?' she asked. 'When a girl has to have her hands all over her boyfriend all the time, to show everyone that he's her property? It's like, okay, we get it, he's yours, now could you just put him down for five minutes?'

Emma took another slug of her wine, only to find that she'd finished it.

'Give me another one of those would you?' she said, holding her glass out to Toby for a refill.

Sarah was looking at her with a hint of understanding in her eyes.

'I heard he was a bit of a player before her ladyship came along,' she said with a touch of sympathy. 'I used to work for someone like him; all the girl grooms fell for him, me included. The trouble is with the bad boys, you know you shouldn't but you can't help yourself because they're so goddam irresistible.'

A black hole of misery opened up at Emma's feet and swallowed her whole. She drained her glass of fizz again and held it out for another refill.

'Whoa girl, you hittin' it hard!' exclaimed Toby.

'I need to get very, very drunk,' Emma said grimly.

'Okey dokey,' Toby said, with a look of mock horror, and filled her glass to the brim.

Emma forced herself to turn her back on the group over by the bar.

'Have you seen Rory's new groom?' Toby asked her.

'No, I don't think so,' Emma replied, grateful for the distraction.

'He's hot,' stated Toby. 'And gay, if I'm not very much mistaken.'

'Can you always tell?' Emma asked.

'Not always,' admitted Toby. 'Sometimes they don't even know themselves,' he smirked. 'Sometimes you just have to suck it and see, if you'll pardon the expression.'

Emma giggled, the alcohol was beginning to take effect and she was starting to feel better.

'Come to the loo with me,' Sarah said, taking Emma's hand.

Emma allowed herself to be led across the room, past the bar towards the loos.

She glanced at Dan as she was towed past him. He was still talking to someone but raised one eyebrow at her with a questioning look. She gave him a small smile.

When they came back from the toilets, Sarah headed straight for the bar.

'I need some brave juice so I can talk to Tom,' she said. 'Let's do some shots.'

She beckoned to Toby to join them.

'Jaeger bombs?' he suggested.

'Yes let's!' enthused Sarah.

Emma wasn't so sure. The last time she had done Jaeger bombs she'd had complete memory loss the following day. But Sarah was already ordering them.

'I thought you weren't coming,' said a deep voice at her shoulder. It was Dan. She jumped almost guiltily. He was on his own; Caroline was talking to one of the American riders.

'I wasn't, but Sarah and Toby persuaded me,' she told him.

His eyes travelled down to the, rather too short, hem of her dress. 'Nice dress,' he said, unsmiling.

She squirmed uncomfortably and tugged the skirt down as far as it would go.

'It's Sarah's.'

The barman was lining up three glasses on the bar, half-filled with red bull, and dropped the shot glasses with Jaeger Meister into them.

Sarah picked up hers and handed one each to Emma and Toby.

'Cheers!' Sarah said brightly, throwing her head back and pouring the liquid down her throat.

'Cheers,' Emma said, pulling a face and knocking it back.

Before Emma had even put her glass back on the bar, Toby had taken a twenty out of his wallet and was ordering three more.

Dan raised his eyebrows.

'Looks like you're going to have a fun night,' he said.

'Either that, or need to get my stomach pumped,' Emma said with a weak laugh.

Caroline had finished talking to her American rider and was coming over. As soon as she joined them, she took Dan's arm.

'Hi Emma,' she said ignoring Sarah and Toby, who were giggling like a couple of schoolkids over something or other. 'That's a nice dress,' she said, although the look on her face told Emma that she wouldn't have been seen dead in it.

Before Emma had a chance to reply, she had turned back to Dan.

'Can you get me a sparkling water?' she asked him.

He nodded, gesturing to the barman who had finished serving Toby. He ordered a beer for himself, and a San Pellegrino for Caroline.

'Do you want anything?' he asked Emma, but she shook her head.

'I'm fine thank you.'

Toby was handing her another Jaeger bomb and Caroline was eyeing the amber drinks suspiciously, a look of subtle disgust on her face as she took her own sparkling water from Dan.

'Are you coming back over with me darling?' she said pointedly to Dan, moving away towards the group they had been with.

'In a minute,' Dan said.

'Cheers!' Emma held her glass up to his. 'Here's to many more days like today.'

He didn't smile, but clinked her glass, and she swallowed the strong, medicine-like liquid, grimacing as she did so.

'Have you had anything to eat?' he asked her.

Actually, she couldn't remember the last time she had eaten anything. 'Um – not recently,' she replied.

'There's food in the other room,' he said.

'Oh right, maybe I'll get something,' she said. 'Although I'm not sure I can fit anything else into this dress.' She laughed self-consciously.

His eyes ran over her dress again. 'Make sure you do,' he said, and walked off.

'Blimey! If he smouldered anymore, he'd set the fire alarms off!' Sarah giggled.

'Doesn't Caroline drink?' remarked Toby.

'She does usually,' Emma replied.

'Ooh! You don't think she's pregnant, do you?' Toby said, his eyes widening.

For a split second, Emma thought her last Jaeger Bomb was going to make an unwelcome re-appearance, but she swallowed and took a deep breath.

'Let's have another one,' she said, getting a twenty out of her own wallet and ordering three more drinks.

'Oh my God,' Toby yelled as "Waiting for a Star to Fall" by Boy meets Girl started playing, 'this is my all-time favourite song!' And he started to dance backwards onto the dance floor, beckoning to the two girls to follow him. He had some serious dance moves and as the alcohol in their bloodstreams took hold, they all danced with more and more abandon.

'You're a Dancing Queen!' Toby sang to Emma when Abba came on.

Emma was actually enjoying herself. It felt so good to just let go and forget everything. They drunk more wine, and things started getting hazy. She was vaguely aware of people up on the tables; some dancing, a couple of lads pretending to fence with two schooling whips that someone had found. Emma kicked off her shoes and Toby lifted her off her feet and spun her around when a song from the film "Dirty Dancing" came on, then they both collapsed in fits of giggles.

At some point, Emma looked around for Sarah; she was over in the corner snogging Tom.

Then Dan caught her eye, over at the bar. She had been having such a good time she had almost forgotten about him. Almost.

Meeting his eye, she realised she was extremely drunk, and hot.

'I need to cool down!' she said to Toby, but he had started to dance with Rory's new groom, a good-looking lad with bleached blonde hair…so Toby would be happy as well.

She made her way unsteadily off the dance floor; the room was sliding all over the place. She was unbearably hot, she needed to get outside.

Trying to avoid bumping into people, which was difficult because they seemed to keep moving in and out of focus, she found her way to an exit and stepped outside into the cool night air.

She felt a hand on her arm.

'Where are you off to?'

Turning in surprise, she found herself looking up into Dan's brown eyes.

'It's you!' she said happily, but when she tried to stand still it was even harder to stay upright, so she started walking again.

'What are you doing Bugs?' he said.

'Just need to cool down,' she said, walking further into the darkness.

'Not on your own you're not. Where are your shoes?'

Emma looked down in surprise at her bare feet, which seemed a long way away.

'I don't know!' she replied baffled. 'I know I had some.'

'Let's go back in and find them, you can't walk around in the dark in bare feet.'

'No, too hot! I can't go back in there.'

'Just stay here a minute then. Do you want me to take you back to the lorry?'

Emma's legs started to fold away beneath her. 'No, just need to lie down a minute.'

Dan caught her in his arms and held her up, steadying her.

She smiled blissfully, closing her eyes and leaning against him.

'Where do you want to go?' he asked her.

'Right here. I wanna be right here,' she said dreamily, laying her face against his chest. 'Don't go,' she said, suddenly needing to cry.

'Go where?'

'To America.'

'What, now?' he laughed softly.

'Not ever,' she said sadly.

'Why not Bugs?'

'Because I want you…here with me.'

He went very still. There were a few moments of sheer heaven, while he stood, silently, holding her in the darkness. She wanted to stay like this forever, breathing him in.

Then someone spoke.

'She alright?' It was Toby who had come outside to look for her.

'She's just had too much to drink,' Dan replied. 'I'm going to take her back to the lorry. Will you look after her while I tell Caroline… and find her shoes? I'll be right back.'

He took her over to a bench by the door and put her down carefully. Toby sat down next to her and put his arm around her. She closed her eyes, leaning against him, and wishing with all her heart that he were Dan, she passed out.

Chapter 36

SHE WOKE THE NEXT MORNING IN THE LORRY, AND INTO A WORLD of pain. She was hot and sweaty and horribly uncomfortable. Her eyes were so dry, her eyelids were stuck down, but blinding sunlight was searing through them, seeming to pierce through to her brain, which had become much too large for her skull.

Finally managing to peel back her eyelids, she found she was still wearing Sarah's dress from the night before. She hadn't even taken out her earrings which were digging into her neck.

She looked at her watch. It was a quarter past nine. *Quarter past nine! Oh my God, the horses!*

She swung her legs over the edge of the bed, wincing in response to the cudgel splitting through her skull. Ouch, ouch, ouch. The smell of the perfume that she had been wearing the night before made her feel sick.

There was a bottle of water by the bed; she removed the lid and drank all of it. The door opened and Dan jumped into the lorry.

'Do I have to ask how you're feeling this morning?' he asked, going to the sink and filling a bottle of water.

'Only if I don't have to answer,' she croaked. 'I'm so sorry Dan – the horses – I'll go and do them right away.'

'No need, they're all done. We're just about ready to load up and get going,' he said.

Emma groaned. 'Oh God, I'm such an idiot! I have no idea why I drunk so much.' In fact, she had no idea about anything much, she could remember hardly anything at all. 'How did I get back here?' she asked.

'Caroline and I brought you back,' he replied. 'Toby offered, but he was dying to get back to that blonde bit of stuff that he was chatting up.'

Emma tried to clear the fog in her brain but nothing would come.

'Did I walk back without any shoes?' she asked in consternation, looking down at her feet, which were revoltingly black and sticky.

'You didn't walk, you were sleeping peacefully, so I carried you and Caroline brought your shoes and your bag, they're over there.' He pointed to the side.

Emma was horrified.

'Oh God, I'm so sorry,' she said again, waves of shame washing over her. 'Was Caroline angry?'

'Well, you might have to hear about it today,' he warned. 'But she didn't have to come, I could have managed on my own. You were like a little Koala clinging round my neck. I think she only came to defend my honour.'

Emma was absolutely mortified, her insides curled up with embarrassment, and her heart, already working overtime to try and rid her body of the poison that was pumping through her bloodstream, started jumping and pounding most unpleasantly.

'I don't remember anything,' she said weakly.

The door opened again, and Caroline bounced in, a bit like an over-zealous Red Setter.

'Well! You've finally come around have you?' she said to Emma, who climbed down from the bed and started to look for some more suitable clothes to put on.

'Yes. I'm sorry about last night...and this morning,' Emma said, genuinely chagrined.

'Oh well, Danny and I coped between us. I guess you don't get the groom of the year award after all!' she said with a little laugh, but there was a hard edge to her tone.

As they drove home, Emma leant against the door of the lorry and tried to close her ears to Caroline's relentless chatter. She seemed particularly shrill today.

The motion of the lorry made her feel even more sick, which added to her general misery. She had made a complete fool of herself, and she was terrified of what she might have said or done in her drunken state.

She closed her eyes and tried to sleep. As she drifted in and out of consciousness, Caroline's voice faded in and out like a badly tuned radio. She heard the words 'America' and 'November' and realised that Caroline was talking about their planned trip to America to meet her family. They must think that she was asleep.

Caroline was saying; 'If we go as soon as the season is over, we could get married at Christmas, in The States.'

Now Emma was fully awake. A wave of nausea surged through her body, filling her mouth with bile. 'Can we stop? I'm going to be sick!' she croaked.

Thankfully, Dan managed to pull over, and before the lorry had even come to a complete stop, Emma had flung herself out the door and was violently sick onto the grass verge.

It was a nightmare journey, Emma had never felt so ill. But her emotional pain was worse than her physical discomfort. It was worse somehow having no idea what it was she had done, just the vague feeling that she had said or done something awful.

She couldn't bear the thought that she might have thrown herself at Dan in her drunken state, and that he might now feel about her the way he'd felt about Becky; pity, or worse, contempt.

She decided that if he wanted to avoid her, she would make it easy for him, so she stayed out of his way, making herself scarce whenever he was around.

There was no reason for her to stay now. She had to get away from here. As soon as she finished work, she rang Lottie.

'Emma?'

'Yes, it's me.'

'What's wrong? You sound upset,'

'I'm okay, but…can I come and stay with you?'

'Of course you can, but why? What's happened?'

'I just need to get away from here.'

'Is it Edward?'

'No…well, yes in a way,'

'I knew something had happened, he called Josh – said he could never get hold of you anymore. What is it, have you had a row?'

'No – Lottie, I can't tell you on the phone – when can I come?'

'Well the thing is, I've got my cousin's wedding in Cornwall at the weekend, I'm driving down there on Friday.'

Emma was silent, wondering what on earth she was going to do. She couldn't go back to her parent's in this state.

'Emma?'

'It's fine,' she said at last. 'I'll wait until you're back from Cornwall.' She would just have to put up with it.

'But I'm so worried about you! You sound miserable. Look, I have an idea – I'll call in on you on the way down. I'll drive down Thursday night, how does that sound?'

Emma almost said no, but she wanted someone to talk to so badly. She wanted Lottie to tell her what an idiot she was being and get her thinking straight again.

'Would you?' she said.

'Yes of course! You've always been there for me. I'll see you Thursday, hang in there!'

She had a shower and made herself look a bit more presentable, before going up to the house and knocking on the door. Malcolm answered.

'Emma, is something the matter?' he asked, showing her into his private sitting room. She took a seat in one of the large armchairs.

Willing the tears to hold back until she was alone, she told him she was leaving after the weekend and asked him if he would talk to Dan about Merlin.

He looked at her with concern. 'I will of course if that's what you want – but has he done something to upset you again?'

She did her best to reassure him; 'No, no, nothing like that. I'd just rather not have to speak to him before I go that's all,' she said.

Malcolm frowned. 'I see how it is, and I'm sorry it's come to this Emma. Don't worry, I'll have a word with him – bloody boy!' he muttered under his breath.

The last thing she wanted was Malcolm having another "word" with Dan. The last time he'd done that, it hadn't turned out too well.

She pleaded with him not to say anything, and finally he agreed he would just sort out the business with Merlin and send the money on to her. Right now, she couldn't care less about the money.

Chapter 37

LEAVING THE HOUSE, SHE TOOK A LONG WALK, DOWN INTO THE fields, and stayed there, talking to Penny until it began to get dark. Then taking her time, she strolled back home. Caroline and Dan had some friends over for dinner, and the sound of their laughter drifted to her ears on the still evening air from the Coach House.

Feeling desolate, she took a seat on the mounting block and rested her back up against the stone wall. The stones, warm from the day's sunshine, gave her back their heat. A few stars were popping out, pale against the inky-blue backdrop of the sky.

Then she saw him. He was coming out of Merlin's stable. Her instinct was to get up and go inside, but he was coming towards her.

'I've been looking for you everywhere,' he said.

He had?

'What are you doing down here?' she asked, her pulse taking off like a lurcher after a rabbit.

'Malcolm called me up to the office just now – gave me a chance to escape for a while – so I came down here to get a beer,' he said with a grin. 'Caroline's on some kind of health binge, she's got everyone on sparkling water. Do you want one?' he asked.

Although she'd sworn never to touch alcohol again, her mouth had suddenly gone so dry. 'Yes please,' she said, sounding a little hoarse.

He went inside, returning with two beers and sat down next to her, his elbows on his knees. Her body immediately went completely rigid, every sense heightened, and she had to remind herself to breathe.

'Have you been avoiding me Bugs?'

How ironic. 'N-No, I…' she stammered.

'We had a long chat – Malcolm and I.'

Oh dear. 'You did?' She took a large gulp of beer.

'Yes. He's told me about Merlin – about the part you played in buying him, and why.'

'I was hoping Malcolm was going to wait until I'd left. But you don't have to buy him from me if you don't want to.'

'Of course I do – I've got a bit of money saved, I just hope it's enough.'

'I don't care about the money, I did it for the horse. I knew if you ever get him right, Malcolm would want to sell him again. I just want you to be in control of what happens to him, so he never ends up in the glue factory.'

He leant back against the wall. Now, his shoulder was touching hers; she didn't move away. She knew this feeling was only borrowed – stolen really – but she didn't care, she was going to enjoy it while she could.

'So, Malcolm says you're leaving.'

She gave a deep sigh. 'Yeah. Lottie is coming down Thursday on the way to a wedding, and then picking me up on the way back.'

'Right.' He was biting his lip. Then he said, 'Malcolm gave me a bollocking that night after the accident, when I tried to talk to you in Merlin's stable. Said I was a selfish bastard.'

She began to tremble and was sure he would feel it. 'Why would he say that?'

His mouth twitched with a wry smile. 'Because he knows me pretty well. Selfish I might be, but I would never pressure you into doing anything you didn't want to – you know that?' She nodded and took another swig of her drink, trying to control her nerves. 'But…you know you have a choice, don't you? Do you want to go?'

That was the million-dollar question. 'Yes…no – I don't know.' She shrugged her shoulders, enjoying the sensation of hers, rubbing against his.

'You have to know what it is you want,' he said. 'Let's do that thing…you know, you have to answer quickly, be honest, try not to think too hard.'

'O-okay…' she said uncertainly.

'City or country?'

'That's easy – country.'

'Office job, or yard job?'

'Yard!'

'Big House or small flat?'

'House – in the country with a big garden! I'd love a dog…and chickens – I've always wanted chickens.'

He laughed. 'Okay, you've got chickens, now…um…beer or champagne?'

'Er…prosecco…can I have prosecco?'

'Fillet steak, or egg and chips?'

'Fillet steak.'

He paused and took a swig of his beer, and she thought he looked perplexed.

'But those things are unimportant,' she said. 'It's more about who you're with and what you're doing.' She tried to be brave. 'Like, when we're backing the youngsters together – I really feel like I'm achieving something, you know? That's *really* important to me.'

He nodded. 'It sounds to me as if you actually do know what you want,' he said.

She did. She did know what she wanted. She wanted him. 'But…I don't know how to get there from here. There are too many things in the way,' she said.

'You don't have to see all the way there, you only need to see the first step.'

'I don't see how….'

'Don't you?' he looked directly at her, and his stare was intense.

Her courage failed her. 'But sometimes, there isn't a choice – not really. There's too many complications, too much to lose!'

'There's always a choice,' he insisted, 'things change – nothing's set in stone.'

All this talk of choice, and yet he wasn't free to do what he chose any more than she was. He was getting married for Christ's sake! He shouldn't even be here, talking to her. Caroline would be livid. He had more to lose than she did.

She shook her head with frustration. 'But at some point, you have to make that choice,' she said fiercely. 'Some things you can't change, once they're done, they're done. There's no going back.'

He drew back a little from the force of her words. 'Yeah, maybe you're right,' he said.

He turned away from her and finished his beer in one long draught. Her heart contracted painfully while she waited for him to say that he ought to be getting back.

Instead, he said; 'I'm not going to America you know.'

The stones beneath her seemed to move, a tremor shook her body. She hardly dared ask. 'Why not?'

'I'm not ready for that kind of commitment,' he wasn't looking at her, he was turning the empty bottle of beer in his hands.

She could barely speak. 'Have you told Caroline?'

'Not yet,'

'Why – when did you make the decision?'

'After the party.'

The party. She looked down at her own half-finished beer. Oh, curse all alcohol! If only she could remember. 'Why after the party?'

Now he looked at her with an uncertain smile, but his forehead was furrowed with a frown. 'You know Bugs – for someone so clever, you really are incredibly thick.'

'What….?' She was overcome with a sudden inexplicable urge to laugh; the relief, the tension, all that pent-up emotion, it had to go somewhere.

She began to giggle. Dan's face relaxed and he started to laugh – just as Caroline walked around the corner. The look on her face sobered them both up immediately.

'We've been waiting for you to start dinner for the past twenty minutes,' she said coldly.

'I'm not hungry,' he said, making no move to get up.

'Oh, so you're just going to sit here and drink all night?' She shot Emma a poisonous look.

Emma squirmed, not knowing where to put herself.

'If that's what I feel like doing,' his voice was dangerously steady.

Caroline turned a most unflattering colour that clashed with her hair and started to shake.

Emma jumped up. 'I'm going in now anyway,' she said. 'Good night.'

Back in her room, she could hear their voices below her window. Dan's deep and resonant; Caroline's rising and getting more hysterical by the minute. Emma put on some music to drown them out, worrying that the temptation to listen would prove too much.

He wasn't going to America, he wasn't going to marry Caroline, and he wanted her to stay. The blessed relief, and the precious, precious, glimmer of hope. She sat on her bed hugging her knees and these new, sweet feelings to herself.

A while later she turned off her light and knelt up on her bed to sneak a peak out of the window. The stars were magnificent now the sky was blacker, and the moon was huge and bright.

Caroline had gone but Dan was still sitting on the block, directly below her. As she watched he tilted his head back and looked up. Instinctively, she drew back a little out of sight, then couldn't resist having another look.

He was getting up. He crossed the yard, but instead of turning towards the Coach House, he went in the direction of the track; in no hurry, hands in pockets. She watched until he disappeared out of sight round the bend. She hoped he wasn't going into town to get drunk. Happier than she'd been for a long time, she got under her covers, curled up and tried to fall asleep.

The next morning all hell broke loose.

Chapter 38

EMMA WAS WOKEN VERY EARLY BY A TERRIBLE SCREECHING SOUND coming from the tack room down below. She sat bolt upright in fright. What the hell was it? Someone was yelling and shrieking – and it sounded like Caroline.

Getting dressed as quickly as she could, she went downstairs. The screeching was still going on accompanied by loud thumps and crashing noises.

Opening the door at the bottom of the stairs and cautiously poking her head around the corner, she was met by a terrible sight. The tack room had been turned upside down. Caroline was whirling around in a frenzy of rage, grabbing armfuls of things and throwing them through the open doorway.

'That's mine!' she screamed, as she hurled a brand new Devocoux dressage saddle out the door. It landed with a sickening thud and skidded across the concrete.

'And that!' as a custom-made Butet jumping saddle went flying out the door in its wake, to land on the heap of various items which was slowly growing on the ground outside.

All the while Dan just stood there leaning against the wall, hands in his pockets, not saying anything, looking like he was struggling not to be sick.

Emma winced every time another beautiful and valuable item joined the pile.

'Don't think for one minute that you're going to keep any of it!' Caroline shrieked at him. '*Any of it!*' And she picked up a tendon boot and threw it at his head. He didn't even bother to duck, but it missed him anyway, hitting the wall behind him with a thwack and then falling to the floor.

She turned on Emma. 'Do you know what he said to me?' Her beautiful face contorted into a hideous mask of fury.

Emma shook her head fearfully.

'He said that he didn't love me, but that if I thought that it was because I hadn't bought him enough stuff yet, then I was welcome to keep trying.'

Emma cringed. God, he was a shocker.

'He is the most heartless bastard I have ever come across in my life,' Caroline continued. 'I wish I'd never met him, and I never want to see him again as long as I live!' And with that, she turned and ran off the yard, wailing.

Emma stood for a minute, not knowing what to say. And then she slowly went over to the pile of stuff lying on the ground and started to pick things up.

'Leave it there,' Dan said, and went into the kitchen.

She dropped the things back on the pile and followed him in.

He was sitting on the sofa, his elbows on his knees and his face in his hands.

Emma went cautiously past him and stood by the table.

'I can't believe you said that to her,' she said eventually.

'Neither can I. And I certainly can't remember saying it, but I guess I must have,' he said in muffled tones from behind his hands. 'I went into town last night after I left here...after that I can't remember much. But Caroline tells me that I came back, told her that I didn't love her in front of all her friends, and then passed out under the table.'

He rubbed a hand across his eyes. 'This morning she said she would forgive me if I said it was all a mistake – that I'd only said it because I was drunk and angry. But I couldn't –because it's true.'

Emma stared at him in shocked silence, and he stared back.

There was a yell from outside and the sound of breaking glass, then pounding footsteps and Rachel appeared, breathless, her face red with alarm.

'Dan, come quick!' she panted, 'Caroline's smashing up your car!'

*

The fallout was fast and brutal, like ripping off a plaster. A recovery truck came to pick up the VW, with its smashed headlights and windscreen. Then a man in a horsebox to take Angel, Beau and Charlie away. In spite of everything, as Emma helped load them up, and the ramp closed behind them, she couldn't help feeling sad. How must Dan feel, after he'd come so far with them and so nearly achieved all he'd ever dreamt of? Without them, he only had a handful of untried youngsters…and Merlin. At least he had Merlin.

She watched him closely for any sign of regret, but if anything, he seemed detached, as if he were a little shell-shocked.

Malcolm was philosophical about the hasty departure of his high paying guest.

'Oh well, back to normality again,' he said cheerfully.

Kitty and Rachel were wide-eyed and talked in hushed voices, giving Dan a wide berth. Simone was complacent; she gave Emma a look as if to say "I told you so", which bothered Emma more than she liked to admit.

Dan was moving back into his old room. He was going to be there, sleeping on the other side of the wall tonight. She was both thrilled by the thought, and terrified by it.

As soon as the others went home after work, she went for a run to clear her head. It had all happened so fast, she needed time to think. Lottie was coming tomorrow and she was scared of how little self-control she had when he was near her. It would be better if she avoided talking to him until after Lottie had gone.

She got back at around dinner time. Cautiously she went into the tack room. The light was on in the staff room, but there was no noise coming from inside. She tiptoed into the kitchen and stopped dead in her tracks.

He was lying on the sofa on his side, his arms folded across his chest, eyes closed as if fast asleep. She could hear his breath was slow and even, his chest rising and falling gently. All she had to do was sneak past and go on up to her room, but she couldn't help stopping for a second.

His thick lashes lay dark on his cheek, his hair curled on his forehead which was smooth and untroubled. He looked much younger in sleep, almost vulnerable, and so beautiful; she couldn't stop staring. Realising she had been standing there too long, she managed to tear her eyes away and headed for the stairs. She'd reached the door when she heard a movement behind her and then his voice.

'Emma.'

She stopped and turned. He'd opened his eyes and sat up.

'Are you hiding from me again?' he asked, running a hand through his hair.

She hesitated, her hand on the door handle, choosing her words carefully.

'I thought you might need some space,' she said.

He frowned. 'That's very sweet of you Bugs, but I'm getting frost bite out here on my own.'

She turned back into the room, her mouth already going dry.

'I've got something for you,' he said, getting up and going to the sideboard. He pulled a large brown envelope out of the drawer and put it on the table. It wasn't sealed, and a quick glance told her it was full of notes, bound in bundles with rubber bands; tens, twenties and even some fifties.

'Oh!' She sat down rather suddenly in a chair.

'For Merlin,' he said.

'Yes – thank you,' she said. Then she had a thought. 'Actually, this is probably going to sound a bit silly but, well – Merlin's competing at Bicton this weekend, isn't he?'

He nodded. 'Merlin and…well, just Harvey now…' he gave a rueful smile and then his expression became anxious. 'My sponsors are coming to watch – to see whether we still have a deal now I've lost Angel and Beau.' He sighed. 'I hope to God Merlin behaves himself.'

Emma felt desperately sorry for him. 'Well – would you mind hanging on to this until afterwards? I'd like to go to one competition with him – see him compete as my horse. I know I'll probably never have the opportunity again, you see?'

He frowned, and sat down opposite her, arms resting on the table.

'Yeah, sure. Malcolm's booked us overnight stabling, as Harvey's class is Saturday and Merlin's Sunday.' He looked down at his hands, splaying out his long fingers on the cracks in the wood. 'I thought you might have changed your mind about leaving,' he said quietly.

This was just the conversation she'd wanted to avoid. This was too difficult. There were so many questions she needed the answers to before she could reply to that; none of which she could ask him. It was too soon.

But she had to say something. 'I don't know, there are a lot of things to consider…' she tailed off.

'Tell me?' he asked.

'It's…' How could she tell him? How could she say; *Because, I'm in love with you and I need to know if you feel the same way*? The thought was terrifying. She needed to know that he wanted her to stay for the right reasons – that he wasn't just going to play with her heart and then move on. Replace her. Leave her with nothing. Was he even capable of love? Or was his heart too badly scarred?

To love someone who was never going to love you back, was such a pitiful state.

She had to say something. 'If I didn't go back, it would mean the end for me and Edward.' She swallowed.

Dan leant towards her, his gaze direct. 'Would that be so terrible?' he asked, in that soft way of his that made her insides feel like they were melting. 'You've been doing pretty well without him for the past six months. Break the shackles? Throw off the chains? As someone who's just done it, I can recommend it.'

She said nothing so he continued. 'Like you've said to me before, you just have to decide what's important to you. I thought having the money and the horses to compete were the most important things to me, but it wasn't worth everything I had to give up – including my freedom.'

He paused, but Emma couldn't speak. His freedom meant that much to him – why on earth would he ever want to commit to her?

'I know you would be giving up a lot if you broke up with Edward,' Dan was saying, 'and I know it probably doesn't seem a very good prospect, swapping fillet steak for egg and chips, and a posh flat in Berlin for a draughty room above a stable…'

'I don't care about any of that,' Emma interrupted. 'It's not that.'

'What is it then?' he asked.

'It's complicated,' she stammered.

He sat back frowning. 'You're not giving much away Bugs,' he said. 'Why can't you talk to me?'

She looked at him in despair. Part of her was burning to open up to him, lay her soul bare and face the consequences, but the larger part of her was terrified to take the leap. Once she had stepped off that precipice, she could never go back. 'I just need a little more time to think about things.'

He nodded. 'Will you come for a drink with me tomorrow? We can talk then.'

Emma wanted to bang her head on the table with frustration. 'Lottie's coming tomorrow.'

He sighed and looked away from her, towards the door. 'Oh yes, I forgot.' He was going to give up on her.

There was a sound of a car pulling up on the gravel outside. He glanced towards the window and swore under his breath. 'She's early.'

'Who…?'

'Caroline.'

Emma's stomach lurched; 'C…Caroline?'

He nodded. 'She rang me yesterday – wants to collect the rest of her stuff…and wants us to have a talk,' he said wearily.

Oh, damn it all to hell! If she'd known that she would have been braver! Too late now. At least she would get the chance to think calmly and rationally about all this in the privacy of her own room. 'I might get an early night then,' she said, reluctantly getting to her feet.

Dan stood up also and stretched. As he did, his T-shirt rode up exposing at least three inches of bare skin between it and the top of his jeans which seemed to be about to fall down off his hips.

Emma nearly sat down again rather suddenly as desire and longing reached straight into her insides and pulled. Apparently, calm, rational thought, was going to be impossible.

'I'd better put this in my room then if you don't want it now,' he said, picking up the money she'd left on the table.

She turned away before he could see her confusion and hurried up the stairs, but he was right behind her, closing the door so they were in almost complete darkness.

Her knees struggled to find the strength to take each one of the steep, narrow steps.

She made it to the top where it was lighter and was at her door, needing to get inside quickly so she could get her pulse back under control, but he spoke again, stopping her.

'Emma.'

Even him saying her name seemed to reverberate through her body, shaking her very foundations. She stopped, her hand on her door, her breath fast and shallow. The narrowness of the passage meant that he was very close to her; the walls seemed to press in around them.

'If you want something from me, you just have to ask, okay? I'll meet you halfway, but trust is a two-way thing.'

And then, before she realised what was happening, he'd leant forward and kissed her, very gently on her cheek, leaving behind a burning mark, each nerve ending electrified. Her eyes closed as she fought to stop herself falling into him. But then, he was gone, into his room and had shut the door behind him.

She stood, rooted to the spot, processing what had happened. Then, letting herself into her room, she stood on the other side of the closed door breathing hard, reliving the moment over and over, her heart pounding. He'd kissed her. Just a friendly touch of his lips to her cheek – but still.

She waited until she heard him leave his room again and go back downstairs. Looking out of her window, she watched him walk towards the Coach House and collapsed onto her bed with a groan. She buried her face in her pillow, her whole body contracting with desire and frustration.

What would he and Caroline talk about? Would she want to make it up; tell him she wanted him back? Make him offers he couldn't refuse? The thought of them being together made her sick with jealousy. Why couldn't she have been brave and told him how she felt? She may have missed her only chance.

If he came back tonight, she would go to him, tell him she loved him. She didn't care about right or wrong, she didn't care about what might happen in the future…if he came back.

But as she lay there, and her breathing gradually returned to normal, reality dawned that Lottie was coming tomorrow. She couldn't meet her friend with a guilty conscience; a cheat and a liar.

'Think, Emma!' she told herself sternly. When had she become this lust-crazed lunatic?

Maybe she could put Lottie off coming. Without giving it a second thought, she dialled Lottie's number.

'Hi!' Lottie's voice came clear down the line, 'I was just about to ring you.'

'You were?'

'Yes, just to say, work is going to let me go early tomorrow – I told them I had to drive down to Dorset and they took pity on me – so I should be with you by six at the latest.'

'Oh, that's just it –,' Emma faltered, 'I rang to tell you not to worry. It's fine – I'm fine now, there's no need for you to go out of your way.'

'I want to come!' Lottie protested. 'It's not out of my way and I'm looking forward to it – it will break up the drive.'

'Oh – well I…' Dammit!

'What's happened?' Lottie asked, her voice suddenly suspicious. 'Why don't you want me to come?'

'I do…it's just…'

'Emma,' there was a warning note in Lottie's voice, 'there's something you're not telling me.'

Emma hadn't counted on her total inability to be anything less than completely honest with her best friend. She took a deep breath.

'Lottie, you're right. I've something to tell you – and you're not going to like it.'

'What?' Lottie sounded scared.

There was nothing for it; 'I…I'm going to break up with Edward, I'm in love with someone else.'

The silence at the other end was deafening – and then an explosion of sound; 'You're WHAT? You can't be serious! Who is it – Joe?'

Emma cringed as she imagined Lottie's reaction to what she was going to say. 'No, not Joe, it's…um…it's Dan.'

'DAN!'

Emma had to hold the phone slightly away from her ear to avoid perforating her eardrum –

'Have you lost your mind? He's… he's…well, you told me yourself what he's like.'

'Lottie, I know how this must sound to you, but…'

'How long has this been going on? When did this happen?'

'Well – nothing has actually happened yet,' she admitted, 'he's only just split up with his girlfriend. But he asked me to stay, and he's asked me to go for a drink with him tomorrow night.'

She thought she heard Lottie breath a sigh of relief. 'Well in that case, I'm definitely coming; talk some bloody sense into you.'

'There's no point really, I've made up my mind to go.'

'You don't know your own mind!' Lottie said furiously. 'Trust me Emma, this is so wrong for you. I can't believe you're doing this. I know it must have been difficult, what with Edward being away so much – but to throw it all away, for the sake of a crush on a piece of ass – a bit of eye-candy; it makes no sense at all.'

Emma tried desperately to explain. 'There's a lot more to him than meets the eye,' she began. 'I know him so much better now – we're friends. I know he doesn't make a great first impression, but when you get to know him, you're going to love him too.'

A brief pause, and then; 'You say he's just split up with his girlfriend?'

'Yes –,'

'Well, how do you know he's not on the re-bound? What if he just wants someone to share his bed?'

This was too close to Emma's own fears for comfort. She gulped. 'Because he asked me to stay before they split up. Because it might even be one of the reasons they split up.' How she hoped that was true! 'And I know he cares about me, he…'

She had been about to tell her that he'd driven her up to see Granddad but was interrupted by a loud, derisive snort from Lottie.

'And you know what?' Emma was furious all of a sudden, 'he's the only damn person that respects me enough to think that what *I* want, is actually important!' she shouted, and hung-up. She'd been gripping her phone so hard her knuckles were white.

Lottie rang back in less than a minute; her tone conciliatory. 'I'm sorry,' she said. 'It's just such a shock. Listen...you say that you want me to get to know him – then how about I come down anyway, and we all go out together?'

Emma was sure that that wasn't at all what Dan had in mind. 'I don't know if that's a good idea,' she said.

'Why not? If he cares about you so much, surely he won't object to getting to know your best friend.'

There was no arguing with that really. 'I – suppose I can ask him,'

'Well that's settled then. I'll see you tomorrow.'

Hours later, Emma lay in bed, but she was wide awake. She couldn't stop looking at the clock on her nightstand. Midnight. Then half-past.

What if Lottie was right? What if he just wanted someone to share his bed? Was she willing to take a gamble on whether his feelings might be real, or would she be letting herself in for a world of pain and heartbreak? The way he behaved made it seem as if he might have some real feelings for her. But it seemed so unlikely that he would want to walk straight into a relationship, when he had just freed himself from the shackles of another. Her thoughts went round and round in circles, never reaching a conclusion.

What if he didn't even come back tonight?

At one o'clock, she heard a car door slam, an engine roar and the sound of wheels, spinning on the gravel. She waited and listened. At last, footsteps on the stairs. She lay still, hardly daring to breathe. They paused outside her door, for half a second, then went into the room next door.

There was nothing more, but she loved knowing that he was there, just the other side of the thin wall. And trying not to think, but just feel his presence, she gradually fell asleep.

Chapter 39

When she heard Dan get up and go downstairs the next morning, she followed him down, desperate to get a word with him. He was putting the kettle on and looked up when she came through the door to the stairs. Then leant against the counter, his expression a little guarded.

'Hi,' she said.

'Hi,' he said.

'Did it go alright with Caroline?'

He hesitated. 'If by alright you mean she left without damaging me, or anything else, then yeah, I suppose so,' he said, rubbing a hand across his face in a weary gesture.

'I'm glad,' she said with a small smile of relief. 'I spoke to Lottie last night,' she began.

'Is she still coming?' he demanded.

'Yes, she's still coming,' she replied, and he began to turn away, 'but she wants to know if you'll come out with us for a drink tonight,' she added quickly.

He turned back. 'Oh.' He didn't seem exactly thrilled by this idea.

'I said I didn't think you'd want to, but Lottie can be quite – um – persistent.'

'Do you want me to?' he asked.

'Well….' She started to blush. 'I'd like you to get to know each other better,' she said. 'Last time was a bit weird if I remember rightly.' Her cheeks reddened even more.

He raised his eyebrows and nodded. 'Yeah, okay – then I will.'

*

Lottie arrived, as she'd predicted at six o'clock, just as they finished work, greeting Emma as if she'd had a family bereavement, or been diagnosed with a terminal illness.

'How are you?' she said with a sympathetic smile, hugging her.

'I'm fine,' Emma said firmly, 'not completely loopy as you seem to think I am.'

'Well, I…' Lottie began.

'Not here,' Emma said firmly, taking Lottie's hand and leading her through the yard, feeling incredibly nervous about the prospect of the evening ahead.

Dan was coming towards them, heading for the feed room door.

'You remember Lottie don't you?' Emma said. He stopped and nodded, with a half-smile, which Emma knew was the best he could do with someone he hardly knew.

Lottie gave him a stiff little smile in return. Dan turned away with a look of mild distaste – this was not going to be easy.

They took Lottie's bags up to Emma's room. As soon as the door closed Lottie started.

'So, is he coming tonight?'

'Yes, and you have to promise you'll give him a chance,' Emma said.

'Of course I will!' Lottie exclaimed, not altogether convincingly, but offered to do Emma's nails; a peace offering maybe?

They heard Dan coming up the stairs and get in the shower. 'You are in very close quarters here aren't you,' she said with an arch lift of her eyebrow.

Emma blushed. 'Yes, although he's been living up at the Coach House – until last night.'

Lottie looked up sharply from the nail she was painting; hand suspended half-way between bottle and nail. 'Last night? Are you sure nothing's happened between you, physically?'

'No,' Emma stated, 'I told you.'

'Well that's something at least. Have you told him you're going to stay?'

'I've told him I'm thinking about it.'

She had just finished Emma's nails when the shower stopped, and they heard Dan going into his room.

'And if you stay, what are you going to do? Live in this tiny room above a stable for the rest of your life?' Lottie said, much too loudly.

'Shh!' Emma hushed her. 'The walls are like paper here,' she whispered. They finished getting ready, saying very little, until they heard Dan go downstairs.

'Be nice,' Emma said as they left her room.

'I'm always nice!' Lottie said.

Why did that remind her of someone else?

Dan was sitting on the sofa reading a magazine.

'Ready?' he asked standing up, his eyes running over Emma from top to toe.

'Yes, let's go,' she said.

She had dressed up a bit more than usual, and now, with his eyes on her she was glad she had, because Lottie always looked so gorgeous.

'I'll drive,' he said picking up the Land Rover keys.

Lottie didn't speak. Dan held the passenger side door open for her, but she ignored him, getting into the back. Emma got in the front, praying that Lottie wouldn't give him the cold shoulder all evening.

The car park of the pub was heaving.

'Thank you for the lift,' Lottie said tersely as she got out.

Dan bought the first round. Lottie had a double vodka, lime and lemonade, the price of which made Emma wince.

Conversation didn't exactly flow, in fact it was painfully awkward. When Lottie spoke, it was all about London and their friends, leaving Dan looking bored out of his mind. And when Emma tried to draw him in by talking about work and the horses, Lottie instantly switched off and started looking at her phone or studying her nails. It almost made Emma wish for Simone and Kitty's company.

Emma got to her feet before they had even finished their first drinks. 'I'll get the next round,' she said, taking her wine with her to the bar, glad to escape from the awkwardness. If neither of them were going to make the effort, then maybe she should just leave them to it.

Barry had gone down to the cellar to change a barrel and there were a few people waiting, so she grabbed a stool and made herself comfortable. 'Face Like Thunder' by The Japanese House was playing on the jukebox.

Emma looked back at the table. At first glance, all seemed to be well. At least Lottie was talking and Dan was listening, a deeply thoughtful look on his face.

But as she watched, Dan's face became a fixed mask. Oh shit. She knew him well enough to know what that meant.

Barry had just finished serving the other customers. It took a very long time for him to serve her, but as quickly as she could she got back to their table.

Lottie said something that Emma didn't quite catch, and Dan seemed to cut her off in mid-sentence as Emma arrived back with the drinks.

'Why are you telling me all this? Dan asked.

'Just making conversation,' Lottie replied.

'Well don't bother,' Dan said, and downing the last of his beer he banged the empty bottle down on the table, making both girls jump. He got up, reaching for his keys.

'I'm going into town,' he stated, making it obvious it wasn't an invitation.

Dismayed, Emma tried to catch his eye, but he refused to look at her.

'O-Okay…' she stammered, 'see you at home?'

But he stalked out of the pub without another word.

'Rude!' Lottie exclaimed. 'What on earth's got his knickers in such a knot?'

'What did you say to him?' Emma demanded.

'Nothing that should have scared him,' Lottie protested.

'What exactly?' Emma insisted.

'All I said, was that I've known you for years and you're my best friend. I said that you were the kindest person – too nice for your own good really – and that you deserved to be happy.' Lottie paused and took a sip of her drink.

'Then what?'

'Then, I asked him what his intentions are,'

Emma was horrified. 'Oh Lottie! You didn't?'

'Well someone had to!' Lottie protested. 'If he's serious about you, that shouldn't have frightened him off. And honestly, I've never seen anyone run away so fast. I'm just trying to look out for you Emma. I seem to remember you doing it for me once – I'm just returning the favour.'

'That was different! You didn't even know him, and you'd only just split up with Josh!'

'And you haven't even split up with Edward,' Lottie said, with some heat.

It was true. She could hardly blame Lottie for judging.

She had a terrible sense of foreboding. She had so wanted them to get on, but now it seemed everything was much, much worse.

Chapter 40

LOTTIE HAD TO LEAVE EARLY THE NEXT MORNING TO GO TO HER wedding.

'You should just come with me now,' Lottie said before she left. 'I hate leaving you here. My cousin won't mind; I have a plus one, and Josh can't come…'

'I need to stay here and sort things out with Dan, I'm not leaving like this,' Emma said.

Lottie pursed her lips. 'To be honest Emma I don't think there's anything to sort out. It seems to me you both want completely different things.'

Emma shook her head, she needed to hear it from Dan himself. 'I'm staying here,' she said firmly.

Lottie sighed. 'Well, I'm coming to pick you up on Monday – that should give you enough time.'

'I'll call you and let you know,' Emma said.

'You have to come home on Monday!' Lottie cried. 'It's your birthday next weekend and – well, I shouldn't be telling you this, it was supposed to be a surprise – but Edward's coming home. For your birthday.'

Oh God. She'd completely forgotten it was her birthday, and she hadn't spoken to Edward in over a week.

'Whatever happens, you owe it to him to speak to him face to face,' Lottie said.

Lottie was right. She did at least owe him that. So she agreed. Lottie would pick her up on the Monday, regardless.

Dan had come home in the early hours, and this morning was

in a horrible mood. Once Lottie had gone, Emma asked him if he was okay, but he just muttered "fine" through tight lips, when it was obvious he was anything but.

Emma was convinced that Lottie must have said something to upset him, but she had no idea what. He avoided her, walking out of the room when she walked in, talking to anyone rather than her, and looking through her whenever she spoke.

By the afternoon, she couldn't stand it anymore, so she cornered him in the kitchen when no one else was around.

'What's the matter? And don't say you're 'fine' again, because you quite clearly aren't,' she said.

'I'm just saying what I think you want to hear,' he said sarcastically.

'What?' she said, baffled.

'I can't tell you the truth in case I hurt your feelings,' he continued in the same vein.

What the hell? 'And what is the truth?'

'I don't know, you tell me,' he replied.

'Dan, you're not making any sense,' she said. 'What did Lottie say to you last night?'

'Just that she's your best friend. How well she knows you. That she knows what's important to you – what you want,' he said, a challenging look in his eye.

'Yes, well, that's true,' she said; she couldn't understand why he seemed so angry with her.

'Tell me Emma, have you talked to Lottie about me? About asking you to stay, and about…what you want?' he said.

Emma faltered. 'Yes, she knew something was wrong, and I didn't know what to tell her…' she admitted.

But he cut her off. 'That's the trouble isn't it? You don't really know what you want, and you can't even be honest with yourself, let alone me.'

There was too much truth in that to deny.

'I have never lied to you Emma,' he went on, a touch more softly. 'I have always been truthful with you – I don't hide anything. You've always known exactly what I'm like, what you see is what you get. True?'

Emma nodded.

'So recently, I had begun to think that… that might be enough for you. You know what I have to offer, and still I got the impression that you might be happy with that – that you might want something from me other than just friendship.'

Emma's heart started to hammer.

'But then I find out from Lottie – and she told me in no uncertain terms – that you want something more. Something I can't give you. Something you have always known I can't give you. And that's why you wouldn't talk to me, because you couldn't tell me the truth.'

Now she understood what he was trying to say to her, and her heart plummeted into her boots. Lottie had been right. He wasn't ready for that kind of commitment. He had told her often enough in so many words – that he wasn't cut out for a committed relationship. Now, he was telling it to her straight. He had just broken one set of shackles; he was hardly going to walk straight into another. And she ought to have known that all along.

What she had thought she'd seen, that he might have some real feelings for her had obviously just been wishful thinking. She'd seen what she wanted to see. There seemed no end to the ways in which she could deceive herself.

'So?' he said, gently now. 'You know what I can offer you Emma. Be honest – is that enough for you?'

Was that enough for her? Just a fling? No. She was always going to want more than that. She wanted all or nothing. To have him and then not have him; to see herself replaced by someone new would be much too painful. She would rather just stay friends.

Emma looked down at her feet, hiding the tears that were welling up in her eyes. She shook her head.

'No, it isn't. I'd rather just stay friends…and I think maybe I should go home after all,' she said in a small voice.

She dared to glance up at him. For a fleeting moment she thought she saw sadness in his eyes, then it hardened and turned to anger.

'So much for fucking integrity,' he growled, and walked past her out of the room.

IT QUICKLY BECAME clear that she was losing his friendship as well. He continued to avoid her, wouldn't speak to her unless he absolutely had to. She couldn't look at him, it broke her heart.

Simone was gleeful. She didn't know what had caused this rift between Emma and Dan, but that wasn't going to stop her making the most of it.

That night, she said to Dan; 'Coming to the pub?'

'Yup,' he replied.

It was like the moment she'd thwacked into the log pile – only worse.

She went to bed and lay awake, her heart aching and aching, her ears straining for the sound of him coming home. Terrified he might not come back at all, or worse; bring someone back.

He came home late, but alone, thank God. Emma couldn't bear the thought of him being with someone else.

She started to feel a little resentful. Did she deserve to be treated so harshly? So, he might feel rejected – something he obviously wasn't used to – but then, so did she. And quite clearly, her friendship hadn't meant that much to him.

She tried to harden her heart against him, obviously she had to get over him because he wasn't going to relent.

But she couldn't let it end like this, there must be some way to make things right. At least salvage their friendship.

Although they hadn't discussed Bicton – difficult when he wasn't speaking to her – it could be her only opportunity to sort things out, so she got up early to pack the lorry and get the horses ready. She had it done by the time he got up, and had made him some tea.

'Am I still coming to Bicton?' she asked him directly when he came downstairs.

His face was dark and closed. 'I'm taking Simone,' he said. And not even bothering to drink his tea, he was on his way out the door.

'Why Dan?' she cried.

'Why do you want to come?' he demanded, turning on her.

She played the only card she had left.

'Because Merlin's my horse and I have a right to come,' she stated.

He blinked and colour darkened his cheeks. 'Whatever. Come if you must,' he said and walked out.

THEY BARELY SPOKE on the journey to Bicton. Reaching the show-ground they parked up. Dan went straight away to sort out the stabling for the horses.

Because it was Harvey's first competition, he would need plenty of time to warm up for his dressage test. Emma rushed to get him ready, but there was no sign of Dan.

She started to get anxious. If he didn't turn up soon, he wouldn't have enough time, and he still had to get changed. She tied Harvey up and went to look for him.

Not too far away, she spotted him. He was leaning against the side of a shiny silver and blue lorry, hands in pockets. He was smiling, showing his dimples. Her heart twisted. She knew that look; he was flirting.

She looked to see who was getting the benefit of his attention. Standing close to him, also smiling and batting her eyes, was a pretty, dark-haired girl, dressed for competition in skin-tight white breeches and long black boots. A third person joined them. Another girl; blonde, also pretty and shapely. They were all talking together and laughing, they didn't see her.

Emma's blood rose. A red-hot spike of jealousy shot through her. She turned on her heel and went back to the lorry, untied Harvey, and folded back his rug. If Dan couldn't be bothered to warm him up properly, at least she could walk him about.

She began walking him in circles, checking frequently over her shoulder to see if Dan was coming. He wasn't. Her circles started to get bigger; closer to the lorry where she knew he was.

He looked up and saw her, but he didn't move, just carried on chatting and laughing. The blonde girl was giggling, leaning towards him, twirling a piece of hair round her finger, looking up at him through her eyelashes.

Emma kept walking, but hot tears of hurt and frustration stung her eyes. She must *not* let him make her feel like this. Right now, she would have given anything not to be there. Why had she insisted on coming? She berated herself for being such a fool.

Eventually, she saw Dan look at his watch and, without hurrying, began to saunter over.

'Finally,' she muttered through gritted teeth. He ignored her, jumping up into the lorry to get changed. If he was quick, he would still just about have enough time, she thought.

He appeared a minute later in breeches and shirt but no stock or jacket.

'Where's my stock Emma?' he demanded.

'I don't know, wherever you put it!' she snapped. He disappeared again, only to re-appear a minute later, still stockless.

'I can't find it, or my number bib,' he said accusingly.

'Oh for Christ's sake!' she cursed. Quickly tying poor, confused Harvey up again, she jumped into the lorry to help him. She found both the stock and the number bib within seconds under the jacket that he'd chucked down on the bench.

'Here!' she practically threw them at him. They hit him in the chest where he caught them.

'What are you so upset about?' he snapped at her.

'Oh nothing!' she said, her voice rising. 'Only that I rushed to get Harvey ready for you because I *thought,* that you would want to ride him in early so you would have a chance of impressing your sponsors. Because I was under the misapprehension that you *gave* a shit. But I don't know why I bothered, I don't know why I gave a flying *fuck*, since you don't seem to!'

He stared at her, shocked.

'In fact,' she went on, warming to her subject. 'I don't know why I bothered to come at all!'

'Well you didn't have to, remember?' he fired back at her, going into the bathroom to tie his stock.

'Oh yes that's right,' she replied, still shouting. The door was open and people around the nearby horseboxes were beginning to stare. 'You didn't want me to come, did you?' The tears had long gone; she was too angry to want to cry now. 'And I don't know why the hell I did, right now I'd rather be anywhere but here with you!'

'Well don't worry, you won't have to put up with me tonight, because I won't be here – I'm going out,' he said from inside the bathroom.

With those two girls no doubt.

'Good!' she shouted back. 'Because quite honestly, the way you are at the moment, I'd rather have Simone for company!'

'Oh, I'm sorry,' he said sarcastically. 'I didn't realise I bored you so much. I guess it's because I don't have a silver spoon stuck up my arse and a fucking degree in being a twat!'

What was that supposed to mean? She picked on the one word that touched a nerve.

'Well I obviously bore you,' she retorted. 'Is that why you wanted to bring Simone instead of me? So you'd have someone to *do* tonight?' She no longer cared what she was saying.

There was a long pause. That must have stung. He reappeared, stock tied, and looked her straight in the eye.

'I haven't been near Simone since we first met, and you know it,' he stated coldly, sitting down to pull on his boots.

She couldn't think of anything to say to that, it was true.

'And anyway,' he went on, standing up. 'Why do you care? What does it matter who I sleep with? You're going home and you'll never have to see me again.'

'Yes, you're right. I am going home, and right now, *I can't wait*!' she said vehemently.

'I'll bet you can't,' he said, angry now. 'I'll bet you can't wait to get back to your stuck-up friends and your stuck-up, snooty boyfriend. You've always thought you were a little bit too good for us down here haven't you? It must have been really hard for you putting up with us carrot crunchers for so long.'

She gasped. She couldn't believe what he was saying. Tears threatened again now at the sheer injustice of it.

'I have never, *ever* thought that!' she protested. 'How can you say that? I've loved every minute of it here, you know I have!'

'So why are you in such a hurry to go home?' he demanded. 'Why are you in such a hurry to get back to Edward?'

She wasn't going to contradict him. She wanted to hurt him now as much as he'd hurt her. 'Because *he* has feelings and *he* doesn't hurt me,' she retorted. 'He *cares* about me!'

'*I* care about you!' he shouted suddenly.

She opened her mouth to reply, but the words dried up on her lips. She stood dumbly staring at him, his words hanging in the air.

She shook her head, a tiny movement of denial.

A single tear escaped from her eye. He watched it as it rolled down her cheek, the anger falling away from his face, but his jaw was still clenched.

'I care about you,' he said again, softly this time. Lifting his hand to her face, he wiped the tear away with his thumb, his hand cupping her burning cheek. In that moment, the wall that Emma had started to carefully re-construct around her heart crumbled and turned to dust. All the hurt and pain that she had blocked out, flooded into her chest, and the ache became almost unbearable. Her throat constricted, and she couldn't breathe properly. After standing for a moment, Dan let his hand fall to his side, with a look of resignation and defeat.

He shook his head, and looking at his watch, muttered, 'I'd better go and ride this test.'

Chapter 41

After sitting for ten minutes with her face in her hands, Emma decided she ought to go and watch. She got up and blew her nose fiercely, squared her shoulders and walked down to the dressage arenas.

He rode atrociously. It was like watching car crash TV. Whether it was due to the lack of warm up, or the fact that Dan's mind was anywhere but on the job, he missed markers, forgot transitions and when he asked Harvey for working trot, Harvey shot forward bucking, and when he asked for canter, he took off around the arena at a flat out gallop and jumped the boards. That meant elimination.

Emma prayed that Dan's sponsors hadn't been watching, but scanning the spectators dotted around, she spotted them. They were standing on the far side of the dressage arena; the white hair of Mr Davies was unmistakeable. They had witnessed the whole thing. She fled back to the box in anguish. Jumping up into the lorry, she shut the door behind her.

It was all her fault. She should never have come. He hadn't wanted her to come and she had insisted. Then she'd fought with him just when he needed to be calm and focused, riding at his best.

He'd said he cared about her, and she'd stood there and said nothing. Furious with herself, she paced up and down inside the lorry, from time to time glancing out of the window to see if he had come back with Harvey. But he didn't come back. She began to get worried. What had happened to them?

Then it occurred to her that he had been eliminated. He wouldn't be show-jumping or going cross-country, he would have taken

Harvey straight back to the temporary stables.

Cursing her stupidity, she jumped out of the lorry and ran down to the stables. Harvey was in his box, rugged up and eating his hay. He was alone. Dan wasn't in there. She checked in Merlin's box as well. Merlin was dozing, resting a hind leg, bottom lip hanging. He looked up and whickered when he saw her, but there was no sign of Dan. Perhaps she was already too late. He might have already gone back with those two girls. She felt sick to her stomach.

In the faint hope that he might have gone back to their lorry she ran back again as fast as she could. But as she had feared, the lorry was deserted.

She sat down heavily on one of the bench seats.

She just wanted to tell him she was sorry, and that she cared about him too. She had missed her chance and she might never get another one. He'd given up on her, and she didn't blame him.

She decided to go and look for him round the show-ground. But after an hour and a half of searching in vain, she went to the stables to feed and bed the horses down for the night, before going back to the horsebox.

In her misery she paced around the lorry. She felt sick wondering what he might be doing. There was no way she could eat anything. She made herself a cup of coffee but couldn't drink it. Eventually she showered and got ready for bed deciding that, at least if she went to sleep, she wouldn't be able to feel anything anymore.

But as she climbed the ladder onto the bed, there was movement outside the door and the box swayed as someone jumped up on the step. The next second the door opened, and Dan walked in. Emma jumped down, all thought of sleep forgotten, so pleased to see him that she forgot that he almost certainly wasn't going to be pleased to see her.

'I came looking for you, but I couldn't find you,' she said.

He glanced at her warily.

'I'm just having a shower and then I'm going out,' he said, grabbing his jeans and a shirt from a locker and going into the bathroom. The noise of the shower pump started.

Waiting for him to come out, she rehearsed in her mind what she was going to say. It felt incredibly important to get the words exactly right, to stop him walking out that door again without at least having a chance to say sorry.

In a very short time, he came out again wearing jeans and buttoning up his shirt. She swallowed hard.

'I'm really sorry about what happened earlier,' she said.

He shrugged. 'Doesn't matter,' he said without emotion, reaching for his wallet from the counter. 'See you later.'

And he was already heading out the door.

'Wait! Please, Dan,' she was suddenly desperate.

He stopped and turned towards her. The look on his face was full of mistrust.

'I just want you to believe that I didn't mean for that to happen. It was all my fault, I should never have come here in the first place, you were right, I'm sorry.' She was aware that she was babbling like an idiot, but she had to stop him walking out that door. 'I don't blame you if you hate me for it, you've probably lost your chance of sponsorship and it's all my fault. I was very unprofessional, and I know I don't deserve for you to forgive me but…' she tailed off, unsure how to continue.

'It doesn't matter,' he said again. 'I've just had a meeting with Mr Davies. They're coming back tomorrow to watch Merlin.'

He delivered this news with a kind of deadpan indifference, looking at a space somewhere to the left of her face rather than at her, but she was so relieved, she was momentarily ecstatic.

'Oh, thank God!' she exclaimed passionately.

He nodded and turned to go again. She couldn't bear it.

'Dan, wait!' she cried again, stepping forward. 'Please don't go.'

He stopped again and turned towards her, waiting, but she couldn't think of anything else to say. And as she stood there dithering, she saw his frustration rising.

'What do you want from me, Emma?' he asked, angrily.

'I just want you not to be angry with me anymore. I just want us to be friends again,' she said, her emotion shining through the tears in her eyes. 'I want things to be the way they were.'

'Well, I don't!' he shouted. She drew back, shocked by the intensity with which he said it. 'I don't want you around anymore,' he said.

His words were like blows. She almost staggered under the weight of them.

He didn't want her around anymore. Her vision blurred and she looked down at the floor. The tears flowed from her eyes and splashed onto her bare feet. She expected to hear the click of the door as he left.

But she didn't.

Instead she became aware that he'd taken a step closer to her. When he spoke again, his voice was much quieter, but still harsh.

'Do you know what it's like for me, knowing you are on the other side of the wall every night. Seeing you every day, watching me with those big eyes. Letting me think I'm getting close, but then pushing me away every time.'

Now his voice and his words sent her stomach into free-fall.

'I'm a man Emma, I'm not made of stone. I can't do it anymore, it's too hard. Just tell me something, I want to know the truth. Did you ever feel anything for me or has it been just a game to you; a way of amusing yourself until you go back to your real life. Back to Edward. Did you ever want me at all?'

She knew that this was her last chance. Unless she spoke up now, she would lose him forever. Whatever the consequences, she had to be entirely honest. She had to bare her soul and he could do with her what he would. If he wanted to crush her and tear her heart up into a thousand pieces, then he could. The choice was clear. She wouldn't hide from him anymore.

Wiping away her tears, she raised her eyes to look up into his with determination.

'Do I want you? Sometimes I want you so much it hurts to even look at you.' Her voice was hoarse. 'I feel as though you've taken my heart from me, piece by piece until there is nothing left. I feel like every time you're close to me I can't breathe properly – but I can never be close enough. I'm only ever happy when I'm with you, and when you're not around I feel like a piece of me is missing. I'm lost. So, do I feel anything for you? Yes, Dan, I do. I love you.'

As she spoke, the look in his eyes changed. At first there was a flicker of something like surprise or disbelief. Then, as the truth behind her words sank in, he blinked and a thousand emotions passed through them like a kaleidoscope of colours, changing them from dark to light, then back to dark.

She heard his sharp intake of breath and only had time to catch her own breath before he had crossed the space between them in two strides. He held her face between his hands, his eyes searching, then his mouth came down to meet hers.

Chapter 42

As soon as his lips touched hers, all thought stopped. There was nothing but powerful sensation. Her lips automatically opened in response to the gentle pressure.

Her mouth moulded to his, her arms went up around him and his kiss got deeper. They sank to their knees, slowly down to the floor, never losing their connection. Emma's emotions were exquisitely painful.

After all the hurt and grief, the sense of loss and loneliness, to have his mouth on her mouth, his hands on her, was like being completely immersed in cool water after being lost in the desert for weeks.

His kiss pulsed all the way down through her body. It was touching a place inside her she hadn't felt before; a place she hadn't even known was part of her. Something was being awakened, like a deep sleeper stirring and stretching, warming and slowly coming alive under his hands.

Emma was almost scared by her body's response; she had no command over these new feelings. They were so powerful, completely engulfing her.

She tried to regain some control, desperately clinging on to some kind of stable solid place in the midst of this raging torrent of sensation and emotion. She clung there for a second until the pull grew so strong she felt herself slipping; gradually losing her hold, until, in a moment of total surrender, she let go.

Whatever happened, would happen. Wherever he was taking her, she must go. She was being swept away by the irresistible current, not knowing if she was going to be broken to pieces or lifted gently to shore. As she gave up, gave in and let go, her body melted into his.

Up until that moment, he had been slow, gentle, holding back, waiting for her to come to him. Then, as she returned the pressure of his kiss with more intensity, hungry and insistent, he pulled her harder against him.

Emma's hands found their way underneath his shirt, she needed to touch his skin, feel the texture. Her hands became bolder, wanting an experience all of their own.

Exploring and delighting in what they found. She started undoing all the buttons of his shirt, sliding it off his shoulders and down his arms. Her hands became her eyes, learning the structure of his body, his powerful shoulders and muscular arms, his chest, his hard stomach, her fingers studying every contour, building a picture in her mind.

Emma had reached a point where the need inside her was becoming almost unbearable. She needed every part of her body to be touching every part of his. She wanted their bodies to merge until they were no longer two separate beings, but together completely.

Her hands moved down to the buckle of his belt and rested there for a moment. She felt his whole body stiffen and he let out a low moan. Then he caught hold of her hands and put them around him, behind his back, holding her tightly against him.

'We have to stop, Emma,' he said into her hair, 'if we go on, I'm not going to be able to control myself and I haven't got anything… any protection –,'

Oh no! She could no more stop now than she could have stopped Arcturus jumping that hedge.

She drew back a little, looking into his eyes. They were dark pools, intense and feverish, the heat was intoxicating. 'I've got an implant,' she whispered, 'and I know I'm clean, there's been no-one else except…' she didn't want to say Edward's name.

'Me too, I got tested…are you sure you want…?' he whispered, his eyes penetrating hers.

She nodded, barely able to breathe, let alone speak.

She felt drunk, the world began to pitch and slide. She closed her eyes, her head coming to rest gently against his collar-bone as she tried to slow her breathing.

Then his hands were moving over her back, soothing but at the same time stimulating new areas of pleasure. They dropped down to the hem of her top, asking.

She replied by quickly pulling it off over her head, dropping it on the floor beside them. He bent down to kiss her neck. It was almost too much for her, she needed him. Now.

Her hands found the buckle of his belt again, sure and persistent this time. She could hear his heart thumping in time with her own.

He stood up, lifting her to her feet. Her legs would hardly hold her, but the pull of his body supported her as she undid the buttons of his jeans. They shed the remains of their clothes until there was nothing left but bare skin.

Emma's eyes, followed by her hands, ran hungrily over his body, wanting to know him completely. Her fingertips traced the scar across his ribs, her touch feather-light and curious, then followed the line of dark hair running from his chest down past his navel.

A tremor went through him, and he gasped. His arms closed around her and he pulled her to him hard, bare skin on bare skin.

He kissed her fiercely, his self-control slipping. And then in one smooth motion, put a hand under each of her arms, and lifted her easily up onto the bed. She looked down at him, pushing her hands through his hair, smoothing it back off his beautiful face.

She kissed him; first his mouth, then his cheekbones, then across his brow, his eyes and finally his mouth once more, with each kiss his name was on her lips.

He kept quite still, his eyes closed until her mouth had come to rest on his again. Then he lifted himself up on to the bed beside her and she lay down, pulling him with her.

He was above her, kissing her lips, her neck and down, running his lips over her breasts.

Her body arched up towards his, her movements instinctive, communicating that she needed him now. She couldn't wait any longer.

As he lowered himself down onto her, she lifted her hips to meet him. She felt the pressure as his body met hers, the moment when hers yielded to receive him.

Breath was suspended for an instant as the most intimate and spiritual connection that can be made between two beings was made: that life creating, merging of body and souls.

Emma felt her world change irreversibly in that moment. There was nothing but this awareness of his soul intertwining with hers. She knew, without any doubt at all, that she loved him, completely, helplessly, infinitely. No matter what.

Then there was the ecstasy of movement, a rhythm, like the pulsing of blood through veins, the pressure gradually growing, pleasure so defined and penetrating it was almost too much to bear.

He was touching that place inside of her, so recently awakened, so new and raw, she cried out with emotion, and the word that she cried was his name. She had the sense that she was being lifted up, up, higher and higher.

She was weightless and floating, the hum in her ears became a roar. She was so high now, she had reached the crest of the wave, it had to break!

Then she felt herself tip over the top and was rushing down the other side.

Exquisite sensation ripped through her body like shock waves, flattening her with the force of their intensity, over and over again. His body responded in answer to hers, every muscle crying out for release.

The tension broke and he shuddered and breathed her name against her skin, and they drifted back down to earth together, becoming still except for their hearts racing. Their breathing gradually slowed.

They lay like that for a long time. Emma didn't ever want him to move. She wanted to stay like this forever, feeling this togetherness, this oneness.

Eventually though, kissing her gently on the lips, he slowly moved and lay down beside her, gathering her to him and wrapping his arms around her. There was no need of words.

She wanted to stay facing him so that whenever she opened her eyes, she could look at him, kiss him, reassure herself that he was real. She wanted all her senses to be full of him. The smell that enveloped them was indescribably sweet.

Lying there, in each other's arms, their breath became deeper and more regular. Emma fell asleep with her lips against his skin.

She wasn't sure which one of them stirred first, not more than a couple of hours later, whether it was his movement which woke her, or the other way round, but gradually consciousness returned and with it dawned the awareness of their bodies.

A very small movement of hers triggered a response in his, and she could feel his need for her growing again.

The night became a pattern of intervals of sleep, richly interwoven with periods of rapturous re-discovery of each other.

Chapter 43

BUT AS THE NIGHT GAVE WAY TO THE NEW DAY, EXHAUSTION finally took Emma to a place of much deeper sleep. She woke with a start, as a shaft of sunlight glanced through the high window onto her closed eyelids, instantly realising that the space beside her was empty. Dan had gone.

Fear like a cold hand closed over her heart. She hastily jumped down from the bed and went into the tiny bathroom. She could immediately tell from the smell of soap and steam that the shower had already been used. He must have had one before he left. How on earth had she slept through that?

As quickly as she could, she showered and brushed her teeth, then got dressed. All the while a kind of urgency was building up inside her. She needed to see him; see how he would be with her now, after…

It was terrifying, the thought that he might be cold and distant with her this morning after the heat and intimacy of the night. It was still only early, and the fact that he had got up and left her caused a fear like a sharp cold pain in her chest.

Leaving the lorry she ran down to the stables, as she got near to Merlin's box she could see the door was open and Merlin was tied up with a hay-net. That must mean Dan was inside the stable with him. She slowed down and forced herself to take a deep breath. She must brace herself for whatever was coming.

If he had shut her out again she must be strong and accept it. She had chosen this, there was no way of denying that she had walked into this with her eyes open.

She went to the open door. He was crouched down re-doing Merlin's bandages. She didn't say anything, just stood watching him for a moment knowing that as soon as he looked at her, she would know. She was almost too scared to betray her presence.

He looked up when he became aware of her standing there, and a smile slowly spread across his face, starting in his eyes and ending with his mouth. That heartbreakingly beautiful mouth. Emma felt almost faint with relief.

'Morning sleepy head,' he said. She smiled giddily back at him.

Finishing the last bandage, he stood up and giving Merlin a pat, he untied him.

Then, turning to Emma he said, 'Come on, let's get something to eat.'

He took her hand and led her out of the stable, closing it behind them.

He didn't let go of her hand.

They walked through the show ground in the sunshine. Emma felt like she was walking a foot above the ground. There were other riders and grooms around; some of them they didn't know, but they exchanged greetings with those that they did. She could feel their eyes looking at her hand in his, and it earned them some curious stares and some knowing looks.

They passed the blue and silver lorry, where the two girls from yesterday were sitting outside on camping chairs with cups of coffee. The dark-haired girl gave Emma a look of pure envy, and Emma thought she might die of pride.

At the wagon selling breakfast – all good hot protein and carbs – Emma realised she was absolutely starving. Dan bought two breakfast rolls with everything in them, eggs, bacon and sausage, and two cups of tea. They found an empty table and sat side by side, the steam from their tea rising into the fresh morning air.

Emma leaned back in her chair, the sun on her face, the breakfast roll possibly the best thing she had ever tasted. Euphoria was mixed with a sense of deep satisfaction. They ate in companionable silence, just their eyes communicating their mutual fulfilment; savouring the enjoyment of their hunger being sated.

Then Dan moved, turning so he could put his legs either side of hers. He had a glint in his eye and a small smile played around the corners of his mouth.

'I had to get up this morning, you were sleeping so peacefully. If I had stayed in bed any longer, I'd have had to wake you up,' he said, exerting a gentle pressure on her thighs with his own.

Emma's mouth went dry and suddenly she couldn't eat anymore, consumed by a different kind of hunger. She swallowed her last mouthful with difficulty, her blood quickening. She could feel her face heating up and was sure he would see her going red. Looking away from him she tried to distract herself from the butterflies in her stomach, which had suddenly gone berserk.

She couldn't cope with feeling like this, not in a public place. It made her eyes water. But then she remembered her promise, never to hide from him again and, steeling herself, she looked back at him; directly into his eyes.

He was smiling – obviously enjoying the effect he was having on her. But he must have seen something in her eyes, because all trace of amusement left his face. Like the hunter, capturing his prey, then realising that he has ensnared himself in his own trap. He put the remains of his food down on the table, swallowing, and leant back in his chair. They sat for a moment, a subtle tension building. Then he said, 'Do you want to go back to the lorry?'

She nodded urgently, and in an instant they were on their feet and moving through the showground, their chairs and what was left of their food abandoned, her hand locked tightly in his. The anticipation of what she knew was coming made her feel weak and light-headed as they wove through the other horse-boxes to their own. She pleaded with God that they wouldn't run into anyone they knew on the way.

The door of the lorry had barely closed behind them before she was pressed against his body and he was kissing her hard. There was no hesitation this time, just a frantic tearing off of each other's clothes and a feverish coming together. A mutual giving of what the other needed, leaving them both blissful and satiated, for the time being at least.

They lay together, hot and panting on the messy sheets of the bed, both staring at the ceiling getting their breath back.

Eventually they turned to look at each other in wonder.

Dan shook his head. 'I don't know what you've done to me girl,' he said laughing, rubbing a hand across his face and through his hair.

Emma thought that actually, it was he who had done something to her. She hadn't known she was capable of experiencing the kind of feelings she was having both physically and emotionally. She had thought that part of her was defunct, broken.

She lay on the bed watching him get dressed. Seeing him put his jeans on was almost as sexy as seeing him take them off.

'*I am a terrible person*,' she thought to herself. '*All my life I've assumed I'm a fairly decent person and now it turns out I'm no such thing. Here I am, I've cheated on my boyfriend, and I don't feel any guilt at all. I don't feel any guilt or any shame, or any regret. I just feel happy. Ridiculously, entirely, completely happy.*'

Dan noticed her watching him. 'If you keep looking at me like that, I'm going to have to come back to bed,' he said.

Everything had taken on new meaning. Even the most mundane, boring little task she performed that day seemed special and significant. She felt like she had been re-born into a new world, unbelievably blessed and grateful; to be alive, to be here, now, with him.

Every time he looked at her, every time he smiled, she was filled with such feelings of love and joy, the like of which she had never known before. She wanted this day to last forever, blocking out any thought of what might lie in the future.

They walked both the horses out in-hand for some grass, and a leg stretch. Then wandered around the showground, watching some of the early dressage, chatting to people they knew.

Emma was seeing everything through a golden haze of happiness. Sometimes Dan would take her hand while they were walking, and when they were watching the dressage, he stood behind her and put his arms round her, resting his chin on her head. It felt so good every time he touched her.

Eventually, it was time to get Merlin ready. They tacked him up between them and Dan warmed him up for his test. He seemed more relaxed than she had ever known him to be before a class. He was riding as if he were at home, and there were no competition involved.

Today, it didn't even seem that important that they did well. But it was as though Merlin sensed that both his humans were as high as kites. In the dressage he was foot-perfect, and in the show-jumping, he jumped with an enthusiasm as if their happiness was infectious. There was no way he was touching a pole today. As he cantered jauntily into the ring, Emma could swear he had a smile on his black face. All was right with the world.

He approached each fence like a springbok, ears pricked and judging the distance perfectly himself, there was no need for Dan to set him up. Then with a merry flick of his tail he bounced over, showing his heels to the sky in a gesture of triumph.

Dan came out laughing. 'He just carried me round, I didn't have to do a thing!' he said, dropping Merlin's reins and patting the big gelding on either side of his neck with both hands. Emma's grin was so wide she thought her face might split. Neither of them could be bothered to check the score boards, it seemed unimportant somehow.

Going into the start box for the cross-country, Merlin had his game face on. Eager and keen to get going, galloping and jumping for the sheer joy of it; doing exactly what he was born to do. Dan rode like he was part of the horse himself, so perfectly in balance that Merlin would hardly have felt him there at all, communicating through unseen channels. That connection that was almost telepathy, which exists when a horse and rider are truly a partnership.

As they came through the finish, he slid down from Merlin's back and buried his face briefly in his mane, hiding some private emotion. Emma had no words; she fed Merlin nearly an entire pack of polos and they led him back between them.

Mr Davies was waiting for them back at the lorry. He took Dan's hand in both of his and shook it warmly. 'Congratulations,' he said, beaming all over his benign face, 'this calls for a celebration. When you've finished here, come and have a glass of champagne in the sponsors tent with us.' He glanced at Emma. 'Bring your young lady too.'

Dan looked a little dazed. 'Thank you,' he said, 'we did our best, but there were a lot of good horses out there today…'

'Haven't you seen the scores?' Mr Davies asked in disbelief. 'My dear boy – you've won!'

As they went to collect their prize, Emma thought her heart was going to burst with pride. Her horse. Her man. Even if only for today. They stood together in the owners' tent, drinking champagne with Dan's new sponsors.

Rory Owens came over to congratulate Dan. 'That was a hell of a piece of riding! That black horse has come a long way, hasn't he? If Malcolm ever wants to….'

'He's not for sale,' Emma and Dan said in unison.

She would never forget this feeling, this would be the way she would define happiness for the rest of her life.

But, as all days do, this one finally came to an end, and they made the journey back to the yard. Emma wished the distance could have been a hundred times longer.

As they drew closer and closer to home, their euphoria evaporated like mist in the morning as reality started to rear its ugly head.

Dan became quiet, his face losing its recent openness and Emma felt him begin to withdraw from her as his eyes took on their usual watchful expression.

With each mile that passed, they left the day behind them and he drifted further away from her. She knew there was no point trying to hold on to him, if he wanted to go, he would go. Trying to cling on would only make him pull away harder.

They drew up into the yard in the late afternoon, just as the others were starting the evening chores. Parking the lorry in its usual spot, Dan let the engine idle a minute before turning it off, and they sat in a silence loaded with unanswered questions.

He turned to face her and, for a second, she thought he was going to say something. She so desperately wanted a word from him, any word just to let her know everything was okay, that it wasn't over. But Rachel and Kitty's' voices could be heard chatting loudly as they approached the lorry; in a second they would be at the door.

He put his hand out and briefly touched her face, and it felt like goodbye.

Then he opened the door and jumped out.

Chapter 44

Dan swept the left-hand side of the yard whilst Simone swept the right. Emma swept outside the tack room and the feed room. Kitty and Rachel were scrubbing the feed bowls and filling hay nets for the morning.

It was all so normal; as though nothing had ever happened. The day had just been a dream. Dan never gave her a smile or even looked at her once. He was silent and withdrawn. He had shut her out. So was this it? Was it over?

Tears started to prick her eyes and the pain became unbearable. She leant her broom up against the wall, went quickly into the tack room and shut the door quietly behind her, covering her mouth with her hand.

'You knew it would be like this all along,' she told herself angrily. 'You chose this.'

Suddenly, Dan came in. Emma quickly turned away from him to hide the fact that she had been nearly crying.

'What's wrong?' he asked her, shutting the door again.

'I don't know,' she replied, trying to make her voice sound normal, but try as she might, she wasn't able to look him in the face. She walked over to the other side of the room and leant against the counter.

'It just feels like this…' she hesitated '…us, is already over. Almost as if it never happened.' She decided she had nothing to lose by being honest in that moment. 'And, I don't want it to be over,' she said in a small voice.

Dan paused for a long moment leaning back against the door, his expression grave and thoughtful. Then he walked across the room, put a hand under each of her arms and lifted her onto the countertop, just like he had lifted her onto the bed in the horsebox the night before. He placed a hand either side of her on the bench.

'Look,' he began. 'It would probably be easier for everyone if we behaved as if nothing had ever happened. It would almost certainly be better for you if you go home tomorrow, back to your real life and just forget about this. You have a good life to go back to, Edward can give you everything you want. I can't. And I don't want to be the reason you have to give all of that up.'

Emma looked down at her hands in her lap. She couldn't look at him. The closeness of him, the smell of him, his voice, was making her senses reel.

She dug her nails into her palms. She couldn't, she *wouldn't* let herself cry until she was alone. This is what she had known would happen all along, she kept telling herself. What had she expected? A declaration of undying love? But nothing had prepared her for just how much it would hurt.

Dan put his hands either side of her face, forcing her to look at him.

'But I can't just let you go like that,' he said. 'I'm too selfish. I've been trying to convince myself to do the right thing and let you go, but I've tried before and I can't. I want you here with me.'

Emma's heart paused in its painful thumping and started to flutter wildly.

'If you stayed,' he continued, 'we could try to make a go of it. Be together properly. I'm not saying it would be easy, God knows I can be a miserable bastard sometimes. I drink too much and do stupid things – well, you *know* me. And I can guarantee it won't all be hearts and flowers. But if you'll have me, I promise you I would try…I would try my hardest to be a better person and make it work.'

Emma felt as though she had received a last-minute death sentence reprieve, her heart lifted and soared. She felt her happiness return with a surge and a rush which flooded her whole being with sensations so sweet as she felt the anguish leave her mind and body.

She made a small sound; halfway between a sob and a laugh and put her arms around his neck.

'Well how can I resist when you make it all sound so appealing,' she said, the unshed tears escaping from her eyes. He chuckled and leant forward for a kiss, wrapping his arms around her. She kissed him back with the newly awakened hunger that lay just underneath the surface.

He pulled her against him, lifting her off the countertop, and she wrapped her legs around his hips – just as Simone walked in the door.

They both jumped like guilty children caught stealing biscuits. Emma slid down until her feet were back on the floor. Dan, without hurrying, turned to face Simone, keeping his hands on Emma's waist. Simone's expression of shock and surprise quickly turned to one of disgust and disdain.

'Oh I do beg your pardon,' she said sarcastically. 'I didn't realise I was interrupting anything.'

And with a parting look, which no doubt was intended to wither their very souls, she walked out, slamming the door so hard behind her, that Emma was surprised it stayed on its hinges.

Emma and Dan looked at each other.

'That's one of the reasons it's not going to be easy,' he sighed.

Simone didn't dare say anything when they ventured back out on to the yard, but she must have bad-mouthed her to Rachel and Kitty because, before they left, they caught Emma alone in the staff room.

'You're a dark horse,' Rachel said, a smirk on her face. 'Just good friends eh?'

'What do you mean?' Emma asked, knowing full well.

'Simone's livid. She said she just walked in on you and Dan snogging each other's faces off, and apparently, you swore to her there was nothing going on between you two.'

Rachel wasn't at all put out – in fact she looked like she was thoroughly enjoying this bit of gossip, but it made Emma feel distinctly uncomfortable.

'There wasn't,' she insisted. 'Not until last night.'

Rachel raised her eyebrows. 'Okay, if you say so.'

'I do say so,' Emma replied.

Poor Kitty looked at Emma with round, astonished eyes. 'Pretty short bargepole,' she muttered.

Once she and Dan were safely upstairs, away from the prying eyes and bitter tongues of the world below, Emma could breathe easy again.

She knew she had some hard thinking to do. How was she going to unravel and unpick her current life, so that they could begin to stitch together a new one? But now, she was just eager to be with him and be able to put her hands on him again.

They opted for her room. Although it was the slightly smaller of the two, Emma had made it more comfortable and homely over the time she had been there.

He pulled her into his arms as soon as they were upstairs, and at first Emma gave in to the delicious sensation of being held and kissed, but she felt grubby from the day's work.

'I need a shower,' she said, gently trying to remove herself from his embrace.

'Sounds good, want some help?' he asked her, his voice muffled as he kissed her neck.

'Er, no, I can manage thank you…for now,' she laughed. Although the thought of taking a shower with him was thrilling, she really needed to get clean.

Once she was standing under the warm water, her body was already shivering in anticipation.

Everything sensation was heightened; the feel of the water running over her skin, the slipperiness of the soap as it turned into a lather under her hands, and the softness of her wet skin. When she was clean, she wrapped a towel round herself and went back into the bedroom.

He had stripped off to the waist and was lying on his stomach on her bed in nothing but his jeans, reading one of her books. His body was so perfect; not thin, but lean and toned, and with just the right amount of flesh and muscle in all the right places, she suddenly felt insecure about her own.

She had always felt that her body was unexciting. Her boobs were too small, and although she was slim and had a small waist, she had always thought that made her bum look too big.

When she came in, he turned on his side, propping his head up on his hand to watch her. She began to dry herself, rather self-consciously.

She glanced at him. He was watching her with that lazy, slightly lop-sided smile which curled up the corner of his mouth and showed one of his dimples.

'I'll never get used to seeing you naked,' he said.

Emma blushed. 'Not much to see I'm afraid,' she said smiling ruefully.

He sat up and reaching forward, he got hold of the edges of the towel, and pulled her towards the bed. Once he had her there, he flipped her over onto her back.

'Rubbish,' he said. 'You're perfect. I especially like it here,' he said, kissing her belly button. She giggled and squirmed. 'And here,' he said, kissing his way up her stomach to her breasts. 'And here,' he said working his way back down. All the way down.

'No!' she squealed, trying to wriggle downwards and pull him up at the same time; she had never let anyone kiss her down there before.

He came back up, but only for a moment.

'Yes, I want to. And as you know, I'm used to getting my own way.' He grinned wickedly. 'And I promise you'll like it, so just lie still, like a good girl.' And down he went again.

Emma gasped. She felt helpless to stop him, and actually, after a second or two she didn't want to. He was like a master musician, expertly getting a tune out of a rather tricky instrument. Holy cow! As someone who had tried to avoid sex all her adult life, over the last twenty-four hours, she had finally learnt what all the fuss was about.

After a while, he got up to have a shower looking very pleased with himself. As he walked out through the door he glanced over his shoulder with a look of smug satisfaction, to where she lay glowing and feeling completely liberated, as if she'd had an out of body experience.

And the best thing was, she didn't feel dirty or shameful at all. Because there was no judgement, just an uncomplicated sense of rightness.

She didn't want to move and lay still, in a state of wonder until he was back, towel slung low round his hips, and still a little wet from the shower.

He came over to the bed and lowered himself down on top of her, holding his weight on his arms, he kissed her mouth. He tasted of toothpaste and smelt like heaven.

She stretched beneath him luxuriously. The towel slipped away and she shivered as their stomachs touched.

But as he began to make love to her again, she decided to take matters into her own hands.

'Oh no, it's my turn now,' she said, pushing firmly on his shoulder so that he rolled over onto his back. She had never been at all adventurous in the bedroom, but her love for him made her brave.

Her slightly open lips and tongue began a sensuous journey of exploration all over his body, from top to toe, brushing, sometimes lightly, sometimes with deeper kisses.

He tried to sit up and take her in his arms but she pushed him back down, taking hold of his wrists and pinning them to the pillow above his head.

'Just lie still, like a good boy,' she mimicked. He groaned, captivated by his oppressor, his eyes pleading with her. This was a new experience for her, and she quite liked the feeling of being in control.

But before too long, instinct took over and all control was forgotten.

Afterwards she lay with her head on his chest and sighed with deep contentment. His arm was around her and his hand gently stroked her back.

'Are you hungry?' she asked him eventually.

'Mm-hmm,' he murmured sleepily.

She got up, giving him a last kiss and got dressed quickly. Going downstairs she made two plates of pasta and tomato sauce with ham and grated cheese. While she was cooking, she thought about what she was going to do – and it didn't make for comfortable ruminating.

She knew she had to go back home. She had to tell Edward to his face that it was over. Tell her Mother, Lottie, everyone that she was coming back to Dorset for good.

It was going to be the hardest thing she had ever done, and although she knew she had to do it, she was terrified.

If she wasn't going to bend and break, she had to have absolute faith that she was doing the right thing.

There was no question at all in her heart how she felt. But at the back of her mind there was a small nagging, niggling voice, spreading the seeds of doubt and fear into her consciousness.

Dan hadn't said he loved her.

He'd said he cared about her, sure, but that was different to saying that he loved her. Why it made so much difference she didn't know, but it did.

Grabbing the plates and two beers from the fridge, she went back upstairs.

He had put on a pair of boxer shorts but nothing else. They sat on the floor on her rug, facing each other and ate.

When they had nearly finished she said carefully, 'You know, I still have to go home tomorrow.'

He put his fork down. 'Do you?' he said.

'I don't want to. But I have to tell Edward to his face that it's over.'

He frowned.

'Can't you just… not go? He'll get the message. Then if he wants to talk to you, he'll come looking for you.'

Emma shook her head vehemently. 'I can't do that,' she said. 'I can't just hide away; I have to face up to him. I owe him that at least. If I don't go it will just make things harder later.'

There was a small silence.

'How long are you going to go for?' he asked finally.

'I don't know. However long it takes to get everything sorted out.'

He sighed and turned his face away from her for a moment, then, he leant back against the bed and pushed his plate away.

'When's your birthday?' he asked her.

'Next weekend, Sunday the 28th…why?' she said, surprised.

He hesitated.

'There's something I have to tell you.'

'What?' she asked in trepidation.

'Lottie told me something when she was here. The night we went to the pub.' He stopped again.

'Yes, go on,' she encouraged.

'She told me that she and Edward are organising a big party for you on your birthday. It was going to be a surprise.'

'Oh.' Her insides curled up. This was getting worse and worse. 'Well, by then everyone will know, and it just won't happen.'

Dan still looked troubled. 'There's something else.'

'What?' Now she was seriously worried.

He looked at her from beneath his frown and seemed to be about to say something, but then he shook his head.

'No, nothing…it doesn't matter.'

'No, what? You have to tell me now!'

But he was steadfast. 'It's nothing. Just… you need to come back before your birthday. If you don't, I'll know you're not coming back.'

'I will. I'll be back before that…but please tell me why. I need to know.'

He got up, reaching forward and took her hand, pulling her to her feet. Sitting down on the bed he drew her onto his lap.

'You once told me that Edward isn't insecure. Well, you need to know that I am. I find it hard to trust people. When you're gone, I know it's going to be hard for me to believe that you're coming back.'

Emma thought of his mother and her heart twisted.

'I will come back. I promise,' she said.

'But when you're at home, surrounded by your friends and family, all telling you not to do such a crazy, ridiculous thing, it's going to be hard.'

'I know.' Emma reassured him. 'I'm ready for that.'

'Lottie doesn't like me,' he stated. 'She's going to go to any lengths to stop you from breaking up with Edward. She's your best friend and she's going to be very persuasive.'

Emma nodded; she knew better than to deny it. 'I know – but she will like you. I know once she gets to know you, she'll love you like I do.'

He shook his head. 'She thinks I'm a low life,' he said. 'She thinks that Edward can give you everything you want because he has money. He can give you a nice place to live, security and everything you want. She'll say that I won't make you happy.'

'What makes you say all this?' she asked him. 'How do you know that's what she'll say.'

'Because it's basically what she said to me at the pub. She more or less said that I wasn't good enough for you – that I had nothing to offer you.'

Emma was shocked. His words repeated themselves in her mind.

They jogged something in her memory. She sat up suddenly with a sharp intake of breath and looked at him wide-eyed.

'Is that what you meant when you asked me if it was enough? If what you had to offer was enough for me?'

He nodded.

'Oh my God,' she got up and started pacing about the room.

'Why? What did you think I meant?' he asked perplexed.

'I think we seriously need to sort out our communication, you and I!' she said with sardonic little laugh.

'Why?' he asked again.

She didn't explain immediately, realising that it wasn't going to sound good. 'So, when I told you that I just wanted to stay friends, you thought it was because you weren't… what…rich enough for me?'

He nodded. 'I suppose so, yeah. I can't give you the things that Edward can give you; money, a home, security. Things that Lottie said were important to you.'

She stopped pacing and knelt down in front of him. 'None of that matters to me!' she cried. 'God, no wonder you were angry if that's what you thought. Now I understand that remark about integrity!' She took his hands in hers. 'Look,' she said earnestly. 'I love you, I don't care what Lottie thinks, and right now I'm pretty bloody angry that she said those things to you, she had no right.'

'She probably thought she was protecting you,' he said.

'Maybe…but she bloody wasn't! She nearly messed up everything.'

He grinned and put his arms around her pulling her up between his knees.

'You're cute when you're angry Bugs,' he said. 'But you haven't told me what you thought I meant – about what I could offer you.'

'Ah,' she said going red. 'I thought you meant that you didn't want anything serious, that you were just offering me….um… no strings, casual sex.'

'Ha!' he laughed. 'Is that what you thought that was, at Bicton – casual sex?'

'Well, there was nothing casual about it – but yes. I suppose I thought you didn't want to get involved with anyone again, after Caroline.'

'Well,' he drawled, 'if I'd known I could have got away with that…'

She smacked his bare leg. 'There is another bed next door you know.'

But she felt suddenly vulnerable. There was so much room for misunderstanding.

'We have so nearly messed everything up because we couldn't communicate,' she said quietly. 'We need to be completely honest with each other. I'll never hold anything back from you ever again. I love you. I'm going tomorrow, but I need you to believe that I am coming back. I promise.'

She held her breath.

He kissed her forehead, but didn't say anything. Not a word. Emma swallowed, the seeds of doubt started to sprout and grow. She searched his eyes, and he didn't look away but the nagging voice in the back of her mind became more insistent. A nasty, sickly feeling grew in the pit of her stomach.

She bit her lip. He looked at her mouth and leant forward for a kiss, but she turned away ever so slightly, getting to her feet at the same time, so he was met with thin air.

'Lottie's coming to get me in the morning,' she said, 'I really should pack.'

She went to the wardrobe and got out her bags, taking her clothes off the hangers and folding them, keeping her back to him. She knew she was being ridiculous but she desperately needed reassurance.

'Emma?'

She stopped what she was doing and turned towards him. His eyes were full of confusion. With a rush of affection and chagrin, she went back to him and dropped down between his knees again, putting her arms around his waist and kissing his mouth. After all, it was her who was leaving – going back to see her boyfriend – it was *he* who ought to need reassurance.

'Sorry, I can pack in the morning,' she said.

She would have to find the courage in her own heart; she would have to be brave. Because tomorrow, she was going to be on her own.

Chapter 45

NEITHER OF THEM GOT MUCH SLEEP THAT NIGHT. THEY SPENT it in Emma's narrow bed; space being the last thing either of them wanted. Dan said he would make himself scarce the following morning when Lottie picked Emma up.

'It will just make things awkward,' he said as the night faded into dawn. 'I'd rather not be here. I'll probably take Merlin for a hack or something.'

Emma understood how he felt.

'I'll call you,' she said.

'No, don't call,' he said. 'I hate talking on the phone – voices never sound the same. Just come back as soon as you can. Text me when you're on your way back.'

They said their goodbyes alone in Merlin's stable; the big black horse a shield from the outside world. But as she watched him ride away, she had a sudden, terrible premonition, that it would be the last time she would ever see him.

LOTTIE GREETED HER in the same, concerned manner as before, ready to console and comfort her. Emma's returning hug was a little stiff, she wasn't ready to forgive her friend immediately for her interference.

She'd left most of her belongings (including the money) behind; her intention being to speak to Edward as soon as he arrived back on Wednesday, and then make her journey back on Thursday at the latest.

As they pulled away down the drive, Lottie kept giving her long sympathetic glances.

'I know you probably feel sad at the moment,' Lottie began, 'but it's for the best, believe me. I know that once you re-adjust to your normal life, you'll realise this was just…'

'Lottie, I'm never going to re-adjust to my normal life.'

'Of course you will! It might take a little time but…'

'I'm coming back here as soon as I've spoken to Edward.'

Lottie shot her a look of surprise and alarm. 'You have to give it more time than that,' she said. 'Give it until after the weekend and then see how you feel. Edward's not getting back until Wednesday, and things are bound to feel strange at first…'

'Lottie, I know about the party – Dan told me.'

'Bloody hell, it was supposed to be a surprise!' Lottie complained. 'What else did he tell you?'

'Just that you warned him off. Tried to make him feel inadequate; like he didn't have a hope. You'll be pleased to know you very nearly succeeded.'

Lottie had the decency to look sheepish. 'Well, considering what you told me about him, I thought I was doing you a favour,' she said defensively. 'I thought I was protecting you.'

'I realise that,' said Emma. 'Which is why I don't entirely blame you – but you have to cancel the party. I'm coming back before my birthday.'

'No! Why? It's all organised and paid for. What if you change your mind?'

'I won't change my mind – I'm in love with Dan.'

Lottie shook her head. 'You might think you are now, but when you…'

'Lottie – I've slept with him.'

Lottie nearly drove her car off the road. 'Oh my God *Em*! How could you let this happen?'

'Lottie! The road…'

'No, no, no Emma! This is so unlike you!' Lottie banged her head on the steering wheel, hitting the horn in a blast of furious sound, then swerved to avoid oncoming traffic.

'Just pull over, before you kill us both!' Emma cried.

Lottie pulled into the next layby and turned in her seat to face Emma.

'So, explain to me. What made you do this crazy, uncharacteristic thing? You've always been the sensible one.'

'I guess I've changed. I'm not the same person I was two years ago. I've never felt this way before.'

'Why? I can see the attraction believe me, but…'

'Because he sees me in a way that no-one else sees me. Because I can tell him anything – things I would never dream of telling Edward. He values me. He respects me. He thinks my opinions matter. And when I'm with him I feel braver, stronger, more myself – I am the person I want to be. I never have to worry about what I say or do in front of him because he accepts me just the way I am. I don't have to pretend to be anyone else.'

Emma told her everything. About the nights they'd sat up talking, watching the mares foal. How when they worked together with the horses it was the most connected she'd ever felt to another human being. She told her about his Mother, and how she had gradually come to an understanding of why he was the way he was, and how they had finally made that connection, mind, body and soul, which now couldn't be broken.

'Do you want me to go on? Because I could,' she asked finally.

While she had been speaking Lottie's horrified expression had gradually softened into one of compassionate understanding.

She shrugged. 'Okay, I get it. I really do. I understand why you feel the way you do about him. And I know how real it can feel – especially when the physical side of it is so good.'

Emma shook her head. 'It isn't about that. I loved him long before he ever touched me physically.'

Lottie pursed her lips.

'But, you said you understand why he is the way he is. Do you really believe he is going to change – just like that?'

'I don't know,' Emma replied honestly.

Lottie frowned. 'Has he said that he loves you?'

This was the one question that Emma had dreaded. Immediately the fear and doubt in her own heart became stronger, fed and watered by Lottie's words.

'No, but….'

Lottie shook her head.

'I just think he finds it so hard to trust because of his bloody mother,' Emma said.

'What if he never learns to trust?'

'Well, that's a chance I'm going to have to take.'

'So you're going into this cheerfully, knowing there's a good chance that it could end in disaster? That you could end up being hurt?'

'Yes. And possibly penniless and friendless.' Emma gave a little laugh.

'Do you know how mad that sounds?' Lottie asked incredulously.

'Yes, but it's worth it.'

Lottie laughed. 'You have changed. You are stronger – crazier, but stronger. I can see that. But I still hope you'll change your mind.'

And Emma had to be content with that, it was more than she had expected. When they arrived at Lottie and Josh's flat, they couldn't talk any-more because of Josh, who was totally oblivious.

Now Emma had to brace herself for Edward's return.

The next few days were something to be endured, like a painful dentist appointment. She could be making the return journey as early as Thursday. It was only three days. She clung to this thought as if it were a life raft in the middle of an angry ocean.

Tuesday evening, she steeled herself to call Edward. It was noisy in the background and she could hardly hear him. She told him that she knew he was coming home for her birthday.

'Lottie tried to keep it a secret, but I guessed,' she lied, feeling horribly guilty.

'Oh well, I'm just glad you're okay – I haven't been able to get hold of you. But listen, I'm not going to be able to catch that flight tomorrow. We've had a flu outbreak here, half the doctors are off with it; they're barely coping as it is.'

Emma's heart sank through the floor.

'When do you think you'll be able to get away?' she asked.

'I don't know yet, hopefully Thursday at the latest.'

She swallowed. 'Edward, I need to talk to you. Please come back as soon as you can.'

'What's that? I can't hear you very well…it's pandemonium here.

I'll call you when I know.'

There was absolutely nothing she could do, but the waiting became almost unbearable.

She desperately wanted to call Dan and talk to him, hear his voice.

On Thursday morning, the thought that by now it could have all been over with, and she could have been on her way back, made Emma feel extremely agitated.

Even though he'd asked her not to, she called Dan.

Her nerves were ludicrous. Listening to the phone ringing, waiting for him to answer, she thought her heart was going to jump through her ribcage.

The ringing stopped, then there was some muffled scuffling noises as if the phone had been dropped.

'Hello?' she heard finally.

'Dan? It's me.'

'Emma?'

He sounded different on the phone, she would hardly have recognised his voice.

'Yes.'

'Where are you? Are you on your way back?'

'No – Edward's not back yet, he's…'

'What? Hang on…' There was some more scuffling noises, and some muffled swearing. She could hear the sharp sound of horse's hooves ringing on tarmac in the background.

'Look, I'm riding Merlin and he's being a git – I can't talk right now.'

'Okay.' Emma floundered; she didn't know what to say. 'Shall I call you later?'

'No, look – don't call. I hate talking on the phone, just…' The phone went dead.

Emma swore to herself. She had called hoping to reassure him – and herself – but had probably made both of them feel worse.

She texted: *'Edward not home yet, haven't had the chance to talk to him, will be back as soon as pos.'* She debated for ages about how to finish the text. She settled for a big X and waited anxiously for a reply. It came an hour later: *'Hate not talking face 2 face. Text me when ur on ur way. X'*

And that was it.

Chapter 46

EDWARD DIDN'T COME HOME THURSDAY. HE CALLED THURSDAY morning to say he was catching the evening flight on Friday. By this time Emma was losing the will to live. Her birthday was on Sunday.

'We need to cancel the party,' she told Lottie.

'I can't! Everybody's coming – what will I tell people? Let's wait and see. Whatever's happened, it's still your birthday. If you're still here by then we might as well go ahead with it,' said Lottie, infuriatingly.

'I told Dan I'd be back before my birthday!' Emma was desperate.

'What difference can one day make!' said Lottie dismissively. 'Wait until Monday morning and I'll drive you myself.'

'So what am I supposed to do? Tell Edward it's over when I'm blowing out my candles?' Emma snapped.

'Talk to him when the party is over. You can stay at my parents' and I'll drive you to Dorset first thing in the morning,' Lottie promised.

Emma thought to herself that she would talk to Edward as soon as he got back Friday evening, and be back in Dorset by Saturday lunchtime.

But when they picked Edward up from the airport late, on Friday night, he was clearly exhausted. It had been an incredibly tough week, he said. He went straight to bed when they got back to Lottie and Josh's flat, not asking her for anything she wasn't willing to give, but also not affording her the opportunity of saying anything. And if he noticed that anything was wrong, he didn't ask what.

As she lay on the sofa-bed, beside his peacefully slumbering form, tears flowed silently from her eyes in the stillness and darkness.

She felt like she was being swept along by an irresistible current, a riptide carrying her further and further away from Dan, from the place she longed to be.

She closed her eyes and tried to remember what it felt like to be held in his arms, the smell of him, the sound of his voice. Nothing would come. Whether it was the guilt, or the proximity of Edward's sleeping body, the memory wouldn't form.

Edward's father picked them up in the morning to take them back. He arrived early and Edward was still asleep. Then there was a rush to get ready. As Emma said goodbye, Lottie took her to one side and spoke to her in a low voice.

'Don't say anything to Edward yet Emma, please! Just give it some time. See how you feel tomorrow.'

Back at Edward's house that evening, they were sitting around the dining room table, listening to Edward telling them all about Germany over cups of coffee. There had been much joy and celebration over his return. All day he had been the centre of attention, people all around him.

Sophie, was already there with her family, and Arabella was expected in the morning. His aunt and uncle were there as well for a welcome home family meal.

Surrounded by Edward's family, talking, laughing – people she was fond of, Emma dreaded what she was going to have to do. As soon as she was alone with Edward she would tell him. Shatter this illusion of happy families.

She almost wished she didn't have to – just yet. Almost wished she had some excuse to put it off – just a little bit longer.

The telephone rang and Edward's mother answered it.

'It's Arabella,' she said frowning, handing Edward the phone. 'Little Joseph isn't very well.'

Edward took the phone and left the room. Joseph was Arabella's youngest child. When Edward came back into the room, he had his car keys in his hand and was putting his coat on.

'What's the matter?' Edward's mother asked, alarmed.

'Joseph has a temperature and a suspicious looking rash,' Edward replied. 'I'm going to drive over there and check it out, just in case.'

There was a chorus of sympathetic noises around the table.

'Let us know how he is as soon as you can,' his mother told him.

Emma got up and followed Edward out into the hall.

'Do you think it's anything serious?' she asked him, concerned.

'Probably not, knowing Arabella,' he replied. 'But you can't be too careful when it comes to unusual rashes. I'll be back as soon as I can.' He bent down and kissed her cheek.

Arabella lived half an hour's drive away; it would probably be at least two hours before he got back.

'Edward, when you get back, we really need to talk!' she blurted out.

He hesitated, hand on the door handle. 'Okay, sounds ominous,' he said with a little laugh.

Emma swallowed, her heart starting to pound. She didn't contradict him.

She saw in his eyes some conflicting emotions.

'Look Emma, whatever it is you're worried about, I'm sure it's not as bad as you think,' he said. 'I know this year has been hard, for both of us, and at times it might have felt like we were drifting apart. But if there's anything that has made you doubt my commitment to you – just give it a couple days and everything will feel right again, I promise you. We can put this year behind us and move on.'

Emma knew this wasn't the time or the place to get in any deeper. 'We'll talk when you get back,' she said.

He frowned, paused a second longer, then left.

She sat up in his bedroom, waiting for him to return, going over and over what she was going to say to him.

The house telephone rang again. Minutes later there was a knock at the door and Emma got up to answer it to find Edward's mother there, wearing her dressing gown. Before she even spoke, Emma got a sense of the inevitable.

'That was Ed,' she said. 'Little Joseph's okay but Bella wants him to stay the night and keep an eye on him – just to be on the safe side. She's always been a nervous mother!'

'Oh, right,' Emma replied. The feeling of helplessness washed the ground away from beneath her feet like the shifting sands on a beach.

Alone, she thought about texting Dan again. To say what? Edward was home but she still hadn't spoken to him? She didn't know when she would get the chance and she still didn't know when she would be back? Make him another promise about being home as soon as she could? There was no point.

*

She woke early in the morning. Her birthday.

Restlessly she jumped out of bed and quickly dressed in her running gear. Grabbing her iPhone and her trainers she went downstairs. No-one else was up.

Out in the deserted street, she put on some music and started to run.

She thought of what Dan had once told her, if you really want to do something you'll find a way, if you don't, you'll find an excuse.

Making a fuss, causing a scene, went completely against her nature. But if she did nothing, she would just be swept along. That premonition she'd had when she'd said goodbye to Dan, that it would be the last time she saw him, might very well come true.

Was she going to let fear control her life? Dictate what happened to her – write her fate?

Her phone buzzed. It was a text from Edward wishing her a happy birthday and telling her that he would see her soon. Joseph was fine and he was coming back with Arabella as soon as they could get organised.

She just had time to read it and her phone battery died again.

Edward and Arabella arrived just before lunch. He was full of apologies that he hadn't been able to be with her on the morning of her birthday, and Arabella was also apologetic and embarrassed to admit that all that seemed to be wrong with Joseph was either a teething rash or a mild virus.

'It's being a mother,' she said to Emma with a laugh. 'Turns you into a neurotic mess! Just you wait until you and Edward have kids.'

'Don't worry,' Emma said, 'if he was my baby, I'd have asked Edward to stay too.'

'I didn't ask him, bless him,' Arabella said fondly, 'he offered.'

After lunch, Emma had to open her presents in front of everybody.

In one box was a jade green dress, long and beautifully made, and shoes with a very high heel to match. They made her put it on and everyone 'Ooh'd' and 'Ahh'd' over it.

Then Lottie and Josh arrived. Lottie gave her a few meaningful glances, but Emma refused to meet her eye.

At five o'clock Edward announced that he was going to take her and Lottie and Josh out for cocktails before they went to eat. Emma knew this was subterfuge for getting her out of the house so that everyone else could get ready for the party. She showered and put on her new party dress.

As she did her make-up she stared at herself in the mirror. The eyes that stared back at her were blank.

She had two handbags; one was very small and didn't hold very much but would go better with her new dress. The other was much bigger. She chose that one.

Just as they were getting in the car Emma hesitated. 'Hang on, I've forgotten something,' she said, going back into the house.

Just by the front door were her trainers where she had left them after her run that morning. Picking them up, she dropped them into her bag and went back out to the car.

*

'Surprise!'

As they walked into the restaurant's function room, Emma was confronted by a sea of faces, all her friends and family. Her Mother and Father were there; but no Maggie, and no Granddad.

She acted as surprised as was expected of her, and the smile she wore seemed to convince everybody that she was as happy as she ought to be.

There were decorations and a band, and the champagne flowed freely. If anyone noticed that Emma was a bit quiet and wasn't drinking very much, no one said anything.

The food was served, and everyone said how delicious it was. But although Emma made all the right noises, she barely tasted anything.

After they had eaten, the waiters walked around with bottles of champagne topping everyone's glasses up and Edward tapped his glass with a spoon and stood up.

Everyone stopped chattering to listen.

'As everyone knows, it's my beautiful girlfriend's birthday today which is why we are all here. But only a few of you know that this is not the only reason that I wanted you all here today.'

A few knowing glances were cast about the room.

'Seeing as we all have champagne in our glasses anyway, and there's no harm in being thrifty.' Here everyone laughed. 'I thought it would be a good time to make this a double celebration.'

With a growing feeling of panic Emma looked up at him. As if in slow motion, she saw him get a small black velvet box out of his pocket. He opened the box and inside was a huge diamond ring.

She saw his mouth move; saw rather than heard the words that he said. It was as if she was locked inside herself and someone had turned the volume down on the outside world. All she could hear was the sound of her own breathing.

She looked around at the happy expectant faces of her family and friends, felt Edward take her hand and slip the ring onto her finger.

Everyone was on their feet now, clapping and cheering, turning to each other with smiles and nods of approval. And she was just sitting there, letting it happen. Being a good girl, not making a fuss. Letting Edward bend down and kiss her mouth. As his lips met hers, his mouth felt so wrong. It didn't fit. His hand was on her cheek and her skin recoiled from his touch.

Her eyes were open, and as Edward drew away he looked into them, and she looked into his, and she knew. He knew she didn't want this, and he didn't care. Didn't care how she felt or what she wanted, as long as she behaved herself, did as everyone expected.

It was as though she had received a massive electric shock.

'I can't do this,' she whispered quietly. No one heard her. She got to her feet.

'I can't do this!' she said much more loudly. This time everyone heard. The sea of faces swung towards her, the smiles slowly, one by one melting into expressions of confusion and disbelief. The room fell silent.

'I'm sorry everyone,' she said. She took the ring off, put it down on the table, and ran out of the restaurant.

Edward caught up with her in the cloakroom, Lottie hot on his heels, followed closely by Emma's mother.

'What's going on?' Edward said.

'I told you. I told you I needed to talk to you,' Emma said, her face a white mask of despair. 'But you never listen.'

'What on earth do you think you're doing?' Sylvia demanded. 'Why are you making such a ridiculous fuss?'

Emma ignored her.

'Emma, not here, not now! Not in front of all these people,' Lottie pleaded.

'Yes, Lottie's right,' Edward said. 'Can we just get through the rest of this evening and we can talk about this tomorrow. We'll just tell everyone you're not well.'

'No,' Emma said. 'We can't.'

'Whatever is wrong, I promise you we can sort it out!' he said taking her hand. 'If it's some misunderstanding, we can fix it,' he said soothingly.

'It can't be fixed,' said Emma.

'Of course it can! Nothing's so bad that it can't be fixed.'

It was as if he were speaking to a child. He wasn't taking her seriously.

'Even infidelity?' Emma said.

She watched the blood drain from his face, and he swallowed hard. But if anything, he held her hand even tighter.

'Look…it was only the once…it didn't mean anything… we'd had an argument, and…'

What was he talking about? He must not have understood.

'Edward!' she interrupted his strange mumbling. 'I've slept with someone else.'

That did the trick. He dropped her hand as if she'd just announced she had leprosy. Lottie clapped her hands over her mouth. Sylvia gasped.

'What?' Edward said, his eyes widening.

'I'm in love with someone else,' she stated.

He looked shocked and confused and she began to feel the full horror of what she had done.

'I'm so sorry Edward,' she started to say. 'I never meant for this to happen…'

'Who?' he cut in angrily.

'Dan.'

'*Dan?*' he said in disgust. 'You've done this? Embarrassed everyone, let everyone down for a roll in the hay with a stable boy? Jesus Christ!'

In that moment Emma realised that it was his pride that was injured, not his heart. The weight of guilt lifted a little…and as it did a thought occurred to her.

'Hang on a minute – why did you say that it didn't mean anything? Why did you say that it was only the once?'

He stared at her, and if possible, went even paler. His mouth opened but nothing came out.

'That girl, – Frieda, was it? – who answered your phone that morning. Just after we'd had that argument?'

He sat down suddenly on the bench. The look on his face told her everything she needed to know.

She shook her head. 'You were going to let me shoulder all the guilt for this,' she said quietly, 'but we are both, equally to blame. We thought we were so above anything like that. We thought we were so much better than everyone else. No relationship can survive that level of complacency – and neither does it deserve to.'

'I don't understand,' Sylvia asked Edward. 'Who's Frieda?'

'Let's just start again,' Edward pleaded, ignoring Sylvia. 'We can wipe the slate clean, start again from scratch!'

'What for?' Emma said. 'We were never in love with each other Edward. We were in love with the idea of each other – there's a big difference.'

Emma sat down and took off her shoes. Getting her bag off its hook, she took out her trainers and began to put them on.

'What the hell are you doing?' said Edward.

'I have to be somewhere,' Emma replied.

'You're going? Now?'

'Yes,'

'Have you lost your mind?' Sylvia said.

'No, I've just started to think clearly.'

'You aren't going anywhere!' her Mother commanded.

She got up, picking up her jacket. 'Goodbye,' she said.

Edward held up his hand. 'Wait. So…if you didn't know about Frieda, you'd made this choice already? Chosen him over me?'

She nodded.

'Why?' he said. And he didn't sound hurt, he sounded incredulous. 'What's he got that I haven't?'

She could have reeled off all those reasons she had given Lottie; tried to make him understand. But in the face of such unbelievable arrogance, she wasn't going to justify her choices any longer. She just wasn't.

She said simply, 'My heart.' And left.

'Emma wait!' Lottie had followed Emma out into the street.

Emma turned on her angrily. 'You knew didn't you? Why didn't you tell me Lottie?'

'I didn't know about Frieda!' Lottie gasped. 'I swear, I would never have kept that from you.'

'Not about Frieda – but you knew he was going to propose, didn't you?'

Lottie looked down at the ground; a picture of guilt. 'I was hoping you might change your mind. It was all going to be so perfect – me and Josh, you and Edward – but I was wrong, I realise that now.'

She looked so upset, Emma's heart softened a little.

'I just thank God that Dan doesn't know that Edward was going to propose.'

Lottie opened and closed her mouth, her face screwed up in anguish.

'Oh Lottie! You didn't tell him did you?'

'I'm so sorry,' Lottie said again.

'Oh my God! That's why he said to come back before my birthday, that if I didn't, he would know I wasn't coming back!' Emma cried. 'I've got to catch that train.'

Lottie looked distraught.

'I'd drive you, but I've had too much to drink. Will you let me know when you get there safely?'

'I'll call you as soon as I can.'

'Will you be okay?' Lottie asked.

'I'll be fine,' Emma said firmly.

Lottie shook her head. 'How can you be so calm? So sure you're doing the right thing?'

Emma thought for a second. 'Because, actually it's not about Dan, or Edward or any-one else. It's about me.'

Lottie looked at her questioningly.

'It's about trusting myself – having a little self-belief. Believing that I don't need Edward or anyone else to make me a valid person. I am okay as I am, and whatever happens – even if the worst happens – I will be okay, I will cope.'

Lottie had tears in her eyes. 'Good luck!' she said.

They embraced quickly, and then hitching up her long skirt, Emma turned and ran as fast as she could towards the station.

Chapter 47

SHE JUST CAUGHT THE LAST TRAIN. FINDING AN EMPTY CARRIAGE, she took a seat, then sat completely motionless, for several minutes, processing what had happened.

A horrible thought occurred to her. With a feeling of dreaded certainty, she fished around in her bag for her phone. Sure enough, it was dead. She had forgotten to charge it.

She felt like hurling the bloody thing out the window. The journey had never seemed so long. With every minute that ticked by, she knew that he must have given up hope.

He would think that she had changed her mind, decided to marry Edward. Would think that she had broken her promise, confirming all his worst fears and perpetuating the beliefs which caused his most self-destructive behaviour.

The thought of it made her sit uncomfortably on the edge of her seat, every muscle tense, willing the train to go faster. But the more she did, the slower it seemed to go.

At last the train drew up in the tiny station and she was running down that well-known road, her bag across her chest.

When she got to the pub, she hesitated. Should she go in and call him from there? But the thought that she might see somebody she knew and have to speak to them stopped her. She was in no fit state to make small talk.

It was raining now. Not hard, but a thick, persistent drizzle. She ran down the dark lane, her trainers making hardly any sound on the tarmac, running as fast as she could.

She saw the lights of the yard up ahead and slowed to a walk.

Having hardly eaten all day, she was running on pure adrenalin, but wet and cold now in her thin jacket, she started to shiver.

She pleaded silently that he would be there, that in mere minutes he would know that she hadn't broken her promise; that she had come back.

The tack room and kitchen were in darkness. Mounting the steep wooden stairs, she reached the top and held her breath. There was a light coming from underneath his door. He was there.

With her heart full, she started forwards, already beginning to feel the sweet sensation of relief …then she froze. She could hear voices. One deep, male, quiet; the other female, louder and disturbingly familiar. They were coming from behind his door.

As if gripped by a horrific nightmare, Emma put her hand out and knocked on the door. The voices stopped. Then there was some muffled giggling and scuffling, and the sound of light footsteps coming to the door. It opened just a little, letting light into the dark corridor.

Emma felt as if she had stepped into some alternative reality. The blood drained from her face, and settled with a congealed coldness around her heart.

Because in the narrow opening stood Simone, with just a thin sheet wrapped around her; legs and shoulders bare. Her eyes were wide, and her mouth opened in surprise.

'Oh! It's you,' she said. She glanced back over her shoulder into the room behind her, and when she turned back to Emma she had a small smile on her lips. She let the sheet slip a little so that Emma could be in no doubt as to her nakedness. 'We didn't know you were coming back.'

Emma felt something collide with her back, hard, and realised she had backed into the wall behind her.

In sheer, blind panic, she stumbled back along the corridor and down the stairs, not seeing but feeling the walls with her hands. All she could see was the image of Simone, standing there in Dan's bedroom doorway; her naked body almost visible through the thin white sheet.

Falling out of the door into the yard, she retched and retched into a flowerpot. Nothing came up.

As soon as she stopped retching she started running, gasping, each breath burning her lungs. She had no idea where she was going, just ran into the night.

When she hit the darkness of the trees, she slowed down to a walk.

Some things were too bad to cry for. If she started to cry, she might never stop.

Chapter 48

THE MOON WAS OUT, BUT THE CLOUDS WERE HEAVY AND BLACK, moving across the sky, only allowing her light to shine intermittently.

Emma trudged on. It all felt like a big test that she had somehow failed.

'But of course,' she thought dumbly. 'How stupid of me. Of course he would turn to the one person who has never left him, who's always there whenever he needs her. She's always said she would be there when everyone else was gone, and she's been right all along.' It was so tragic, such a senseless waste.

Perhaps you couldn't change your fate, no matter how hard you tried. You would always keep falling into the same trap, over and over again, driven by the demons from your past, things that were out of your control. Choice was an illusion; you were just a puppet, moved by the masters of early conditioning and circumstance, cold and indifferent.

It seemed so unfair somehow, so unjust, so pointless. The universe was broken. The moon hid her face behind a cloud in shame.

Emma heard the sound of a heavy vehicle approaching; a lorry. Its noisy diesel engine ripping through the quiet night. It was coming fast. She had nearly reached the corner where she would be able to see the pub up ahead. The road was narrow here, the hedges on either side high. She plodded mechanically on.

What was the point of anything when you didn't really have any choice; it was all so futile and hopeless. As she rounded the corner, the lorry's headlights cut through the blackness on full beam, dazzling Emma. She was wearing dark clothes, it didn't see her, it didn't slow down. If she didn't move it was going to hit her, she thought numbly.

In an almost trance like state, induced by shock, exhaustion, lack of food and misery, she stared straight into the blinding beams of light.

It would be so easy, she thought, just to stand here and let it hit her. It would be over in less than a second, and then she wouldn't have to feel this pain anymore, wouldn't have to deal with this mess.

The lorry bore down on her, its sides crashing through the low branches of the trees.

This was all her fault, she deserved this, she was being punished for her weakness. And Dan would be punished for his, because he could never love Simone, he would be miserable. He had only done this because he was hurt, because he thought she had broken her promise. She knew this to be the truth, she felt it deep in her bones.

With this certainty taking a hold of her mind and body, her spirit surged with new life. No. She wasn't going to allow it to end like this. She wasn't going to allow all that she knew to be wrong, to triumph over everything she knew to be right. It wasn't fair. It wasn't right.

She wouldn't have it!

A rush of adrenalin fired her muscles with new energy, and she threw herself backwards into the hedge, just as the lorry crashed past her, splattering her with wet mud. The wind from the close encounter with its massive, hurtling bulk like a solid mass; flattening her into the tearing branches of the hedge.

The lorry roared off into the night, unconcerned and apparently unaware of the precarious balance of life and death it had so nearly played a part in. Emma extracted herself from the hedge, its thorny twigs clutching and tearing at her skin and clothes.

She stood still for a few moments, shaking uncontrollably. She couldn't see. Her eyes were still blinded from the headlights, her ears still deafened by the roar of its engine. Slowly, she regained her balance and her senses started to work again, gradually adjusting to the dark and quiet.

But as they did, with cold fingers of fear creeping up her spine, she became aware of the sound of boots scraping the tarmac, of the outline of a dark figure coming towards her out of the blackness. There was a person, walking along the road from the direction of the pub, surprisingly close.

The primal terror of meeting a stranger on a deserted road at night took her by the throat. Her instinct was to turn and run, but she was too late. Hands gripped her arms, she struggled to free herself. They were strong, but then, suddenly, they let her go.

She started to run, but then she heard a voice. A voice so familiar it penetrated through the black wall of her panic.

'It *is* you…Emma stop! Come back, where are you going? Stop. It's me!'

She stopped trying to run and turned. She thought she was dreaming. Perhaps she was really dead. Because, as the moon came out, she thought she was looking up into Dan's face.

It had been his hands holding her arms, his voice telling her to stop, to come back to him. Her desperate and distraught mind wouldn't take this in, wouldn't accept that this was real. She shook her head.

'How can you be here?' she said.

'Emma, what's happened to you? What are you doing here? Did that lorry nearly hit you?' he said, stepping forward and catching her just as her legs gave way.

'I don't understand…you were back there! In your room…,' she said, leaning heavily on his arms, her legs had about as much strength as chewed string.

'I was at the pub,' he said. 'Bloody-hell Emma you're freezing!' He took of his jacket and put it around her. 'Come on, we need to get back.'

'But Simone!' Emma practically sobbed. '*She* was in your room, she answered your door, she was with someone…who...?'

He stopped and seemed to grasp what she was saying.

'Jamie, the new groom. Your replacement. He's got my old room. I couldn't stand for someone else to be in yours, to sleep in your bed – especially a man – so I moved in there. Simone must be with him.'

Emma buried her face in his jumper. 'Oh thank God!' she sobbed, in muffled tones.

'Oh shit! You thought…?'

She nodded, her face still firmly buried in his jumper. He wrapped his arms around her tightly, rocking her. She couldn't breathe very well, but she didn't care. It felt so, so good.

Everything started to make sense again, the universe wasn't broken after all. 'Thank you, thank you, thank you,' she prayed silently.

'Why didn't you ring me – tell me you were coming?' he asked, still rocking her.

'Phones dead,' Emma said, turning her face slightly to the side so he would be able to hear her. 'I came straight from the party.'

He held her slightly away from him and looked at her. Her deathly white face in the moonlight, streaked with mud and tears, her torn party dress, the hem soaked to her knees. He felt her freezing hands, scratched and bleeding.

'Jesus, we need to get you warm,' he said. He took off his coat and put it around her, then scooped her up in his arms and began to carry her back along the road towards the yard.

Emma didn't know whether to laugh or cry. How was it possible, she thought, to be in the depths of the deepest, darkest despair one minute, and the next, for everything to change so dramatically, that you found yourself in the one place you wanted to be more than anywhere else? The one place you felt happiest and safest in the world.

It was as if, in that moment, that she had looked inward and found that last ounce of inner strength, something had shifted, like the focus of a lens. She had focused on what was important until it had become sharp and defined, and everything else had blurred and faded out of existence.

Perhaps it was never any use looking outward for help, it had to come from within. Shock was starting to subside.

'It's okay, I can walk,' she began to laugh. Although she still felt light-headed, strength was beginning to return to her limbs.

He gently set her down, but kept his arm around her. She looped her arms around his waist, and they walked like that all the way.

She told him how Edward hadn't come back, and how she kept trying and failing to speak to him. She told him about the nightmare of the party, the sickening moment when she realised Edward was going to propose.

'Is that what you wouldn't tell me, before I left?'

He nodded. 'Lottie told me...but I didn't want that to influence you one way or the other.'

They had reached the yard now and Emma marvelled again at how she could be so happy to be back at a place that, only a short time ago, she had fled from as if the hounds of hell were was chasing her.

In the kitchen, Dan made her sit on the sofa while he lit the gas fire and put the kettle on.

'Are you hungry?' he asked her.

'Starving,' Emma admitted. Her appetite was back with a vengeance.

She watched him while he made her a cheese toastie and heated up some soup. He was just wearing his old jeans and a chunky knitted jumper, the sleeves pushed up to his elbows, his dark hair curled damply onto the nape of his neck, but to her, he had never looked so irresistible.

All the while the love she felt for him grew and grew, flooding every inch of her being until she could hardly sit still. Fierce, burning, extraordinary love.

He turned to find her watching him. Smiling, he brought her food over to her, sitting facing her. She took the plate and mug, and ate, gratefully. Nothing had ever tasted so amazing, she couldn't remember the last time food had tasted this good.

'I was so worried you would think I wasn't coming back,' she said between mouthfuls. 'Edward kept delaying and delaying his flight back.'

'And I thought that when you saw Edward again, you might realise you still loved him.'

Emma put her hand out and took his. 'I'm sorry, I should never have gone back, I realise that now. I should have just called Edward and told him I wasn't coming home.'

But Dan shook his head.

'No. I think it had to happen this way. At least it's proved something to me – to both of us maybe?' he said.

She looked into his face, there was no need to ask what that was. She knew.

She finished her food and was warm now, through and through. He looked a little troubled.

'What is it?' she asked.

'Tonight, I was in the pub with Joe and Hannah…Amy was there,' he said.

Emma felt her chest tighten ever so slightly at the mention of Amy. She didn't say anything, just waited for him to go on.

'I was having a moment of serious doubt, about whether you were coming back. Feeling pretty cynical about the world in general. I knew tonight was your party, and that Edward was proposing. Lottie told me, that you'd said, if Edward proposed, you would accept. I knew it was now or never. If you didn't come back tonight, and I didn't hear from you, you wouldn't be coming.'

Emma squirmed uncomfortably at the thought of what must have been going through his mind.

'I kept looking at my phone, but there was nothing, and the obvious thing to do was to get drunk and try to forget about it. Then Joe and Hannah left.' He leant forward, elbows on knees. 'I knew I probably shouldn't be in there with Amy on our own. So I told her I was going. She tried to make me stay with her – said she didn't want to drink alone. I was tempted. I mean – really tempted. It was getting late and I thought you weren't going to call, I just wanted to get so drunk I wouldn't feel anything anymore.'

Although it hurt her to hear this, Emma couldn't blame him for feeling like that.

'She offered to get me another drink, and I so nearly said yes. But then she said, if I just had one more drink with her, she promised she would let me go home. She promised. And I thought…we both know that's not true. She had no intention of letting me go home – knew if I stayed for another drink, I would stay in there all night…would probably end up going home with her.'

Ouch, that hurt! But she was glad he was being honest with her.

'And then she said it again. "I promise". And I know it was only a flip remark, people say it all the time – but I thought; why say that when it's not true? And I thought of you, and how you would never say something like that, unless you meant it. Not even just a casual comment. You would never promise something you didn't mean. That's when I knew you were coming back, no matter what. If it were at all possible, you would be here. I knew that was the truth. I felt it, in my gut. That made me ask myself what the hell I was doing in there. So I left, and that's when I found you on the road.'

All the while he was telling her this, Emma felt tears pricking her eyes.

It could so easily have all ended so differently. If Amy hadn't said those exact words to trigger that response in him, and he hadn't left the pub when he did and found her on the road – what would have happened? She would never have found the courage to go back to the yard.

And Simone. As far as she was concerned, it had been the perfect revenge. There was no way she could have planned it, but she was an opportunist – she would never have told Dan that Emma had come back.

Emma would have left, thinking that Dan was sleeping with Simone. Dan would think Emma had decided it was all a big mistake and was going to marry Edward.

They would both have been too hurt; too proud to call each other. They would never have seen each other again.

And worse; if she hadn't got out of the way of the lorry in time.

Sitting here, in this warm room, full of food and love, Emma couldn't believe she had nearly allowed herself to get hit by that lorry. She shuddered, goose over her grave.

'You look spooked,' Dan said.

'I was just thinking – it's all about near misses isn't it, life? I mean, a split-second wrong decision could change your life forever – could mean the difference between happy ever after, or tragedy.' It was a scary thought. 'It just makes me think, I really should pay more attention,' she said.

Dan chuckled. 'I think we all get plenty of chances. If we keep fucking it up though, eventually life gives up on us.' There was a pause and he looked into her face intently. 'So, did you have any moments of doubt?' he asked.

Emma thought she should be as honest as he had been.

'Not about my own feelings no.' She swallowed hard. 'But… I must admit, there have been moments when I doubted yours.'

'And now?' His eyes searched hers. She could only hold his gaze for a second before she knew her eyes had given her away. 'You still doubt them?' he asked.

She got up quickly and took her mug and plate to the sink. Why was it so important to hear those three little words? Maybe she was the insecure one after all. She kept her back to him, rinsing her plate, whilst she waged war with her emotions.

'Bugs, leave that,' he said.

She was being ridiculous – after all, Edward used to say it all the time, and it meant absolutely nothing…

'Emma! Come here.'

Hesitantly, she turned and went over to him, letting him pull her down onto his lap. 'You need to hear me say it – is that right?' he asked.

Emma went sharply into reverse.

'No, it's okay honestly…'

She struggled in his arms, trying to free herself but he held her tight.

'Emma, look at me,' he said.

'No, please don't say it…I don't want you to say it if you don't mean it!'

'I love you.'

On second thoughts, it actually felt amazing to hear him say it. At once, all the resistance deserted her and she allowed herself to be crushed against his chest, feeling an inexplicable urge to cry.

'I thought you knew – thought you felt it. I think I fell in love with you that first night at the pub, when I offered to buy you a drink and you stood there, looking disapproving, and rudely asked me to buy Kitty one as well.'

She stifled a sob, which turned into a giggle.

'I didn't admit it to myself for the longest time though. I knew you didn't like me and I couldn't work out why it bothered me so much. I'd never cared what anyone thought of me before. I've never known anyone so tough, but so kind at the same time. The way you stood up for Kitty – stood up to me. Standing there in the feed-room, telling me to my face that I was a bully. It made me question everything about myself for the first time.' He laughed a little self-consciously. 'You seemed so untouchable. I thought you would never leave Edward, so I told myself to get over it. Got myself involved with Caroline.'

At the mention of Caroline she remembered how she had learnt for the first time what it was to be jealous and had fought against the realisation of what that emotion meant.

But he was hers now. Putting a hand up to touch his face, she looked at his mouth. She watched his lips part and then closed her eyes as they connected with her own, and she felt again that unmistakeable sense of rightness.

But while she loved what he'd said, it also made her feel a little sad. She drew away from him a little to look into his face.

'All that wasted time,' she said. 'Why's it taken us so long? Why's it so hard for us to let ourselves love and be loved?'

'Part of the human condition I suppose,' he said softly. 'We're all so busy trying to protect ourselves. And it was hard for me to believe that someone like you could want someone like me.'

Emma was incredulous. 'Huh! I'm a lousy catch, look at me; I cheated on my boyfriend, let down all of my friends and family. I've got nowhere to live, no job – at least you have a job.'

'I don't actually,' he said.

'What?' Emma said faintly.

'I gave my notice in, this afternoon, when I was having one of my more serious moments of doubt. Things wouldn't have been the same.'

They sat, just looking at each other until Dan said, 'For two people who are trying to make a go of it, we haven't got off to a very good start have we?'

And suddenly, it seemed completely hilarious. Emma started to giggle. Dan caught it from her and began to laugh and Emma laughed harder and harder until neither of them could stop. Because none of it mattered, not in the least.

Just then, the door to the stairs opened and Simone appeared, dressed in a man's T-shirt and nothing else. Their laughter dried up pretty quickly.

'Oh,' she said, her eyes flicking from one to the other of them.

'I wondered what all the noise was.' She looked at Emma. 'You found him then?'

'Yeah, she did, no thanks to you,' Dan growled.

Simone smirked. 'Don't mind me,' she said, going to the cupboard. She got out a bottle of wine and two glasses.

'But I do mind you. A lot,' Dan said, the threat in his voice was clear.

Simone turned to face them. She seemed to be trying to think of a retort, but she just turned red, crossed the room quickly, and went back upstairs with the wine.

It felt like the mood had changed with Simone's interruption.

'Where are we going to stay though?' Emma asked. 'We can't stay upstairs with…' she shuddered. The thought was intolerable.

'No, we can't.' He thought for a moment. 'But I still have the keys to The Coach House.'

'Won't Malcolm be cross?' She remembered how he had reacted when he'd found them in Merlin's stable together.

Dan smiled. 'Malcolm, will be over the moon.'

'Really?'

'Mm-hmm. Do you remember that talk he gave me? Before I broke up with Caroline?'

'Yes.'

'He gave me the third degree; asked me exactly what was going on. I told him how I felt – but that I wasn't sure how you felt. And he told me then, that I would be an absolute fool to let you go without a fight. But that if I ever messed you about – he would kill me with his own hands.' He grinned.

Emma was unbelievably touched.

'He's definitely got a soft spot for you,' Dan laughed. 'Oh… that reminds me.' He got up and went to the side-board. When he came back, he had something in his hand, which he put down in her lap. 'Happy Birthday,' he said.

She picked up the plastic booklet, 'Is this….?'

'Yes. Penny's passport.'

She was speechless. 'I can't believe you've done this…this is the best present I have ever, ever been given,' she said truthfully.

'Better than diamonds?' he grinned.

'A million times…a gazillion times!'

'Malcolm let me have her ridiculously cheap, knowing she was for you. And I know he'd let us stay if we wanted to, but I think it's time to move on. Don't you?'

Emma had to agree.

'We'll find something – I don't know what yet, but we'll think of something.'

There was a moment's silence while they both contemplated the future.

'I know what we could do though,' Dan said, his smile returning.

'What?' Emma asked him.

'First, you need a hot shower. And then – we could go to bed.'

Epilogue

DAN PICKED UP HIS TOOLS, SURVEYING HIS HANDIWORK. HE HAD replaced a couple of broken rails in the post and rail fencing, so that when the new crop of foals were born the following spring, there would be somewhere safe for them to be turned out with their Dams.

There was an awful lot more work to be done, but they were getting there. Now, at last, he didn't feel the relentless pressure that he had the first two years they had been here.

Looking at his watch, he began to stroll back to the house in the evening sunshine. He went through the gate into the paddock by the house, where Merlin and Penny were turned out.

Merlin carried on grazing, he would only come for Emma, but Penny came over to meet him, nudging his pockets for treats. Dan gave her forehead a rub and a grass nut out of his pocket.

Standing here, on the rise of the slope, Dan looked down on the house and the garden, and to the yard beyond. He got a rush of satisfaction. It was all starting to come together.

The house looked picturesque in the golden evening light, smoke pouring from the chimney, it was getting cold enough to have to light a fire in the evenings.

He could now look at the house without the wave of anxiety it used to give him.

This summer they'd finally had the money to get the roof repaired and the stonework re-pointed. The year before, the priority had been getting the stables repaired and the school re-surfaced so that Dan could work the horses and teach. The teaching brought in much needed money.

He could almost laugh now looking back, remembering how they'd had to sleep in the kitchen in front of the fire that first winter; the only warm, dry room in the house. God knows it hadn't seemed funny at the time.

When Malcolm had first showed them the house, and the land, Dan had been overwhelmed by the amount of work that needed doing. It hadn't been lived in for years, not since Malcolm's parents had died.

But Emma had looked at the sagging roof, the broken windowpanes and the ancient, filthy lino on the floor. 'It's perfect!' she'd said. And you couldn't look a gift horse in the mouth.

Malcolm let them live there for nothing that first year whilst they found their feet. The deal being that they would do up the house themselves and gradually pay him some money when they could afford to. Malcolm definitely had a soft spot for Emma.

And now they could afford to. Gradually, their income was increasing.

It was all worth it, but God, they'd had to work hard for it. It had nearly broken them.

He could still picture Emma, on her hands and knees on the floor of the kitchen, trying to scrape the rotten linoleum of the flagstones, scrubbing the mould off the walls in the bedrooms, pulling up the ancient, mildewy carpet in the living room, choking on the dust. All this, while trying to get the business off the ground. He'd felt enormous guilt that she'd had to work so hard.

Things hadn't gone to plan at all that first year. They'd had to borrow so much money to put into the house, and because he couldn't afford to compete much, his sponsorship deal had fallen through. They'd been so broke, they'd barely been able to afford to eat.

But she'd never complained. Not once.

Giving Penny a last pat, Dan walked back through the garden. The apple trees that they had planted three years ago were getting big. The apples needed picking, a few of them on the ground already. Emma's chickens were scratching around the base of them, pecking at the fallen fruit.

Dan looked through the kitchen stable door, the top half of which stood open. He could see Emma standing at the AGA, stirring a huge pot of something. The steam from the pot rose into the beam of sunlight coming through the door, which glanced onto the gleaming flagstones. His son was on her hip, his head leaning against her shoulder, his curly brown hair mingling with her blonde hair. As always, he was flattened by a wave of love for them both.

It had definitely all been worth it.

He paused in the doorway, savouring the moment before they were aware of his presence. Sometimes the best things happened as a result of things not going to plan he reflected, remembering that night two years ago.

She had been stirring something on the stove – much like she was at this very moment – when, without warning, she'd put her hand over her mouth and rushed out of the room, running for the bathroom. He'd been so worried. She'd been looking so pale and wan recently.

'Are you alright?' he'd asked her when she'd come back. 'What's wrong?'

'Nothing, I'm fine,' she'd replied.

'No you're not. You're exhausted. You should go and stay with Lottie, or even go to Maggie, in Spain.'

'I'm not going anywhere Dan,' she'd replied wearily.

The guilt and worry were too much for him. 'Yes, you should just go! I can't do this anymore, it's not working…and it's making you ill.'

She'd gone and sat down at the table and put her head in her hands.

'I'm not ill Dan…I'm pregnant. I'm so sorry. With everything that's been going on, I forgot to get my implant changed.' And she'd burst into tears.

With those words came a deluge of conflicting emotions: immense relief that there was nothing wrong with her; shock, amazement; desperation, because they were only just keeping their heads above the water as it was – and immense joy. She was going to have his baby.

He'd gone and put his arms around her, lifting her to her feet and holding her tightly.

'It's alright, I'm sorry, I'm sorry,' he'd said over and over again. 'Don't worry, we'll work something out. It'll be alright.'

'I know it will be,' Emma had replied.

And it was. From then on things got better.

He didn't know where she got her unflagging faith in him; that he could achieve anything he set his mind to, but somehow it had the effect that he could. He didn't know where she got her strength from either, but he knew he could draw on it whenever he needed to.

Once the morning sickness had subsided, Emma had regained her health and her happiness and when Thomas had been born, she'd been in her element. Together they built the business: competition livery, backing and training young horses, gaining a reputation of producing some of the best horses in the country.

Slowly, the money had started coming in. Dan was able to compete more, and Merlin just got better and better, winning everything in sight. Because of this, Dan got offered the rides on several good horses and then, got a new sponsorship deal on the back of his success. Now, three years on, Merlin had qualified to do Badminton in the spring, and they had several exciting youngsters.

He always said he didn't believe in being lucky, but by God, they had been.

Going in quietly, he went up behind his wife and son, putting his arms around them both, kissing the nape of Emma's neck, and the top of Tom's head.

Dan inhaled the delicious aroma of herbs, garlic and red wine.

'Smell's good. Are you sure you've made enough?' he said sardonically, eyeing the enormous pot.

'Joe and Hannah are coming for dinner,' Emma replied, grinning.

It was amazing how often people wanted to visit now the house was warm dry and welcoming. No one had been very keen when it had been cold, damp and mouldy.

Malcolm came over most weeks, Maggie had come over from Spain to stay, and even Lottie was a frequent guest. She and Josh had broken off their engagement when she'd discovered that the fling with a girl from work had become a full-blown affair.

Despite their bumpy start, she and Dan had found common ground, initially in their mutual love for Emma, but then in the realisation that they were actually quite similar.

'Yes! You're both bloody minded and entirely unmanageable!' Emma insisted. They even had the same birthday.

Emma's Granddad had been down to stay too. Emma drove up herself and picked him up in her little Ford Fiesta, which she was so proud of. He was full of admiration for what they'd achieved, and besotted with his great grand-son.

'Da-da-da,' Tom said, holding his arms out towards Dan, and he lifted him off Emma's hip.

'I'll take him out into the garden for a while,' he said.

Emma smiled at him gratefully, turning her face for a kiss.

He carried Tom outside, setting him down so he could practice his new skill of walking on his own.

Dan sat on the wooden bench by the kitchen door, the sun in his face, watching his son toddling around, trying to catch the chickens, a look of sheer determination in his eyes that were so like his own.

Kitty came through the garden gate closely followed by Henry, their black Labrador.

'Everything's done Dan,' she said.

'Thanks Kitty,' he said.

Nowadays he could be more-or-less confident that she had done everything properly. She had come to work for them when Emma had the baby, living in so she could help Emma with Thomas, as well as working on the yard. What she lacked in competence she more than made up for in devotion to Emma and Tom.

Always on hand when they wanted a babysitter, she enabled Emma to ride out with Dan, groom for him at competitions and help with backing the youngsters.

It was the perfect arrangement.

Kitty went over to Thomas, who'd found Henry's ball in the long grass. She helped him to throw it, and Henry bounded after it.

Tom adored Kitty. He had plenty of people in his life despite the lack of grandparents.

It had been nearly two years, after Emma had come back to Dorset before she'd had any contact with her parents at all. She didn't even tell them when she found out she was pregnant.

Then one day she had received a letter.

When she'd read the writing on the envelope, she had opened it with a look of dread. As she read, her face paled, and she'd sat down heavily on a kitchen chair.

'What is it?' he'd asked.

'It's from my father,' she'd replied, her face as white as the paper in her hand. 'He's left my Mother. But that's not all.'

She'd handed him the letter. Once he'd read it from start to finish, he'd looked up at her. The colour had returned to her cheeks and she there was excitement and hope in her eyes.

'I have a sister!' she'd said.

In the letter, her Father had revealed that he'd been having an affair for the past twenty-five years, and that he had a twenty-four year old daughter with this other woman. Emma was more excited about this than she was upset about her parent's separation.

'No wonder he wasn't around very much when you were growing up!' Dan said in disbelief.

It had apparently been an even bigger shock to Emma's Mother, she hadn't even suspected.

'All those years!' Emma was incredulous. 'How could she not have known?'

'She wasn't paying attention?' Dan had suggested.

She had come close to a mental breakdown and Emma had relented and gone to see her. She was no longer the fire-breathing harridan; Silvia was a broken woman.

Now there was an uneasy truce, and although there was as yet little affection between them, there was more honesty than ever before.

Emma came outside and sat down next to Dan on the bench, handing him an open bottle of beer; another in her hand. She leant back against the sun-soaked wall, closing her eyes with a sigh of contentment.

'What time are Joe and Hannah coming?' he asked her.

'About an hour,' she said. 'Tom needs a bath.'

'I'll give him his bath,' volunteered Kitty, picking up the little boy.

The perfect arrangement.

Kitty went inside with Thomas, chatting to him cheerfully, heading for the downstairs bathroom.

'Thanks Kitty, you're a star!' Emma called after her. 'In that case, I'm going to have a shower.'

They now had two, fully functional bathrooms, one en-suite.

'Sounds good – need some help?' Dan said with a grin.

She smiled and turned to look directly into his eyes with "that look". The look which, even now, never failed to get his pulse racing. Getting up, she went indoors, looking back over her shoulder at him.

He sat a moment longer letting the happiness soak into his soul, like the sun into his skin. Then he got up quickly, went into the house, and bounded up the stairs two at a time.

THE END

ACKNOWLEDGEMENTS

I'M SURE MANY books never make it to publication because new writers get discouraged along the way, whether because they lose faith in their own ability, or don't get the kind of support they need to finish the publication journey. I have been very fortunate to have some amazing people who have given me much needed support and encouragement. All those beta readers who had to plough through my first drafts: Danielle Simpson, Rebecca Connell, and Julie Wood, right through to Alyce King who proofread my final draft, and made sure I hadn't left in any embarrassing mistakes.

I was very lucky to get a place on the RNA's New Writers' Scheme, and even more fortunate to get Janice Horton (*The Backpacking Housewife*) as my reader. Her advice has been so valuable and her words so encouraging, that I still read them often when I need a bit of a boost. I'd also like to thank Becky Warrak (Ravencrest Books) for reaching out to me, and without whom my book may never have got its cover.

Finally, and most importantly, I owe a huge debt of gratitude to my family. My children, Jack and Mary, who didn't ridicule their mother for wanting to write a book, and who have given generously of their opinions and advice whenever called upon. And my husband Fred, who must – countless times – have been frustrated by the inordinate amount of time I have spent neglecting my responsibilities, and ignoring him, whilst furiously tapping at my keyboard, but who has just quietly picked up the slack and never complained – not once.

About The Author

Lucy Ann Huxter lives with her husband, two children, and many animals on their farm in West Dorset. Her love for horses began earlier than she can remember, and as a small child, she begged her non-horsey parents to be allowed to ride. They thought it was just a phase and waited patiently for her to grow out of it – they're still waiting. Patricia Leitch was her favourite author as a child, and when she wasn't riding, she read the "Jinny and Shantih" books countless times. She still knows them by heart.

Age 10, she helped her neighbours start, and train, their homebred filly. Being lightweight she was the ideal person for the first "sit on", and it was only luck that through these neighbours, she ended up with her first pony on loan; a hot-headed Prince-Philip Cup pony, who went from halt to gallop and gallop to halt, turned on a sixpence, and taught Lucy how to stay on – if nothing else!

After leaving school, she went from agricultural college to working in the equestrian industry, many of these jobs involving starting and training young horses. In her twenties, she was lucky enough to be offered a job at the yard of probably the most famous Event rider in the world; Lucinda Green.

There her love of Eventing began, grooming for Lucinda and Canadian rider Diana Burgess who was based at Lucinda's. Diana was the most encouraging and kind person she was ever fortunate enough to work for, and Lucinda was extremely generous with her time and knowledge, giving Lucy one-to-one tuition, and even allowing her to compete one of her horses, Lucky Secret, aka "The Grey Horse".

Lucy's passion for writing was born from her passion for reading, and inspiration for *A Matter of Trust* started as early as twenty years ago, when she moved to West Dorset and met her now husband, Fred. She gave up working in the equestrian industry when she got married, starting a business with her husband, which enabled them to buy their own farm. This allowed Lucy to take in young horses for training and eventually realise her dream of breeding her own foal. And so "Minty" was born; a now six-year-old Irish Sport horse mare, with a gregarious nature and a penchant for polo-mints.

Printed in Great Britain
by Amazon

33750549R00209